LOST
MOTHER

BOOKS BY CATHERINE HOKIN

The Fortunate Ones
What Only We Know

CATHERINE HOKIN

THE
LOST
MOTHER

bookouture

Published by Bookouture in 2021

An imprint of Storyfire Ltd.
Carmelite House
50 Victoria Embankment
London EC4Y 0DZ

www.bookouture.com

ISBN: 978-1-83888-953-1
eBook ISBN: 978-1-83888-952-4

For Vera,
the best kind of old friend

PROLOGUE

Central Park, New York, November 1935

Anna felt the sound in the same moment she heard it. The ripple of notes caught in her throat and left her unable to open her eyes. It was so like the gurgle that ran through her dreams, she wondered if she had dozed off for a moment. And then it came again, richer this time, rising up to meet the birdsong which normally rang out unchallenged this early in the morning.

Four months. That's when they start to laugh. It could be her. If it's a little girl, it could be her.

A hopeless thought, a desperate thought. And yet…

Anna opened her eyes. There was a baby carriage parked beside the opposite bench, and two women arm in arm cooing over it. It was such a jolt to see anyone sitting there, Anna wondered for a moment if she was still sleeping, if she had somehow conjured them up.

In the four weeks since she had first found this little corner of Central Park, she had been its sole occupant, besides the birds and the occasional curious rabbit. At seven o'clock in the morning, which was Anna's preferred time to slip away – or, more accurately, the one time in the day she could carve out for herself – Central Park was a haven. It was too early for the office workers seeking a moment's solitude before the demands of their day engulfed them, or for the children who, come afternoon, would spill from their classrooms into its playgrounds. There were no honking car horns, no whooshing subway vents; none of the clamour which filled the rest of the city. The air was so still, Anna could hear the lions in the park's zoo roaring their good-mornings. The tree-shaded nook had become her place to breathe, and to remember. To be herself away from prying eyes, with all the longings and the pain that shedding of her outer skin brought. And now that sound, that beautiful sound, had slipped out of her imaginings and she was struggling to hold on to the day.

'She's only recently started doing it.' The young woman rocking the boat-shaped pram caught Anna looking and smiled. 'The laughing, I mean. The slightest thing sets her off. If we could get her to start sleeping as happily, life would be perfect!'

It was clear from her shining eyes that life was already quite perfect.

Anna nodded – all her words seemed to have left her – as the older of the two women beamed.

'My first grandchild, such a beauty and always up before the rest of the world. We thought a little fresh air might help, but she's far too curious to settle.'

It should be me rocking the pram. It should be my mother bragging about her precocious grandchild.

The image of the three of them sitting together, her holding her baby, her mother holding her – an image Anna had been running from for months – hit her so hard, she gasped.

The real mother and grandmother moved instinctively closer to the pram.

It could still be me. If I could only find her. If I had my own baby back, I could make a home. I could find some way of contacting Mutti. If I had my own baby back, I could do anything.

She got up, wanting nothing more than a closer look at the child. The baby was lying on her back, her satin-edged blanket kicked off, her face all circles and smiles. She peered up at Anna and chuckled.

'*Sie ist sehr schön. Sehr schön.*'

The German came from nowhere.

The mother was suddenly on her feet, her body thrust between Anna and her child, her arms outstretched as if to fight Anna off. 'Get away from her.'

It was the same order that had torn Anna apart in Berlin's Charité Hospital. Delivered in the same staccato tone. Time slipped away and took reality with it. All Anna could see was the ward, and the cot, and another woman reaching out for the child that was really hers.

'*Aber sie ist mein. Ich bin ihre Mutter.*'

The blow stung Anna's cheek and broke whatever bad spell had gripped her.

'I am sorry. I am so very sorry.'

She had recovered her English, but it was too late. There was nothing she could say to make amends for the fear in the other woman's eyes.

'I know she's your baby, not mine. I never meant any harm or to frighten you. But my daughter is here in America. She is somewhere here. And I need to get her back.' The words came out in a tumble, her accent all heavy and tripping them.

The older woman pulled the pram away and began shouting for help.

'I really am sorry.'

The apology was pointless, insulting. Her words had no weight here. Her pain, so raw and alive, had lashed out and hurt someone else. She had made another mother feel as wretched and afraid as she had been. It was unforgiveable; it was not who she was.

The mother was sobbing, clutching her baby. Footsteps were coming, the grandmother's cries had been heard.

Anna turned and, still stumbling over her apologies and her longing, she ran.

PART ONE

CHAPTER ONE

Rhode Island, August 1957

When had casseroles become the currency of death?

Peggy slammed the fridge door shut and slumped against it, convinced she could feel the metal bulging beneath her back. In the week since her mother's burial, the fridge's shelves had mutated into walls of Pyrex. There was enough food crammed between the groaning racks to feed two high school football teams, never mind a girl of twenty-two who barely scraped five-feet-five in heels.

Peggy had begun to dread the doorbell ringing. No one had warned her about these neighbourly rituals. Fruit Hill, where the Baileys had lived since their move from New York, was a close community – like every part of Rhode Island. Everyone's lives had become intertwined years ago by the demands of school calendars and potluck suppers. But, when Peggy's father, Jack, had died five years earlier, the street had simply dropped round cards and praised her mother for being 'so capable' and 'such a trooper'. Not this time. Now Peggy was no longer her parents' 'bright spark' but a 'poor little soul', pushed back into childhood and apparently incapable of coping. Well meant or not, it was wearing her down.

It had been a week since Peggy had managed a proper night's sleep. She kept lying awake, unable to switch off, not thinking about her mother as she wanted to be doing, but fretting over the stupidest things. Worrying whether her *thank-yous* sounded as mechanical to her neighbours as they increasingly did to her. Worrying whether there was some order of value ascribed to this procession of *a little*

something to tide you over that everyone but she knew, and that
her ignorance was failing her mother. She had lain sleepless, lost
in the ridiculous task of trying to determine whether tuna noodle
carried more affection in its crust than hamburger bake. Whether
the declarations stirred into a home-made marinara sauce topped
those tipped in with a can of condensed soup. Standing in the
kitchen now, pressed against the fridge door as if she was holding
back a dam on the edge of erupting, Peggy had a sudden vision of
ice rinks and scorecards. Of casseroles pirouetting.

'Which one would you put your money on, Mom? I bet you a
dollar to a doughnut the noodles would take it.'

The kitchen shivered, the fridge turned hollow. Peggy gripped
tight to a chair and tried to remember how to breathe. When would
it stop? This calling out, this speaking aloud to someone who was
so painfully, so obviously not there? This turning, expecting to see
her mother's answering grin, expecting her to jump into whatever
nonsense Peggy was spinning?

She groped her way to the sink, poured a glass of water, lowered
herself into the chair as if her bones were brittle.

'This is all your fault, Joan Bailey. I'm drowning in pot roast
and who am I supposed to laugh about that with?'

She sipped at the water until her eyes stopped stinging. *You don't
have to be on your own.* All her friends had said it. She could pick
up the phone and find someone in an instant who would listen.
Nancy, who had been her room-mate during the final year Peggy
had just completed at college, who had kept her standing during
the diagnosis and the first few weeks of her mother's illness and
helped her see out that last impossible term. Any of the gang from
their corridor. Barbara and Kathleen who she had known since high
school, who still lived a handful of blocks away. She wasn't short of
people. *But none of them are you.* None of them could pick up one
of Peggy's ideas or a throwaway comment the way that her mother
could, flipping it into a tale they tossed back and forward between

the pair of them, as her imagination ran even faster than Peggy's. None of them had that hug that wrapped like a blanket, no matter whether Peggy had brought bruised knees or a bruised heart for mending. And none of them carried such warmth in their smiles.

'You talk about her as if she's your best friend, not your mother.'

Her first-year room-mate had dropped that comment with a fair portion of envy. Peggy hadn't argued. She had smiled and explained, possibly a little smugly, how Joan had always been her confidante and how, until his death at the hands of a distracted driver when Peggy was sixteen, her father Jack had been her hero.

'You describe it all so perfectly, it makes me wonder what you're hiding.'

She had forgotten that little barb, delivered by an older girl less bothered about being liked than the hungry-for-approval freshmen.

Were we really that close? Or were we too scared not to be?

Peggy couldn't remember fighting with her parents the way her school and college friends described the flare-ups in their own homes. She couldn't actually remember any rows at all. Her mother and father preferred, in her mother's words, to keep 'the mood pleasant'.

And I was always eager to please. Always determined to do the right thing and keep us all happy.

Unlike her girlfriends and their mothers, she and Joan had rarely found themselves at odds, especially after her father died. And on the few occasions they were, it was always Peggy who crumbled.

'He would have been so proud of you. Of all the universities he taught at, Brown was his favourite.'

'I know. But I'm not going.'

Sitting at the kitchen table where they had opened the acceptance letter, Peggy remembered her mother's sudden shift from smile to snort, and winced.

'How can I, Mom? When it means leaving you rattling around here on your own?'

'Well, that's very sweet, Peggy dear. But don't you think it's also a little insulting?'

Peggy remembered blushing scarlet at that, but Joan's tone had remained gentle and the hands that caught hers had held tight. And her mother's logic had been, as ever, inescapable.

'I'm fifty-three, sweetheart, not eighty-three. And I hardly *rattle around*. I've taken on extra teaching this term; I've the chance to take on more. And, besides, when is this house ever empty? Between my bridge night and my book club night and all the wives who end up here looking for "a bit of space without men", as they so *tactfully* put it, when am I ever alone? Who knows? I might enjoy a bit of peace. I'll never stop missing your father, Peggy, and I will miss you too, you know I will. But I want you to go and get your degree, the way we all talked about. I want you out in the world, doing what you've always dreamed of. Besides, it's Brown, not Berkeley; it's an hour's train ride away, if that. And it's not as if I'm going anywhere.'

Except she had.

Peggy opened her eyes and wished she had opened them sooner, wished she had properly looked. How had none of her mother's constant stream of visitors spotted it? How had *she* not spotted it? The weight loss, the tiredness, that was surely more than 'I've been overdoing it' or 'I just need a holiday'? Why had she accepted the excuses so readily?

Because it was easier than facing the truth.

That Joan wasn't 'fine, stop pecking at me', but riddled with a cancer that would leave her bedridden in three months from the diagnosis, dead in barely six.

Leaving so much unanswered and unsaid.

The doorbell chimed, shocking Peggy back into the present. She froze. She couldn't bear another sad-eyed neighbour, another overfilled dish. She shrank into her chair. How would she ever get through the summer? And, if she did manage that without turning herself into a hermit, what would she do when September arrived without the safety net of classes?

Despite the shock of Joan's illness, Peggy had graduated as one of the youngest and one of the highest placed students in her class – her mother had forbidden anything less than her completing her degree. The ceremony in May had been the last time Joan had made it out of bed and back into the world. So Peggy had her degree, but she hadn't thought a moment past that. Her application letters to the newspapers whose desks she had imagined sitting at in a white shirt as crisp as Katherine Hepburn's had gone unwritten. Her portfolio of college articles had gone unsent. For three months, Peggy had been a nurse, her world reduced to a bedside and trips to the pharmacy. Now she was rudderless, with no idea what to do next.

Except that isn't strictly true.

Ignoring the still buzzing bell, Peggy crept out of the kitchen, clinging to the edges of the hallway to avoid casting a shadow across the half-glazed front door. She couldn't stay in the house; it was still too full of her mother. And there was no college waiting, no job; nowhere else she was expected to be.

But there is a puzzle I could try solving, if I'm brave enough to do it.

Crouching below eye level, and feeling foolish for doing it, she slipped into the curtained front room. Ignoring the now stripped single bed, she crossed to the bureau and pulled open the top drawer. The photograph was still lying where she had left it on the night of her mother's death, tossed face down on top of countless years' worth of jumble.

'I should have given it to you a long time ago. I'm sorry.' Joan's voice that night had been barely a whisper. 'It was tucked inside the blanket you were wrapped in. Your real mother must have hidden it there.'

Your real mother. Joan had never used that expression before. It was hateful.

'Don't say that, not now. You don't need to say anything; you need to save your strength.'

But Joan had caught at Peggy's hand and kept going.

'You don't understand. I should have been kinder. I was taking her child. But we were desperate, your father and I. All those years trying, and longing. That's why I could never tear up the picture, even though I wanted to. She wanted to leave you some piece of her. I couldn't deny her that.'

Every word was born with such a struggle; in the end, Peggy had begged Joan to stop trying. She had only taken the photograph her mother was clutching because rejecting it had caused Joan unwatchable distress. She had barely looked at it. At that moment, she couldn't bear the thought of attaching *Mother* to anyone except the woman too quickly slipping away.

'I've got it. It's fine. You can tell me whatever it is you need to tell me in the morning.'

Except the morning, for Joan, never came.

The doorbell had finally stopped ringing. Peggy shook herself and returned to the kitchen's mint-green and cherry-red cheerfulness and placed the photograph carefully on the table. It looked even older in the sunlight, its black-and-white images fading to yellow. When she picked it up, the thin paper curled and a tiny tear in its middle threatened to spread. Two girls gazed back at her. Both of them were young, no more than eighteen or nineteen, and both were wearing fluted skirts that hugged their hips and flared out in pleats and frills at the calf. It was a narrower silhouette than the nipped-in waists and circle skirts Peggy and her friends ran around in. Based on the fashions she had seen in old photographs of her mother, Peggy guessed this one must have been taken in the late twenties or early thirties.

It wasn't a studio shot. The people milling in the background – under a sign that read *Hoppegarten*, a word that meant nothing to Peggy – their shoulders and elbows jutting into the frame, suggested that the picture had been snapped, not staged. Both the girls were standing with their bodies turned in towards each other, their faces looking directly at the camera. One of them was slightly tight-lipped, although her eyes were sparkling. The other was positively glowing: looking slightly past the lens, her gaze measured, her mouth smiling but in a subtle way that was almost a pout. She seemed to Peggy as if she was cultivating a 'look', trying to project an air of mystery and sophistication that was dazzling but a little too old for her face. That the two were friends was obvious in their looped arms and tilted heads. But there were spaces between them too, and a stiffness in the smaller girl's shoulders and elbows; hints that, for all their apparent closeness, there may have been differences that ran beyond the shape of a smile.

So which one is she? My mother? Which one do I want her to be?

Peggy dropped the photograph, the questions stinging. This was wrong. This was a betrayal of Joan.

Except that she kept it. And then she gave it to me when she was too ill to explain what it was. Isn't that the real betrayal here?

For the first time in years, Peggy allowed the surge of anger she normally swallowed to surface. Her childhood had been happy because her parents had managed her, wasn't that the real truth? Hadn't everything been kept *pleasant* because the alternative – the everyday arguments and jealousies that other families were strong enough to deal with – was too frightening for them?

Peggy's pulse was racing. She traced her finger up and down the tablecloth's checks, using the rhythm to steady herself. She had spent so long not thinking about her past, she wasn't sure she knew how to reach out to it. She had loved her parents, and they had loved her. She had no doubt about that; she had never been allowed a moment's doubt about that.

But we were all equally afraid of testing the bond. Especially once I knew.

Before she knew; after she knew. They were two separate stages in her life, not that Peggy had ever admitted that. Or admitted how often she had wondered if her parents would have told her the truth if she hadn't prompted the telling.

'What does this word mean?'

Peggy could see the day her world shifted as clearly as she could see the current one. It had been a Saturday morning. Her parents had been drinking coffee in the kitchen of their cosy house on 81st and Columbus Avenue on New York's Upper West Side; the house where they had lived since Peggy was a baby. Planning a trip to the market, consulting the weather forecast and debating whether they should take a wander round the Planetarium or risk the open spaces of Central Park. When she came through the door, Father had been making his usual weekend suggestion of a detour to Kirsch's Bakery for Linzer Torte Cookies, and Mother had been looking pointedly at his waistline and shaking her head. Both of them knew they would end up there anyway.

There had been nothing remarkable; nothing to mark it out from any other Saturday. Until Peggy had waved the newspaper article at them and asked what *I Am An Adoptive Mother* meant and why the slightly fearsome Joan Crawford was saying it.

Peggy pushed at the tablecloth and remembered the look that had flashed between her parents, and the awkward pause that followed it. Jack had coughed and looked away, leaving Joan to answer her, with a smile so alarmingly bright, Peggy had instinctively taken a step back from it.

'It means she chose her children, sweetheart. It means they were very much wanted.'

Peggy remembered liking that. *Chosen* sounded lovely, especially if it was a famous film star doing the choosing. She had been about to share that thought, and start what her father called her 'story weaving', when there was another look. And then there was a nod and a whisper she couldn't catch, and her parents were suddenly holding hands so tight their knuckles stuck out like stones. She had gone to slip out of the room, not comfortable with whatever was hovering, but her mother had stopped her retreat.

'Sit down, Peggy dear. Your father and I think it is time we told you something. It's nothing to be scared of. Quite the opposite in fact.'

Her mother's smile was still too bright and her voice was pitched too high. Peggy had dithered, sensing this *something* was too big for the room, but her mother patted the empty chair beside her, so Peggy did as she was asked, the same as she always did. And then out it all came. How Peggy had had a different mother first, *in Germany of all places*, who loved her very much, *how could she not*, but who couldn't care for her and was *terribly grateful* when the Baileys stepped in. How lucky they all were that *Daddy had been on secondment to the Humboldt University at exactly the right time, which meant that Peggy was surely meant to be theirs after so many years waiting for a child of their own.* How Peggy too had been *chosen* and *wanted*, which made her *extra-special*. And *how terribly lucky they all were* because *hadn't everything worked out for the best?*

Sitting in the silent kitchen, Peggy remembered how her mother's voice had quickened. How still her father had been.

'Am I a German then?'

It was the only thing she had managed to ask. Her mother's laugh at the question was too shrill for her to risk asking anything more.

'Of course not! You were barely there. You're completely American. You're the same as us.'

Except that wasn't true, and, after that day, it never would be again. But her mother's eyes were saucer-sized and her father's shoulders were trembling, and they were both so desperate for Peggy to agree that, yes, everything was wonderful, that she did.

Her parents had clapped and grinned and declared that today wasn't a park or a Planetarium day after all, but a day to go to Schrafft's for butterscotch sundaes. They had swept Peggy out in a whirlwind of chatter that blocked her voice up for weeks. And then her father had been offered a post at Brown and the bustle of a move from New York to Rhode Island had whirled everything else away. Everyone was happy, everything was settled and secure in its place.

Except for Peggy, who was confused and couldn't find a way to admit it. Who was still her parents' daughter, and yet not. Who was suddenly German, and yet not.

Germany. It was a country she didn't know, with a language she didn't speak. A country which had started a war and lost it, and done terrible things to its people that no one spoke about except in hushed tones. A country which had spawned the monster-man Hitler and his goose-stepping Nazis. Whose dreams of world domination and master races had once, according to her father, nearly infected America. Peggy still had a vague memory of a march she had seen the tail end of as a small child in New York. Of being bundled away from shouting and from banners that bore the bent cross she later learned was a swastika. Germany came with such dark shadows, Peggy hadn't dared ask how deep its claim ran on her.

I should have asked more, but I didn't. They should have told me more, but they didn't. They said it didn't matter, so I made it not matter. And then she drops this bombshell on me, and it does.

Peggy picked up the photograph again. Why would Joan have given it to her, and at such a time, unless she wanted her to act on it? Unless it was some kind of permission to go looking? Peggy was certain her mother had intended to tell her more, that she had been struggling to do just that when Peggy made her stop talking because she couldn't bear the pain of watching Joan agonise over every word. Perhaps stopping her had been the wrong thing to do – giving a key with no clue to the lock it fitted was a cruelty her mother wasn't capable of – but it was too late to regret that decision now.

Maybe there's something I'm missing.

She held up the picture to the window to better see the faces. There had to be some familiar feature, some trait that one of the two girls shared with Peggy, that would identify her. One of the girls was dark-haired and dark-eyed, which was promising, but then she was tall and Peggy definitely wasn't. *Pint-size* was still a nickname that plagued her. The other girl had elegantly high cheekbones, which Peggy had been told she had too. One of the girls...

She gave up. Every feature she imagined forged a link could be a trick of the light, or a coincidence, or her own longing. Peggy turned the photograph over and scraped at the back with her nail. There were still no names, no date.

I might as well rip it up for all the good keeping it will do.

She flipped it over again, angry and frustrated, and started to pull at the slight rip in the middle. And then something caught her eye. The girl on the left had a brooch pinned to her collar: a ballerina with her skirt and arms spread out; it caught the light as if it was made out of rhinestones. It was beautiful, and unusual; and it was memorable. As something about the wearer's face was suddenly memorable.

Peggy leaped up from the table and ran out of the kitchen, taking the stairs to her bedroom two at a time. Please God, her mother hadn't thrown them all out. She whirled through drawers and under the bed, flinging her belongings everywhere. And then, finally, there they were, her film magazines, tidied away neatly into a box at the back of her closet. Peggy upended the carton and began digging, looking for the oldest editions, the copies of *Movieland* and *Modern Screen* dating from 1947 and 1948 that she had stored up her precious pocket money to buy.

'There you are. I knew it!'

Peggy sat back on her heels, grinning at the cover shot. It was dated March 1947 and featured Louise Baker, one of Hollywood's brightest stars at the time, and a screen legend now. Peggy knew every detail of the actress's face. The scarlet-slicked trademark half-smile; the high curving cheekbones; the famous curls, tumbling like a treacle waterfall over one eye. Louise Baker at the height of her fame and utterly breathtaking. And wearing the ballerina brooch in the deep plunge of her gown, exactly as Peggy had remembered it.

It could be a coincidence; it could be a copy.

It could be. But that didn't matter.

Taking the stairs more carefully this time, Peggy went back to the kitchen and lined up the magazine next to the photograph. The brooch might not be unique, but that crooked smile was. And that glance up under the lashes that was so casually done it was clearly deliberate.

Except it doesn't make sense. I was adopted in Germany. If my mother is one of the girls, surely that's where the photograph must have been taken. And Louise Baker isn't German, which means it can't be her.

But it was. *Impossible, illogical,* whatever words she chose to deny it, Peggy was certain: the girl on the left, looking straight into the camera as if she was daring Peggy to recognise her, wasn't a stranger any more. She was a star.

CHAPTER TWO

Berlin, May 1931

'UFA have requested you both this afternoon for screen tests. It's most irregular. I explained that your classes aren't completed yet, that you don't have your diplomas, but Herr Reinhardt agreed to the request, so here we are.'

'How much pain do you think she is in right now?'

Anna ignored Marika's deliberately overloud whisper and smiled at the Reinhardt Drama Academy's formidable secretary. Her attempt at friendliness wasn't returned.

'Take these. They are your attendance records and your proofs of good conduct.' The secretary pushed two envelopes across the desk with the tips of her fingers. 'You are expected at Babelsberg at 1.30 p.m. Do you require train passes for the journey?'

'Goodness me, no. What a thought. Papa will send a car the minute I call him.'

Marika scooped up the letters and whirled Anna away before she was halfway through her *That's kind, but no thank you.*

'Seriously, Mari, do you always have to be mean to her?'

Marika rolled her eyes. 'Shouldn't the question be, why does *she* always have to be such a misery? Did you hear her? It's hardly *most irregular* to get called up by the studios: what a nonsense. How long has she worked here? She knows the final-year productions are showcases, or why on earth would the casting directors attend those rather than all the other shows we've done in the last three years? You know what her problem is, don't you? She's jealous and bitter, and do you want to know why?'

'Not really, but I imagine you're going to tell me.'

'Because no one would ever pay to watch her on a screen, and because she's in love with Max and he never sees her. It's all very tragic, but how is any of it my fault?'

'Stop it.' Anna couldn't help but laugh at Marika's unconvincingly innocent expression. 'It's totally your fault that she loathes you, and me by default. You needle her, you know you do. And when Herr Reinhardt is around, you're shameless. You call him Max, as if the two of you are best friends, and the way you flirt with him in front of her is cruel. I'd be jealous and bitter.'

'No you wouldn't.' Marika linked her arm through Anna's and pulled her down the corridor. 'I flirt with Eddy all the time and you never care a bit about that, do you?'

Oh but I do. You have no idea how much I do.

Not that Anna had any intention of admitting that to Marika; nor would it stop Marika if she did, although she knew how crazy Anna was about him. Eddy Hartmann was – as Anna had once described him to her friends after one too many cheap cognacs and was now never allowed to forget – 'the Romeo to my Juliet, except without all the dying'. She had met him in their third term at the Academy, when she and Marika had been selected to help the trainee director polish his outdoor filming technique. He had taken them to the Grunewald horse racing stadium, expecting to shoot a few reels of film and some stills in an hour and then enjoy an afternoon's betting. Marika, however, had unleashed her best film-star flirting routine on the beer-soaked crowds and the resulting chaos had almost lost Eddy the day's light.

Anna still had one of the photographs Eddy had taken of the two of them that day. It wasn't one of his best pictures – Marika was smouldering at the camera like Gloria Swanson; Anna was trying not to laugh at Eddy's increasing exasperation – but it was one of her favourites. It was a memento of the day she had first felt the spark that had deepened over the last two years into a love that was as vital to Anna as breathing. Vital, but not always easy. They were both ambitious, they were both hungry to make their mark on the world; their affair had been, at times, a rollercoaster ride that Marika refused to believe was worth it. The men Marika collected were adoring puppies she could boss about, or older, more cynical suitors who did what she wanted, as long as she put up with the price. She insisted she found Eddy 'far too much like hard work, despite those dreamy eyes', but that didn't stop her flirting with him at every opportunity. It niggled at Anna, but Eddy shrugged it off, so she did her best to do the same.

'Marika flirts with every man under eighty; she can't help herself. But she's going to be a star, anyone can see that, and I want to direct stars, which means I plan to stay on her good side, no matter how ridiculous she gets. You know how this world goes; you know my heart's yours.'

When Anna had repeated that to her mother after a night when Marika's relentless attention-grabbing had led to a fight, Frau Tiegel had defended Eddy as squarely as Anna had needed her to.

'He means it; the way he feels about you shines out of him. And he's right about Marika: I don't think she cares one way or the other about Eddy, but she needs to feel every man is in love with her. The last time she was here, she flirted so much with your father, she terrified him. She's a good girl, with a good heart most of the time, but keep an eye on her. No matter how much you value her friendship, keep a little bit back.'

Frau Tiegel's advice had been gently given, the way it always was, and Anna had listened, the way she always did, although she hadn't perhaps followed it as closely, or kept Marika as distant, as her mother wanted her to. And it was true that she valued the friendship, although, given how difficult Marika could be when the mood was on her, Anna couldn't always explain why. Perhaps it was because Marika Bäcker was different to anyone Anna had ever met, and that made her interesting. She was a brilliantly talented whirlwind: charming and witty and capable of filling the air around her with colour. And she was ambitious and nobody's fool, both traits Anna had always admired, in men and women. She was also selfish and spoiled and ruthlessly competitive. That should have triggered enough red lights to keep Anna away, but the mix was too intriguing, and too interesting a challenge to ignore.

Anna had deliberately kept pace with Marika from their first day together in the Academy's highly competitive acting classes, matching whatever tricks Marika pulled out to grab all the attention. At the end of the first week spent dancing round each other, Marika had linked arms with Anna, the way she still did, and declared her verdict.

'So, Anna Tiegel of Mitte, you're clearly the main competition in this place. As far as I can see, it's be best friends or kill each other. Which one do you think we should choose?'

Anna had burst out laughing and they had been inseparable – and dividing the class trophies between them – ever since. It was a strong bond; there was mutual respect and a rivalry Anna believed was healthy, even if her classmates didn't quite see it that way. But she still drew the line at talking about Eddy.

'Where are you dragging me off to now?'

Marika was too swept up in her own plans to notice that Anna hadn't answered her question.

'To Costume, of course. You look like you're about to service the heating, and I'm not going to turn up at Germany's biggest film studio in slacks and a waistcoat as if I'm a wannabe Dietrich.'

Which you obviously are, today at least. Goodness knows who you'll come as tomorrow.

Anna turned her head so Marika wouldn't catch her grinning. For all that Marika kept claiming how *unique* her talent was, she was a chameleon. Her obsession with learning every mannerism of the leading actresses she worshipped was legendary among the other students. And her obsession with the ones, like Dietrich, who had swapped Germany for Hollywood, and her determination to join them, was a topic that, once started, could run on for hours. More than one tutor had reprimanded her for 'disloyalty to her homeland'. Not that Marika ever took any notice. In the same way that Anna usually took no notice when Marika shuddered at her practical, rehearsal-ready clothes. Today, however, she had to concede that Marika knew what she was doing.

As the Bäcker family's Mercedes swept the girls under the Babelsberg Studio's stone archway an hour later, she was glad that she had given in. Her daisy-sprigged lemon silk bolero and matching tiered skirt – plucked from the Costume Department by way of Marika's generous wallet – was far better suited to the elegant reception area than her blue overalls would have been. And Marika's wrapped and pin-tucked peach dress was, as Marika had put it herself, 'quite perfect'.

Universum Film AG – better known throughout Germany as UFA – was the country's oldest film company; it claimed to be older than Hollywood. It was also, since it had sucked up most of the smaller studios in the 1920s, Germany's biggest. Some of the largest production facilities in Europe were concentrated on the sprawling Babelsberg compound, and every star in Germany – and many from America – had shot films there. A UFA contract meant the start of a glittering career and every drama student craved one, or was meant to. Anna knew that Marika had been living for the studio's phone call since the day she entered the academy – she had made no secret of it. One step over the threshold and it was clear she already considered herself part of the place. Halfway down a corridor lined with giant posters for *Metropolis* and *The Blue Angel* and her shoulders were back. By the time they had passed the third backlot rigged up with lighting towers and cameras perched on tripods like curious insects, Anna would have sworn Marika was two feet taller than when they came in.

'It's our world, what did I tell you? Can't you already feel how much we belong?'

Anna didn't answer. She couldn't deny the energy: the air buzzed with it. But as to it being her world? The sheer scale of the sets and the crowds of scurrying extras had her longing for a stage's more intimate lines. When she stayed silent, Marika came to a halt with such an exaggerated sigh, Anna almost looked round for the camera. Before she could launch into a lecture, however, a voice cut across the bustling lot.

'Fräulein Bäcker, what a delight. Are you here for your screen test?'

The man approaching the girls had a voice far bigger than his slight frame and a limp his quick pace couldn't fully conceal. He took Marika's hand and kissed it, bowing so deeply he almost bent himself in two. The gesture was so ridiculously theatrical, Anna almost laughed, but then he straightened and caught her eye and the impulse left her. He dropped Marika's hand; he did not pick up Anna's.

'And you must be Fräulein Tiegel?' He smiled as Anna frowned. 'Darling Marika mentioned your name at one of our parties. And when she said how good an actress you are, I took the liberty of also suggesting you to the studio. That is why you are here today.'

He stopped, clearly waiting for Anna to respond. His manner was so condescending, she wasn't sure how. Luckily, Marika jumped in first.

'Joseph, how could you! You promised you would only recommend me.'

The pause before he smiled was slight, but it was long enough for Anna to catch the shadow that clouded his face before he repositioned his smile. There was something familiar about his dark hair and thin face, although she knew they hadn't met. Then she made the connection between his first name and his limp and had to stop herself from stepping back. Joseph Goebbels. The propaganda chief for the National Socialist Party, whose aggressive and demanding style of politics had suddenly, and loudly, burst onto the streets of Berlin. Or the *hoppity little thug in a too big suit*, as her father called him. How on earth did Marika know a man like Joseph Goebbels? Anna would have asked, but Marika was still complaining.

'It's not as if Anna even wants to act in the movies. She wants to be on the stage, I told you that. Which, I keep telling her, is a pointless affectation. Who wants to fritter away their talent on a play where your performances go unrecorded and forgotten, when cinema can turn you into a goddess?'

Goebbels laughed; Anna couldn't hear any mirth in it.

'Don't pout, Marika dear, not until your test anyway. And why wouldn't I encourage another beauty to appear on our screens? There's plenty of room for both of you.'

The ownership that ran through his voice turned Anna's stomach and loosened her tongue.

'Actually, Marika's right. I don't have any great desire to do a screen test and I would far rather perform in the theatre. It's more real. The thrill of the audience in front of you, reacting. Not cut off from the actors' emotions by weeks of filming and a camera's filter. Drama breathes in the theatre, I really believe that; the cinema freezes it.' Anna had meant to sound passionate; she sounded smug. Goebbels turned towards her; this time it was Anna who stumbled into the pause he left. 'What can I say? I'm a theatre brat, I can't help it. It's what I was raised on.'

It was a clumsy recovery.

Marika, who was clearly irritated at losing her admirer's attention, sniffed. 'Not the joys of the dusty wings again. If your father's theatre was as wonderful, and always as packed as you insist it was, why is it a cinema now? Do you think it might be because the world has moved on?'

Anna flinched. The dig was a keen one, the kind Marika excelled in. She knew exactly what his changed position had cost Anna's father. She had sat in their kitchen on enough nights, listening to Franz tell his stories about the theatre he had managed for twenty-five years, about the casts and crew who had stolen his heart there. She knew that heart had been broken when the owners, more concerned with their wallets than the sentiment Anna and her father had clung to, had converted the elegant old building and blocked out the stage with a screen. Anna itched to remind Marika of that, but she had no desire to lay her family open in front of a man her father despised.

Goebbels shrugged as if Anna's objections didn't concern him; his narrowed eyes, however, told a different story. 'If I had known you felt this strongly, I wouldn't have wasted my time putting you forward. It is a little awkward, of course – I had asked for a favour and now it's not needed – but the director is a Party man and I'm sure this won't reflect badly on Marika. He is a professional – he won't judge her by your rudeness.'

Marika's gasp was loud enough to turn heads.

'Anna, apologise to Joseph for goodness' sake! And be a bit more grateful: he didn't have to do this for you.'

So why did he? Why does it matter to him where I perform?

But Marika's eyes were bright with tears and Anna had no choice but to say sorry and follow Goebbels to the shed-like studio, where the director greeted him with a hand that shook as he offered it. Anna doubted Marika noticed – she was too busy checking her make-up – but she knew Goebbels did. She saw him smile.

Marika was her irrepressible self again on the ride back into Berlin. Her test had been *wonderful*. She was a *shoo-in* for a contract. She was completely uninterested in listening to Anna's reservations about Goebbels.

'He likes actresses, what's the big deal? And he's obsessed with *creating the right image for the Party,* whatever that means, which he says is the cinema's job. To be honest, he can be really boring about it – I go to nightclubs to dance, not listen to lectures – but, with the amount of champagne he's willing to pay for, I'm happy to at least look like I care. Now, can't we talk about something more interesting?'

Anna knew by that, Marika meant herself, but she wasn't quite ready to give up. Germany was becoming increasingly unsettled, and the rapid rise of Adolf Hitler's National Socialist Party was to blame. Anyone who spent any time with the newspapers was aware of it; unfortunately, as Anna well knew, Marika's taste ran more to fashion magazines.

Which is why someone needs to look out for her.

'Mari, honey. Are you sure it's a good idea to get mixed up with a politician? There's some disturbing people trying to get into power at the moment. I'm not saying his attentions aren't lovely, and useful, but maybe you shouldn't be around him so much.'

It was a pointless effort. It always was when Marika had bagged a new conquest.

'Don't be a bore, Anna. Papa mixes with politicians all the time; most people of our class do. It's hardly as if Joseph is some thug in a brown shirt, running round the streets picking fights. But can't we focus on celebrating my rather wonderful day? We should go for drinks. What about Ciro, or shall we be daring and brave the crowds at Efti?'

Going for drinks with an over-exuberant Marika was the last thing Anna wanted to do, especially when she refused to make the connection between Goebbels and the Brownshirts. She was about to try and explain, but the effort was too much. She was exhausted. Unlike Marika, she had hated the screen test: it had made her feel like a show pony.

Turn this way, turn that. Walk quicker, walk slower. Tilt your head. Take off your hat; put it back on again. Smile.

It had taken them so long to stop parading her and actually give her a script, Anna had begun to wonder if silent movies had come back into fashion. The director, however, had loved her and told her an offer was in the bag. It was flattering, but, last week – not that she had told Marika yet – she had had auditions with Berlin's three biggest theatres, and the directors there had loved her too. Now that she had seen first-hand what a cinema audition was like, she couldn't imagine changing her mind about where her ambitions lay.

Marika was still bubbling on about which bartender mixed the best gin fizz as the car swept into Tiergartenstraβe, the enclave of private mansions and embassies flanking Berlin's biggest park, which included the Bäckers' huge house. The villa was a magnificent place, all wrought iron and carved columns and crenellations. It wasn't, however, a home Anna wanted to live in. Given how often she invited herself to the Tiegels' far more modest apartment in Mitte, she doubted Marika cared much for it either. She couldn't: for all its grandeur, it was staff who filled it, not family or friends.

Anna, like Marika, was an only child. But unlike Marika's, Anna's home was a busy and warm one. It played host not only to herself and her parents, but also to the students her mother tutored and fed, and to her father's card-playing cronies, and the waifs and strays both the Tiegels regularly acquired. The number of plates set for dinner was never a constant. Anna imagined that Marika's detached banker father and social butterfly mother would hate all the living and laughing that went on inside its cosy walls.

But it's what I need now. A heaped plate of Mama's paprika stew and an audience who will appreciate how ridiculous the whole studio experience was. And maybe a little detour first to see Eddy.

He had said he would be at his flat all night, getting his notes in order for the school production he was directing next week, his

own big-break showcase. It was still early. Time enough to drop
into Wedding before she went home, or, perhaps, didn't.

She gathered up her bag as the car eased to a stop and opened
the door before the chauffeur's slow walk round to it delayed her.

'I'm tired, I'm sorry. Go and have fun without me.'

She was out in the street and heading for the subway before
Marika could argue.

The warm May evening had brought couples and families out
strolling, heading for the Tiergarten's leafy pathways. Women
nodded as she passed by; men tipped their hats. It was peaceful
and quiet; there was hardly a sound to disturb the twilight, other
than children laughing and the occasional clip-clop of a horse.
What Marika had said was true: it was hard to imagine a group
of Brownshirts sauntering here, even though they seemed to be
popping up all over the rest of the city.

Especially in Wedding.

Anna quickened her step towards the station, knowing how
cross her father would be if he knew where she was heading. He
loathed the SA, the *Sturmabteilung* – the official name for the
brown-shirt-wearing military wing of the National Socialist Party
– who took their orders, in Berlin at least, from Goebbels. Franz
Tiegel loathed the whole Party.

'They're criminals, the whole lot of them, from Hitler down to
his ignorant bully boys, not some proper political party like they
pretend to be. They say they're battling communists? That's rubbish,
an excuse for beating up anyone they don't fancy the look of. And
they don't care who they frighten. They attacked a cinema last week,
for goodness' sake. Who in their right mind attacks a cinema?'

Now that Anna had met Goebbels, however, that episode made
a little more sense. There had been an almost childishly vengeful
streak in his threat that her lack of gratitude at the studio would
rebound on Marika, and the outbreak of violence at Berlin's Mozart
Hall that had upset Franz had certainly felt childish. Goebbels' SA

mob had disrupted the premiere of the war film *West Front 1918,* claiming that the movie was 'an insult to good German soldiers and unpatriotic'. They hadn't done it with their fists like they normally did, but by unleashing stink bombs and mice onto the audience. Anna and her fellow students had thought the whole thing was ridiculous, but Goebbels got his way and the film was banned. That he could wield so much influence without any official position had been far more unsettling than the release of a few mice.

Some of the students, Anna among them, had reacted to the uproar by deciding to investigate the Nationalist Socialist movement. They had gone to the Neukölln neighbourhood – a known Brownshirt stronghold – on a cold February morning, to watch a march and try to understand what was winning Adolf Hitler and his allies so much support. After an hour spent shivering on a windy street corner, all Anna could confidently say she knew about the Party was that its marchers were angry men. Beyond getting rid of 'the Reds', she was no closer to understanding what they actually wanted. All the slogans seemed to be about who they intended to attack, not who they intended to help. She gave up listening after the first few columns had tramped past. She couldn't fathom why anyone would waste their breath on a group of people wrapped round with such hate.

'They act strong and they're tapping into everyone's fears about unemployment and another economic crash, but there's no substance there. The novelty will wear off soon enough. They'll crawl back under whatever rocks they crawled out from.'

Neither Eddy nor anyone else who went to the march had argued with her assessment and Anna had given the Brownshirts little thought since. Wedding, however, unlike Neukölln, had always been an area of Berlin with strong socialist sympathies and had therefore been a target for SA attacks for months, and meeting Goebbels – and realising how strongly he had got his claws into Marika – had unsettled her. That was a connection that needed breaking, not that she had any clue yet how.

Anna emerged from the Seestraβe station in the heart of the district, trying not to get distracted by her worries over Marika, holding tight to her bag and ready to move fast. The streets, however, were as peaceful as the ones surrounding the Tiergarten. Anna relaxed. It was barely a ten-minute walk to Eddy's flat, straight down Müllerstraβe and then one turn into Gerichtstraβe. The route was so familiar, she could do it with her eyes closed.

She continued down the street, running the next day's rehearsal scene in her head, taking no notice of her surroundings. She was so absorbed, she barely registered the first crash. She presumed someone had slammed a window shut too firmly. And then the violence exploded, in a hail of broken glass and flying tables that dropped her to her knees.

Some kind of beer hall or restaurant had erupted. Anna stayed crouching and scuttled into the protection of a dark alleyway as a brawling mass fell out through the gaping doors and splintered windows. At first, she could hardly tell arms and legs apart; she certainly couldn't separate one side from another. And then she realised one group of fighters was moving in a synchronised pattern, their movements as deliberate as if a choreographer had schooled them.

A beer mug caught the street lamp's glare as it flew up and plunged down. Batons and broken table legs crashed hard into bone. Spikes sprouted from fingers; metal blades flashed like struck matches. There was blood, so much blood the gutters were running, and screaming that was so loud Anna had to plug up her ears. And then there was a whistle, so piercing and high-pitched she curled up against it. Two blasts, a shout, and it was done. The Brownshirts formed up into two columns and were gone, with a speed that matched their fighting. The bodies they had smashed lay still.

Moments passed without any sound beyond groaning. Anna didn't dare move. Gradually, as the street stayed quiet, doors further along from the wreckage inched open. People appeared, moving slowly towards the bodies, staying in the shadows. Someone checked the alleyway, asked Anna if she was all right, if she needed help. She shook her head, stepping away from the man, who might be worth trusting, and might not,

'That's the third night this week we've come under attack. Goebbels' boys call this place "Red Wedding"; they won't be happy until there isn't a meeting hall still standing.'

Anna kept quiet: she couldn't believe the ferocity of what she had seen, but – given how uncertain the mood in the whole city was, never mind these streets – she had no intention of discussing the night's violence, or anything to do with Goebbels, with a stranger.

He could be one of them. He could be trying to work out whose side I'm on.

She shuffled away as a police siren began wailing. Once she was a dozen yards away from the gathering crowd, she started to run; she didn't stop until she fell breathless against Eddy's doorway. With the solid wood against her back, she closed her eyes and finally breathed deeply, using the techniques learned in her classes to stop her heart hammering. She couldn't ring the bell, not yet. She didn't want to pore over the details, or have Eddy fly out into the night, clutching his camera. There was a darkness to what she had witnessed, a pleasure taken in violence that was more shocking than the beatings themselves. She didn't know how to explain that, without sounding hysterical. She didn't know how to put into words what she had sensed. That the brutality she had seen was precise and deliberate, and wasn't going to vanish with the summer as most disturbances did; that it had roots which were burrowing their way deep into the city. That these men, these terrible men with their uniforms and their fists, had crawled out from under their rocks to stay.

CHAPTER THREE

Rhode Island to California, August 1957

Everything was ready, which was hardly a surprise: Peggy had made list after list and double-checked every item. The house was spotless; the shutters were latched; the contents of the fridge now filled the freezer. She had dropped carefully crafted notes through the neighbours' doors – *an extended vacation to get over my grief, no need to worry or call anyone* – watching the house lights go out first to avoid the inevitable questions. Every inch of her mother's Plymouth Convertible that could be serviced had been serviced. The tank was full, the tyres were plump. She had packed a collection of Esso and Standard Oil road maps – the ones that came with the gas stations marked – into the glove compartment, ready to take her to Chicago and the start of Route 66, the highway that would then take her all the way west. She had made a note in her journal to buy the next maps in the set as she crossed each state line. She had cash in her purse and more stowed in the trunk, and her chequebook was folded into her suitcase. Peggy had no intention of being derailed by desert breakdowns, or any other damsel-in-distress dramas; this journey was going to go firmly to plan.

Except she couldn't seem to get started on it. Everything was ready and she was still sitting on the porch swing, half an hour after her planned departure time, trying to work out why she couldn't get into the car.

Perhaps it's the weather that's bothering me, the heat I won't be able to avoid in the desert.

That was a perfectly reasonable concern. The temperatures in Arizona and New Mexico in August could climb over one hundred degrees. Only a fool wouldn't be nervous at that, no matter how well-serviced their car was.

Peggy's neighbours would no doubt pick up her notes and imagine her *extended vacation* to mean a quiet few weeks in New England. If she had told them where she was actually heading, their jaws would have dropped.

The one person she had told her real plans to – about her planned destination at least – was her old college friend Nancy, who she planned to look up in Chicago, rather than trying to attempt the whole drive without the guarantee of one friendly face. Peggy had contacted Nancy by letter, however, and hadn't had to deal with a reaction.

She got that from the mechanic at the garage: he had been shell-shocked. He had asked her half a dozen times if she knew that the journey from Rhode Island to California was well over two thousand miles. That it would take her a fortnight's solid driving to do it, if she was lucky and didn't linger, or hit all the trouble he clearly thought that she would. She had taken refuge in polite nodding. When he had pronounced such an undertaking 'unsuitable for a girlie' and suggested it might be time for her to 'find a nice boy who would settle her down', she had given up trying to respond. But when he had begun to probe into her finances and ask how 'a pretty girl like you plans to keep herself fed and watered all that way' with a leer that made her skin crawl, she had cut him down. Her curt 'I'm using my dead mother's money' had shut up his concerns.

The heat is a worry, I can't pretend that it's not, and so is the distance. But they're not the problem; they're things that I've planned for.

Peggy still couldn't move.

It wasn't the thought of travelling alone that had stalled her either. Or spending every night in different motels and eating her meals at silent tables. Peggy had been brought up by a father obsessed with chivalric quests and King Arthur's knights. As practical as she could be, there was a part of her that had picked up, and expanded, his romantic streak. The idea of striding out alone into the hills and the deserts – fighting her own battles, overcoming her own obstacles – with nothing but her wits between her and the world was quietly thrilling. When she pictured herself telling the tale of her cross-country drive to her astounded friends and being thought of as *resourceful* and *plucky,* her heart skipped a beat.

So if I can manage all that, why am I still sitting here?

She closed her eyes and leaned back against the swing's smooth wood. The morning was quiet. It was too early for dogs to be barking, almost too early for birdsong. Her breathing slowed. The last few days had been a whirlwind of *doing*. Ever since she had married up the magazine cover with the photograph, she had been consumed with the idea of going to Hollywood. Now she had time to reflect, and that wasn't an entirely comfortable thing to do.

This isn't a crazy impulse; I've thought it through. And it isn't only about tracking down Louise and confronting her. It's also about getting a job. I love the movies and I want to be a journalist, so combining the two makes perfect sense.

All of that was true, but Peggy knew it wasn't as true as: *if I can turn this into a job, that's a bonus – I'm going to Hollywood in search of my mother.* And that was where she was stuck: at the truth.

It isn't the journey that's the problem; it's where its ending puts me.

Getting into the car meant leaving; going in search of Louise Baker meant another *before*, another *after*. A change in her life's direction that, this time, she had put knowingly in motion. And leaving this house meant leaving Joan, while the pain of her death still sat as raw as a burn.

Maybe all I'm really doing is running away from my grief, and spinning a story round that to make me feel better.

Peggy didn't know what to do with that. What she did know, however, was that, whatever the outcome, the journey would throw up more questions than answers. How could it not? Questions Peggy couldn't prepare for, no matter how many lists she wrote.

Whatever I find, whether Louise is the woman who gave birth to me or not, I won't come back the same.

Peggy opened her eyes and stared along the street. At the manicured lawns and the up-and-down skyline the mix of colonial houses and spread-out bungalows created. At the familiar palette of cream and yellow and blue woodwork and walls, and the white wraparound porches. This was home. Despite her father's death, she had always felt safe here, watched over here.

And maybe that is why I have to go.

The claustrophobia of the last fortnight, and the months of her mother's illness, coupled with the thought of any more time spent at the mercy of the constantly chiming doorbell, pushed her up and out of the swing. She had to go: if she stayed, the weight of her loss would bury her.

'I want you out in the world, doing what you've always dreamed of.' Her mother had said that after her father died and had said it again when she was dying. And Peggy's circumstances might have changed, but not the future she – no, *they* – had always wanted for her. Peggy still longed to be a journalist as much as she had when she first saw Rosalind Russell lighting up the screen in their local cinema's re-showing of *His Girl Friday*. She had been spellbound by the sparkling whip-smart reporter; unlike her swooning friends, she had barely noticed Cary Grant. She had spent years imagining her fingers rattling across a clattering typewriter while the headlines were held for the zinger of a piece no one but her could write. She had spent hours slaving over her school and then her college newspaper, churning out reviews of student plays that smoothed out stumbling casts; turning interviews with dry and dusty professors into sparkling prose. What was all that for, if not for this?

If I'm going to do this, I have to think like a journalist.

This was a real story – no, it was *a heart-warming story* of a mother and child torn apart and finally reconciled. It wasn't even a story, it was a *scoop*, with the writer herself there at the heart of it. It was the stuff movies were made of. So she had to go, with everything that entailed, and, if a different Peggy came back, if no kind of Peggy ever came back, what did it matter? Her mother – her real mother, not the one she had made up from a photograph, but the one who had been brave enough to take a baby into her life and love it as if it was her own – would surely have cheered her on.

I can do this. She made me strong enough to do this.

Peggy grabbed her suitcase and bounced into the car, willing herself not to look back and falter. She pulled on her cream leather driving gloves and reached to adjust the mirror. And then she stopped and properly looked at the face looking back. Why was she worried about turning into someone different when she had already taken the first step?

'Make me into someone new.'

She had gone into the hairdressers on a whim and said the line with a swagger that mortified her the minute it came out of her mouth. The stylist, however, hadn't laughed. She had gone to work, refusing to let Peggy sneak as much as a glance until the transformation was complete.

Peggy had emerged from the salon with her long chestnut ponytail chopped away, sporting instead the thick curls and bare neck of the newly popular, and still rather daring, Italian Cut. Perhaps the stylist's claim that 'you and Liz Taylor could be peas in a pod' was a little dramatic, but Peggy had to admit the change was striking. The shorter style accentuated her cheekbones and widened her gold-flecked brown eyes. It made her look older, and more glamorous. Like a girl who walked towards adventure, not away.

*

Her excitement faltered and finally failed her somewhere on the edges of New Mexico.

The first few days on the road had been a novelty. Peggy wrapped a chiffon scarf round her curls, snapped on her tortoiseshell sunglasses and drove with the top down, singing along to Elvis Presley and the Everly Brothers at the top of her voice as one local radio station merged into the next.

Louise Baker might be my mother.

The thought grew more exciting with every mile that she covered. The papers and film magazines might be filled nowadays with pictures of Marilyn Monroe and Natalie Wood, but everyone knew Louise Baker. She was one of the old Hollywood greats, who had shot to fame before the war and remained a mystery in the way the new girls didn't. She rarely gave interviews; she rarely appeared in public without dark glasses and an entourage wrapped round her. She was glamour personified. Imagining being welcomed into such famous arms kept Peggy's smile glowing even when the first two motels she checked into were a little disappointing. Their interiors were not quite as modern as their flashing signs suggested they would be, and the delights of their in-house diners sat a lot duller on the plate. Then Peggy arrived in Chicago and her wearying spirits bounced back.

The city was exactly as Nancy had described it: bold and brash, shoulders squared for a fight. It was similar enough to the New York of her childhood to be familiar, and different enough to add the edge to her journey Peggy craved. And Nancy was the delight she had always been. She burst into the bar full of consoling hugs and gossip from the *Chicago Tribune,* where she was employed 'as the lowest of the low, putting commas in the personal ads', and made Peggy long even more for a newsroom. Three cocktails in, and Nancy was promising to put in a good word for her as the *Tribune's* new LA correspondent as if she was the newspaper's editor. Her proclamation – delivered to the entire room – that

Peggy was a 'pioneer and an adventuress and everyone should drink to her' was exactly the springboard Peggy needed to launch the rest of her journey.

She pushed on, buoyed up by friendship, determined to gather exciting snippets to report back from every stage of the drive. She stopped in St Louis and sent Nancy a postcard filled with enchanted descriptions of its antebellum buildings and French-looking churches. She sent another when she fell in love with Tulsa's art deco curves and spires. The scenery she crossed as she headed towards Oklahoma City was *breathtaking*, the Ozark plateau and the splayed-out ranches and oilfields *unlike anything she had ever seen*. And yet…

For all that Peggy told Nancy that this was the *Mother Road,* a route soaked through with America's history, and that the landscapes she passed through were magnificent, the telling soon became rather hollow. In all her preparations, Peggy had forgotten to consider one very important fact: she was, at heart, a city girl, or, at the very least, a big town or campus girl. She liked buildings and bustle, being part of a crowd. The further she drove, the more the huge spaces unnerved her. By the time she reached New Mexico, with its endless brown deserts and its jagged-teeth mountains, she was longing for sidewalks and skyscrapers. The population-light towns she pulled into for gas stopped looking quaint. The flashing neon signs topped with bluebirds and wigwams shining outside the dusty motels proved to be all glitter and no gold. After almost a fortnight of travelling, nothing felt solid or certain.

Her senses were overloaded trying to adjust to vast skies and changing time zones. The conversations she had hoped to strike up had stayed in her head. Families and couples formed impenetrable units; men on their own took one look at her and slipped off their wedding rings. Peggy grew self-conscious and stopped smiling. Even her choice of book was the wrong one. She had brought along a copy of *The Grapes of Wrath* to be her mealtime companion, thinking it would provoke discussion with fellow travellers following in the Joad family's footsteps. After too many days on her own, however, the Joads' miseries had become unbearable and instead she sat in faceless restaurant after faceless restaurant, wishing she had brought *Peyton Place*. Wishing, if she was honest, that she had never set out.

Peggy Bailey, are you really going to be a quitter? Didn't we raise you stronger than that?

Joan's voice jumped so loudly into her head, Peggy almost choked on her hamburger.

You're lonely, sweetheart; you're not used to it. Count your blessings; this will pass.

'Are you all right, dear?' A heavy-set waitress wearing too much eyeliner was hovering, clutching a coffee pot. 'You've turned pretty pale.'

Peggy swallowed hard and waited a moment before answering, horrified that such a casual encounter could bring her close to tears.

The waitress leaned over and refilled her empty mug. For a brief, irrational, moment, Peggy imagined folding herself inside the broad arms and asking for a hug. She sat on her hands and tried to focus on what the woman was asking.

'Long day, or long drive?'

Peggy sniffed but managed not to sob. 'Both.'

The waitress nodded as if she was listening, but she was already scanning the rest of her section. 'That's often the way of it down here. You heading away from something or towards?'

'Both.'

This time, the waitress looked properly at her.

'Well, that's a different answer to most. Two sets of problems then. Do you know which of them's worse?'

Peggy hesitated, not sure how to measure up the death of one mother against the chance of finding another.

'No. No, I don't. Whichever way you look at it, something gets lost. I was thinking maybe I should give up, go back to what

I know?' She stopped, hoping that the woman would realise how much she needed an answer, but another customer waved their coffee cup. The waitress nodded absently and moved on.

Peggy stared at her plate and stopped herself from spinning the moment out, imagining the woman's return and a heart-to-heart full of homespun wisdom. It had been an offhand enquiry, Peggy had momentarily piqued a bored waitress's interest; there was nothing more to the encounter than that.

Which at least means I walk away with my dignity intact.

Her skin suddenly burning with an unaccustomed blush, Peggy scrabbled in her bag for bills enough to pay for her meal and leave a substantial tip.

Whichever way you look at it, something gets lost.

When had she become such a pessimist? And when did she start sharing her problems with strangers?

Peggy wrapped the remains of her hamburger in a napkin and went outside. The sun was setting, in a riot of crimson and rose. She found a bench and sat down to watch it. The sky swirled above her in a triumph of technicolour; there were even shooting stars. It was such a perfect Hollywood-reveal moment, Peggy started to laugh.

'It's time to get a grip, Peggy Bailey; it's time to see the big picture.' She said it out loud in her best Jimmy Stewart voice.

So the journey had been a little harder than she thought it would be; she had still manged most of it. Yes, there was still a long way to go. The Mojave Desert was still in front of her, and Arizona, and the worst of the summer's heat. She doubted she would drive the rest of the way more enraptured by the wonders of nature than she had already been. It didn't matter: she had come this far without mishap; she could surely do the rest.

And so what if she had been embarrassingly naïve? Thinking she would do well with solitude, refusing to admit how deeply lonely she was. Wasn't that a lesson worth learning? Wasn't she doing this in the first place because she didn't want to be alone in the world? If she gave up and went back, wasn't that what she would be?

Peggy watched the colours shift across the darkening sky, watched the stars darting and imagined Joan up there, blowing some of the stardust down to brighten her daughter.

'You're right, Mom: I'm not a quitter. Whatever is coming, bring it on!'

Heads turned across the parking lot. This time she had shouted. She didn't care. Her voice cutting through the night air sounded good.

Blue wasn't a wide enough word to describe the Pacific. Even at the shoreline, its waters rippled through cobalt and sapphire. Peggy trailed her fingers through its warmth and laughed at her disappointment when they resurfaced still pink.

Santa Monica, a small town wrapped round a long beach and the last stop on Route 66, was perfect enough to send Nancy an overdue postcard. From the moment Peggy had arrived on the sprawling edges of Los Angeles, everything had finally fallen into place. The city had an energy, as though it was determined to push back the desert clinging round it, and the mountain ranges too, if it chose. The streets and sidewalks pulsed. The signs that lined the long boulevards promised food for the soul as much as the body – cinemas and theatres, bookshops and nightclubs all crowded together, claiming their space. Peggy had been tempted to stop at the first hotel and jump into the bustle, but she had joined the road west at its start and had made a promise to herself to see it through to its end. When she reached the ocean and couldn't catch her breath, she knew she had made the right choice.

She stopped moving forward. She slowed down. She looked around her. Instead of choosing a place to stay based on how exhausted she was, she stopped at a cheerful-looking gas station and asked for a recommendation. Ten minutes later and she was on

Santa Monica's Ocean Avenue, outside the pristine white apartment blocks of a motel nestled into the side of a bougainvillea-draped park. She could barely drag herself away from the hummingbirds long enough to register for one of the spacious apartments.

That night, she took a drive up Laurel Canyon into the hills and watched another crimson-streaked sunset, this time with the Hollywood sign, not a garish neon motel advert, at her back. Somewhere in the tangle of lights below her was Melrose Avenue and Paramount Studios. Tomorrow, if the copy of *Film Daily* – the industry trade paper she had scoured in the hotel lobby – was accurate, Louise Baker would be on set there filming. Not for a major role, she didn't land those any more, but she would be there and she had been easy to find, something Peggy hadn't expected. There had to be a good omen in that.

The next morning, Peggy was up early, incapable of eating breakfast, dressed for the stylish crowd she expected to meet. Ankle-skimming gingham capri pants and a toning lemon tie-waisted shirt; cats-eye sunglasses and, despite the heat that was already building, a satin-edged baby-pink cardigan draped over her shoulders, the thin material suspended from two diamanté clips and a delicate chain.

She parked the car on the corner of Melrose and Van Ness and wound her way up to Bronson Avenue and a set of gates so famous she could describe them from memory. Wrought iron as intricate as lacework, set inside an elegant cream-and-gold arch decorated with scrollwork, and topped off with the curling *Paramount Pictures* sign. They were fabulous; they wouldn't have looked out of place on a temple. They were also smaller than they looked in the magazines, which made them far easier to guard and more intimidating than Peggy had supposed they would be.

After half an hour standing and staring, she still hadn't plucked up the courage to go in.

Which is fine. And sensible. It's not nerves: you're being careful, checking out the lie of the land.

Wise words she kept repeating; she still didn't believe them. No one on their own was getting through without checks. And it no longer mattered that she looked the part – so did everyone else.

As the sun rose too high to keep standing in it, she took refuge in a drugstore that overlooked the gates. There was a group of girls at the counter, collecting bottles of soda and cigarettes, flicking their ponytails and clutching folders; talking loudly enough about production schedules and directors' demands to be noticed. Peggy sidled closer. As soon as they gathered up their last orders and headed out, she pulled her journal out of her purse and tagged on behind them.

Smile like you own the place and no one will dare ask.

A college classmate dripping generations of Boston privilege had offered that advice. It worked: Peggy glided through the gates at the back of the group without a glance from the guard. Once they were inside, however, the girls splintered off in a hail of goodbyes, heading up a fan of rickety staircases which led to a walkway and a long row of offices. None of the doors marked Reading Room or Writing Room or Production were open or inviting, so Peggy walked on.

The trade paper had said Miss Baker was shooting her latest picture, *Higher Than the Moon* – one in a series of love-triangle movies in which she, as the older woman, was perpetually wronged – in Studio Four. Peggy had no idea where that was. The little she knew about the Paramount compound was the same as every film buff could recite: that it covered twenty-six acres and included eighteen studios plus dozens of backlots, far too many to cover on foot.

Peggy couldn't risk asking for directions and being asked her business. She could, however, see signs for Studios One and Two a little way ahead of her, so she did the most logical thing and headed in their direction. She kept her stride purposeful; she avoided eye contact. It was hard, however, not to get distracted when each side of the road peeled off into shooting lots. Within two blocks of the gate, she had caught glimpses of a very convincing row of New York brownstones, a medieval market, and the dusty sidewalks of a frontier town. The studios, however, were all firmly sealed up and covered in *shooting in progress, do not enter* signs.

Studio Four, when she finally spotted it, also came with its own guard, a burly-looking man she had no clue how to approach. Peggy turned the corner, walked the length of the building, walked back. The guard didn't move; the solid white walls didn't get any less challenging.

I'll say I've got a message. From Mr Hitchcock. He's sure to be filming here somewhere. No one's going to argue with an assistant to Alfred Hitchcock.

She began to cross the road, her best smile in place, and was only saved from making an almighty fool of herself by the sudden blast of a siren. Doors burst open all round her as if the sound had released a coiled set of springs. Peggy jumped back against the wall as a tide of people emerged, dressed in costumes that mingled more centuries and countries than her brain could pick out.

It must be lunchtime.

She had read it was a communal affair, stars and secretaries alike all eating together in the commissary, albeit in heavily demarcated sections. She hadn't realised, however, that communal meant everyone downing tools, or how accessible that suddenly made the film compound.

Forcing herself to stand still, she let the first surge go. Her patience was rewarded. A few minutes after the siren had disgorged the bulk of Studio Four, a smaller group emerged from its shadowy interior. They came out in a huddle, hands raised against the sun's glare. Peggy craned forward, convinced her heart was thumping out of her chest like a Disney cartoon. Another few seconds and there she was: Louise Baker, out in the open, a small entourage flitting around her, her eyes hidden under a pair of elegant sunglasses with rhinestone flowers set into their frames. Apart from the glasses, she was clearly in costume – Peggy couldn't imagine such a glamorous woman would wear that drab grey dress out of choice – but she walked as if she was dripping in mink. The group moved closer to where Peggy was standing. One of them turned to speak to Miss Baker, who didn't reply.

This is it.

Peggy had planned as carefully for this moment as she had for the journey that led to it; she had even rehearsed her lines. A quick introduction, a request for a moment or two of Miss Baker's time, preferably in private. A carefully pitched tone that wasn't demanding, that carried a slight hint of deference. Delivered properly, the way she had practised, Peggy couldn't see how her approach could fail. And now the actress was barely three feet away. Peggy stepped forward.

'Miss Baker?' Peggy smiled and stuck out her hand.

The actress shied a little, but she stopped.

'It's such a pleasure to meet you.'

'It's a fan. Nothing to worry about. Give her this.' One of the entourage handed the actress a signed photograph, a close-up of her face, all slick crimson lips and tumbling chestnut hair.

And then Peggy's mind went blank but, unfortunately, not her mouth.

'No. That's not why I'm here. I don't want another picture. I want to know what you were doing in Germany, years ago, before the war!'

Peggy was bundled back through the gates at ten times the speed she came in.

Louise Baker had screamed, actually screamed. And then, when Peggy tried to gabble out an explanation, one of the world's most famous film stars had slapped her. Peggy could still feel her cheek stinging. She had reared back, horrified by how spectacularly badly the long-imagined meeting had gone, and then there was shouting and running and two uniformed men lifting her half off her feet. They had dumped her so roughly onto the sidewalk, her ankles throbbed, their 'come back again and it will be the cops' sending tourist cameras clicking.

Peggy fled down Melrose Avenue with no idea which way she was going. Then the realisation of how spectacularly she had failed caught up with her and she froze.

I'll never get near her again.

She was so shocked, the sounds of the street disappeared; all she could hear was the word *failure* beating through her head. And she was wound so tight that, when she felt another hand grabbing at her elbow, she swung round, palm raised.

'Woah there, tiger! There's no need for more violence. I come in peace, I promise.'

A boy – no, a man on closer inspection – was now standing a more measured distance away, his hands up in surrender. He was handsome – his green eyes wouldn't have looked out of place on a movie poster – but he had the scruffiest hair Peggy had ever seen. The straw-coloured mop stuck up at odd angles, as if a flock of birds had spent the morning pulling at it. The only word she could think of to describe it was *thatch*. He was tall too, his frame hanging rangy beneath broad shoulders. And he had an impossibly wide grin, which lit up his face and made his eyes twinkle. Peggy resolved to ignore that. She stepped back from him, but he carried on talking.

'That looked terrifying, to be honest, being scooped up and thrown out, never mind setting La Baker off like a siren. I thought you might need a bit of company, and somewhere quiet to take stock, or lick your wounds.'

The offer of help, rather than a barrage of questions, caught her off guard.

Which is probably precisely what he intended.

If he had seen what happened, he must have been at the studio. And there were ink stains on his fingers, which suggested he was a writer, not anyone she wanted to speak to at all. Peggy took another step away, but he wasn't dissuaded.

'I get it. You don't know me. But I do know a café a few minutes away where the owner is a friend of mine. It's a small place; it stays below radar. It's a good spot to hide if you need it, which, trust me, you do.'

Peggy had half-turned, ready to walk away, but that brought her back round. 'Why would I need to hide?'

'Because the whole press pack is about to come searching. They're milling round La Baker for now, but you're the real prize.'

She hesitated. None of his body language suggested he was lying.

'Even if that's true, why would I go with you?'

'Because I'm not after anything except the chance for a cup of coffee with a pretty girl?'

That grin again. It was infectious and he knew it. But that didn't hide the fact that his chat-up line was appalling and he could be part of the pack he'd outpaced, hungry for a scoop and thinking a charm offensive would land it. Peggy was about to refuse – she had no intention of handing over her story to anyone else's ambitions. The others coming after her, however, sounded believable. And she was tired and thirsty and the thought of a quiet café was too tempting to ignore.

'All right. But a coffee – that's all.'

He didn't attempt to take her arm again. With a quick look behind him, he led her down a side street to a place that was far shabbier than any she would have chosen. And far cosier inside than its dull awning implied it would be.

'Are you hungry? I missed lunch and I'm starving, which is, admittedly, my permanent state. You probably wouldn't eat it, but Sammy does the world's greatest grilled cheese.'

'Why wouldn't I eat it?'

Peggy's companion, who had finally introduced himself as Charlie Fisher – a name Peggy quickly decided perfectly matched his charm-coated curiosity – grinned.

'Well, that answers one question: you're not an actress. Not if your culinary interests extend beyond lettuce.'

The comment was so cheap, Peggy grimaced.

She went to the counter where she ordered grilled cheese for them both, much to his evident amusement. It wasn't until she turned back to the table, however, that she realised she had left the journal filled with her notes about Louise out on view. When she snatched it up, Charlie's grin disappeared.

'I didn't look at it, I swear. I'm not that kind of writer. I've got my own material; I don't need to steal.'

'What kind of writer are you then?'

He ran his fingers through his hair and scratched his head. He suddenly looked boyish again and far more endearing. Not that Peggy had any intention of being drawn in by that.

'Honestly? Without the spiel? A hopeful one, I suppose. I've done bits and bobs same as most people trying to make a name here. I was a stringer first for whatever paper wanted a cheaper source of gossip than their usual hacks. Now I'm a very lowly scriptwriter, who sometimes gets to keep one line in a movie. Not quite the dream of Oscar-winning success, but a step on the way to it.' He stopped and nodded at the journal Peggy was now holding. 'Is that what you are too? A writer, out here to get famous?'

'Maybe.'

She put the book down as their food arrived and took a bite of the sandwich. It was mustardy and melting and glorious.

'You could have brought me straight here and not wasted time with all that grinning. The promise of this would make anyone talk.' This time, to Peggy's amusement, he pressed his lips deliberately tight and left the smiling to her. 'I want to be a writer, yes. For the papers though, not the screen. But I'm not anywhere close yet. I've done school stuff, college stuff; I've an English degree. But I've a way to go before I set the world on fire.'

Charlie leaned forward. 'But you've got something that might carry a spark?'

Peggy finished one half of the sandwich and forced herself to take a breath before demolishing the other. She had to face facts: today's misstep had been a disaster. Getting onto the Paramount compound again would be impossible, and she had no other way yet of reaching Miss Baker. A Hollywood scriptwriter wasn't her ideal confidante, but he might still have connections if he'd once been a journalist, and she could do with that in her corner.

'What do you know about Louise Baker?'

Charlie, clearly recognising when he was being stalled, sat back again. He turned his attention to his fries, scooping them up and dredging them in ketchup.

'Not much more than anyone else. She's known as *La Baker* because she's old-school grand. I don't mean in some creepy *Sunset Boulevard* way. She might be pushing fifty and out of the running for the big parts, but it's not like she's some forgotten Norma Desmond. Everyone at the studio says she's the consummate professional, even though it's no secret she hates the older, abandoned-woman roles she's forced into now. But, whether she's a Norma or not, she's got to be afraid – her best days are long behind her and she doesn't have the range to play mothers or character roles, not in Hollywood anyway. If she's spooked though, she never lets anyone see it. She's tough. She's also glacial and she intimidates everyone.' He swallowed the last of his fries and stared straight at Peggy. 'And then you turn up and the ice maiden cracks. What did you say to rattle her like that?'

'You're good, your training still shows. Softening up the subject and then tacking on the key question.' Peggy turned her attention pointedly back to her food.

'Then we're well matched: you're equally as good at not answering. You're asking me for info, but you know something about her, don't you? Something the other hacks don't.'

If you want something out of someone, you have to give something first.

The advice from her first-year journalism module had always made sense, but now Peggy added a mental coda: *just don't give it all.*

'I don't know. I suspect. I could be very wrong.'

She wiped her fingers and pushed the journal across the table.

'These are my notes about her. There's not much, because there doesn't seem to be that much to find. She's never revealed many details about herself, and no one seems to have looked at her very hard, despite all her fame. I know she was born in Nancy, in the north-east of France and she came to America before the war. That any family she had back home were lost in the conflict, and that she was married once, briefly, but her husband died. And that she has no children, or at least...' Peggy stopped. 'That's all I've got.'

A telephone was ringing in the room behind them. Peggy waited while Sammy came to answer it and Charlie skimmed through her notes.

'I'm not surprised it's light. She keeps herself close – she's famous for it. There's never been a breath of scandal about her. The older stars are good at that; they manage to be untouchable in the way the newer ones aren't. Is this really it?'

Peggy watched him running his finger across her scribbles, lingering on the key words. There was an intensity about the way he studied it that she liked, that reminded her of herself. Focused and thoughtful.

Maybe don't give it all won't get me anywhere.

'No. I've also got this.' Peggy pulled the photograph out of her purse and handed it to him. 'Do you recognise either of them?'

Charlie pulled at his hair and held the picture closer to the table's dim light, squinting as he pored over it. 'Maybe. Yes. I'm not sure. Where did you get it?'

'My mother gave it to me. Before she died. She wasn't actually my…' Peggy stopped. It wasn't just that she was wary of giving too much away; the word *died* had momentarily derailed her thoughts. It still sat too heavy in her mouth when she used it.

Charlie was frowning.

She recovered herself and hurried on before the frown turned into a question. 'It was taken in the early thirties, from the clothes and, well, other clues. And in Germany, if that word *Hoppegarten* is what I think it is, which is the name of a racetrack in Berlin; anyway, definitely not here.'

'Germany?' Charlie's hand went back to his hair. 'Then it can't be who I think it is. Why would she have been there? She's French. And I can't imagine it was much of a holiday destination in the thirties. Wasn't that when Hitler was on the rise?'

Peggy slipped the photograph out of his fingers before he twisted it into shreds.

'The Nazis were coming to power then, yes, but that doesn't have to mean anything. She was from an area very close to the German border. She could have been on holiday, or filming there if her career had already started…'

'Did you show her this today?'

'No. But I asked her if she had been in Germany before the war.'

'And then she slapped you? That's quite an extreme response. What am I missing here? What's your connection, or your mother's, with her anyway?'

Peggy was saved from trying to work out a simple answer to that by Sammy's reappearance.

'There's a call for you, Charlie. I think it's one you'll want to take.' She smiled at Peggy as Charlie got up. 'Mr Hotshot here uses this place as his office so often, I'm thinking of charging him rent.'

She started fussing with the plates, making small talk about the weather Peggy couldn't take in. When Charlie was still at the table, talking to him had seemed a good idea. Now that he had got up and broken their connection to take a telephone call, which suggested someone might have seen where he had taken her, her nerves were back on edge.

I've told him too much. What if he starts piecing this together the way that I did? Maybe he's already started. Maybe that's a contact on the phone now and he's selling whatever he thinks is going on here.

She jumped up and was sweeping the photograph and the journal back into her purse as Charlie re-emerged.

'I have to go, I'm sorry.'

'Peggy, wait. I know what you're thinking, but I told you: I'm a scriptwriter now, not a journalist. I've no interest in going back to that world. And even if I did, this is your story – I respect that. But you need to hear this.'

If he had switched on the grin, she would have walked away. He didn't.

'That phone call was Louise Baker's manager. They tracked you here – don't ask me how, these people have more webs than spiders. Anyway, she wants to see you.'

Peggy's knees wobbled. She sat slowly back down.

'What, now? They're going to let me back into the studio?'

'No. Not at the studio.' His voice had lost its confident edge. There wasn't even a threat of a grin. 'She wants you at her house. Tonight.'

CHAPTER FOUR

Berlin, May to November 1934

You are requested to attend a reception at the Ministry of Propaganda and Public Enlightenment on Wednesday 27 June at 3 p.m. in the presence of Reichsminister Goebbels.

Tea will be served.

Tea will be served. As if that made the whole charade any better.

Anna stuffed the invitation into the bottom of her handbag where no one would see it. Marika's offhand comment at UFA three years ago that Goebbels 'liked actresses' hadn't even been close. From what Anna had heard, the monthly tea parties the Minister held to, in his words, 'celebrate our brightest and loveliest young talent' were no better than casting-couch sessions, even if the couches were grander than the average film set could provide. In the short time since Goebbels had brought the film industry under his close scrutiny, his patronage had come to be recognised as a double-edged sword. Even Marika had admitted that he could make or break an actress's career with a word, and that he was easily slighted and quick to take offence. Marika, however, was one of his 'darlings'. She was frequently photographed in the groups of laughing girls clustered round him at premieres and nightclubs, and Goebbels had named her as *one of Germany's most promising new sweethearts*. She also believed she could manage him, which was a claim Anna neither believed was true, nor wished to have to try copying.

Anna hadn't seen the Minister since their brief brush against each other at the UFA screen tests. Both the girls had been offered contracts that day – Anna hadn't asked if Goebbels had had any influence over that; Marika hadn't cared. She had snapped hers up; Anna had politely requested a hiatus which she was still extending three years later. From that point on, their careers had followed the different paths Anna had always said they would, one on the stage and one on the screen. Both of them had started to enjoy success the way stardom measured it, in red carpets and glowing reviews and any table in any restaurant they chose. Despite Marika's views on the theatre and Anna's on the cinema, and the very different circles they moved in, their friendship had also not only survived, it had flourished. Even if Marika's wilfully blind behaviour when it came to the men she encouraged sometimes threatened to derail it.

Anna no longer tried to explain their bond to the actresses she worked with in the theatre, who found Marika showy and overbearing and far too full of herself. Who didn't trust their boyfriends anywhere near her. She understood it, and so did Eddy. It was no more complicated than *because old friends matter*. The world had moved faster than any of them could have imagined since they had left the Academy; old friends, whatever their flaws, at least brought stability with them. Marika was maddening, Marika was fun; one side didn't come without the other. Anna had decided to accept that the day they first met, and nothing had changed. Besides, as her career, and Eddy's, had gone from strength to strength, and their relationship with it, old jealousies seemed too childish to feed.

Anna had no urge, however, to follow Marika into Goebbels' circle, although she had no idea how to wriggle out of the invitation, and no one to ask for advice on how she might manage that. Her parents, who had no more love for the National Socialist Party now than they had when Goebbels was wrecking film screenings, would tell her to refuse it. Eddy would be angered and horrified by the vulnerable position it put her in, and would know that she couldn't. He worked at UFA – he had no illusions about how demanding the Minister was, or the consequences that would result if those demands weren't met.

Since Goebbels had expanded his Propaganda Ministry and set up the Reich Chamber of Film the previous year, every part of the industry came under his scrutiny. Scripts were scrutinised line by line and anything that hinted at an anti-Party or, worse, pro-Jewish stance, was rejected. Set designs, costumes and background music had to reflect a set of *German values* that were rapidly narrowing. Artistic freedom, as Eddy loudly complained, had become as mythical as a dodo. It was a culture of control he railed against, that he wanted Anna to stay free from in the theatre for as long as she could. It was a culture that had crept into every aspect of life since the National Socialists had been elected to rule Germany.

The new Chancellor, Adolf Hitler, had swept into power a year ago, in 1933, with a far clearer vision of the country he intended to rule than Anna remembered hearing from the Brownshirts marching through Neukölln. Or, perhaps more honestly, than she had chosen to hear.

'It was all there, wasn't it? This idea that *true Germans* are a superior race who deserve more space in the world. It was in the slogans and the speeches all thick with this idea of *blood and soil* we all thought were too ridiculous to listen to.'

Eddy had winced at the phrase that was now everywhere, but he had nodded. 'The *right people* bound by blood and loyalty to the *right land.* The Brownshirts used to chant it when they marched through Wedding.'

'Then why didn't we realise it was serious?'

Anna's question came up time and again, in her parents' home and in the cafés and bars her friends frequented, and it always went unanswered. None of them had shared Hitler's vision of the future;

no one they met in their social or work lives had any time for it. How, therefore, were they supposed to realise that anyone else would listen to, never mind vote for, the National Socialist Party?

Except people had, and in overwhelming numbers. Nearly forty million of them, and what did it matter if those votes were won through violence and banning all opposition, when such a decisive outcome had swept any hope of protest away? Germany had chosen Hitler. Germany had therefore chosen to embrace the love of *homeland* he brought with him; the mistrust of *other.* The whole country was starting to learn how the first would be encouraged, how the second would be discouraged, and both at all costs. And how that learning would be painful for many when *other* did not mean simple things like American films, or English novels; when it also meant people. *Aryan* had become the country's most sought-after prefix, its yardstick for judgement, its way of determining value. *Aryan* was the new ideal, the basis of a Germany all its good citizens were to unite in striving towards. And not accepting that, or not meeting that ideal meant…

Anna snapped her handbag shut. So far it had meant book burnings. Great pyramids of fire consuming Marx and Freud and Kafka and hundreds of others, that had started in Berlin's Opernplatz and fanned out through every German city. And constant, unpredictable outbursts of carefully targeted violence. Against shops selling goods not deemed sufficiently patriotic. Against anyone too slow to stiffen their arm and shout out *Heil Hitler!* And against Jews. Always against Jews.

She had a script to learn, but she couldn't concentrate. The invitation had unsettled her. Too many things these days unsettled her. The communists were crushed, their party banned the day after Hitler had seized power. That didn't mean there was no longer an enemy. The National Socialist machine had turned all its ample resources against Germany's Jews with a hatred that was visceral. And the hatred had stuck, gathering momentum quicker than a snowball rolling. Antisemitism had become a trait as prized as love of country; Germany's language had changed to embrace that. Anna felt sick even thinking such a thing, but the evidence was everywhere. There were slurs thrown on the streets and newspaper headlines on open display that would have invited fury and shame a year ago. Now they were encouraged, supported. Laws were already appearing, restricting access to once tolerant institutions, introducing new rules for workplaces. *Aryan clauses* that dug deep into families, including her own.

She and Eddy no longer spent Sunday evenings with their friends debating directing techniques or who the next great German playwright would be. They pored over the papers instead, trying to understand what was happening to their country; feeling increasingly, frighteningly, powerless. Whatever the sector that was under the spotlight, the core of each new regulation distilled down to the same question: *how German are you?* A question which, as they all increasingly knew, actually meant *how Jewish?*

Everyone in the entertainment industry was suddenly required to fill in a profiling form, explaining the racial background of themselves and their families. People had begun to talk in the press and on the radio in terms of scales and percentages. One parent being something *other than German* – the new shorthand for *Jewish* – meant a person couldn't be classified as totally *Aryan*; two meant they weren't Aryan at all. The discussion was cold, bound up in maths, not in people. It turned Anna's stomach. None of their group could understand why the scrutiny mattered, or what consequences would come from all the information gathering. Then the *Aryan Clause* had been unleashed on UFA and dozens of writers, technicians, actors and directors were tossed out of work the same day it came in. Anna and Eddy scrutinised the names of the sacked and almost drove themselves crazy trying to work out a pattern.

'Declaring yourself as a practising Jew, or having two Jewish parents seems to be a definite negative strike. Most of the people who lost their jobs in the first hit fit into those categories. But then they've issued permits to continue working for some of the most popular actors and directors who should, if the profiles were rigidly applied, have been dropped. And there's no clarity on what it means to have Jewish grandparents and one Jewish parent, practising or not, like you and Marika. Some people in those groups have been dismissed; others haven't.'

Eddy had passed the list to Anna, but she could make no better sense of it, although the threat to her family made her desperate to try.

'Half of what's happening seems to be getting done on a whim, as if they're still working out a formula. And this *weeding out*, as Goebbels so horribly put it, is happening across the whole industry. Everyone at the theatre was asked to complete the same question-naire as you were at the studio. No one has acted on it there, or not yet. I haven't told you this before – I can't bear to think about it, never mind put it in words – but Father has had to tell his employers for the first time that his parents were Jewish. He doesn't practise, but he's never hidden his heritage and it's never mattered before. But now the cinema owners have started dropping hints that he should think about retirement, even though he's not even close to it. They've known him for years and now he's somehow beneath them, someone they would rather not deal with. And the effect of that is spinning out. Mother has lost some of her students. They don't give a reason, but it's not hard to guess it when they refuse to talk to Father. The only way to feel safe is to be able to prove your family tree runs back *purely* through Prussia for hundreds of years, and who can do that? Who knows what *pure* even means? And who should have to? We're all German citizens, what else should matter?'

Eddy didn't have an answer to that any more than Anna did. And Marika refused to accept there was a problem at all, even when it came to her own father's Jewish ties.

'All this fuss about religion, about proving who your grand-parents were or weren't, it's dreadfully lower class. Papa is rich. All this nonsense about whether people who are long dead wasted their time in a church or a synagogue has got nothing to do with him. Besides, he was some kind of officer in the war, and his father gave the government so much money, he was treated as a hero. No one's going to touch him, he's too well connected. And so am I. Seriously, Anna: who would dare upset me, with all the powerful men I know?'

Anna had dropped the subject then. She was too sick with worry about her own father to listen to Marika dismiss the crackdowns as nonsense. And she had no interest in mingling with *powerful men*. She had seen all too clearly, from an alleyway in Müllerstraβe, exactly what they were capable of. Except one of them, it seemed, had her back in his sights, and she had no idea how to turn off the spotlight.

'I won't go again. If he asks me, I'll feign illness. I know I should have done it this time, but Marika would have had a fit.'

Eddy was still tense. He had barely spoken on the drive out of the city.

Anna sighed. The day was supposed to have been a very differ-ent one. They had both been working such long hours, they had barely seen each other for weeks. Eddy had been locked in the studio agonising over the final edits of *Auf Wiedersehen, Marianna,* the romantic comedy he hoped might make his name. Anna was deep in rehearsals for the lead role in Schiller's *Maria Stuart* and feeling the strain of carrying the play. A whole Saturday together was a treasure. They had woken early and reached for each other. Breakfast had been broken up by so many kisses, they had gone back to bed. When Eddy had said he hoped there would still be mornings like this when they'd been married for ever, they'd both smiled. And then Anna had mentioned the Ministry tea and the day disintegrated.

It had taken Anna the best part of an hour to calm him, and then herself, down. The day, however, was a sunny one and she had spent too much of June cooped up indoors to waste it. Anna had insisted on continuing with their plans to drive to the Wannsee lakeshore and picnic at the smaller and quieter of the area's two lakes. The journey had been an uncomfortable one, but the combination of sunshine and sparkling water had gone a long way to easing bruised tempers. They had agreed not to talk about anything that mattered. They had swum, slept, gorged themselves on fresh bread and thickly sliced ham, and slept again. By late afternoon, they were back in each other's arms and kissing. The day had, in the end, turned out much better than Anna had hoped it might; it would have been easier to forget the whole issue of her trip to the Ministry, but she couldn't. It had disturbed her and she needed to share it.

She took a sip of raspberry beer and passed the bottle to Eddy, who was stretched out on the blanket beside her. His bare skin had picked up coppery tones from the sun. She let her fingers trail feather-light circles across his chest and quivered as he traced the same pattern round her wrist. She leaned over and kissed him so deeply he shuddered.

'I need to talk to you properly about what happened, Eddy, and about Marika. It was too odd to keep it to myself, and who else would I tell if not you?'

He sighed, but he nodded.

'I know. And I'm sorry I got angry. I hate the thought of you anywhere near Goebbels, that's all.' He took a swig of the beer and kissed her again. 'Tell me again what you said before about Marika being nervous – I'm struggling to imagine it. She's been going to those teas for months now. She won't shut up about them when I see her at the studio, or about how *special* she's always made to feel when she goes.'

Anna rolled onto her stomach, aware that a tanned face would hardly endear her to the theatre's make-up department. It was hard to swap the Wannsee's soft treeline for the bristling flags of the Wilhelmstraβe, but she made herself do it.

'I think that's the problem – I think the stakes get higher the more often you go. She was brittle from the moment I got into the car, all eye-rolls and drumming fingers at everything I said. I swear I was ready to jump out after ten minutes.'

'Why didn't you?'

Anna had threatened to. When she had suggested that the day was such a pretty one perhaps they could walk not drive down the last block of the Unter den Linden and Marika had accused her of 'having all the social graces of a shop girl', she almost had.

'Because it wasn't simply one of her moods. She was strung so tight, if it had been anyone else, I would have said they were frightened. She was dressed as glamorous as ever, and rigged out in her warpaint, but she looked drawn. She's lost weight; I'm not sure it suits her.'

Eddy sat up and began rummaging through the picnic basket.

'She never eats, you know that. And she's on a tough schedule. Three films back-to-back and Goebbels with his fingers in them all and constantly arriving on set unannounced. All the actresses are edgy.'

That didn't surprise Anna, not with all the gossip she had heard. She suddenly realised, however, that none of that had come from Eddy – he was at UFA every day, but he never mentioned the Minister.

'Have you ever spoken to Goebbels yourself?'

Eddy flexed his fingers. 'I keep out of his way; I don't want to get on his radar. He's a nightmare. He has to know every detail of every project down to the dialogue. And he's got the whole studio buried in directives that are a mass of contradictions. One minute he's demanding that all UFA films "must be saturated in the new German spirit, binding our people to the nation with the most heroic of feelings", whatever the hell that means. The next he's insisting that we make American-style screwball comedies to keep the audiences happy and "don't under- but don't overdo" the National Socialist message.'

He took a swig from his beer bottle as Anna laughed. 'I know, I know, but that's how he speaks: as if he's permanently addressing a rally. It's a load of nonsense, and it's all impossible to deliver. His latest slogan is the worst: *subtle propaganda*. None of us have a clue what that means, never mind how to make it.'

He bit into an apple with a crunch that almost split it in two. 'The trouble is, it's not just the actresses who need his approval to get on; we all do. So any pearls of wisdom you've collected that might make Mr Almighty happy, or at least manageable, would be gratefully received. What did you think of him?'

Anna wriggled into a sitting position and hugged her knees.

'That he's even more sure of himself than the first time I met him, which it's hard to imagine he could be. That he's learned how to present himself, so you only see the public face and don't get a single glimpse of the private one. It's more than hiding his thoughts, although he's good at that. He can wrap himself in a bigger physical persona than he actually has – it's uncanny. People who hate him talk about how short he is, and about his club foot, but even I didn't really notice those this time. He's grown very poised, and there's an elegance about him – the suit he was wearing was probably worth more than your flat. He's attentive too. He has this way of switching his attention onto you, like there's no one else in the room. It's easy to see how some people could be charmed by him, and he knows how to use that.'

'You sound as if you found him attractive.'

Eddy was staring hard at her, a frown creasing his forehead.

Anna flinched. 'No. Not at all. I said *some* people. I was repelled. There's an energy coiled beneath the surface you'd be a fool to

disturb: I sensed that before, but I'm sure of it now. His beliefs
are odious, but he's clever and that's a dangerous combination.
You've heard his speeches, how he can use his voice to make the
worst sentiments sound, well, not reasonable – comparing Jews to
parasites could never be reasonable – but you know what I mean.
He knows how to create an illusion of normal. I spent two hours at
the Ministry and there wasn't a moment when he didn't understand
the impact of whatever provocative thing he was saying. Or wasn't
watching to see how you reacted. And the more you hold back
from him, the more he pushes to get your approval.'

Eddy opened another bottle of beer and offered it to Anna.
She waved it away, her stomach lurching as she remembered how
the afternoon at the Ministry had played out. Goebbels was self-
involved and demanding, but he was also shrewd and manipulative.
Anna had been well aware that every moment of their visit to the
Propaganda Ministry had been choreographed.

Wilhelmstraβe itself was a stage set. Identical scarlet banners
stamped with swastikas trooped across the stately old palaces Hitler
had transformed into his seats of power. Identical black Mercedes
hunkered shiny as beetles outside each solid square entrance.
Every Ministry – whether it was the Presidential Palace, or the
Department of Justice or the Reich's Chancellery – was flag-draped
and guarded, each building a copy of the next so that the street
resembled giant blocks of troops drawn up in formation. There
wasn't a man out of uniform; salutes snapped up and down the wide
avenue like pistons. Soldiers had lined the spotless steps outside
the Propaganda Ministry; more had flanked the marble staircase
inside. Bronze eagles brooded at the top of the stairs, which were
draped, like everything else, in banners. Every statue and flag was
oversized; every movement was seamless and hushed. Walking into
the building had silenced her, as she was assumed it was meant to.

By the time Anna and Marika entered the reception room,
with its gold mirrors that stretched to the ceiling and fireplaces big

enough to roast an ox in, Anna could feel herself shrinking. When
Goebbels rose from his chair, hands behind his back in the manner
of a king admitting grateful guests to his presence chamber, it had
taken all her self-control to stop herself from bowing.

'It was all perfectly stage-managed. His chair was even placed
on a small platform, although I was too overwhelmed to notice
that at first.'

Anna had noticed, however, how he kept them all standing until
the full party arrived. How he spread his arms like a conductor
when he invited them to sit and waved them to their places one
by one, starting with the seats furthest away from him. And the
way Marika trembled as they waited, and how some of the women,
the ones who, from their whispers, had attended these receptions
before, eyed the chair on his right with such hunger. Marika was the
last woman he left standing. When Goebbels finally gestured her
forward to the privileged seat, her whole body relaxed. Her smile
returned. She spent the rest of the afternoon playing the hostess,
with every ounce of the sparkle she unleashed on the screen. It
was a magnificent performance; it had made Anna want to cry.

'Marika told me when we left that she has been given that place
by his side at the last six film teas. That sitting there is a sign of how
much Goebbels respects her talent and how invested he is in her
future success. She was clearly dreading it being given to anyone
else. She made it sound as though being chosen to sit next to him
was an unimaginable honour; I think she's convinced herself that's
true. But the whole time we were there, she was so tense, it was
hard to watch and…' Anna stopped.

'What?'

'I overheard a couple of the other girls talking. The actress
Goebbels sat there before he selected Marika to be his handmaid
was Luise Ullrich.'

Eddy fumbled with his beer bottle and nearly dropped it. 'But
she's his current mistress.'

Which is why my stomach is spinning.

'I know. And he runs through his mistresses quickly. The others were talking about Marika as if she would be next.'

'For God's sake, Anna! Couldn't you have told me this sooner? Someone needs to stop whatever game Marika is playing before she ends up in over her head. She can't get involved with him – she's too good for that.'

His sudden burst of anger sat Anna up straight.

'I know that. But I'm her best friend, not you. If anyone is going to try to stop her, it'll be me. And why are you mad with me anyway? I couldn't have told you sooner; I've hardly seen you since Wednesday. And when I first tried this morning, you wouldn't listen.'

He muttered something she couldn't quite catch and then turned it into an apology.

'I'm sorry. What you said was a worry, that's all. Mixing with him exposes her to circles filled with people I don't want her, or you, near.'

'I don't want her mixed up in them either, but you don't need to storm to her rescue.'

Eddy grabbed her hand and kissed it. 'Don't frown, don't let's fight again. Tell me more about Goebbels. Did he speak to you directly?'

Anna let him hold her hand as she stared out over the lake's smooth surface. There wasn't a ripple to be seen; the water was as blue and peaceful as the sky.

And yet all it takes is a storm and all this beauty vanishes.

Goebbels had spoken to her. He hadn't whispered into her ear, the way he did with Marika, or invited her to perch briefly on the chair he kept vacant on his left, although a handful of the others were temporarily granted that honour. He had addressed her across the room and then sat back, as if he was waiting to assess her performance.

'Fräulein Anna Tiegel, we meet again. And what a success of your career you are making. You are becoming quite the star. So, given your very different experience from the ladies here, I have a little question for you: are actresses in the theatre the same as these beauties who grace our screens? Loveable of course, and delightfully enthusiastic about their craft, but also, let us face facts, children in need of firm guidance?'

Heads turned; there was a flutter of appreciative laughter and a smattering of applause. It was such a ridiculous question, Anna couldn't think what to say.

'We are all actresses, Herr Minister, wherever we work. I imagine we all feel lucky to do what we do.'

'A charming answer, very diplomatic. Do you know why I asked you?'

Anna's smile had started to ache. Speaking to him was like inching over slippery ice, trying to be the quickest to spot the cracks. She shook her head. Goebbels patted Marika's hand.

'You see I can't help thinking back to the first day we met. I confess that what you said that day has really stuck with me. Do you remember? That acting for the cinema was rather beneath you, that nowhere except the theatre – how did you put it? Ah yes – lets drama *breathe*.'

This time there was such a chorus of exaggerated gasps from the other girls, Anna had half-expected one of them to slip into a prettily staged faint. She gave a laugh she hoped was suitably charming.

'Perhaps we should put that down to the snobbishness of youth, Herr Minister. I hope I have widened my tastes since then.'

She kept her smile in place; so did he.

'An excellent response that puts my mind at ease. I have watched your career and it has been troubling me, I must confess, that one of Berlin's most widely talked about young actresses would refuse to grace the screen and share her talents. What better way to reach out across our nation's community than through the cinema?

Surely every true German has a part to play in uniting our country? Wouldn't you agree?'

He's pompous, and sure of himself. And he's waiting for me to trip.

Anna had no desire to see what he might do if she did, so she said what he wanted to hear. 'Of course.'

'Excellent.' His smile was so wide he looked like he could swallow her. 'Then I will expect to hear that you have signed the UFA contract you keep refusing. I'm sure your director boyfriend will be delighted to have you step into the fold.'

Anna had faltered then. Wondering how much the man knew about her; realising he would always know as much as he chose.

'I would be honoured; of course I would. But I am contracted to play Maria Stuart.'

Goebbels brushed an invisible crumb from his mouth and wiped his hands.

'And you will be done in three months and ready to start in September. Sign the contract, my dear; be the good loyal citizen I am sure that you are. And then I have the perfect role for you. A delightful little number about a young couple turning their backs on the lives they thought they wanted in America and choosing to return instead to the joys of their homeland. Such a powerful message. It would do your Herr Hartmann's career no end of good to be involved in such an important film. Which he will be; if you are.'

He had turned back to Marika at that, accepted the cake she had picked out for him as if it was a ruby, and hadn't spoken to Anna again.

'It's an honour, Anna. To have his eye on your career. You do understand that? It will be good for you, and for Eddy.'

Marika had kicked off her shoes the moment they climbed back into the Mercedes which Goebbels had provided to take them both home. Her manner was less intense than it had been on the way to the Ministry, but it was far from relaxed.

Anna had waited until they turned out of Wilhelmstraße's forest of flags before she replied.

'Is it though? He has his eye on you; it's clear you are his favourite. But you don't look well on it.'

For a moment, the mask had dropped. Marika's face crumpled. 'That's the thing, though, isn't it, with being the one at the top? There's always someone waiting to step into your shoes. If I bore him, or if one of these lead roles I'm starting to get bores the audience, where am I then?'

'What about Hollywood? Wasn't that always your dream?'

Marika's sharp laugh at that had torn at Anna's heart.

'How would I get to Hollywood now? I'm one of his *darlings*. I don't get to leave. I don't get to be safe and to be a star on my own merits – nobody who catches his eye gets to do that. I get to stay and keep him happy; whatever that means.'

Marika must have noticed the chauffeur watching her. Even though the partition between them and the driver's seat was closed, she suddenly perked up and started talking about how Anna's career would 'finally be on the movie map, where it should be'. It was a false brightness that was as disturbing as her vulnerability had been. Anna knew Marika had heard the threats in Goebbels' offer that Anna had. She also knew Marika would refuse to acknowledge them, and would refuse to remember she had admitted to not feeling safe, or that part of her wished she could still run to America.

But I can't hide his threats from Eddy.

Anna turned away from the water and squeezed Eddy's hand. 'He did. And he has a plan which involves us both…'

By the time they returned to the car and set out for Berlin and home, Anna was exhausted. Despite his deep dislike for the Minister, Eddy had almost jumped out of his skin with delight when he heard he was in the running to direct Goebbels' pet project. She didn't blame him; she knew as well as Goebbels had what a career boost it would be.

'I knew it was happening but never expected to be involved. You should see the budget figures for it. They're going to build a replica of downtown Chicago on one of the lots. This will be the biggest film UFA has shot since *Metropolis*. I do this well and, never mind Goebbels, Hollywood will be yelling for me.'

And then she had explained her part in the deal and his smile had disappeared.

'You can't do it, Anna. You can't sign. We've just talked about how dangerous he is. You don't want to be a film star, or be beholden to him. Once *Maria Stuart* opens, every theatre in Berlin, and probably on Broadway, will be clamouring for you. That's everything you've ever dreamed of.'

'I know. But I have to take up the contract. Goebbels won't stand for me going against him. He's got some bee in his bonnet about me making a film, probably because I wasn't grateful and subservient enough three years ago. It's a whim. He'll move on soon enough to trying to control someone else. I'll negotiate one, maybe two, movies and then a break to go back to the stage. It won't harm my career.'

She wasn't convinced of that. There wasn't an actress she knew who moved successfully between stage and screen, but it surely couldn't damage her prospects as much as a refusal would damage them both. And then, if she really did make her mark and Broadway came calling, perhaps that would be a way to get them all out from under Goebbels' influence and safe.

'It's the best for all of us, Eddy. Marika included. I'm worried about her. At least if I'm at UFA, I can keep a better eye on her.'

He had grumbled a bit more, but the sun was still shining and it was easier to imagine success than failure on such a lovely day.

Anna watched as the trees danced past, waved at children playing in their front gardens and decided to feel at peace with the world. She tucked her head onto Eddy's shoulder and drifted off to sleep.

'What was that? Was it thunder? Or hailstones?'

Anna jerked awake as the staccato sound crackled around them and realised that the car had stopped. Nerves made her whisper; her voice still sounded too loud.

'I think it's gunfire.' Eddy's hands were still gripping the wheel; his voice was as tight as hers.

Anna tentatively wound down the window, torn between wanting to hear the noise more clearly, and the fear that a gun might suddenly appear, poking through it.

'That doesn't make sense. Where's it coming from?'

Eddy shook his head. 'I don't know. We're near Lichterfelde and there's an army barracks there, but why would anyone be firing a gun this late on a Saturday evening?'

Another volley split the air, making them both start.

'It's not random shots. It's a group of guns and precision bursts. It could be target practice. Logically, that's what it must be. But it sounds like…'

'Executions.' Anna finished his sentence and then half-laughed and shook her head with the impossibility of the idea. 'Which is ridiculous. We're tired, that's all this is, and we watch too many films. There'll be a perfectly normal explanation. This is Berlin, not the Wild West.' She wished she sounded more convincing.

And then another co-ordinated burst rang out and what else could it be?

'I'll take the back roads, stay off the main drag. Best to be safe until we can find out what's happening.'

Eddy drove on, tense and silent, taking a winding route up through the city. The gunfire faded. The streets were quiet. They began to relax, started speculating about prison breaks, although they both knew they were nowhere close to a prison. It wasn't until they reached the outskirts of the Tiergarten that they encountered traffic and started to grow nervous again. The cars were moving impossibly slowly, backed up in a snail-paced crawl.

'Something's going on. Look.'

Eddy looked where Anna was pointing. Army trucks blocked every junction, a machine-gun post positioned between each pair. Soldiers fanned out to form checkpoints. Cars were being swept inside and out with flashlights and sniffed at by dogs.

'Maybe it was a prison break after all, and someone has escaped.'

They inched through the cordon and surrendered their papers. Anna tried to ask what the problem was and got no answer except a second sweep of the flashlight straight into her eyes. They continued in silence, past streets that had ropes slung across them and soldiers standing guard.

'There's no Brownshirts, have you noticed?' Anna twisted round as they passed another checkpoint. 'Normally trouble of any kind would have them out in swarms, but all I can see are black SS uniforms and those green ones some of the new security forces wear.'

There was no one to ask for an explanation, not that they would have dared stop. There was no one at all on the streets, which were still sun-filled and should have been bustling. Anna gave up trying to work out what was wrong; it was enough that something was.

'Take me back with you – your flat is closer than mine. The city's like a ghost town, but that doesn't mean there isn't more trouble brewing. I don't want to be out here any longer than we must.'

They continued the journey in a silence that they couldn't break, even within the safety of the flat. They went through the motions of making a meal and going to bed, but neither of them ate, or properly slept. It wasn't until the next morning, when they tentatively re-emerged from the apartment, that they began to piece together some of what had happened the previous night.

Needing news and the company of others, they went down to a café they visited so often most of the faces were familiar. Instead of the usual barrage of greetings, however, everyone was quiet, clearly in no mood to talk; jumping each time the door opened in case a stranger walked in. And everyone was glued to the radio broadcasts that grew increasingly strident as the morning wore on.

Anna had been right about the lack of brown uniforms. The SA was no more. Its Chief of Staff, Ernst Röhm, had, according to the official bulletins, been plotting against Hitler, planning to use his brown-shirted troops to rise up and topple the regime. He was a *traitor*. He was dead. His men were traitors too and as dead as their leader, or arrested, or soon would be. The uniforms in charge of the streets now were black, the ones worn by the disciplined ranks of the SS, loyal to no one but Hitler. The change was, according to Goebbels, who was now the sole voice on the radio, 'a wonderful thing. A cleansing, which leaves the Führer as Germany's supreme leader, loved and unchallenged, as all our good citizens want him to be.' So it had been gunfire, and executions, that they had heard the night before. And dozens, or hundreds, or maybe thousands, were now dead.

'Goebbels ordered it.' Anna pushed away another undrunk cup of coffee. 'You heard him crowing. He gave the order for the first shot, or he claims he did, which amounts to the same thing. It's not just what they do that's terrifying, it's their efficiency that makes my skin crawl. How does anyone in their sights escape?'

They spent the rest of the day unsure of their city. There were SS men everywhere, unsmiling, challenging anyone who was foolish enough to linger in one spot too long. The only vehicles on the street were military ones. There was no more gunfire, but they saw men being bundled into trucks, their faces bloodied. After the third corner revealed another frightened group being hustled away, they crept home.

Eddy went to work the next morning, subdued, no longer delighted by the project he had been offered; wondering how many ripples the purge would send out. Anna moved round the flat in slow motion, then walked to the theatre without meeting anyone's eye. When she arrived, there was another crested envelope and a politely formal courier, with instructions to wait for her signature on the UFA contract it contained. Anna did as she was asked, trying to ignore the whispers and nudges behind her. Then she went into the bathroom and was violently sick.

There were no other cars. From the way Marika had described the weekend, Anna had expected a parade of Mercedes lined up along the villa's snow-dusted forecourt. The compound, however, was deserted.

'Are we here first? Are the family and the rest of the guests arriving later?'

Marika sighed as Anna opened the glass panel to speak to the chauffeur. 'Why do you always have to fuss? There'll be a simple explanation.'

There was, but it wasn't the one Anna wanted.

'Bogensee is the Minister's private retreat. The family do not use it. Frau Goebbels prefers to remain at the Göringstraße residency when her husband… entertains. As for the other guests' – the driver's smirk was unmistakeable even when viewed through the mirror – 'they usually prefer to arrive after dark.'

'That is enough.' Marika's voice could have dissolved sheet metal. 'Open the doors and remember your place.' She turned to Anna as the chauffeur scrambled out of the front and round to her side. 'This is what happens when you talk to the help as if they are equals. They get familiar.' She stalked out of the car without a thank you and left Anna to shrug off the chauffeur's stony glare. Half a dozen paces from the car, she stopped again. 'This is amazing. We could be in the Alps.'

Anna could see why Marika was entranced. The villa was long and low, nestled in the shadow of fragrant pine trees and painted a rich creamy yellow. Both the main entrance and the two angled wings were topped with pitched roofs that sloped down to head height. The architecture, together with the November snowfall, could have been lifted straight from Bavaria. That the property looked as if it had been designed to meet Party guidelines on how to build the perfect Germany did not make Anna feel better.

'It's gorgeous, yes. But I'd be a lot more comfortable if his wife and children were here, which is what I assumed would be the case. Or if I knew who the other guests were.'

'Does it matter?' Marika waved the chauffeur ahead with their bags and began picking her way over the snow-flecked cobbles. 'Honestly, Anna, you can be such hard work. You've barely been at the studio for six weeks and already he's singling you out – don't you get how envious the other girls are? Do I need to keep repeating how important it is to be inside his circle?'

It was as if the car ride back from the Ministry in June had never happened. Marika was hiding again behind her Party-loving stance, or at least her Goebbels-loving stance. Any time Anna, who was still overwhelmed by the studio's bustle, raised the slightest doubt about the move she had made from stage to the screen, Marika embarked on another lecture. About the stratospheric salary Anna could command if she stayed in Goebbels' good graces. About the privileged lifestyle that was hers for the taking. About the benefits that would pass on to Eddy. After the visit to the Ministry, Anna suspected Marika was mostly trying to convince herself that the rewards were worth the price they surely commanded. That didn't mean, however, that the lectures were any easier to listen to. Or that Anna was in any mood to hear another one in such a secluded location.

I can't keep hiding from this. I have to tackle her.

'Don't you worry what he wants from you in return?'

The main door opened and a housekeeper appeared, her stiff black dress a sharp contrast to the sparkling snow.

Marika sighed. 'Fine, let's do this, and then it's done. If you mean sex, why don't you say so? When did you become such a prude? So he wants to sleep with me? Of course he does. Is that such a big deal when you consider what's at stake?'

The words were tough enough, but Marika could barely meet her eyes. Anna paused, looking for the right words, the ones Marika wouldn't dismiss out of hand.

'Maybe it wouldn't be if you genuinely liked the man. If he had your best interests at heart, if there was mutual respect and it didn't all sound so transactional, maybe then an arrangement would be... understandable. But not this, Marika. This is an entirely different thing.'

'Oh for goodness' sake, stop grabbing for the moral high ground. Just because you've settled for Eddy and you never give a thought to anyone who could actually help your career, that doesn't mean I have to do the same.'

Marika turned away. Anna caught her arm and stopped caring whether the words were right or not.

'How dare you. I haven't settled; I love Eddy. And I'm not some naïve little idiot, so don't treat me like one. I know all about casting couches – what actress doesn't? But this is Goebbels, Marika, and the stakes aren't the same. Never mind his reputation for sleeping with actresses and ruining their lives when he's done. What about the rest? That he's a rabid antisemite who thinks Jews aren't human. And don't forget that classification – given both our fathers are Jewish – now includes, by his reckoning, us. Or that he orders executions. Or that he thinks Hitler is some kind of a god. Doesn't that scare you? Don't the National Socialists scare you? They should: they're terrifying. And he's there, in the heart of it all. Is that really a man you want to share a bed with?'

'Ladies, is there a problem? You're turning my lovely home into a refrigerator.'

Anna jumped. Goebbels was standing barely a meter away, his footsteps muffled by the snow. She hadn't a clue how long he had been there – his expression was too bland to read.

'Joseph, darling!' Marika ran straight to him and kissed his cheek. 'We were just admiring the wonderful view. It's positively Alpine and utterly delicious.'

Goebbels bowed and took her arm. 'Then, please, come inside, where it's even more enchanting. Before we all turn into an ice sculpture.'

Anna followed them, keeping a pace behind, making sure nothing else came out of her mouth except praise as they toured the house. The oak-panelled movie theatre and banqueting hall; the electronic patio doors facing the lake that vanished into the floor at the flick of a switch; the chandeliers and the checker-board flooring and the blue-and-gold tiling were all *astonishing* and *breathtaking*. She said all the right things, but she hardly took any of it in, except for the sixty telephones Goebbels was inordinately proud of.

It wasn't until he showed them to their rooms and suggested they freshen up that Anna plucked up enough courage to ask who the other guests were, and when they might be arriving.

'In a little while. When we are ready for them. As to who they are? Important men, my dear, who expect to be well looked after. What else do you need to know?'

She waited until his footsteps had disappeared back down the stairs before she rounded on Marika. 'This is ridiculous, and very probably dangerous. We can't stay. I'd call Eddy to come and get us, but I don't want to put him in a difficult position. You need to call your father; get him to send a car. We can pretend someone's ill if you want, whatever you need to save face.'

Marika began fiddling with her compact. 'That's not going to happen. Even if I wanted to call Father, which I don't, I can't. My parents aren't in Berlin; they're still in France.'

'What? Mari, that makes no sense. They went on holiday in August; it's November. What's going on?'

Marika blinked hard. For one shocked moment, Anna thought she might cry, but she pulled herself back together.

'Don't make a big deal out of it. It turns out it wasn't a holiday they went on, that's all. Apparently Father finds Hitler and his plans for Germany *tedious,* so they're not coming back. We have family in France, on Mother's side. He can do whatever it is he does as easily from Paris as Berlin, and she can spend her days in the fashion salons. I imagine it's all working out for them very well.' Marika's tone was nonchalant enough, but the hand holding the compact was shaking.

Anna was horrified: Marika's parents had always been careless with their daughter, but this behaviour was cruel. She knew if she said that, however, Marika would go on the defensive and they'd never get away.

Despite the effort it took, she managed to keep her voice steady. 'And what, you've been rattling round that huge house by yourself all this time? Why didn't you say something?'

Marika snapped the compact shut. 'Because I'm twenty-three, not a child in need of Mummy and Daddy. And besides, I haven't been rattling around, as you put it. They've rented it out, left me with the top floor. It's fine, although it's put a bit of a dampener on entertaining.'

It was another brave performance, but Marika's eyes were glistening.

Anna reached out to take her hand, but Marika slapped her away.

'Don't. I don't want your pity. I don't need it. But I do need my career. You're making too much of everything as usual. Joseph is a gentleman, and, as you said yourself, we're hardly naïve little girls. Whatever tonight is, it won't be anything we can't handle. I'm going for a bath; I suggest you do the same. Or have a brandy. Or both, but, for God's sake, relax.'

Anna tried, for all of five minutes. She wanted to believe that Marika had everything under control. She wanted to believe the night wasn't going to descend into a chaos that could swallow them both. But she had seen the predatory way Goebbels had watched them, and nothing, not even Marika's beloved career, was worth whatever *entertainment* he was clearly planning.

Anna made a decision, not because she wanted to, but because she had to. She knew Marika would be cross, she knew Goebbels would be furious, which was a far more dangerous proposition. She placed the call anyway.

The three of them were in the drawing room, drinking coffee and nibbling on squares of cloud-textured cheesecake as if they were at a post-church Sunday social, when the phone call came. Anna was requested, Goebbels took it. When he re-entered the room, his face was, once again, unreadable.

'Frau Tiegel, I am afraid I am the bearer of bad news. It appears your mother has been taken ill with an influenza severe enough to warrant a hospital visit and she is asking for you. The young man who rang – your cousin apparently – was most insistent I release you from your stay.'

Anna didn't need to act out dropping her cup. She had presumed Eddy would be put straight through to her; she hadn't considered he would have to try and fool Goebbels.

The Minister looked at the mess of crockery and coffee splashes, looked at her and smiled. She managed not to shiver.

'It is a shock to you then? Well, my car and driver are, of course, at your immediate disposal. I imagine you would prefer to leave at once, before the snow sets in?'

He rang for a maid to clear up the mess and call for the car. He never once took his eyes off Anna.

'Thank you, that's most kind.' It was all she could do not to stutter. 'And Marika. Marika should come too, don't you think? Obviously I know she would be perfectly safe here, but for the sake of propriety, wouldn't it be best for her to leave too?'

'What? Why is that necessary? I'm very happy to stay.'

Goebbels reached for Marika's hand and raised it to his lips. 'As much as I am enchanted to hear that, Marika my dear, Anna is, of course, right. It could harm your good name if word slipped out that you had stayed here alone. And reputation, as I am sure your dear friend agrees, is everything.' He was still watching Anna; his gaze was so intent, she felt speared by it. 'I, for one, am pleased she is solicitous of you, although I expected nothing less: my poor heart was resigned to your departure the moment I answered the call.' He kissed Marika's hand again. 'Now the car is ready, and your bags are repacked and you really must go. I would hate poor Frau Tiegel to suffer unnecessarily.'

'You aren't cross with me?'

Marika's pout made Anna shudder and Goebbels laugh. He led them both into the hallway, where the maid was waiting with their coats and helped Marika into hers.

'Run to the car, sweetheart, and don't catch cold. I need to give Anna the name of a doctor I would like her mother to see.'

She blew him a kiss and was gone. Anna's instinct was to grab her coat and follow, but Goebbels was too quick. He caught her wrist so tight, her skin burned.

'You must think that was very cleverly done. Except she won't thank you for this little stunt and you, my dear, are finished.'

'I don't know what you mean.'

He dragged her through the front door before she could fasten her coat. The sharp wind and the sting of the now heavily falling snow whipped her breath away.

'Don't insult us both. I can have Marika whenever I choose, or I can choose not to have her at all. This little trick of yours makes

no difference to that. Although it will make her more desperate
to secure my good favour, especially when I add my regrets at her
parents' rather sudden departure to her worries.'

His mouth was so close, Anna could feel his lips brushing her ear.

'Jewish grandparents. You do understand that means at least
one parent shares the stain? Both, if you consider, as you should,
intermarriage to be a crime. It fascinates me how easily your kind
seem to think being Jewish is something you can put on and take
off, or leave in the past, as the fancy suits. It really doesn't work that
way. You, my dear, both have Jewish fathers, whatever your fathers
might think of that. That might be a problem for her, it might not.
I haven't decided. But as for you? Now that is a very different issue.'

Anna could no longer control her shaking hands. Goebbels
laughed.

'Look at her, in the car, warm and cosy, not quite certain I'll
forgive her, so already planning how she will make sure that I do.'
He raised his hand and waved at Marika, who waved enthusiastically
back. 'And here you are, at the mercy of the wind and the snow.
It's cold, isn't it, on the outside? And it's lonely. I wonder if you'll
ever get used to it. I do hope that you don't.'

He pushed Anna away with such force she slipped and wrenched
an ankle.

'I have instructed the driver to take you both to your parents'
home. I don't believe for a moment your precious mother is ill,
but it's always useful to have an eye on a place.'

Anna limped slowly to the car, her knees shaking. The chauffeur
did not come to help.

Marika's smile lasted until the car turned the corner out onto
the empty road back to Berlin, and then she slumped against the
seat as if someone had punched her. 'What on earth where you
thinking?'

Anna was so close to tears, it was hard for her to reply. 'I was
trying to look out for you.'

Marika stared at her as if she was stupid. 'How was that *looking out for me*? He'll punish me for this. It wasn't my fault, but that doesn't matter. This could cost me my career.'

'It's not you he's angry with. He threatened me; he knows about my father and he's not going to overlook it, whatever dispensations he offers anyone else…'

But Marika was still talking, her voice as jagged as smashed glass. 'I can't do this anymore. I'll go mad with the strain of it. I have to get out. I have to get to America. Eddy can do it; Eddy can help me. He'll have to, when I explain how I'm drowning.'

Anna jolted out of the fog she had fallen into, full of soldiers bursting through her parents' apartment and dragging them away.

'What do you mean? How can Eddy help you?'

Marika stopped babbling at the window and swivelled round again. 'He really hasn't told you? I know you like to make your own way, but I thought he would have at least shared that.'

Her eyes were feverishly bright. Anna recoiled.

'What are you talking about? What hasn't he told me?'

Marika refused to answer. She lapsed into a silence Anna's questions couldn't break. When they arrived back at the Tiegel home in Mitte, however, and Eddy opened the door, she quickly recovered her voice.

'It was you, wasn't it? Who thought up that clever idea, and telephoned the house? Oh, Eddy darling, you saved me! Goodness knows what Goebbels had planned. He can be such a monster and, well, you're one of us, you know how it is: if you don't meet his demands, you're finished. I've been keeping him at arm's-length for months, but I knew time was running out. And if you hadn't rung when you did… oh, Eddy, you're really and truly my hero!' Marika burst into tears and fell into his arms.

Eddy caught her and held on as if she was as fragile as thistledown.

Anna watched the spectacle with her mouth open, her own fright temporarily forgotten.

She can't be serious. He can't be fooled.

Marika continued to sob and hang round Eddy's neck as if Anna was invisible. Anna waited for him to disentangle himself, to explain that he had simply followed Anna's instructions and was hardly a *hero*. For someone to explain what the mystery Marika had alluded to in the car was about. Eddy was busy mopping up Marika, however, and seemed to have forgotten Anna existed, and Marika was deliberately ignoring her. Their behaviour was infuriating and humiliating. Anna's temper was about to snap, and then her parents appeared in the hallway, half-asleep and confused by the commotion and in need of reassurance.

There had been too many unexplained incidents in the neighbourhood lately – beatings and broken doors and disappearances that were never solved – and it took Anna a while to convince her parents that there was nothing to worry about. By the time she left their bedroom, Eddy and Marika had retreated to the kitchen. They were both sat at the table, their hands wrapped round coffee cups. To Anna's relief, Marika had stopped crying, although she was still staring wide-eyed at Eddy as if he had sprouted wings and a halo.

Anna sat down and reached for the coffee pot. Neither of them spoke to her, but Eddy, at least, had the manners to look embarrassed.

'I don't know what Marika's said to you, but our story didn't fool Goebbels. He knew it was a ruse to get us both away, and he threat—'

Before Anna got any further, Marika broke into a fit of coughing. Eddy jumped up at once and began fussing with water and glasses. Anna stared at Marika, who still wouldn't meet her eye.

Eddy can help me. What was this thing she didn't know?

'Eddy, is there something going on? Something you haven't told me?'

He sat back down at the table, picked up his cup and set it aside again.

'I suppose there is, yes. But it wasn't something I meant to tell you like this.'

He stopped, clearly groping for words.

Anna knotted her fingers to keep herself from drumming on the table.

'Tell me, Eddy. Whatever it is, it can't be that bad.'

He latched onto that as if she had thrown him a lifeline. 'No, it's not bad at all, I promise. It's a bit more complicated now than it was, but it's actually wonderful really. Do you remember that I told you Max Reinhardt has been given permission to go to Hollywood to film *A Midsummer Night's Dream*? And that he wants to take me as one of the assistant directors?'

'Not exactly.' Anna put her own cup carefully down. 'I remember you said that there had been an approach, an initial conversation. You didn't say it had gone anywhere.'

Eddy rubbed his face. 'Well, if I didn't, I meant to. These things go so fast and we've both been busy, maybe I thought that I had. Anyway, Max wants me to go to Hollywood pretty much straight after Christmas, to start looking at locations and sets. I know it's short notice, and I don't know how long I'll be gone. But it's an amazing opportunity. And a solution too perhaps.'

Anna nodded, knowing she was missing something but not wanting to spoil his delight. 'You're right, it's incredible. I'll miss you, of course I will, but yes, it's wonderful, career-changing. But what is it a solution to, Eddy? I'm sorry, I don't understand.'

And then she looked at Marika's face and she did.

'You're going to take Marika with you.'

Eddy looked so pleased with himself as he poured out the plan, Anna could have cried.

'That's what we were talking about while you were in the kitchen. Marika needs to get away from Goebbels and, obviously, she wants to stay working in the movies. She can't do that in Germany if she upsets the Minister who controls the whole industry. America, however, would be a new chance entirely. And the thing is, I've been told to select the group who will come with me – a couple of technicians, a writer maybe, and an actress – to set up early shots and start organising the production and costume meetings. The Chamber of Film has agreed the whole thing. I was going to ask you to be the actress, obviously I was, and I still really want you to come. But, given what has happened, I'm sorry, but I think the person who goes with me first has to be Marika.'

He's going to be a hero; he can't help himself. How do I tell him he's saving the wrong girl?

Eddy continued, however, before Anna could stop him. 'Which might sound risky, I suppose, given she's his favourite, but the beauty is that Goebbels won't need to know. Warner Brothers has arranged all the visas and the agreement with UFA is that we take one of the studio stock company actresses. We don't need to submit names in advance, and I am the one sorting out the travel dates and buying the tickets. I was going to wiggle things and stick you on the list at the last minute. I wanted you with me; you must know I did. But I'm coming back, even if Marika isn't. Given Max's plans, this won't be the only trip and I'll take you next time. It will all work out fine, I'm sure of it.' Eddy's face split into a grin; Marika stared at him adoringly.

Anna hated to be the cold voice of reason, but she was more comfortable using that than the panicked one she was struggling against. 'It's a kind idea, but it's not as simple as you're making it sound. Never mind the repercussions if you do make it work, Marika would have to be very careful before you even left. Goebbels could get wind of her plans no matter how open-ended the travel documents are – you know what he's like for sniffing out secrets. She would have to avoid him for weeks. I don't see how that's possible.'

Then Marika finally spoke and it was clear that she had thought through every detail. 'That won't be a problem. Christmas is coming: Joseph has already said Hitler will be cracking the whip for all his ministers to be very publicly with their families. He doesn't expect to be at the studio for a while. I can manage him for the time that is left.'

No wonder she was quiet in the car; she was working all this out.

Anna folded her hands to stop them shaking. Marika was in a difficult, a horrible, situation, but it wasn't life or death. Whatever she needed to do to keep her career, Marika would do it, and she would survive it, Anna was certain of that. But her own danger was still real, and there was no way out of it but this. She had no choice – she had to put herself first.

'Eddy. You can't take her; you have to take me. It's me who needs to get away from Berlin, for good.'

She meant to sound calm and logical; instead, she sounded needy and she hated herself for it.

Eddy stared at her. 'Anna, come on. Firstly, I'm helping a friend, our friend. There's nothing more to it. I'm not choosing her over you. And, secondly, what do you mean *get away for good*? If you went to America with me, why wouldn't you want to come home again?'

'You don't understand. It's nothing to do with what I want. Goebbels knew I was behind today's escape. He said I was finished and he'd make sure I would always be *on the outside*. I'm afraid of him. I've no idea what he's planning to do, but I think he intends to harm me.'

'Don't you think you're being rather dramatic?'

Marika looked so poised, Anna wondered – at least until Marika spoke again – whether she understood what Anna was asking Eddy to do.

'Joseph was angry; he'll get over it. He'll probably ship you back to the theatre, that's all, and you'd be perfectly happy with that. You said yourself you were worried about me, about what it would cost me to sleep with him, which I haven't done, but I'll have to do if I stay. This is my only way out. Do you really want to abandon me to a man who you called *rabid*, over some vague threat? He'll forget about me once I've gone, and surely you don't think he'll spend his time plotting his revenge on you? No one's that important to him, not even me.' Marika shrugged.

Anna was speechless.

Eddy scratched his head. 'I could try and take you both. If you're really worried, I mean. Are you, Anna, honestly?' Eddy took her hand, but he didn't stop frowning.

Anna nodded. 'Yes, I am. The threat wasn't vague – he meant it. And it's not that I think I'm important…' She stopped.

I sound like a child.

Eddy squeezed her hand; the gesture was uncomfortably paternal. 'I don't want you to be afraid, of course I don't. I never wanted you near that man in the first place. I'll do it: I'll take you both. I'm sure I can fix it. And it will be fun. The three of us in Hollywood. It will be an adventure. As for not coming back, well, let's not worry about that now. I'm sure a few weeks away from him is all you need. Besides, I don't believe you could leave Berlin and your family so easily.'

Anna could tell from his too hopeful tone that he wasn't sure about any of it, but he smiled, so she smiled and decided to at least act as if he was right. His embrace was warm. She felt almost better, and then she caught sight of Marika's frown.

CHAPTER FIVE

Los Angeles, August 1957

'That's all I have: a photograph with half an explanation and a deathbed apology. It's barely enough to build into a paragraph, never mind a feature.'

Once Peggy had decided that trusting Charlie was a far better option than battling on alone, he had proved himself to be a more thoughtful listener than his scruffy appearance suggested. She waited while he pulled out a packet of Marlboros, lit one and blew a smoke ring into the palm trees that fringed the apartment block's garden. 'It's a hell of a paragraph though. Louise Baker could be German and she could be your mother. It's a whole different slant on her image.'

'*Could,* Charlie. That's the key word here.'

'That's pretty much proof by movie-world standards.' He stubbed out his cigarette and unfolded himself from the plastic lawn chair. 'It's six-thirty – you ought to get going.' He hesitated, clearly not wanting to overstep the boundaries of their newly formed friendship. 'Do you want me to drive you there? I'd be glad to.'

Peggy nodded. She was doing her best to act calm, but her skin felt clammy despite the ocean breeze, and she doubted her hands were steady enough to navigate the winding road up to Bel Air. It would be far simpler to curl up on the swing seat nestled under a bank of gardenias and pretend this was no more than a holiday.

Charlie got up and then, when Peggy didn't, he paused with his hand on the gate. 'You don't have to go. I know she insisted on meeting tonight, but you could put her off until you feel ready.'

It was kindly said, but he clearly didn't believe Peggy could back out any more than she did.

'No, it's fine; I'd rather get it over with.' She smiled with more confidence than she felt and followed him to the car.

Charlie did his best to distract her as they crossed Sunset Boulevard and began the climb up Bundy Road. He pointed out the house used in the eponymous film and the sprawling celebrity estates, filling her silences with anecdotes. Peggy barely listened. None of this was going as she had imagined it; none of it felt in her control any more. The summons after such a dreadful first meeting had foreboding stamped all through it, and the location was hardly welcoming. For all Bel Air's reputation as the most sought-after residential area in Hollywood, all Peggy could see was a community enamoured by its own wealth. Even the simplest set of gates was carved out of glistening marble. The few houses near enough to spot from the road were so overdone they could have been borrowed from the set of *Gone With the Wind,* or a giant's version of Georgian England. Everywhere had pillars; everywhere was gilded. Everywhere yelled *Keep Away.*

'This is it.'

Charlie turned a corner into a narrower road and up to a surprisingly simple low gate. To Peggy's relief, the house visible on the other side wasn't square and forbidding, but a gentle mix of terraces and wings fanning out from a curved two-storey centre.

'Don't be fooled by the lack of show. This is one of Bel Air's oldest, most expensive houses. She inherited it from the dead husband she chose very wisely. Rumour has it, the inside is a palace.' Charlie leaned out, pressed a discreetly placed buzzer and gave Peggy's name. The gates swished open. 'I could wait in the car if you like. It's you she asked for.'

Peggy had always assumed that she would broach the delicate question of 'are you my mother?' without witnesses. After the morning's debacle at the studio, however, going in alone and posing that question suddenly seemed rather rash. As much as she wanted Charlie's backup, however, she was concerned that Miss Baker would recognise him from the studio and would refuse to speak to her if he was there.

'She won't know you, will she?'

Charlie laughed, although none too gracefully. 'Are you kidding me? I'm a writer: in movie terms, that's the lowest of the low. I barely rank better than a bug to her.'

As they came to a halt and Peggy opened the car door, a maid appeared, her black dress stark against the pink roses and greenery trailing round the arched entrance. The woman barely managed a stiff 'good day' as she ushered them inside and Charlie's whispered, 'I didn't know Mrs Danvers worked here too; should I call our hostess Rebecca?' did nothing to settle Peggy's nerves.

They were whisked straight through an entrance hall empty of anything except a dramatic chandelier. To Peggy's disappointment, the doors which marched down each side were firmly shut; only the marquetry-inlaid set they were heading towards stood open. The maid motioned them inside and left, leaving Peggy and Charlie to enter a room that was so breathtakingly beautiful they almost stumbled into each other. The room was twice as long as it needed to be, the ceilings impossibly high. At the far end, huge and perfectly polished glass doors led out onto a sweep of emerald-green lawn. More light flooded in through a central dome. The walls were painted in a rich cream, and every upholstered surface was wrapped in the same delicate shade. Peggy blinked.

'A snow palace for a snow queen.'

'I shall assume that is a compliment.'

The throaty purr was as unexpected as it was familiar. Peggy jumped. The room was so still, she had assumed it was empty. Instead, Louise Baker sat watching them from a cushion-thick couch, a grey-haired man perched on an armchair at her side. There was no invitation to sit, no offer of refreshments. Miss

Baker – Peggy couldn't begin to think of her in such surroundings as Louise – didn't waste her time on greetings or pleasantries.

'I presume this is about money. It usually is with your sort. Whatever gossip you have picked up, however much you think it matters, I have no interest in it.' The actress waved her hand over a glass-topped table. 'There is a letter here requiring your signature and guaranteeing a small sum on the undertaking that there will be no repeat of today's disturbances.'

She sat back and nodded to the man Peggy now assumed was her lawyer. He produced a pen, which he held out to Peggy.

'You slapped me.'

'I beg your pardon?'

The mood in the room was so cold, it was trance-like. Peggy shook herself and ploughed on before her nerve failed.

'You've got this wrong. Whatever you expected, I didn't come tonight, or this morning, for money. And, I'm sorry, but I don't believe you. If you've no interest in what I've got to say, why did you slap me, why did you ask me here, and why is your first impulse to offer me some kind of pay-off?'

The bland expression flickered, although Miss Baker held on to her bored tone. 'All right, if that's how you want to do this, if you need some attention, I'll humour you a little. Why are you here then?'

Peggy stood as straight and square as she could. There wasn't going to be any softness in the woman facing her, that much was clear. There wasn't going to be the outpouring of joy at a lost child rediscovered that she had naïvely imagined.

There's nothing to be done but get through this.

'My mother died recently.' She paused and left Miss Baker a space to offer her condolences. When the actress said nothing, Peggy ploughed on. 'I call her my mother, and she was, if you measure that by the amount of love she gave me, but I was actually adopted, as a baby. And I was born in Germany, where I think you spent time when you were young. And also, well, here's the thing, I think you might be my mother, I mean my real one, the one who gave birth to me.' The declaration hadn't sounded half as smooth spoken aloud as when Peggy had practised it in her head, but at least it was out.

There was a sharp intake of breath, from Charlie not Miss Baker. She didn't flinch. The lawyer, however, was half on his feet.

'That is preposterous, young lady. You need to retract that at once.'

Miss Baker gestured him back down again. Peggy was watching her and saw the tightening round her eyes, the way she hid her locked fingers under the drape of her scarf. To anyone not looking closely, however, the actress looked, and sounded, perfectly at ease.

'I don't need you to speak for me, Leo, although you are right: this is ridiculous. And I am sorry to derail your story, my dear, but I am French, as anyone will tell you. I have never been to Germany. And as for the gift of children, sadly I have never been blessed.'

Charlie coughed and Peggy knew he had heard it too. The subtle pause on *children* and *gift*. The faint edge of sadness she pushed through the words.

She's good. And she's lying. She won't meet my eyes.

The famously husky voice dropped another register and took on more warmth. 'Your mother's loss has clearly upset you deeply. I am sorry for that. But I'm not the woman to help you.'

It was a dismissal. Peggy opened her purse instead.

'But I think you are. You see, I have this.' She held out the photograph.

The effect on the actress was electric – her whole body contracted.

'Where did you get that?' The voice wasn't husky anymore, it was strangled.

Peggy instinctively pulled the picture back out of reach. 'It was with me when my parents got me from the hospital, before the war, in Berlin. I believe the girl on the left – underneath that sign which locates the picture in Berlin – is you.'

The actress was on her feet, her face the colour of parchment. She tried to recover herself, but her words fell over each other. 'Why would you bring that here? What am I meant to do with it?'

She hadn't denied it was her, but her response was so strident, Peggy stumbled and sounded far less sure of herself than she meant to.

'You're meant to say that one of them is you. And you're meant to tell me who the other girl is. And which of the two of you is my real mother.'

Every last hope she had for a tender-hearted reunion went out of the window as the actress screamed, 'Get out!'

Charlie and Peggy stared at her, rooted to the spot by the switch in her face and voice.

'I said get out. I'm not German. I'm not your mother. Whatever game you are playing, I want no part of it. Get out of my house now!'

Miss Baker was shaking so hard, Peggy thought she might faint. She didn't care.

'But it has to be you – I recognised your brooch. And Charlie knew you too. And if you're not my mother, then the other girl must be, or why would this picture have been tucked in with me? How can you think this is a game – how can you? This is my life.' She was shouting now too, and, to her horror, she was crying.

'That's surely enough, Peggy.' Charlie's voice was full of concern, but his grip on her elbow was tight. 'This is going to get out of hand.'

'Let me go, I'm not finished with her…'

The vase would have hit her full in the face if Charlie hadn't dragged her back in time. He pulled Peggy into the hall as another missile came crashing.

'Get in the car, quick, before she does anything worse.'

He screeched away and wouldn't stop until they were back at the beach again.

'That was crazy. Are you all right?'

Peggy's chest was so tight, she could barely breathe. 'I don't know. If she is lying and she is my mother, then God help me. If she's not and the other girl is, it's as bad. The one person who knew her just threw a vase at my head.'

Charlie's hair looked as if he had been electrocuted. 'It wasn't ideal, I'll grant you. But it was certainly a reaction. What do you want to do now? Back off, or carry on?'

They both knew there was only one answer to that.

It took them a week to come up with a plan that wouldn't tip off the actress, or her lawyers, that they hadn't backed off at all.

'She'll be keeping tabs on you, trust me, and she'll have spies on her payroll. Everyone is paranoid at the moment. Between scandal sheets like *Confidential* digging for dirt, and the fallout from McCarthy digging for communists, no one trusts anyone. You need a cover story that's wider than her. And you'll need to be careful who you ask.'

Charlie had decided to become Peggy's partner in uncovering Louise, as Peggy was now determined to call her, to bring her down to a manageable size. Peggy – who was far more taken with Charlie's grin and green eyes than she was ready to let him know – had decided to let him. Most evenings, after Charlie had finished at the studio, would find them either ambling along the waterfront before going for dinner and drinks at cheap diners like Leo's Place or Jack's at the Beach, or huddled in the dark spaces of the Frolic Room, which was a favourite screenwriters' hangout. Charlie's crowd of colleagues were more than happy to include Peggy in their gossip and good-natured complaining, especially when they heard she had writing aspirations. It was on them, therefore, that Peggy road-tested the core of the plan she and Charlie had cooked up: that she was working on a history of Hollywood's early years and the stars who had shaped it.

'With a particular focus on the 1930s and all the incomers from Europe. If you have any thoughts on the best people to talk to, please fling them my way.'

They came up with such a flurry of suggestions, Peggy initially thought uncovering the information she needed would be done in a week. Except, as she moaned to Charlie in the privacy of the apartment after one too many disappointing nights, it wasn't.

'It's the same dead end every time. The same cast of characters that go nowhere. *Salka Viertel* – Austrian screenwriter, wrote scripts for Garbo. Knew everyone. Left America four years ago. *Max Reinhardt* – German director. Whole legions of actors passed through his drama academy. Dead, fourteen years ago. It's pointless. Anyone of any use is dead or gone, or has become as important as Billy Wilder and is too lofty these days for mere mortals to speak to.'

'It's hardly surprising. It's Hollywood: people pass through, and on, quicker here than in the rest of the world.'

Peggy grimaced as Charlie flicked through her notebook. His man-in-the-know manner could be infuriating, particularly as he was generally right.

'Don't scowl. You need to be patient, that's all. People are interested. We have feelers out. Someone will come through. Although then you'll have a different Hollywood problem: if we do get anyone to talk about what we actually want to hear, whoever they are, they're going to want money.'

'Money's not a problem. I have plenty of that.' She threw a coaster at him as he raised his eyebrows and called her *Mrs Moneybags*. 'I'm an orphan, remember? And my parents were both savers. The one thing I'm not short of is money.'

His 'excellent, all the drinks are on you then' did not help her sour mood.

Contacts, however, did come in. They were, without exception, charming, long out of the business and happy to ramble. And not one of them could remember Louise Baker in any other version than the one they knew from the screen.

'*The Californian.* That was her first picture. She played a girl in the bar. Hardly enough lines to earn her a credit, but, boy, did the camera love her. She got more close-ups in that movie than the leading lady.'

Every tale they heard was already part of the legend. Peggy was beginning to think she had imagined the scene in Bel Air.

When Charlie arrived unannounced at Peggy's motel apartment one Sunday morning three weeks after they had first floated the plan, waving another coffee-splashed sheet of paper, she struggled to dredge up any excitement.

He's like a puppy, the way he always bounces around. A great big shaggy mongrel puppy.

Albeit one it was becoming rather hard not to pet.

'This one could be a worth a punt. Clara Sokoll. She worked for Max Reinhardt as his secretary at the Workshop of Stage, Screen and Radio he ran on Sunset. And, get this, at his theatre school in Berlin before he was forced to flee here from the Nazis.'

Peggy scanned the crumpled note with a lot more interest.

'She's in Brentwood? That's what, fifteen minutes' drive from here?'

Charlie nodded.

'And there's no phone number…'

'So all we have to do is show up…'

'Catch her off guard…'

'And it's lunchtime, so chances are she'll be home…'

She had the car started before Charlie could finish.

The small house they drew up at was one of the neighbourhood's older Spanish-style buildings, bordered front and side by a neatly clipped lawn. The woman who answered the door matched her home perfectly. She was, Peggy guessed, in her well-preserved seventies. She was dressed in rigidly pressed tapered slacks and a blouse tied with a neat bow at the neck despite the heat.

Peggy explained about the book and their interest in Max Reinhardt; Miss Sokoll corrected her title from the *Mrs* Peggy had automatically used and welcomed them in. She proved to be another enthusiastic talker. She recounted her memories of the Hollywood drama school, showed them some stills from Reinhardt's 'spectacular' production of *A Midsummer Night's Dream*, provided them with coffee cake and sodas and was the perfect hostess. It was no different to any of the other frustratingly cosy afternoons Peggy had sat through. And then, as Peggy was trying to frame a question about Louise that was sufficiently nonchalant, Miss Sokoll leaned forward.

'This is all terribly nice, but what do you really want? You haven't asked a thing a dozen other Hollywood oldies couldn't answer. So, who are you really after?'

The question was too direct for Peggy to waste time prevaricating. 'Louise Baker.'

There was a moment's silence; Miss Sokoll adjusted the chain on her glasses and peered at Peggy over the black frames. 'Why?'

She could be my last chance, it's not like there's anyone else clamouring to talk to us.

Peggy was suddenly so tired of edging around and playing it safe, she decided to jump in and tell the truth, whatever the consequences. 'There's a chance she might be my mother.'

The old lady's steady gaze didn't flicker.

Peggy ploughed on. 'So I'm trying to find out if she could be German, not French, and if she ever had a child.'

'Those are two very interesting questions to ask about a famous, and famously private, woman. If I answer them, what's in it for me?'

Charlie called it correctly: everyone does have a price, even the old and respectable ones.

'Don't frown, dear. This is Hollywood: nothing comes free.'

Charlie snorted. Peggy ignored him.

'If you have information that's really of use, then I can pay. Tell me what you know and I'll tell you what it's worth.'

Miss Sokoll laughed. 'You are funny. But no, I don't want a negotiation, I want three hundred dollars.'

Charlie whistled. Peggy got up.

'Sit down, dear. What's that to a bright girl like you? A month's salary? It's a nice little vacation for me. It's surely a lot less than a mother is worth.'

It was an outrageous amount, far more than anyone else had asked for, or considered their memories were worth. There was nothing to do, however, but count out the last of the cash Peggy had withdrawn to cover the interviews and pray that, this time, the price would be worth it.

'Lovely. Well, where to start? Your suspicions about where Louise came from are correct, so perhaps that's the best place. She is indeed German. I knew her in Berlin, or I knew Marika Bäcker, as she was then. She attended Max's theatre school and was quite the leading light. She made a handful of films in Berlin in the early 1930s, not major ones, but she was about to break into real stardom, and then she decided that Hollywood's sparkle was far more enticing. She came over here, although the circumstances of that, I'm afraid, are a little bit muddy. A kind of "here one minute gone the rest" episode, if I recall, and no one was quite sure when she did it. But she came, and the rest, to use a well-worn cliché, is history. There we are: you were right, well done.'

She had rattled through the story so quickly, Peggy was still trying to process what the old woman had said at the same moment she realised Miss Sokoll was finished.

Does she think I'm an idiot? If she knows that much, surely she's got to know more.

Peggy snatched the banknotes back up from the table. 'What you've said is helpful, I'll give you that, but it's not worth three hundred dollars. I could have got that much out of her. I almost did.'

The old lady almost smiled. 'You didn't, or you wouldn't be sitting here with your mouth unattractively open. But am I to assume you spoke to Louise about this? That was a bold step. That must have given her a fright.'

Fright was an interesting choice of words. Peggy nodded.

'It did.' Peggy decided to take a chance and put the bills back down, although she kept them out of Miss Sokoll's reach. 'It was a heck of a response. Stronger than if she'd simply decided to come here to Hollywood all those years ago and do a little reinventing – the way I imagine many people did then and still do. But you knew her before, and I assume you met her again over here. Did you never question why she had suddenly turned French?'

Miss Sokoll was still watching the money. 'When I arrived in Hollywood, Louise had already been here a few years. Max knew who she was and so did I, of course. But he went along with her charade when she asked him, and he always paid me well enough not to question his decisions. Besides, that was Marika all over: used to getting her own way, especially around men, and always with something to hide.'

It was hard not to hear the bitterness, and hard not to hope it would lead to spilled secrets. Peggy nudged the bundle of notes a little further across the table.

'Could the things she had to hide include a baby?'

The old lady sighed as if she was in no mood to be pushed, but her gaze strayed back to the payment. 'You really are quite the terrier. No, not a baby; I'm fairly sure of that. She was always too clever to get caught that way, in Berlin anyway. I assumed changing her birthplace to France was more to do with being German and what that meant back then. You have to remember that Germany was a very different place in the 1930s, a very dangerous place. Once the Nazis took power, well, they removed anyone who didn't fit into their new world order and controlled the ones who did, and they did it fast. Max and I fled because we were Jewish. We were lucky – we had resources and connections, so we could.' She stopped for a moment, her eyes clouding over. 'Well, that's a long time ago and nothing to be done now. But the Nazis ran every aspect of our lives, never mind film-making, although they twisted that to their own ends as successfully as they did everything else. And it is possible, if rumours are to be believed, that Marika – Louise – got herself in, with one of them at least, a little too deep.'

That was so far from anything Peggy had expected, all she could manage was a slightly shaky, 'Too deep with who?'

Miss Sokoll waited and then she smiled, as if she was already enjoying how much she was about to shock them. 'Goebbels. Hitler's propaganda minister.'

Charlie sucked in his breath; Peggy froze.

'You didn't see that coming, did you?' The old lady took advantage of their shock to scoop up the notes. 'The surprise reveal: it was always one of Max's favourites. Well, there were rumours she was Goebbels' mistress, or lined up to be next. I don't know how true it was: the movie world there, same as here, was always fuelled on gossip and jealousy.' She sat back. Despite her obvious delight in the impact her news had made, she looked a little winded. 'Perhaps that makes it easier to understand why she got out when she could, and why she was keen to become someone else. And now, I really do think we are done.'

'The photograph. Show it to her.'

Charlie's hiss pulled Peggy back from the wild scenarios she was picturing. She dug the picture out of her purse and slid it across the table.

'I believe one of these girls is my mother. And I believe the one on the left is Louise. Can you confirm that's who it is?'

The old lady picked the photograph up and nodded.

Peggy could barely get the next question out.

'And the other girl, do you know who she is too?'

Miss Sokoll looked at the picture again. 'Well I never, it's Anna Tiegel. I haven't thought about her in years. She was an actress too, far better, in my opinion, than Louise, although she didn't have quite the same movie-star glamour. They were at Max's academy together in Berlin. They were friends, good friends, although they were very different and sometimes the sparks flew. Close as kin one moment, not speaking the next, from what I remember. But drama-school friendships were always like that: dramatic.'

'Do you know where this Anna Tiegel is now?'

Charlie must have heard the tremor in Peggy's voice as she repeated the name: she felt his arm slide round the back of her chair.

'I don't, my dear, I'm sorry.' This time, there was no bite to the *my dear*. 'I really don't. She disappeared. There was a rumour that she came to America, or maybe it was more that she was planning to. Her boyfriend certainly did, for a while at least; he worked on *Dream* with Max, he must have been here when Louise first came out. Anyway, I don't know if Anna came or not. If she did, she can't have picked up her old career. I haven't heard her name since I left Berlin, and she would have been a star here if she had tried.'

Miss Sokoll stopped suddenly. 'No, wait. I do remember hearing Max mention her, to Louise. It must have been around 1938, not long after we'd got settled and opened the Workshop on Sunset, when Louise came to ask him not to reveal her background. My desk was directly outside his office and the door was open. He asked her what had happened to Anna, because Eddy – that was the boyfriend's name, Eddy Hartmann – had gone back to Berlin and hadn't been able to find her, and was there any chance that she might have come to America. Then he called for water and, when I went in, Louise was in quite a state.'

There were so many questions Peggy wanted to ask, but she could sense from Miss Sokoll's twisting hands that time was running out.

'You mean she was upset? But why?'

There was a pause.

Peggy resisted the urge to repeat the question as the silence stretched out. It was clear from Miss Sokoll's frown that she was thinking hard, not being evasive.

'I'm not sure. She was feeling guilty about something, I felt that at the time, although I can't explain why. I never liked her, perhaps that's all it was. She left shortly after that and I never saw her again, except on the screen. And then the war started and Max died and everything fell apart.' Her face and body sagged. 'I'm sorry, but that really is all I have.'

Miss Sokoll looked drained. Peggy knew she should stop, but she couldn't give up without one last push.

'Are you sure there's no one else? Not one other person from those days who might be prepared to talk about Louise, or who might remember Anna, or even Eddy?'

The old lady, who now looked every inch of her years, sighed. 'Well, you said you'd been looking, and you haven't unearthed anyone but me. Doesn't that suggest that, if there was anyone, she's paid them off and shut them up?'

Miss Sokoll was probably right; Louise herself had hinted as much – *'I presume this is about money. It usually is with your sort'* – but Peggy still wasn't ready to give up.

'She never tried that with you.'

Miss Sokoll shook her head and gave a sigh that was almost a laugh. 'I missed my chance. I was too loyal to Max. And then, when I did think about approaching her and maybe earning a little payout, she'd got too popular and powerful. I'm too old to be making enemies like that.'

'Come on, Peggy, she's exhausted.' Charlie kept his voice low, although Miss Sokoll's attention had drifted. 'She's given you more than you had when we came.'

Charlie got up; Peggy reluctantly followed.

They had said their goodbyes and were about to close the parlour door when Miss Sokoll suddenly called them back.

'Wait a minute. Maybe there is something else, not someone who knew Louise, at least I don't think so, but who knew Eddy. There was a man I remember, a lighting director from UFA, who also worked on *Dream*. Him and Eddy were as thick as thieves at one time. Give me a minute.'

Miss Sokoll closed her eyes; Peggy hovered in the doorway, clutching Charlie's arm, doing her best not to urge the old woman on.

'Manny, that was it. Manny Brettenheimer. That's not a name anyone would risk taking back to Germany, not then. He could have stayed. If he carried on working in the business, someone might know him.' She sank back into the chair as suddenly as she had come alive again. 'And now I really have earned my money.'

She didn't respond when Peggy said goodbye for the second time and suggested a further meeting. Peggy didn't care. Miss Sokoll had given them a thread to follow, a very thin one perhaps, but it was still a thread.

It took Charlie a week to spread the word through his studio contacts and track Manny Brettenheimer down. A week which Peggy spent staring obsessively at the photograph, trying once again to trace herself in either of the girls, but mostly, this time, in the unknown face that was Anna.

'He's in a home in Echo Park for industry workers who have fallen down on their luck. He's not in great shape apparently, although I don't know what that means: seems no one has actually seen him in years. Maybe you should do this one alone: if he's not doing so well two visitors could overwhelm him.'

The home was a small one and as run-down as its patients, but the nurse who met Peggy at the main entrance was motherly and kind.

'He has emphysema, which makes it hard for him to breathe. He was also a drinker, I'm afraid – a lot of the men in here were –

which means his memory can be a little muddled. And he doesn't get visitors; I don't think he has any family. But he's a nice old boy, always polite; I'm glad someone's remembered him. Are you a niece or something?'

Peggy hadn't known what to say, so she gave a vague nod, which seemed to satisfy the nurse. The room she led Peggy to was a spartan one. The man hunched in a chair too big for his body was frail; Peggy couldn't imagine he had many years left to him.

She introduced herself and chattered as brightly as she could about the old days of the film industry, but, for the first few minutes she spoke, he didn't seem to be clear she was there. She was beginning to think that her journey had been a wasted one, that all she was doing was confusing him, which hardly seemed the decent thing to do. Then she mentioned Louise's name, and his watery eyes focused.

'I never said anything.' His voice was a wheeze, the words forced out in gasps. 'I swore I wouldn't when I took the money. I stuck to it.'

'I know.' Peggy repeated it until he eventually believed her. 'And it's not really her I'm interested in; it's an old friend of yours: Eddy Hartmann?'

For the first time since Peggy entered his room, Manny's sunken face smiled.

'The cupboard. Open it.' He pointed to a small chest of drawers in the corner of the room. 'It's in the top one.'

The drawer was pitifully empty apart from a cardboard box. Peggy lifted it out.

'Under the photos.'

Peggy pushed the handful of black-and-white snaps aside. There was a pile of cards underneath them – she counted at least a dozen – all printed with the same message: *Fröhliche Weihnachten*.

'Eddy. Every Christmas, he never forgot me. Even during the war, he still stayed in touch.'

It was so much more than Peggy had hoped for, she hardly dared ask the next question.

'Do you have an address for him?'

Manny nodded and waved for her to pass him the box. He dug under the cards and pulled out a piece of paper. 'Take it. I know it by heart.' As he passed it over, a coughing fit struck and the nurse bustled in.

'You'll have to go now; he's worn out.'

The old man was gasping for breath as if he couldn't imagine catching another one. It was too painful to watch for Peggy to argue. Then she realised he was trying to get her attention.

'Is it Anna?' It was so hard to pick the words out, Peggy thought she'd misheard. 'Is it about his lost Anna?'

This time, there was no mistaking the name. *His lost Anna.* Peggy nodded; she was too choked up to speak.

Manny finally managed a strong breath and a weak smile. 'Help him find her. What he did broke his heart.'

His voice was too thin to handle all the questions bursting through Peggy, but she couldn't hold back. 'What do you mean? What did he do?'

She could see in his red-rimmed eyes that he wanted to answer, but his coughing returned with a vengeance and the nurse shooed Peggy away.

If Anna really is my mother, and Eddy was Anna's boyfriend in Berlin, could he be my father? Could I have found them both? And, even if I suspect that's true, is it in my power to say anything to him?

It took Peggy five attempts to write a letter that was restrained enough to send.

The writing was hard enough, but the waiting was worse: she had no idea how long it would take for a letter to reach Berlin, or for a reply to arrive, or if Eddy Hartmann could read or write

English. After two aimless days spent wandering the beach while her brain spun through hoops, Peggy had had enough of waiting and wondering and doing nothing, a state of affairs which had never suited her. She decided, therefore, to fill in whatever blanks she could for herself and to turn herself back into a student.

She haunted the movie theatres on Montana Avenue and Westward Boulevard which specialised in retrospectives, watching every one of Louise's films she could find. She buried herself in the Los Angeles Public Library, checking out every book and old newspaper which would educate her about World War Two, and, more particularly, the conflict's impact on Berlin.

The information she unearthed made for sobering reading. The statistics from the bombing raids were horrific: 363 air raids; over 67,000 tons of bombs dropped; 80% of the city destroyed; 35,000 dead and hundreds of thousands left homeless and injured. The photographs of the obliterated city reduced her to tears. Seas of rubble replacing homes and lives; buildings ripped open and gutted; people and places pounded to dust. She wondered what the Baileys had made of the damage that had been wreaked on the city they had once lived in; if that had been what had made her father so angry when he saw Nazi supporters marching through New York. That Eddy had survived such devastation seemed little short of a miracle. When his reply finally appeared in her mailbox, Peggy could barely open the flimsy blue envelope for fear it would crumble.

His letter – to her relief – was written in English, although it was clear from the stilted phrasing that it wasn't a language its author regularly used.

Dear Miss Bailey,

I have received your letter requesting information about Anna Tiegel. It was not a request I expected – I am not sure I understand why an American wishes to write about cinema in Germany, or the actresses who worked in it, in the period of the last regime or the war. That was a dark time. Is it not better forgotten?

In answer to your question, however, yes: Anna Tiegel was known to me. As to her whereabouts, all I can answer is that I wish that I knew. I have not seen, or heard from, Anna since December 1934. I do not know for certain whether she is in America, but I believe it to be more of a possibility than her being in Germany still. I am as certain as I can be that she is not in Berlin. I searched for months for her here in 1935 and 1936, without success, although that may be because she did not want to be found, or at least by me.

I have never stopped hoping she is alive, that someday I might find her. I came once to America myself, and it is not impossible that Anna may have gone there to find me, although I did not deserve that. If things in my life had been different, I would have come back and searched there myself, but the circumstances I found myself in for many years did not allow it. And then I was afraid my attempts would be too late, or not wanted.

I wish you luck. I have never forgotten Anna; I have never wanted to. If I may, I also have a request: if your search uncovers anything of her, will you share it? I cannot help you, I am sorry for that, but you could, perhaps, help me.

With regards,
Eddy Hartmann

'I don't know what to make of it. I do know that the dates add up: that, if they were still together in December 1934, Eddy could well be my father. But I can't tell how he felt, or feels, about Anna, although he clearly went searching and the whole thing is dripping in guilt. I'm pretty sure he didn't know she was pregnant, if she was, so I can hardly write back and tell him that Anna may have had a child, which, by the way, may have been me. Not without knowing what I'm stirring up. I honestly don't know whether this moves me forward or back.'

What Peggy wanted to do was to go running back to Bel Air at once and confront Louise, with Clara Sokoll's vague accusations that Louise was hiding some mistreatment of Anna, and with Eddy's letter, which may or may not back that up. Charlie had a hard fight to talk her out of it.

'I agree he sounds guilty, but you don't know if Louise has any part in whatever that is. And Clara and Manny have both proved that Louise is a master at covering her tracks. She's kept her past hidden for over twenty years and done it so well, no one's had an inkling that there's anything to find. Louise isn't going to roll over. And you've seen her temper. If you're determined to tackle her again, you need real proof, not hunches and suspicions, and any meeting has to be in a place where she's visible and she has to behave. And she needs to understand that, if she doesn't turn up, you'll go public with Clara's information.'

'She won't believe I'd do that.'

'She won't dare take the risk. Leave it with me: I'll get a message to her lawyer via the studio, see if I can ruffle some feathers and smoke her out.'

Peggy wasn't convinced, but she agreed to let Charlie try. When he did, the response was immediate.

'She's agreed to meet tomorrow, which suggests she's definitely rattled, and at the Bel Air Hotel. That's secluded rather than public, but it's the best I could do. She's bringing Leo the Lawyer with her, so you need to be clear on what you are going to say. And clear on what you want.'

Peggy hadn't needed to think about that: she had thought about nothing else since their Bel Air meeting. 'I want to know for certain which one of them is my mother and, if it's this Anna Tiegel, as I suspect, I want to know where she is. It's a simple enough ask, given what we've got on her.'

Charlie took a swig of his beer and lay back on the sand. 'And what about the other stuff. Why she pretended she wasn't German. And what happened with Goebbels.'

Peggy gazed out at the ocean, her stomach in knots. She'd woken up two nights in a row worrying over what *a little too deep* meant. Had lain awake staring at the possibility that one of the Reich's most notorious ministers, a man who had poisoned his own children in the last days of the war and then killed himself to avoid capture, could somehow be her father. If Louise suddenly recanted and announced that, yes, she was Peggy's mother, Peggy was afraid that she would be physically sick.

'If it's Anna who gave birth to me, I don't need to know about any of that.'

'I do not appreciate being summoned. Or being treated like an equal by a nobody.'

Louise had crackled with hostility from the moment Peggy and Charlie slid into the shadowy high-sided booth. Even her outfit – a tightly fitting skirt suit in a bronze material which the candlelight turned metallic – was forbidding. Peggy had no doubt the armour-plated effect was deliberate. The actress was sipping an olive-studded Martini; Leo was drinking whisky. When neither of them offered Peggy and Charlie a drink, Peggy summoned a waiter and ordered them the same round. The frown that darkened Louise's face was deeply satisfying.

'If this is about me being your mother again, you won't have time to drink those. I can assure you that I'm not. I've never had a child. By the time I realised I might want one, it was too late.'

That there was no self-pity in Louise's voice, and no attempt to win sympathy, was what convinced Peggy, this time, that the denial was true.

She sipped her drink: the relief that she was neither Louise's child, or Goebbels', was overwhelming.

'Fine. But I think you know who is. Do you remember the name Clara Sokoll? She was a secretary years ago, when you were first starting out.'

'I meet a lot of secretaries. You can't expect me to notice them all.' Louise's shrug was enough to imply *or any.*

She makes it very easy to dislike her.

Peggy fished the olive out of her drink and crunched it.

'Well, this one remembered you. She was Max Reinhardt's secretary. She knew you in Hollywood, and in Berlin.'

Louise's studied air of boredom shifted a fraction.

Peggy continued. 'And she recognised you in the photograph.'

'Young lady, we have already done this and I see no purpose in continuing…'

'It's all right, Leo.' Louise put her hand on the lawyer's arm. 'Let them have their little bit of fun. So they've discovered my *terrible secret*, that I'm not French but German.' She picked up her Martini and took a delicate sip. 'What of it? I came to Hollywood at a difficult time and I fudged my past a little. It's hardly a crime.'

Louise looked perfectly poised and totally sure of herself, but she was holding the stem of her glass so tight Peggy was sure it would snap.

She thinks I'm not brave enough, or that she holds enough cards to wriggle away. Well, not this time.

Peggy decided to cut straight to the point. 'Nobody is saying it is. What you pretend to the world is your own business. But you were in that photograph, and Miss Sokoll also recognised the other girl. She called her Anna Tiegel.'

Louise gasped.

Peggy registered that and pushed on. 'And if you're not my mother, then surely she is? I was born in 1935. Were you and Anna still friends then?'

'What? When did you say you were born?' Louise's voice was no longer steady.

Peggy sat back. 'In July 1935. My parents got me from the Charité Hospital in Berlin when I was about a week old. I had the photograph of you and Anna with me.'

'That's not possible. That would mean Anna was…' Louise put her drink down so abruptly, the clear liquid splashed over her silk gloves.

Peggy's neck prickled. 'Was what?'

'Nothing.' Louise's voice had steadied but not her hands. 'I don't know how you came by this photograph. I don't know why you've come up with this nonsense about adoptions in Berlin and linked it to me. If it isn't for money, then perhaps you are simply a fantasist, a silly little Walter Mitty. Whatever it is, it has gone beyond anything worth my attention.' She clicked for the waiter without looking his way. 'Enough of my time has been wasted. This is done.'

She's afraid, and she's not a good enough actress to hide it.

'No it's not.' Peggy leaned forward, forcing Louise to look at her. 'You know something. You knew Anna had disappeared from Berlin back in the thirties. Miss Sokoll heard Reinhardt tell you – she said you were in quite a state when you heard. Did you have something to do with that? There were rumours, apparently, that she might have come here, like her boyfriend Eddy did.'

This time, Louise didn't gasp, she gaped.

'Is that what Anna did? If you know, you have to tell me.'

'I don't know and I don't care.' Louise was on her feet, pushing out of the booth.

'You're lying!'

Peggy jumped up. She knew this was it, that she wouldn't get close to Louise again; that she had nothing left to lose.

'Your words say one thing, but all your reactions say different. And I've found Eddy – I've had a letter from him that's all twisted up with guilt. Something happened to my mother, I know it did. She disappeared. He thinks he was to blame for that, and I've a hunch you were too. So, tell me the truth, tell me what really went on twenty years ago. Did you leave Germany because you were a Nazi? Because you were sleeping with Goebbels, like Clara Sokoll hinted you were? Did you fall out with my mother because she knew? Were you afraid that, if she really had come here, she would uncover you and wreck your career? Did you hurt her?'

Charlie gasped; the lawyer jumped up. Peggy had eyes for no one but Louise. She didn't know a face could change so fast. The twist in Louise's from beautiful to ugly was shocking. Peggy braced herself for another blow; the verbal attack that came instead was worse.

'You poisonous little bitch. You don't have a clue. All you've got is a load of nonsense spun by a dried-up old hag desperate for a bit of attention. I remember Clara Sokoll all right. She hated us all, for being prettier and wittier than she could ever be. She was always jealous, in love with Max and too plain to be noticed. And as for Eddy Hartmann, he was a spineless fool.' The actress's face was mottled with red, her neck stretched and sinewy. 'You know what? Maybe you are Anna's daughter after all. You're certainly as easy to fool.' She turned on her heel and was gone, snapping her fingers for Leo to follow.

Peggy slumped back onto the banquette.

'Are you all right?' Charlie pushed her Martini towards her. She gulped it down in one swallow.

'I'm not sure.'

He picked up his glass and drained the last of his whisky. 'You shook her, you really shook her. That was a hell of an exit.' He covered her fingers with his; Peggy let him.

'There's a story in this, isn't there?'

Charlie laughed. 'Are you kidding? *Famous Film Star's Nazi Past*. It's the best kind. God knows how she kept it quiet this long; she must have been very convincing when she first came here. And very clever. So yes, it's a story. The question now is what are you going to do with it?'

Peggy waved to a waiter and nodded at their empty glasses.

'I came to Hollywood to find my mother. And now I know her name, and I know there's a chance she could be in America. I've no idea how to piece the bits together yet, or how high to get my hopes up, but I've got enough to start pushing. If the truth about Louise became public, it could flush Anna out. What else can I do then but make the truth public?'

Charlie was staring at her as if he was weighing her up. 'And if telling the story destroys Louise?'

Peggy picked up her fresh glass. 'She's had a good enough run, better perhaps than my mother. Whatever is coming her way, she deserves it.

CHAPTER SIX

They were gone. Without a trace, without a word. Eddy's flat was deserted; the whole of Marika's house, not just her floor, was locked up, awaiting the arrival of new tenants, according to the gardener, who was the only person still at the property. No one had seen either of them, no one had any idea where they were, although Anna had a very good idea. Not that she could find anyone to confirm her suspicions. Max Reinhardt's office was closed up for the Christmas holidays; the Babelsberg studios were shut down the same. It would be January before the crews and the casts and the secretaries who might be able to help her reassembled properly again.

We weren't supposed to be leaving Berlin until the New Year.

The more Anna picked at that, the more hollow it sounded. What the three of them were *supposed* to be doing suddenly mattered far less than what they had done.

'Is it true that Eddy's disappeared? And Marika too? Surely they haven't run off together, have they?'

It didn't matter who asked, she didn't have an answer. The pitying looks and the nudges became unbearable before her first week of searching was done.

The only people Anna dared tell the truth to about their plans, and the collapse of them, were her parents. They were so heartbroken for her, and so disappointed with Eddy, it made her misery worse.

'I knew Marika could be a selfish piece, but I expected better of her with you. And it has to be her doing, sweetheart, I'd lay money on it. Eddy doesn't have a secretive bone in his body. Leaving quicker than intended, without any word? Marika's at the bottom of it, mark my words. He'll be back with his tail between his legs before you know it, trust me.'

Anna wasn't sure she believed the last part, although she badly needed the rest. But then her mother's protective hackles flared higher than Anna needed them to and her upset for her daughter spilled out in a wave of *I did warn you* and *I told you to watch her.* Anna knew it was well meant, but she was too soaked in fury herself to hear anything that, even inadvertently, implied that she was at fault; that her foolishness, not their betrayal, was the sin.

She had longed to sob out her misery for her mother to soften it. She had wanted to confess that she was spinning in circles. That she had got no nearer to spotting the clues, to pinpointing the moment when the decision to abandon her had been taken. She had wanted to offer the excuse that the three of them had seen so little of each other in the weeks since the disastrous trip to Bogensee that perhaps the problem was simply one of communication. Eddy had been away on location in the Dolomites, filming a mountain-based epic. She had spent as little time as she could at the studios outside her designated filming slots, to minimise the chance of running into Goebbels. Her schedule and Marika's had never seemed to coincide. Maybe she had missed some signs?

But, then again, when they had finally met up a little over a week ago, their plans had seemed solid. Eddy had requested permission to take a second actress, and was almost sure he would get it. Marika had studied the train and the ocean liner timetables for the route that would take them via Hamburg to New York. All three of them had agreed to leave on the first January sailing, the week before they knew the rest of the small group planned to go out. Eddy had promised to buy the tickets on the twenty-third of December – the last day the bureau would be open before the holidays. They had pooled their money for the fares and agreed how much luggage they could take without attracting suspicion; everyone had felt confident they could keep the details secret.

Anna had been waiting until the last minute to tell her parents what she was planning, and to float the idea – if they would even listen – that they might be able to come and join her in America one day. Now she wanted to tell her mother all the secret plans, not to share the possibility of a new future for all of them, but as proof that she and Eddy and Marika really had all been working together. Except it was the twentieth of December, and Eddy and Marika were gone and she was confused and hurt and still looking for excuses. And then Frau Tiegel had grown angry and was too careless with blame, and pride had choked Anna up.

'Marika was frightened of Goebbels. She was desperate to get away from him.'

It was the last thing she had left to try. She didn't even convince herself.

'That is utter rubbish, Anna. Marika Bäcker isn't frightened of anyone. She's always been desperate to make her name in Hollywood. She would sleep with the Devil himself if she was guaranteed that; she would certainly seduce Eddy, which is what must have happened. Besides, don't you have more to fear from Minister Casanova than she does? You said he knew it was you who spoiled his fun at the villa.'

Later, when everything had fallen completely apart, Anna wished she had told her mother the truth about Goebbels' threats, and hadn't continued to hide them the way she had done on the night she and Marika had fled from Bogensee to the safety of Mitte. She also wished she had explained that Eddy had known how frightened she was that night, and how desperate she had been to run to America and safety. That him knowing all that had made his desertion so much harder to bear.

Instead she gave up. She stopped trying to explain it all to herself, or anyone else. She swallowed her tears. She hugged her mother, and let her go, and wandered off into the night with no sense of where she was going, or who she was anymore, until the ice in the wind defeated her. It was too bitterly cold to roam the streets; she couldn't face going back to her memory-packed flat in Prenzlauer Berg. She slipped instead into a cinema and sat mindlessly in front of the flickering screen as star-crossed lovers and wittily warring families were miraculously healed. Anna knew her mother's anger wasn't really directed at her, that it wasn't really directed at Marika either. That it came from a far wider fear of the future unravelling. Frau Tiegel might call Goebbels names and make light of his predatory ways in the safety of her own home, but Anna knew that the Minister – that the whole Party – terrified her. Every time Anna went back to her parents' flat, it was a little shabbier, a little emptier. Her parents refused to talk about how they were managing as their world shrank; they refused to take Anna's money. She took more and more groceries with her when she visited, and the three of them pretended potatoes and carrots were normal things for daughters to give as presents. None of them were ready to admit how precarious the Tiegels' lives were becoming as the Party clamped down on Jews.

Anna also knew that, if she went back and told her mother everything, the warm arms she needed would hold on to her without question. Her pride, however, still wouldn't let her. To be deserted was bad enough, but to be deserted and pregnant? No matter how kind she knew her mother would be, there would be pity first, and then fear of what Anna's condition might mean for them all, and that would undo her.

Unable to go back, unable to go home, Anna sat on in the dark, watching couples sneak kisses and families share sweets. It was only a few days since she had pieced together the tiredness and nausea she had thought was stress and realised what was actually happening to her body. In another week or two, once she was far enough gone to be sure that the pregnancy was safe, she would have told Eddy about the baby. He would have taken her with him without question if he had known, Anna was sure of it, no matter what tricks Marika pulled. And he would have stayed in America with her and the child, if that was what she had wanted; Anna was sure of that too. He would have treated her like porcelain until he drove her happily mad.

He still will. He'll come back. In a month, or two at the most. And he might write, or send a telegram, to the studio at least if he can't face me. There's still time to make us into a family.

Given the love she had to believe had always bound them, that scenario was more likely than not. And yet… There was a part of Anna that didn't want to, or couldn't, believe it. The part that was eaten up by anger. The part that whispered how turned Eddy's head must have been by Marika's flattery. And how turned it would be by the freedoms Hollywood could offer. For all she might want it to be, the part that loved him still – that wrapped her hands around her middle, searching for a thickening or a fluttering it was too soon to find, that she wanted desperately to share with him – wasn't strong enough to fight back.

Anna picked up her bag as the main feature finished and the newsreel started, sending lines of soldiers goose-stepping across the screen. Goebbels' voice rang out, twisting her stomach. She pushed her way out of the row, afraid she would be sick. Someone sneered at her; someone spat. It was a mark of loyalty now to stay and applaud the Party's troops and promises. Anna didn't care. She elbowed her way through the crowds milling through the foyer, one arm protectively across her body, and burst out into the freezing air. It was snowing, the flakes falling in thick heavy curtains. She stood still and let it surround her.

My heart is broken.

How many times had she heard that line? How many times had she looked out over the floodlights and said it? And now here she was, standing in the dark and the ice, with a pain gripping her chest like a fist. Cars raced past her; trams clanged by. Anna could envisage the dramatic ending. The step forward; the slow fall into the traffic. The audience gasping, dissolving in tears. She pulled up her collar, tucked her scarf in tight.

My heart is broken; it still has to beat.

Whether Eddy came back to her or not, the damage to their relationship was done. But the baby was hers to take care of; the child's life depended on hers. She couldn't fall apart, no matter how much she wanted to; she couldn't be selfish, no matter who else could. The pregnancy wouldn't be easy to hide, not with the visible life that she led. She had four months, maybe five at the outside, before her body would force her to step back from the cameras and costumes. It wasn't long. It was a film, it was a season on the stage, if she could balance them both. But, with the salary she was currently commanding, she should be able to salt enough money away to bridge the gap between the baby's arrival and her return to work, and pay for help when the child came. It would be difficult. In this new Germany, with its tightening morals and narrowing codes of conduct for women, an actress with a child and no husband might not be allowed anywhere close to a screen. She couldn't get rid of it, however. She would never condemn anyone who did, but, from its first days, this pregnancy had seemed too real to wish it away. It would be difficult, but the baby was here and difficult had to be done.

Other cinemas and theatres were spilling out; there were queues at the tram stop. Someone had already turned to look at her twice. Anna couldn't risk a prowling journalist or press photographer, not with her skin so raw. She hailed a cab, and closed her eyes when the driver tried to talk. She would go home and make a plan and she would sleep – she had to. She couldn't afford any more nights wasted on tears or days spent pointlessly searching. She didn't have another moment to waste.

*

'Fräulein Tiegel, a moment please. Herr Ritter wishes to see you.'

'Now? Why? What does he want?'

Anna blushed as the receptionist raised her eyebrows. She always made a point of being polite to everyone at the studio; she took pride in it. Now she sounded like the worst kind of diva. She smiled and forced her shoulders to relax.

'Forgive me, you know how the first day back after a break is. I have a costume fitting before shooting and a session with my voice coach. I'd be happy to meet with him later?'

As long as the morning sickness lasts only as long as the morning. As long as the wardrobe mistress's eagle eyes don't spot my chest has grown half a size bigger. As long as nobody asks me about Eddy.

The receptionist's frosty expression hardened. 'Now, Fräulein. He was most insistent.'

Anna went down the long corridor to the production offices with her heart sinking. She had never met Karl Ritter, although she knew him by reputation. Nothing she had heard made her comfortable with this summons. Ritter was one of UFA's newest and most powerful producers. He was also Goebbels' man – the Minister's eyes and ears across the whole Babelsberg complex, if rumours were to be believed – and he was a staunch supporter of the Party. Anna had loathed Ritter's most recent film, *Hitlerjunge Quex*, which sang the praises of National Socialism without any attempt at *subtle propaganda*. She had no desire to work on one of his Party-infused productions, or to encounter his notorious temper. Which, if her guess was right and she was about to be interrogated over Eddy and Marika's ongoing absence, she was surely about to be.

She knocked sharply on his door and entered the minute he barked, 'Come in.'

The producer didn't get up; he barely looked at her.

'There is no need to sit, Fräulein.'

Anna breathed a silent sigh of relief and took her hand off the chair she had started to pull out. A short meeting must mean a production matter, perhaps a change to the January schedules which would delay the comedy she was currently working on. Anna hated the film – a ham-fisted attempt to recreate the American movie *Bombshell* starring Jean Harlow – and would be perfectly happy to take a break from its clumsy set-pieces.

'This is notice of the termination of your contract with UFA, with immediate effect.'

'What?' Anna stared at the letter lying on the desk, its few sentences stamped over with an eagle and swastika. She stared from it back to Ritter. His bullet-shaped face was set in hard lines.

'You no longer work here, Fräulein. Or at any other studio. You will be escorted from my office straight off the premises. You will not return.'

The room wobbled. She didn't dare sit. 'I don't understand. Surely no one has complained about my work?'

Ritter sighed. 'What does your work matter? There are dozens of girls who could do your work. Girls who do not have Jewish fathers. Girls who do not encourage once loyal German citizens to betray their country. Girls who have not thoroughly, and carelessly, upset the Minister.'

Everything he said was so unjust, Anna didn't know where to start. 'This dismissal is Goebbels' doing?'

Ritter tapped his thick fingers on the table and tutted as if she was a child incapable of following the simplest lesson. 'This is your doing, Fräulein Tiegel – the fault is all at your door.'

He's done what he promised he would: he's pushed me out; he's ruined me.

Anna focused on holding her face and body as still as she could. She had tried hard to stay below Goebbels' radar since Eddy and Marika disappeared. She should have known it was pointless.

Even on her brief forays outside her flat, she had picked up the rumours. That Goebbels had flown into a furious, desk-toppling rage when he discovered that Marika was gone. That Hitler had been so furious at the loss of another popular actress to America that he had publicly screamed at his minister, accusing him of carelessness. She had heard the word *traitor* whispered and attached to both the runaways.

Despite the baby, she had begun lately to hope that Eddy wouldn't come back, fearing the danger that returning could plunge him into. As for herself, she had hoped that staying quiet, and staying away from the film world until she had to reappear in it, would stop the ripples spreading her way. She had been naïve. She wasn't, however, prepared to be desperate.

'Whatever Marika Bäcker has done was her decision. I did not encourage her. I did not know that she had left. I do not deserve this treatment. You – and he – cannot hold me to blame.'

It was a good performance. She managed to sound angry, not pleading.

Ritter sat back in his chair and let his gaze travel over her. Now Anna had the full force of his attention, all she wanted to do was get out from under it.

'That was well said. One of your better deliveries; not as stilted as I have heard you can be. But he can, my dear. I think you will find Minister Goebbels can do whatever he chooses.'

By the end of January, he had chosen to close every door.

Anna had left the UFA studios with her head up – despite the shocked stares as she was marched away – and gone straight to the Metropol Theatre. As Eddy had predicted, after her sell-out season in *Maria Stuart*, every theatre in Berlin had showered her with offers, the Metropol chasing her the hardest. Now, however, the director's diary was full and so were his cast lists. It was a shock, but she was gracious. She left her card and moved on. Berlin was stuffed full of theatres; she doubted they would all be inflexible.

She went from one to the other, her voice growing increasingly crisp. No one would meet her. The agent who had handled her before she signed with UFA was 'awash with new clients, dear' and unavailable. After a week filled with rejections, Anna was forced to face the truth: the theatre wasn't her world to command any more.

In the five months since she had been away from the stage, Goebbels' grip had stretched around every aspect of it. New names marched across old buildings. Audiences flocked now to theatres with suitably patriotic titles – the Volksoper, the Deutsches Theater, the Theater des Volkes – to watch State-approved German playwrights and nothing that was foreign except Shakespeare and Shaw. New directors and theatre managers 'didn't know her'. Which Anna quickly came to understand meant that they knew her very well, that their ignorance was as decreed as the plays they could perform. No one would employ her. Not even – as she discovered when pride started to become an expensive luxury – to sell tickets, or programmes, or to sweep the stages she once stood on bathed in applause. Anna had become *other*, an undesirable; worse than invisible.

Anna retreated further into herself. No one sought her out. She couldn't burden her parents with the car crash her career had become. Her father had finally lost his job at the cinema, her mother's last students were gone; they were existing on whatever odd hours either of them could pick up in factories or warehouses, their pitiful incomes steadily dwindling. No matter how much she longed to, with her own income vanished, Anna couldn't carry on helping them, and she couldn't bring them her misery until she had found a way out of it.

By the middle of February, her rainy-day saving pot – which she had dipped into far longer than she should, for the gifts she hoped would fool her parents that her circumstances hadn't fallen as badly as theirs – had shrunk to the point where there was nothing to be done but sell the Prenzlauer Berg apartment. Leaving it was frightening: she was afraid she would fall apart without the apartment's security and, once the buyers got wind that her father had been classified as Jewish, she barely got a tenth of its worth. But she kept herself going; she had no choice. She found a tiny flat to rent in Wedding in a building where the neighbours fought all night and the stairwells stank, and which was so close to Eddy's old flat, she couldn't drive away thoughts of the happier days she had spent there with him. That didn't help her to sleep or to settle. Neither did her rapidly emptying purse, even though she stretched out every mouthful of food the growing baby demanded. It wasn't until she managed to find a job in a small grocery shop, where the owner didn't care about her heritage or her straining skirt and was no fan of the theatre, that she finally felt able to breathe.

'Goebbels didn't win after all. He didn't beat me. I'm still here, I'm still standing. And one of these days, these Party men will be seen for the monsters they are and I'll take my life back.' She said that out loud, to the baby who was now so utterly part of her, to make herself braver, and pressed her hands against her stomach until something fluttered back.

It was almost March; spring was in the air. Sunday was her day off. It was time to face her parents and explain her changed circumstances. To introduce the idea of the baby, which might at least give them some hope for the future, despite the further difficulties a new mouth would mean. Which might make them feel properly like a family again.

And then Goebbels dropped the last hammer down.

'Another beating. Another poor man dragged off the streets to be killed. No one will be charged; no one ever is. What have we done to our country?'

Anna nodded, but she was barely listening. Herr Gessler hated Hitler and the Party and he didn't care who knew it, despite his wife's constant pleas that he take more care. Anna was thinking about the daffodils she planned to pick and take to her mother. About the plum cake she would bake that night in her tiny kitchen as a surprise for her father. It was almost two months since she had seen her parents – that wasn't unusual, especially when she had been at the mercy of the theatre's long hours, but it was too long. She barely glanced at the copy of the *Berliner Tageblatt* Herr Gessler threw onto the counter. If it hadn't been for his grumbled next comment, she wouldn't have noticed the short article at all.

'A decent sort too, from the sound of it. A family man out of Mitte, used to manage a cinema until the Nazis ran him out of work. Not the kind to deserve such an ending.'

The newspaper had spelled the name wrong. *Tegiel.* They had got everything else correct. Anna lowered herself off her high stool behind the counter onto legs that were thick and clumsy.

'I have to go.'

Herr Gessler took one look at her white face and waved her away.

She got on the train at Seestraβe, changed lines, exited at Börse, every movement as automatic as a factory line.

Anna had worn a deliberately loose dress and coat, but her mother was too lost in grief to notice Anna's changing body. When she opened the apartment door, Frau Tiegel had aged thirty years.

'He took the same route every night. Out for one beer, it's all we can run to. One game of cards. Home. There's never been a breath of trouble on this street before.'

Anna held tight to her mother's hand long after Frau Tiegel's tears had stopped. She was too numb to add her own.

'What happened?'

'Nobody's sure. Someone said there was a group of men clustered on a corner by the pub, but no one can remember what time that was. Someone else said they thought they heard a scream, or maybe a shout. He didn't come home at his usual time. That worried me. When it got to midnight, Gunther from next door went out to look. And there he was, in an alleyway. Every bit of him broken.'

Another wave of tears hit. Anna held on to fingers that had grown frighteningly thin and tried to find the words that would help them both.

'I am so sorry…'

Before she could stumble on any further, her mother's voice rose.

'Where were you, Anna? I couldn't find you. I sent word to your flat, but the neighbours said you'd been gone for weeks. No one knew where you had got to. I had to bury him on my own.'

The loss was so raw it tore at Anna's heart.

'I was… I had to…' She couldn't speak: what could she possibly say to repair this?

She pulled away, ran to the bathroom, fell to her knees on the freezing-cold floor and sobbed. It was him. Anna had no doubt about that: Goebbels had taken her father away, and ripped her family to pieces.

How can one man contain so much hatred? At what point will he stop? Why can't he be content with ruining me, rather than destroying the lives of people who can't possibly matter to him?

She got up slowly and wiped her face before returning to the too empty room. He had killed her father; she knew who his next target would be, even if she didn't know when. And there was nothing she could do to make the telling of that bearable.

'You can't stay here, in Berlin, Mama. I'm so sorry.'

'What are you talking about?'

Anna sat back down on the worn sofa next to her mother. There was no way to do this but quickly. She took her mother's hands in her own and pulled her in close.

'I wish I could pretend Father's death was some random attack; it would be easier to do that, but it wasn't. Goebbels ordered it; I know he did.'

'I don't want to hear this, Anna.' Her mother tried to pull away, but Anna kept on holding her.

'I know you don't, but you have to. I've kept too much from you, and that's taken Papa away and it's put you in danger. I can't lose you too, I won't, so, as hard as this is, please listen. All this misery goes back to that night at Bogensee, when Goebbels warned me to keep out of his business and I didn't. He blames me for Marika leaving, and he's obsessed with revenge. He destroyed my career, and he won't stop coming after me until everything, and everyone, I love is ruined. Which means he had Father… attacked. And he'll come for you next. It's all my fault, and the only good thing I can do now is to get you out of Berlin.'

This time, her mother pulled back too strongly for Anna to stop her. 'That's ridiculous. My life is here; your father's grave is here. And it's where you are, unless you've got it into your head again to go running to America. Where on earth would I go?'

The fear that her mother would refuse to get away and get safe made Anna frantic. 'Anywhere, it doesn't matter, as long as it's somewhere far away from me. What about to Aunt Trude's in Hamburg, couldn't you go there? Or to one of the cousins further south? It doesn't matter, it really doesn't, as long as you go somewhere, and you go at once.'

Even if Frau Tiegel had wanted to ignore the words and the advice, she couldn't have ignored her daughter's out-of-character panic.

'Are you really telling me that Goebbels had your father killed? That it was him who had my husband beaten like an animal and left to die in the street? And that he did that because of you?' There wasn't a shred of colour left in her mother's face.

Anna nodded. 'Yes. And it's why you have to leave Berlin. I'm sorry, Mama, I truly am.'

There was no anger. Anna could have dealt with her mother's anger – it was what she deserved. Instead there was nothing but an exhausted despair.

'Anna, Anna, my pet, what have you done? I know you meant none of it, but how could you have brought that man into our lives? He has taken my heart from me. And now I have to lose my home and lose you? How am I meant to bear it?'

'I don't know.' Anna knew there was no apology or defence she could offer that would make this right. All she could hope was that, with time, her mother would forgive her, even if she would never forgive herself. 'I don't know how either of us can. But you will go? I know I've no right to ask you to do anything for me, but you will?'

Her mother nodded; she was clearly too worn out to fight. 'I will go to Hamburg; at least I will try, if that is what you want. I will arrange the ticket today. Will I see you before I leave? Will you come and see me off?'

Anna said yes, she had to say yes, although she knew she couldn't risk doing either. She kissed her mother, and held her as tight as she dared without giving her secret away. She stumbled out of the flat and barely made it out onto the street before her knees buckled.

'Are you all right? Do you need help?'

She waved the man away and carried on clutching the railings. How had this happened? How had she fallen prey to such hatred and let it spill out so terribly around her?

I don't think he'll stop until everything is ruined.

Her hand flashed round her middle, gripped tight to its swelling. 'He can't have you. I won't let him have you.'

She had spoken aloud; her grief drew unwanted attention.

'Fräulein, you are making a scene. Good German women do not do that. Calm yourself or come with us.'

A harsher voice. A black uniform. No offer of help.

Anna pulled herself away from the railings and ran.

'You cannot care for the child?'

'I want to.'

The stiff-faced matron tidied the papers on her desk and sighed. 'That wasn't my question. *Want* has very little place here. You were found on the street, fainting, clearly malnourished. My nurses tell me you are days away from giving birth. I asked you if you can care for the child you are shortly about to deliver.'

Anna's head ached. She hadn't intended to walk around so long in the sun, or to go for so long without eating. But the convent-run hostel she had a bed in didn't allow residents inside during the day and she had no money for food – she had to rely on the two small meals she was given. She spent her days now sitting in parks or hiding in libraries, or sitting at her father's graveside, trying to hold on to some semblance of the girl she once was but unable to pull herself out of the nightmare she had sunk into. Everything had collapsed before she had a chance to cling to it.

Barely two weeks after her father's death, Herr Gessler's shop had been fire-bombed and he had been flung into prison. The charge was anti-Party activities, the sentence ten years' hard labour. His wife had blamed her husband's own foolishness, but Anna knew better. Anna knew his fate was her fault. She had seen the dark-suited men lurking on the opposite pavement; she knew that they followed her. Frau Gessler was kind and said she could stay in her spare room, but Anna couldn't risk the woman losing her home as well as her business.

No one else would give her work. The excuse was always her pregnancy, but Anna knew the real reason. If she could see the shadows she trailed, surely everyone else could? When she could no longer afford to pay her rent, she was so desperate she went back to Mitte. The new tenants who reluctantly opened the door told her that all they knew of the previous tenant was that she had left and they had no idea if there was any letter or forwarding address, because they had thrown out the 'rubbish' she had left behind. When Anna burst into tears, they closed the door as sharply as they had opened it. It was a relief to know that her mother had got away, but it was also an ending.

Anna had no money and she had nowhere to live. She was, however, carrying a child and that child needed protecting from Goebbels the same way that her mother had, so that was the only thing that could matter. With no other choices left, she threw herself on the strained mercy of a moralising priest and the nuns he sent her to, and now she lived on charity, and in fear. So, no, she couldn't look after her baby.

'I will take it from your silence that you can't.' The matron's face suddenly softened. 'You're not the first girl who's got into this mess, and you certainly won't be the last. It is a good thing you were brought here when you fainted. The Charité Hospital is well named. We won't judge you. We will give you a bed. When the time comes, we will find your child a good family. After that? I don't know who you are, or were, or what has brought you to this, but I am certain, my dear, you can do better.'

Anna was given into the care of nurses who treated her with more kindness than she had known in months. One of them even went to the hostel and retrieved her meagre belongings. And when her daughter was born, the same nurse, who Anna now knew as Kerstin, let her hold the baby. Just for a few minutes. Just for long enough to breathe in the child's sweet vanilla scent and kiss her impossibly soft skin and feel the love that surged through her body like a fire as she held on to her daughter. Then Kerstin gently unpeeled Anna's clutching fingers from the tightly swaddled blanket and eased the child away.

'We have to take her now.'

'Is that it? Is she going to her new… people?'

Kerstin had the baby on her shoulder, her tiny head turned away from Anna. 'No, sweetheart, not yet. She's too little. She'll stay in the hospital for a while, but it won't do you any good to see her. Let her go now; let me give you something that will help.'

Anna was still crying when the sedative took hold. It didn't help at all.

*

A week passed. A week in which every new baby's cry tugged at Anna like a chain. She slept when they told her to and ate what they gave her and focused on staying calm. It was easier to be a good patient than a troublesome one. Easier to avoid attention than attract it. Nobody watched good patients. Nobody asked where she had been when she sneaked to the nursery for a few precious seconds to stare hungrily through the viewing window at the cots, wondering which – if, please God, any – of the blurred bundles were hers. Nobody paid any attention on the night she scribbled Franziska Tiegel across the napkin that came with her dinner, as if the name might keep a scrap of her father alive. She was so well behaved that, when they told her that her recovery time was done and they were discharging her, sending her back into a world she no longer had a place in, she hadn't argued. There was nothing to be gained from making a fuss.

No one realised her polite manner was a performance. That, underneath her docile surface, she was burning with rage. That she dreamed each night of knives and bombs and murder. That, if she could find a gun, she would march straight into Goebbels' office and shoot him dead. She was dressed and sitting in a chair by her bed, imagining how she might walk into the nursery and walk out with her daughter, when she heard two of the younger nurses whispering.

'They're coming for that one's baby today. An American couple. I met them: he's handsome enough, if quiet; she's pretty, but a bit highly strung.'

'I heard the wife tell someone they've been trying for a kid for over ten years. That's probably why they made such a generous donation. The desperate ones always do.'

They moved on, the clattering medicine trolley masking the rest of their conversation.

Anna didn't care about donations – she wasn't fool enough to think the hospital entirely lived up to its name – and she didn't care who was handsome or pretty. The only important thing was that Franzi was still here. She got up carefully, her body still not quite her own, picked up her bag and fastened the flower-sprigged coat Kerstin had brought her. Whatever came next, she was going to see her baby.

Nobody stopped her. She moved quickly. Two well-trodden turns of the corridor and she was at the nursery. The door was open, the nurse who normally sat scribbling at the desk in the corner with her back to the window wasn't there.

Anna slipped inside and peered into the cribs. Two were empty; two contained babies who were startlingly blonde. She hesitated. What if she didn't know her own child? What if a week had changed the baby's features enough to wipe away the few minutes burned into her memory? And then Anna looked into the next cot and she knew. Her daughter was awake. She had a fuzz of dark hair, the same shade of brown as her grandfather's, and the deepest brown eyes, with tiny flecks round the pupils that glittered in the light.

Eddy's eyes. Treacle and gold.

She leaned closer in; the baby squinted up at her. The blanket wrapped round her was looser than when Anna had held her. A tiny fist emerged, curling and uncurling as if she was trying to wave.

'Hello, beautiful.'

The baby's head jerked, the hand reached out more definitely this time, as if it was searching.

'You know my voice.' Anna had to cling to the edge of the cot to steady herself. 'You know I'm your mother.' The word was so perfect, and so forbidden, it caught at her throat. 'I am. I'm your mother. And you won't remember.'

The loss she thought she had made small enough to carry reared up again.

'You can't go with nothing of me.'

Panic washed over her. She grabbed her bag, started searching for a pen and paper. She could leave a note, her name at the very least, maybe the address of the hostel, or the name of the priest. Perhaps if the people who were coming for her were good – and they surely had to be good – they would keep it; they would share her with her child. She dug deeper, but there was nothing. No paper, not even an eye pencil or a lipstick sharp enough to make a mark.

Heart racing, she pulled out her purse, in case there was an old business card or a UFA pass – anything with her name on it. There was nothing there but an old dog-eared photograph tucked into an inside pocket. The picture Eddy had taken of her and Marika at the Hoppegarten racetrack, a lifetime ago. She had forgotten she still had it.

A trolley wheel squeaked along the hall; Anna could hear the faint slap of footsteps. Not knowing what else to do, she stuffed the photograph down into the baby's blanket. And then her fingers touched skin, and the baby cooed. It was the softest sound, but it rang through Anna like bells.

'What am I doing? You can't go anywhere. I can't let you.' Her hand curved round the small body.

'Get away from that cot. The baby in there is mine.'

It was unmistakeably an order, barked out in a stiletto-sharp tone.

Anna's hand instinctively tightened; the startled baby cried out.

'I said get away from her. Now.'

The woman in the doorway wasn't a nurse, and although she spoke the language confidently, from her accent, she wasn't German. She was slightly built, no bigger than Anna, but her body was poised for a fight and her dark eyes were dangerous.

'I am her mother.' Anna said it in German and then again in English, to ensure her meaning was clear.

The woman took a deliberate step closer.

'No. You are not. She was promised to me, and I have been visiting her. You gave birth to her perhaps, but that means nothing. Any animal can do that. You gave her up; that was your choice.'

Anna took a deep breath. There was no compassion; there was nothing in the woman's face but a longing as fierce as her own.

'I didn't want to. I made a mistake. I'm her—'

'Do not use that word again. Not to me. You chose not to keep her; you chose to give her away. To strangers. No real mother would do that. A real mother would do everything in her power to keep her child with her and safe.'

Part of Anna knew that the woman facing her was desperate, that she would say anything to get what she wanted. No one could look into that strained face and not see the hunger filling it. A bigger part of her knew the accusation was true. She couldn't keep the child safe; she couldn't keep anyone safe.

As if to prove it, the baby began crying and pulling away from her hand.

She knows that I'm dangerous. She doesn't want me near.

Anna hesitated and moved her caressing fingers away; the woman pounced.

'It's for the best – you know it is. Step back. Let me have the child I was promised.'

Anna's body obeyed before she could summon another argument. The woman immediately streaked past her and grabbed the baby out of the cot.

'Don't you want to know my name? Don't you want to know anything about me at all?'

But the woman was gone, and the child was gone with her. And all Anna could do was sink down, and howl.

PART TWO

CHAPTER SEVEN

Cuxhaven – New York,
September to December 1935

The pier was crowded with people frantically scanning the ship, desperate for one last glimpse of their loved ones.

I must be the only person hoping there's no one searching for me.

Anna hung back from the railings. She couldn't see any black uniforms, but that didn't mean the danger was gone. Not all the Party's watchmen made themselves visible.

He's forgotten me; he must surely by now have forgotten me.

She was no longer as confident of that as she had been a fortnight ago, not with the new legislation the Party had unleashed. The National Socialists seemed determined not to overlook anyone whose existence offended them; their attention to detail was terrifying.

A shudder ran through the ship. Chains dropped. Metal scraped against metal and the gangplanks released their grip; the ship's horn blew. As the liner finally began to move, a babble of voices flew up from the lower decks, flinging promises and sobs back to the crowded jetty. Even from Anna's elevated position, the noise was astonishing. First class, by comparison, was far calmer. Many of the passengers had already begun to melt away, preferring the comfort of their staterooms to the stiff September breeze. The few remaining watchers fluttered their hands politely, but no one shouted or cheered as the ship glided away.

Anna could hear Frau Berger's voice as loudly in her ear as if the old lady was standing beside her: 'Decent people always behave decently. Stay on the deck if you must, but kindly remember that. I will not permit you and, by extension, me, to be the subject of common amusement or gossip. That is a rule I will not tolerate you breaking.'

Frau Berger's rules – as Anna had learned after a handful of days in the old woman's company – were rigid and extensive and quicker to multiply than rabbits. They covered every aspect of Anna's day – from what type of tea was appropriate at any given hour to the length of her skirt and the state of her hair and who she could, and, more importantly, could not, directly address. Kerstin's comment that her aunt could be 'a little difficult' had been so wide of the mark, it was almost comical. Anna's new employer was so imperious and demanding, *a little difficult* sounded enchanting.

But she is my passage to safety, and to the country where my baby is, and she will have to be borne.

The lower decks quietened, the upper ones emptied. Anna knew she should also go inside: Frau Berger was sure to have a long list of duties waiting. Anna didn't care: standing on deck when she shouldn't might be a small rebellion, but it felt like a good one. She moved forward and leaned on the railing. There would be a long list of duties waiting every day of the seven or eight it would take the ship to make its way via Southampton and Cherbourg to New York. There would be plenty of time to fetch and carry for Frau Berger. Anna, however, was well aware that she wouldn't manage any more of the subservience the old woman expected unless she stood still for a moment and remembered exactly why she was putting up with Frau Berger's rudeness and constant bad temper.

To make a new life safe from danger and live it. To start searching for my daughter.

The last eight weeks had been a whirlwind, full of decisions. Now there were no more changes to make – for a short time at least – it was time to stop worrying over what had brought her to this point and start considering what needed to follow.

Although they were barely out to sea, the breeze was growing stronger. Anna pulled her cloche hat tight around her ears before its narrow brim was plucked from her head. The sky was heavy, the clouds huddled and angry. The pier they had sailed from was barely visible. The huge port of Cuxhaven, which served the ocean liners of the Hamburg–America line, was already blurred. The sea stretched out on all sides, coating the ship's solid bulk in a sheet of gunmetal grey. Salt gathered in the wind, so thick Anna could feel her cheeks tightening.

She closed her eyes, concentrating on the rhythms of the ship, the thrum of its engines and the vibrations under her feet. Despite the sea's gathering swell, Anna felt a sense of peace she hadn't known in months.

I shouldn't have left her. I should have gathered her up and run.

Her eyes snapped open; her fragile sense of calm shattered. The pain of the child's loss had become as much a part of Anna as her skin. That didn't mean it no longer stabbed. The first time she had properly woken after collapsing in the nursery, her head thick with a chemical sleep, the pain had sliced through her. That she had to find her baby had been her first conscious thought. Her second was that she was too tightly bound to the bed to do anything at all.

'We had no choice.' The Matron's voice was stiff, but not her face. There was such pity in her expression, Anna's initial panic, and then fury, at being restrained subsided a little, or at least enough for her to listen. 'You were desperate to hurt yourself – we had to calm you. Scratching at your face, punching at your chest. We had to stop you, my dear, and this was the only way.' She paused, coughed. 'And we should have taken better care, not let you see the new mother or the child being taken. I am sorry we failed you in that.'

'How long has it been?'

It had been an effort to ask even that much. Anna's throat had grown raspy, her tongue dry and swollen.

'You have been under heavy sedation for four days.'

Four days?

'Then she is gone?'

'Yes, my dear. She is gone. To America, and with good people. Take what comfort you can in that.'

When Anna didn't cry out, or struggle, the Matron motioned to an orderly to untie the leather straps.

'What happens to me now?' Anna tried to move her loosened arms, but they were clumsy and awkward. She tried to imagine them clasping a baby and couldn't. 'Do I leave?'

The Matron waved the orderly out and Kerstin, the nurse who had been kind to her, in.

'You are not physically ill, so, strictly speaking, yes, you should. It has not been easy to keep you here this long. If the doctors had seen you restrained, they would have demanded your transfer to a psychiatric ward. They still could.'

Kerstin gasped, the Matron hushed her.

'I won't permit that. Providing you continue to stay calm, no one will suggest it. If you can do that, then I will be able to keep you for a few more days, until you have your strength back at least. After that…' She stopped.

Anna stared at the crumpled sheet. *After that* was too big and too empty to contemplate.

'Well, those concerns are for later. For now, you must concentrate on your recovery. Good food, gentle exercise; not brooding on what cannot be undone.'

She bustled out. As soon as the door closed, Kerstin sat down on the edge of Anna's bed.

'Not brooding is good advice, about the baby at least. But, as for what is waiting for you outside… I think you may have more challenges there than we guessed at when you first came in.' She picked up Anna's right hand and began massaging the limp fingers and wrist. 'You talked. In the moments when the sedation was wearing off. Some of it made sense, a lot didn't.'

What does she know?

Anna could feel the room tightening around her. She tried to ease her tingling fingers out of the nurse's grip, but Kerstin wouldn't let her.

'You don't need to be afraid, not of me anyway.'

'What did I say?'

Kerstin began working on Anna's other hand, her fingers moving in slow circles.

'You talked about your life before, although what you said was muddled and disjointed. You spoke about the theatre, and I realised that I had seen you on the stage, although I didn't recognise you when you came to us. You cried for your baby and for your mother, more than once, but you didn't seem to have any hope she would come. You believe you are in danger, and that your existence puts others in danger. And you talked, a lot, although not always clearly, about the man you believe is responsible for that.'

This time, Anna had pulled back so quickly, Kerstin jumped.

'Did I say his name? Did everyone hear?'

Despite the order to stay calm, Anna couldn't. Kerstin didn't reply until she had fetched a glass of water and propped Anna up into a sitting position where she could drink it without soaking herself.

'You did say it, yes. But I doubt anyone heard but me. I won't repeat it and it doesn't matter that I know. I've no love for the Minister, or any of that pack. You are very scared of him, that much is clear. And you don't have to tell me anything more now if you don't want to. But, if you did, perhaps I could help? I know about fear, Anna, and I know about loneliness. Why not trust me with the whole thing?'

Kerstin's voice was as convincing, and her tone was as kind as ever, but Anna still hesitated.

'Why would you help me? You barely know me.'

'Does that matter? I know you are in need.' Kerstin squeezed Anna's hand and let it drop. 'I said I knew about loss – maybe it would help you to hear what I mean. I also had a daughter once. She died, when she was still a child. She wouldn't be far from the age you are now. And if she had lived and ever found herself in the kind of distress you are in… well, I couldn't bear to think of her anywhere alone and afraid. If that had happened, I would like to think someone would have stepped in.'

There was so much pain in the older woman's eyes, Anna momentarily forgot her own.

'What happened to her?'

Kerstin looked away. When she answered, all the warm notes had leached from her voice.

'The influenza epidemic that followed the end of the war took her, and my husband too. They died within hours of each other. I was in the house alone with them – no one would come, not even a priest. The anger at being spared devoured me… I thought I would go mad with it. But I didn't. Time passed. I started to breathe again. Eventually I became a nurse.' She turned back to the bed. Her eyes were bright with tears, but she blinked them away. 'And now it helps me to help people, Anna. Not because I am particularly good, but because it wipes away, for a while at least, how helpless I was then.'

Kerstin's kindness was genuine and it deserved the same honesty; as soon as she stopped talking, Anna began. It was hard to be vulnerable – by the time Anna got to the end, she had twisted the sheet into knots – but she told the whole story, while Kerstin quietly listened.

'I can't think about Franzi or I will never get out of this bed. I don't know what to do next. I have to believe Goebbels will get bored tracking me, or hurting those I love, but I can't. I have seen how obsessive he is. Berlin isn't safe; Germany might not be safe. But I can't leave. Even if I had the money, which I don't, I could be flagged up on a list somewhere. The moment I apply for a visa, I potentially step back into his sights.'

'But would you go away to America, like you told me after the baby went that you wanted to, if you could?'

'Of course.' Anna hadn't had to think about her answer. 'Not to chase after Eddy. I'm done with him. But it's where my daughter is, so where else would I want to be? I know the odds of finding her aren't great, even if you could break the rules and tell me the name of the couple who took her, but isn't going there worth a try? Or does everything I've told you, including how much I long to find Franzi, make me sound mad?' The weight of all she had said was suddenly too much, as was the fear that she might have put Kerstin at risk simply by saying it. 'I shouldn't have told you. My messed-up life isn't your problem. You should forget it. Or perhaps you should get a doctor and have them send me to a psychiatric ward after all.'

It was a clumsy attempt at a lightness Anna didn't feel. Kerstin responded with a switch from sympathy to anger that was so swift, it left Anna reeling.

'Don't say that. You of all people should know how dangerous these times are. Never mind people in the film world being thrown out of their jobs, there's discussions taking place between doctors about the "right way" to treat psychiatric patients that would make your blood run cold. Oh, they think we don't hear them, or don't understand the terms they use – there isn't a doctor in this place who credits a nurse with a brain. But whatever they call it, euthanasia or eugenics, it all amounts to the same thing. Killing. Doctors who follow the Party here, and no doubt all over Germany, are considering killing, or at least sterilising, patients with even the slightest mental impairment. We all pretend it's not true, but it is. Don't make jokes, Anna; don't give them excuses. Especially if you are on one of their lists. Do you hear me?'

Anna had been too shocked to do anything but nod.

'I watched you in the days before the baby went, when it was clear that your heart was broken, but you never said a word. You are good at being a good patient. You need to stay that way. Do you promise?'

'Yes. Yes, of course. I'll do whatever you want, whatever it takes.'

Kerstin's clenched face finally relaxed. 'All right. Well then, I have an idea and I think I can help you, but it will take a day or two, maybe more, to arrange. I have some time off owing; until I come back, do whatever you are told and keep yourself to yourself. The young nurses are cinema fans – I doubt they've ever been inside a theatre – but, now you're not pregnant and you're on the road to recovery, you're going to start to look more like yourself. Try as much as you can not to.'

It was the strangest direction Anna had ever been given, but she followed it. She scraped her hair flat, roughened her accent and kept the window curtains drawn. At the slightest hint of a doctor, she curled deep under the covers. She kept quiet and still, but she barely slept. By the time Kerstin returned to duty – after a two-day break that felt like a week – Anna hardly had a fingernail left. Kerstin, however, was fizzing.

'It's done. You are going to New York. You sail on the SS *Hamburg* on the twenty-second of September. All you have to do is convincingly play the part of a lady's maid for one short interview and you're in. Can you do that?'

Kerstin spoke so quickly, Anna was still two steps behind when she finished. 'I can do whatever you need me to do, but slow down! Tell me what exactly you've done.'

'I've got you a job.'

Kerstin's sudden burst of laughter was so pure, Anna wished she could catch it.

'You might curse me, though, as much as thank me. I have an elderly aunt who is booked on that sailing, going to visit her sister in New York. It's a pity it is Aunt Helga travelling not Aunt Brigitte, but beggars can't be choosers, and Helga was the one who stayed here. Anyway, Aunt Helga – or Frau Berger as you will need to call her – is of that generation who won't make such a long journey without a travelling companion. Unfortunately, she struggles to keep anyone very long in her employment – she can be… a little difficult. I knew that the girl due to travel with her has already quit – the whole family knows that, probably the whole of Berlin – so I suggested that the daughter of an old friend of mine could take her place. In other words, you. All you have to do is mind your manners long enough to pass her scrutiny and the position, and the ticket, is yours. And then, when she comes back to Germany, you don't. What do you think? Will that work for you?'

Anna was still trying desperately to keep up.

'But what about the visa? There's still the problem of my name attracting attention, and I don't have my birth certificate, which you surely need to apply for travel papers?'

Kerstin didn't falter. 'And all of that can be sorted. Aunt Brigitte is married to someone high up in the American State Department. Aunt Helga is always boasting that all she has to do is snap her fingers and she can sail whenever she wants. You will have a medical certificate from here and we can type up a letter explaining your birth certificate is lost. If you are going as a companion, Uncle Fred will push the application through from his side and won't question anything: he's as scared of Aunt Helga as the rest of us.'

Kerstin stopped suddenly, her face clouding. 'And it would be best, anyway, not to mention your father's name, or his heritage. Use your mother's name for the visa; give the impression your father died in the war. My aunt has prejudices I promise you I don't share. It's not ideal, but it's not as though you will have to stay with her long.'

Everything Kerstin said made sense, but it wasn't comfortable. Lying about her father, trusting her future to a woman who she assumed was an antisemite; the finality of leaving. Anna knew it was what she had said that she wanted, that it was her only safe option, but, now the thought of it had become a reality, she was suddenly uncertain.

'I am very grateful. It is a brilliant idea and you know I will do everything you ask, but…'

'It's hard to leave, when you don't know where your mother is, and you won't be able to say goodbye.'

Anna nodded, grateful she hadn't had to push the words round the lump in her throat.

Kerstin patted her hand. 'I understand, I do. But you might be able to come back one day. If people come to their senses and vote the National Socialists out with as much enthusiasm as they voted them in, you might get the chance to pick up your old life.'

Except there's no opposition left to vote for, the SS will make sure it stays that way and that old life is long gone.

Anna didn't say it. She knew Kerstin was thinking it. Sometimes it was better to hold on to dreams.

Despite every reservation, Kerstin's plan had worked. No matter how difficult Frau Berger could be, Anna had to be thankful for that.

The interview with the old lady had not been pleasant. Frau Berger had sniffed and scrutinised Anna as if she was a stale slice of bread. With Kerstin's advice to 'smile and say yes to everything' ringing in her ears, Anna had, however, managed to convince her prospective employer that her credentials were good – for the length of the interview at least.

She had spent the six weeks between her hospital discharge and the crossing date, when Frau Berger required her presence, staying in Kerstin's spare room. Nobody had come knocking. When Anna had finally plucked up the courage to slip out early in the morning and walk to the park two blocks way, no one had followed her. After a few days with no one lurking in the shadows, she began to wonder if there had ever been anyone there. There was even a moment, a day or two perhaps, when Anna felt so safe under Kerstin's wing that she wondered about staying in Berlin. A moment when the thought of trying to find Franzi in a vast country she didn't know a single inch of seemed as daunting as she was desperate to do it. And then the world finally tipped the way the National Socialists had long been pushing it and her choices – which Anna in her heart knew had already vanished the moment she looked into her baby's eyes – truly were gone.

On the fifteenth of September, the Party held a rally in Nuremburg and unveiled the framework for the citizenship formula it had been doggedly concocting since the first profiling questionnaires were sent out. Radio announcers and newspaper headlines were triumphant with the new laws which would 'protect German blood and honour and the future of the Reich'. Which would determine exactly, in the eyes of those with the power to decide it, what a German citizen was.

The rules were simple: only those of *pure* German blood were German. Not Jews; not anyone descended from Jews; not anyone married to Jews. Not anyone with a trace of Jewish blood or kinship at all. And the rules were to be underpinned by new social classifications: clear-cut categories that would give everyone a measuring stick to attack their neighbours with. That would excise – without exception – anyone with the slightest hint of Jewish heritage from all aspects of German life.

The new definitions were chilling; the reception they received was as bad. Anna walked into shops where people waved the latest headlines and cheered at the rulings. She walked out of cafés where *honest citizens* raised their glasses to toast their country's bright future. She started to watch the shadows again and stopped pretending she had any kind of future in Berlin. She helped pack Frau Berger's bags. She got on the train to Hamburg, knowing that, as desperate as she was to try to find her mother there, the risk was too great.

As they left Berlin, she didn't look back. She bit her lip every time Frau Berger attacked her clothes and her manners and her general shortcomings. She walked onto the boat and prayed no one would come after her. And then they arrived at the port and her tourist visa – made out in the name of Anna Brandt – passed without scrutiny and it was done.

Germany is closed to me; there is no going back. My child is in America, so that is where my future must be.

She repeated the words every night of the crossing. And kissed the piece of paper Kerstin had given her on the morning of the sailing. The one with the single word *Bailey* on it that breathed life into her dreams.

The leaves were turning, swapping summer's greens for November's crimson and rust. Anna wrapped her scarf tight and tried to lose herself in the changing colours. The stretch of grass overlooking the grey sweep of the Hudson River lacked Central Park's charm, but, since the incident with the mother and baby, that was no longer safe ground. The trees were scrubbier, there were no shaded nooks to shelter in from the wind's sharp tug, but it was quiet and it was open, and Anna was grateful for that: it helped ease her homesickness.

New York, as Anna was quickly discovering, was so far removed from Berlin, it was hard to believe the two places inhabited the same planet. Berlin was a city filled with spaces and air: the parks and the waterways that ran through it, and the lakes that ringed its edges, were well loved, part of the lifeblood of its people. It was also a city which wore its history in its streets and in the elegant museums and palaces which dominated its centre – even if their classical lines were scarred now by red flags and swastikas.

New York, as far as Anna had seen, was a city of concrete and steel, with no sense of age in its stones. It was a city that looked forward, and looked up. Every building and monument – from the Statue of Liberty which towered above New York Harbour to the skyscrapers punching their way up and out of Manhattan – seemed to throb with its own core of energy. There was an urgency in New York that Anna could not imagine encountering in Berlin, even under the National Socialists – a greedy, uncontrolled push for the new the Party would never have tolerated. To an outsider like her, who had encountered America mostly through the cinema and novels, it was as if the pioneering spirit she associated with the Wild West had seeped into the city's fabric. New York had forced the conquered land it stood on and the rivers it clustered round into submission, and everything it built was as big as it could be. The Statue of Liberty looked as if she was holding up heaven.

Nothing about their arrival – with the exception of the Statue and the skyscrapers cutting into the skyline – had played out in the way Anna had expected. In the movies, everyone was processed in bustling crowds through the immigration control centre on Ellis Island. Anna had waited on deck for that to appear, and had stayed up there watching while the *SS Hamburg* sat at anchor for two days and ferries full of passengers bobbed between the ship and the government compound. Anna had used the time to practise her best English accent, ready to impress the officials. When Frau Berger had heard her efforts, however, she was horrified.

'Ellis Island is for steerage. We are first class. We are not *examined*. Why must I keep explaining the world to you?'

Frau Berger's sniff and exasperated sigh had punctuated the entire crossing and it had not stopped in the time since they finally met land. Everything – and Anna most of all – exacerbated her permanent state of irritation. The dockside she had been expected to step onto was 'impossibly filthy'. The cream Buick sent to collect them was 'ostentatious in the extreme'. The McGregor family's sandstone and marble mansion, set in the elegant neighbourhood of the Upper West Side's Riverside Drive, was 'too obviously new and therefore horribly vulgar'. Of all the many rules Frau Berger clung to, her belief that 'family and heritage are the lodestones we live by' was her most precious.

The sentiment was as out of place in New York as a bear wandering down Broadway. This city's lodestone was wealth. One bag-carrying trip to the dazzling department stores on Fifth Avenue and one reception – which she had attended to help serve the drinks – was all it took for Anna to understand that. And that the admiration and pursuit of wealth wasn't confined to the rich. None of the servants she shared her quarters with came from anything remotely connected with money, but they all believed that – with enough hard work – they would one day reach a place bursting with dollars. Anna could see no practical reason why that would come true for any of them, but it would have taken a harder heart than hers to point that reality out.

The city wore such a brash and confident veneer, it was hard for an outsider to imagine anyone in it feeling afraid, even though Anna knew that couldn't be true. The Wall Street crash of 1929 had set a chain reaction in motion that impacted economies all over the world, Germany's among them. Her father's theatre was one of countless businesses that had never recovered. Not that Anna could bear to dwell on that, or on her mother trying to restart her life in Hamburg, or on the roses wilting over her father's grave. The homesickness even the smallest memory conjured up would have swamped her.

Anna and her friends had followed America's plight in the newspapers. They had looked in horror at the photographs of the miseries that had followed the collapse of the stock market. The hordes of people queuing desperately outside closed banks, and then outside soup kitchens. The men wearing placards begging for jobs. The children with eyes far older than their faces. One of the maids in the McGregors' employment had told her about the Hooverville shanty town that had sprung up in Central Park in 1930. About the rows of tin-covered shacks where the homeless, until barely two years ago, had lived in the shadow of the mansion blocks that surrounded them, whose owners were blind to the shanty-dwellers' plight.

Anna knew there had been terrible suffering, but it was hard to see it in a city which seemed to have sealed over its scars. As it was hard to imagine anyone in this city waking up sobbing from the kind of nightmares that had gripped Anna since the ship had landed. The sea had acted as a physical barrier between her old life and her new, but not a mental one. The dreams that plagued her were so vivid she could taste them. Dreams in which black-suited men bundled bodies into vans and babies were constantly crying. Dreams which left Anna clumsy and light-headed from lack of sleep and reinforced her status in Frau Berger's eyes as a constant disappointment.

A drop of rain landed on her cheek, pulling her back into the morning. A dog walker hurried past, followed by a man buttoned into a raincoat and clutching a briefcase. Anna pushed back her glove and made a fervent wish, but the hands on her wristwatch were far further past eight than they should have been. Frau Berger's bell would start ringing precisely at nine. If Anna hadn't memorised the day's diary by then, picked out an appropriate selection of outfits and folded the newspaper neatly onto the society pages, the day would start with a litany of complaints.

Which it will regardless, anyway.

That Kerstin's pairing had not been a success had been evident within two days of sailing. It couldn't continue. The old lady was impossible to please, Anna was exhausted and – if she was honest – completely fed up trying to get one thing a day even halfway close to right. If they had been in Berlin, she would have walked out long before now. Except this wasn't Berlin. This was an unknown city where Anna's accent – no matter how hard she used her acting skills to soften it – marked her out as different and other. She wasn't sure yet how much that mattered, or if it mattered at all. The cook had described New York as a melting pot: perhaps there wasn't a right or wrong kind of different here. It was a hopeful thought, but not one Anna was ready to trust. It was also a city where she currently had no right to be longer than the three months on her tourist visa – almost half of which had already been eaten up – and that wasn't a situation she could rectify in Frau Berger's employment. Anna knew she needed to set her new life in motion; she had no plan, however, for how she might do that. She needed, therefore, to stay in Frau Berger's good graces until she could take her next careful step.

Which being late won't help me to do.

She jumped up, rammed on her hat so that wet hair wouldn't be added to her list of misdemeanours, and set off back to the mansion at a clip. A month. That was as much time as she had left before questions of returning would arise. A month to learn the city and turn Anna Brandt into someone who could fit seamlessly into it. Surely she could manage one month?

In the end, she barely managed one more week.

'There is a story around you, Miss, that I do not want to hear and have no more patience to live with.'

Frau Berger's summons had come on a Saturday morning, far earlier than Anna had expected. That she arrived breathless and windswept, with no time to tidy herself, simply sealed her fate.

'Why are you never where you are meant to be? And what respectable girl goes out alone at this time of day? Don't answer, don't deny it. This is not a house where the servants go unseen. My poor sister is beside herself that a domestic under her roof could behave in such a cavalier way and risk everyone's reputation.'

Anna doubted that was true. Brigitte McGregor was a far kinder woman than Frau Berger. Anna had encountered her once on her way in from an early-morning wandering; all Mrs McGregor had commented on was 'the pretty colour' in Anna's cheeks. She didn't argue, however. Frau Berger was too puffed up with indignation to hear any defence Anna was foolish enough to give.

'I do not know what my niece was thinking, recommending you. She is too kind-hearted and people take advantage. It was a convincing performance at the interview, I grant you that, but you have never been a lady's maid before, have you?'

For a moment, Anna considered telling her interrogator that her performance had been so good because she was actually an actress; only the thought of the tongue-lashing that revelation could land on Kerstin's head stopped her.

'No, I haven't.'

Frau Berger's shudder was as theatrical as if Anna had confessed to a life of crime.

'I knew it. You are far too impressed with yourself. Whatever I ask you to do is beneath your abilities, in your own head at least. You do not possess a scrap of humility. Everything in your manner is insolent, young lady; thoroughly insolent.'

It was clear a dismissal was coming. For one moment, Anna thought about begging, about trying to buy herself an extra week. And then all the pent-up days and bitten lips crashed back.

'That is as untrue as it is unfair. I may not have done my job to your standards – I doubt anyone could – but I have never been rude to you, although, believe me, you've deserved it. Your niece is one of the most generous women I know, and you are the most impossible. If you are going to fire me, then fire me, but could we do it without the lecture?'

Frau Berger's eyes narrowed. She made no attempt to hide her smile.

'With pleasure. And without the rest of the wages you would have earned had you completed your time with me. Get your things and get out of here today. I won't wish you luck. I am sure, with your unbecomingly loose attitudes, you will have no problems making money.'

There were too many insults chasing through her head for Anna to be bothered choosing one. She slammed out of the room and down the main central staircase, not caring who saw her. It wasn't until she reached the warmth of the kitchen that the reality of her situation hit.

'Sit down. Drink this.'

A chair appeared under her; a cup of coffee materialised. It was too hot to sip, but blowing on it at least calmed Anna's breathing.

'What's happened? Have you been given notice?'

The housekeeper, Mrs Michaels, waved the hovering cook back to work and waited.

Anna nodded.

'Well, that's no surprise. That woman is a monster. She has always been the same: spoiled and impossible.'

Anna looked up from her steaming cup, confused by the accent that had crept into Mrs Michaels' usually polished tones.

The housekeeper smiled. 'It doesn't go, not entirely. Even when you have been here twenty years and you are married to an Irishman with a brogue he spreads thick as butter. I came to New York with Mrs McGregor from Berlin when she married, and I remember dear Helga well. We were all glad to be away from her temper, and now we dread her visits. This is the fifth and, trust me, age and distance do not improve her. Did she give you money for your ticket home?'

Anna hesitated, wondering how honest she could be about her intention to stay. Mrs Michaels had struck her from her first day in the McGregor home as a good-hearted woman. Discretion, nevertheless, seemed safer.

'No. She may have been going to, but my tongue ran away with me first.'

The housekeeper snorted. 'She didn't pay the last one she cut loose, so I doubt it was your tongue that kept her purse closed. Drink your coffee, eat some of the pastries Cook is desperate to pile on you, and wait.'

When Mrs Michaels returned, she was carrying a small envelope.

'This is from Mrs McGregor. It is enough to cover your ticket home and to keep a decent roof over your head while you wait for a sailing. You cannot, I am afraid, stay here – Madame has no wish to endure the rows that would bring down. I have, therefore, included the address of a boarding house in with the money, and a short note recommending your character. The house is on the other side of Central Park and is run by a decent woman, a friend of a friend who came out from Berlin on the same boat as me. Once she sees my name on the note, she will find you a room with her, or somewhere equally suitable, I am sure.'

Anna opened the envelope and gasped. 'But there's a hundred dollars in here – that's more than six weeks' wages. It's too much.'

The housekeeper shrugged. 'It's the price of a second-class ticket and a month or two's board. You may need that if the crossings are full, although I sense that the ships that come here nowadays may be far busier than the ones that leave. It is, anyway, what *my* employer thinks is reasonable. But, if you want to swap it for the steerage passage *your* employer would have offered if she had offered anything, you are, of course, at liberty to do so.'

A hundred dollars.

Anna could hardly believe how quickly her prospects had changed. A hundred dollars, together with the money she had held back from what Frau Berger had already paid her, bought her months of rent and perhaps a resident's permit, or the pathway to one. It bought her the chance to start searching.

She pushed the envelope into her pocket and finally relaxed enough to smile. 'No. Of course I will accept it. Please thank Mrs McGregor for me. Tell her I am more grateful than she could know.'

*

The address Mrs Michaels had given her – 89th Street and Lexington – was in the Yorkville area of the Upper East Side.

'It is an hour's walk, if that, but, if you prefer, I am sure Madame won't begrudge you a cab.'

It was a kind offer, but the day was dry and Anna's suitcase – which she had packed carefully enough to make a three-month trip rather than a permanent stay believable – was no heavier than she could manage.

Anna thanked the housekeeper and said goodbye to the cook. There were no other farewells needed; there was no one else she had had time to grow close to. She left through the front door – there was no one interested enough in her movements to reprimand her. A few paces down the driveway, she stopped and looked back. The lacquered black door had closed silently behind her. The curtains were drawn. The building sat square and shuttered, like a box sealed tight against prying fingers. For all Mrs McGregor's generosity, Anna knew that – whatever might happen to her next – this house was no longer open to her.

She walked steadily away, heading down 81st and across Columbus Avenue. The further she went from the wide lots of Riverside Drive, the more diverse the streets became. Houses and gardens were smaller, although the properties were still determinedly respectable. The streets closest to the gateway that led to the park's Planetarium were lined with brownstones – pretty family homes with high stoops decked out with plant pots and shrubs. Anna slowed her pace and peeped through the lower windows as she passed by, envying the sleepy Saturday mornings unfolding inside. She tried to imagine herself playing a part in this neighbourhood's script. Cooking eggs in a neatly arranged kitchen. Waiting to eat breakfast with a husband as kind-looking as the one cradling a baby to his chest as he picked up the newspaper. The image was both everything Anna wanted and impossibly out of reach. The pain of it was unbearable.

Keep walking. Stop looking. This isn't your life, not yet, but it will be. When you find Franzi, it will be.

She focused on the words, matching their rhythm with her footsteps. The trick got her across the park without crying. Then she reached the East Side and the change in the air was so immediate, her darkening mood fell away.

Two miles from Riverside Drive and she was in another city, one that better matched the New York she had spied from car windows and shopping trips than the sedate enclaves of the Upper West Side. The streets here weren't wandering into the day, they rushed. Although it was only a little past eleven, the sidewalks on 5th Avenue were crowded.

Anna hurried along, swept up in the bustle. Dodging shopfronts whose produce spilled out in stacked crates that threatened to trip her. Dodging gesticulating family groups who all seemed to walk five abreast. She had never walked down streets filled with so much noise. Apart from when the National Socialists whipped it up, Berlin wasn't a city much given to shouting. And she had never heard such a muddle of accents and languages.

Anna knew she had moved within a very small social circle since her arrival in New York. Other than on the dockside, most of the people she had encountered spoke in tones that had been softened by wealth. They rarely raised their voices; they didn't need to: even their gentlest orders were obeyed. The mansions on Riverside Drive were as stately and quiet as their owners. The East Side streets, however, were unashamedly loud, their languages layered one over the other like the lasagne Anna could see advertised in a nearby delicatessen. She could hear English but coated in the strong brogue she had heard in the cook's voice and guessed was Irish. What she presumed was Italian flew around her, its music sailing across a jumble of harsher sounds that Anna recognised from

Berlin as Polish and Russian. The effect was vibrant and exciting and so life-affirming, Anna was entranced. And then she turned onto 86th and her heart stopped.

The smells caught her first. *Apfelkuchen* and *Roggenbrot*; hop-heavy beer and a briny pickle that had to be sauerkraut. As she stepped further onto the street, the other languages fell away, and all she could hear was German. She stopped, put her suitcase down. Geiger's Konditorei, Ehret's Bar, Rudi's & Maxi's Brau-Haus, Café Hindenburg. The names marched on and on down both sides of the street.

Anna sniffed and stared, her head and her heart suddenly filling with her parents and Eddy and home. She blinked and rubbed at her prickling eyes, and then she noticed that some of the signs set above the shops were so traditional they looked almost impossibly Alpine.

How much of Germany have they brought over here?

She froze and didn't dare look up, in case the floors above the storefronts were draped in swastikas.

'Sind Sie verloren, Fräulein? Kann ich Ihnen helfen?'

The man who approached her was small, and rounded and looked to be in his seventies. He was wearing a green loden jacket and a small feathered hat and looked as if he had stepped out of a poster advertising the delights of Bavaria. Anna gaped, wondering if she had somehow wandered onto a film shoot, shivering at the sudden flashback to the Bogensee villa. And then, before she could answer his question, a sharp noise ricocheted round the street. She didn't think; she acted on instinct. She flung herself into the nearest doorway, shielding her face from the squad of SS officers she was certain were about to come marching towards her.

'It is a car. Nothing but a car. There is no need to be frightened.'

The old man had switched into a heavily accented English.

Anna took her hands from her face and followed his pointing finger. The culprit was a baker's van, stuttering and banging its way up the street. Nobody but her had taken any notice. There were no bodies being bundled into the back; no black uniforms raking the crowds; no guns. Anna shuffled back onto the sidewalk and picked up her suitcase; even though she could see the van, her hands were still shaking.

'I am sorry. I was startled. You were right, it was nothing.'

She spoke in German – the street somehow demanded it.

The man frowned. 'Are you newly here, from the old country?'

She nodded.

'Then tell me, what has Germany come to, if its daughters shake in terror at a misfiring engine?'

Anna didn't know how to reply. He was smiling. He looked innocent enough. But how – in this *Alice Through the Looking Glass* version of Germany – was she meant to know where his political sympathies lay?

You need to calm down. You're letting your imagination run away with you.

She found a smile she hoped was convincing.

'I overreacted. Traveller's nerves. And I am not lost, but thank you for asking if I was and if you could help me.'

She moved away before he could ask her any more questions and tried to look at her surroundings with a kinder eye. This was an immigrant area, that was all. People who missed their homeland were trying to recreate it. It wasn't sinister; it wasn't dangerous. It was, however, a relief to round the corner into the far more ordinary-looking Lexington.

The boarding house itself proved easy to find, and the building was so pretty, Anna instantly felt better. It was one of what she later learned the Americans called row houses: a cluster of narrow terracotta-coloured three-storey buildings, pressed together on a tree-lined street and rather dwarfed by a block of flat-roofed tenements. The house, and the ones neighbouring it, had a flight of steep steps leading to a doorway recessed inside a cream-coloured archway. The upper windows were topped with a triangular pediment which gave the building a jaunty air, and the windowsills were edged with delicately carved mouldings. It was elegant, and homely, and solid. It looked like the kind of place she could regroup in.

A scrawny maid lost inside a voluminous white apron answered Anna's knock. She led Anna into a narrow, spotlessly clean hallway furnished with a dark wood telephone table. A vase sat on top of it, containing orange and yellow carnations. A gilt-framed mirror hung at the bottom of the stairs, next to a painting of boats bobbing in an old-fashioned harbour. It was so perfectly ordinary, and so exactly as it should be, Anna wanted to laugh. She realised she had been holding her breath, half-expecting the front door to open onto a photograph of Hitler and a large bunch of edelweiss.

She straightened her hat, smoothed her gloves and quickly wiped off her lipstick, not wanting to give the landlady any excuse to reject her. All it took, however, was the note from Mrs Michaels and the landlady, Frau Möller – who was dressed in a simple blue housedress, not the dirndl skirt Anna's imagination had put her in – was all smiles. Anna introduced herself in English, but, when Frau Möller noted her accent and switched into German, Anna was glad to continue the conversation in her first language. The day had been filled with so many changes, there was an unexpected comfort in her mother tongue.

'You are in luck. One of my young ladies is leaving me to be married and has already returned to her parents. It is a first-floor room; you will share a bathroom with Fräulein Strasbach. The rent is ten dollars per month, breakfast and dinner included. No gentlemen callers are permitted. Do you have your ticket home booked?'

'No.'

Frau Möller waited, and pursed her lips when Anna would not be drawn further.

'Well, that is your business. Shall we say three months' rent in advance?'

Anna agreed and handed over the money.

The maid – who introduced herself in a mumble as Molly – reappeared and began leading her up the stairs.

'Do you need a job, Fräulein Brandt?'

Anna stopped, surprised at the question.

Frau Möller smoothed her tightly rolled hair. 'You are clearly intending to stay in the city. I do not imagine your pot of money is endless. And I find it simpler to deal with problems before they arise. Can you do shop work?'

'Yes.'

Frau Möller nodded. 'Good. Let me see what I can arrange. This is a close community; we look after our own. I hope that will suit you?'

Anna had no idea if that would suit her or not, and she did not want a shop job – she had other ideas – but she thanked her new benefactress and followed Molly up the stairs into a room whose high ceilings and tall windows filled it with light. The bed was covered in a pale green flower-sprigged quilt. When Anna sat on it, she sank. The windows overlooked an immaculate courtyard, picked out with blue and red plant pots. Anna pushed open the lowest pane and leaned out. The air smelled of fresh rain.

I could breathe here.

Her shock at how bizarrely German 86th street had been, and the episode with the van – an event which now made Anna feel foolish – had worn off. Being fired from Frau Berger's employ suddenly felt like a blessing. She had somewhere safe to stay, where she wasn't expected to play a role she couldn't possibly fit. She even had the promise of a job, although she had no intention of taking it: for the first time since she had been pushed into signing the contract at UFA, Anna had a plan that was entirely her own. A plan that made her heart lift, not plummet. It had slipped into her head as she walked through the East Side's babble. What she needed to recapture herself and give herself the courage to begin looking for her daughter was colour, and life, and work that she knew and was good at. Which meant a return to the theatre. Her old career – her old love – reinvented.

Tomorrow she was going to head out for Broadway. There were shows there, hundreds of shows. There would be auditions. Surely somebody somewhere would listen to her story and give her a chance?

'You keep yourself too much to yourself, Fräulein Brandt, which, trust me, is not an overused phrase in this house. It is not healthy for a young woman to do nothing but work.'

Anna stared at the parsley-flecked potatoes steaming untouched on her plate. The landlady's eagle-eyed scrutiny had, so far, largely avoided her. She would have preferred to keep it that way.

'I am on my feet all day, Frau Möller, and that tires me. Perhaps when I am more used to the bakery's hours, I will be able to manage a social life.'

'What utter nonsense! You slice plum cake and wrap bread for a living. You are hardly building a bridge.'

One of the other three lodgers gathered for dinner rather unsuccessfully stifled a giggle. Frau Möller ignored it.

'I told you when you first came to us that Yorkville is close-knit. I would have thought a girl as far away from home as you – and one who seems set on staying – would have been grateful to play a more enthusiastic part in our community.'

Anna had no answer she could comfortably give. She could hardly explain that it wasn't her body that the job at the bakery exhausted but her spirits. Or admit that having to stand behind the high-topped counter or serve at the small cluster of tables felt like the worst kind of failure. How could that sound anything other than ungrateful?

She would be dismissed – quite rightly – as spoiled. She wasn't. Her dreams of returning to the stage had been trampled so conclusively, there was barely a grain of them left and she was sad. Not crushingly so: the loss of her child was a mountain of grief compared to this. But she was sad, she couldn't pretend otherwise, in a way that made her feel old and drained down to her bones.

She had made such a fool of herself. Everything she had done had been wrong – starting with her assumption that Broadway was one long, easily navigable street. Anna still smarted when she realised how naïve she had been, even though it had been weeks since she had tried uselessly to reignite her career.

She had left the boarding house the morning after she had hatched her plan as optimistically as Pollyanna. Everything had felt like an adventure. She had ridden on the El train's elevated tracks as if she was flying in a plane; she had lost a morning wandering round Times Square and the streets that led off it, marvelling at the crowded billboards advertising every shade of entertainment from melodrama to musicals. New York's theatre land was as brash and bold as Berlin's, and it felt like home. Anna had imagined herself breaking audience hearts as the poverty-stricken mother in *Moon Over Mulberry Street,* or terrifying them with the cruelty of her Lady Macbeth. The dream-weaving had been the best part.

It took her half a day to realise the scale of the task facing her – that Broadway was, in fact, not one avenue but a sprawling web of streets fanning out from West 41st to West 65th which contained over forty theatres. It had been a surprise, but not one that daunted her.

Instead, she had embraced the challenge. She had bought a map and a pen from a kiosk and made what she believed was a logical list, starting with the theatres on 42nd and circling out from there. In the end, it took her three days to cover them all – it would have taken longer had they all let her in.

She had worn her most professional outfit: a navy-blue rayon dress with a pleated skirt and a row of large white buttons that accentuated the tiny polka-dot print, and a coat with a tawny-coloured fur collar. She had felt glamorous, part of the world she was trying to walk back into. It did her no good. She was as unwelcome as if Goebbels ran Broadway.

The few stage managers she managed to meet refused to understand her accent. The ones who listened to more than a sentence waved her away when she couldn't produce something called an Equity Card. No one was interested in who she might once have been. No one would give her information about companies or upcoming productions or audition arrangements. 'Buy a paper and check the listings same as everyone else' was the kindest thing said to her. 'We've no room for Nazis' was far from the worst. Living in the McGregor house and then in Yorkville had given Anna no clue as to the hostile attitude towards Germany her accent increasingly unleashed. Her insistence that she was no more a lover of Hitler than they were, that she had left her country because of him and his party, went unheard. For the first time in New York, she felt *other*.

In the end, she gave up on the theatres and tried to make appointments with casting agents. The only one who would see her told her to take off her dress. She had gone home, cried for an hour, been furious for an hour, and then she had accepted the position Frau Möller had secured for her at the Heidelberg Bakery. It was a wage. It covered her rent and her few expenses. If she was frugal, she should be able to add to her nest egg and save up for the resident's permit and the acting and voice classes she planned to bury herself in. She was temporarily beaten, but she wasn't broken: she still had a plan. There was no space or spare cash in it, however, for socialising.

'It's not that I don't want to be involved, Frau Möller, but I really need to save up my money.'

The landlady sniffed. 'Which is a laudable enough aim, I suppose, but I won't have it said that I don't look after my girls. What are you? Twenty-two? Twenty-three?'

Anna blushed. 'Twenty-five.'

'Well, you look younger, which is something. But looks do not last.'

Somebody at the table snorted. Anna could feel her skin burn. Frau Möller took no notice.

'You are not getting any younger. Independence is all very well, but what you need is a husband.'

'It really isn't…'

Frau Möller kept on talking. 'This Saturday night there is a dance at the Casino. The League of German Wives has arranged it and there will be young men there from some of our very best families. The rest of my girls are going; I would see it as a personal affront if you don't attend too.'

'There's no point in arguing. She sees it as her duty to get us all settled with a *suitable man*. She's worse than my mother.' Romy – the Fräulein Strasbach Anna shared a bathroom with – used Molly's door-banging entrance with the pudding to cover her whisper. 'The dance will be more fun than it sounds, I promise. And, if it's not, at least if you go, she might leave you alone for a while.'

'Well?' Frau Möller was still looking at her.

Romy was right: it was one dance, four dull hours at worst. If it would buy her some peace, surely she could manage it. Anna drenched her rather dry-looking strudel in cream and lit up a smile.

'Of course, Frau Möller. If you think it is for the best, I would be happy to go. Thank you for thinking of me.'

The landlady swallowed Anna's performance and smiled with delight; Anna wished she could have convinced Broadway of her talents as easily.

The Yorkville Casino was built on a far grander scale than Anna had imagined it would be. The club on 86th was six storeys high and towered over the rest of the block. Patrons entered through a canopied walkway, and three huge arched windows took up most of the facade. The flagpole on the top – from which the black, red and gold German flag streamed – was so high, Anna had had to crane her neck when she looked up – foolishly she knew, but she couldn't help herself – to check which symbol was flying.

'Isn't it amazing?' Romy slipped her arm through Anna's as she steered her through the chandeliered foyer. 'There's pretty much everything going on here you might want to do: book groups, singing societies, drama clubs, politics, if that's your thing. There's a cinema too, which shows German films, and two massive dance halls, as well as the private dining rooms.'

Anna nodded: the enormous dance floor that awaited them through the crystal-bright glass doors had left her too stunned to answer. Anna was no stranger to nightclubs. Although many of them had closed down since the National Socialists took power, she had visited most of Berlin's best, including Efti with its Moorish arches and corridors linking bars that were designed to resemble carriages from the Orient Express, and Resi where love notes and cigarettes – and cocaine – flew backward and forward between the tables along snake-headed pneumatic tubes. She had not, however, expected to find anything on that scale in an area like Yorkville. She had presumed they would be going to something smaller and more intimate, on the lines of a neighbourhood *ballhaus*, with a small stage and seating for two or three hundred. The stage she was looking at now was big enough for an orchestra, and three hundred dancers would barely fill up one corner of the polished floor.

Romy pulled her into the room and dropped their purses on a table. 'It's wild, isn't it? And this isn't even the biggest hall. There's one upstairs that apparently spans the whole building, not that I've seen it. And the Tuxedo Room across the foyer can fit a couple of thousand onto the dance floor alone. This one tends to be for German dances, but the Tuxedo is one of the city's most popular nightclubs. You never know who might be wandering about here, which is why I told you to wear your best outfit.'

The other girls entering arm in arm and waving at the boys clustered round the bar were all so immaculately turned out, Anna was glad she had heeded Romy's advice. She wasn't interested in anyone who *might be wandering about* – her heart was still too bruised from Eddy for that – but getting ready for the evening had reminded her that, whatever the theatre managers on Broadway might think, she was still an actress, and she knew the importance of looking the part. Her rose-coloured dress had always been her favourite one to go dancing in: it had a handkerchief hem which fluttered perfectly when she moved.

As they gave their drinks order to a passing waiter, the band started up a new song. Anna's toes tapped as she recognised it.

'You know this one? It's reached Germany?'

'Yes. It was really popular. "We're in the Money".' Anna smiled back at Romy. 'From the movie, *Gold Diggers of 1933*. I saw it at the—' She stopped. She was about to say: *at the studio*. It had been one of the films Goebbels had brought in for the actors and directors to study and copy, as part of his plan to make German films more audience-winningly American. She settled instead for, 'I saw it and I liked it a lot.'

Romy's grin spread. 'Can you Lindy Hop?'

When Anna nodded, Romy whooped and pulled her straight onto the dance floor. Three beats in and Anna was spinning, every dance lesson she had taken rushing back. Romy shrieked with delight and matched her step for step. By the third song, a space had cleared big enough for the girls to show off in. By the fourth, partners were queuing. Anna dropped Romy's hand and danced with one laughing man after another, barely looking at any of them but feeling happier, and younger, than she had done in months.

'Oh no. I don't get one and then done. We're the best dancers here; we're meant to be partners.'

The man who hadn't let go and stepped aside when the music stopped was slim and dark, and far more handsome than Anna had noticed when she first took his hand.

'That's better; at least now you're looking at me. Do you always slip into a world of your own when you're dancing?'

Anna frowned. He was attractive, and an excellent dancer, but that did not mean she wanted his attention. 'I didn't know that I did.'

The band started up again. The man pulled her in close. Before Anna had time to think, she twisted back out, her body automatically finding the song's rhythm.

'You dance as though you are alone, even when you are in step with your partner. It's what makes you good: you're completely involved with the music.'

He stopped talking as the tempo increased. There was a challenge in his eyes Anna realised that she liked. She bent slightly forward, kicked her feet out to the side in a complicated series of half-jumps. He smiled and followed her lead. Their kicks grew faster. Every time Anna changed her footwork and added a hop or a sidestep or a spin, he was there. She could hear clapping and cheering; she was conscious that there was no one dancing near them anymore. She kept her eyes on his. And then he lifted her – with a swoop so smooth she felt like she was flying – and dropped her back down, sliding her under his legs and back out as perfectly as if they had been practising the move for months. The watching crowd erupted.

'I told you.' His mouth was so close, she could smell peppermint on his breath and lime cologne on his cheek. 'You and me. We're the best in the room.'

It was just dancing, a few hours of fun; it didn't need to mean anything. She let him hold on to her hand for the rest of the night.

CHAPTER EIGHT

Yorkville, April to December 1936

Frank Gellner was an elusive man.

Perhaps that is part of his attraction – that he's different from Eddy.

Anna clipped a tortoiseshell comb into her newly set waves and straightened the bow fastening the neck of her coral-pink blouse. She didn't know exactly what kind of an event she was attending tonight, or what the dress code might be, so she had erred on the side of simple and elegant.

Marika would be proud of me.

She pushed the thought away before it forced her to change her whole outfit. She did not want to think about whether Marika would have approved of her choice; she had no desire to think about Marika at all.

Focus on Frank instead: whatever tonight is about, it clearly matters to him.

He wanted her there; he might not have been clear about what he was launching at the Casino tonight, but he had been very direct about that. His invitation was more personal and intimate than most of the conversations they had had. It read as if – for him at least –whatever this thing was between them was a relationship, not a series of almost casual encounters.

Anna located her lipstick and coloured in her mouth, making her top lip slightly darker than the bottom in the way that was currently in fashion. She wasn't used to not being able to read a man. She wasn't entirely sure that she liked it. She and Eddy's relationship had been so intertwined, there had been no mystery about him. Until their last few weeks together, Anna would have said she knew him inside out.

Thinking about Eddy wasn't something Anna often let herself do: her feelings for him were still too clouded in confusion and anger for her to know whether there was still love for him there. Now that she had some distance on the way things had ended, however, she had realised that Eddy finally succumbing to Marika's flattery and to her casting him as her rescuing knight had saddened but not surprised her. Eddy had never cheated – Anna would have staked her life on that – but he was a romantic and far too susceptible to a woman pleading distress, especially if that woman was as seductive as Marika. Eddy had been many things – not least misguided – but Anna would always have called him an open book; that was one of the reasons she had fallen in love with him. Frank, on the other hand, was a charming but closed one.

They had met half a dozen times in the four months since the December dance. Their attraction, Anna was convinced, was mutual, although it hadn't progressed physically beyond goodnight kisses Frank was always the first to pull back from. His self-control had made her crave his touch more – she wasn't sure if that was deliberate.

They had partnered each other three times in the swing competitions that were held monthly at the Casino. They had won them all, without any practice. Frank had taken her to the cinema twice. Once to see the musical *Anything Goes,* once to see *The Petrified Forest*, which was a far darker drama. Anna wasn't sure which, if either, he preferred.

They hadn't yet gone out alone for dinner, or spent any time talking about anything much beyond their daily lives. Anna had been vague about Berlin and hadn't mentioned her acting career; she had said nothing yet about her family. She knew – although mostly from Frau Möller – that the Gellners were brewery owners, who were proud of their still strong ties to Munich. Frank himself had said very little about them, apart from a younger brother, Stefan, who he seemed to dote on. And she knew that he wasn't a college man – he had worked in the family business since he was fourteen – but that he was a reader. Wherever Anna met him, he had a book stuffed in his pocket – usually something to do with military history that she thought looked very dry and wasn't interested in asking about.

Frank's main interest outside his work and his books, as far as Anna could tell, was Yorkville. He sat on a number of committees he said were to do with preserving the neighbourhood and retaining its character, although he never mentioned anything about politics, other than at a local level. In many ways, they were still strangers to each other, still sketching their lives out. It was, however, early days and Anna was happy to proceed at the slow pace Frank appeared to favour. She had no desire to jump too fast into anything that could distract her from her plan to find Franzi, or to re-establish the career she would need to support her child when she was found. Especially now that she had managed to put a little money by to help her pay for the acting classes her experience on Broadway suggested she would have to invest in and, more importantly, to start the process of seriously tracking down the Baileys.

It was enough then that he made her pulse race when she saw him. And that he was handsome and good company and attentive, both when they were together and when his meeting schedule and frequent trips on brewery business meant that they couldn't be. The huge bouquet of cream roses he had sent by way of apology for a recently cancelled Saturday night had given Frau Möller palpitations.

And that he knows people. Who might have contacts with the docks, or with immigration, and might be able to track down the name Bailey on a passenger sheet.

That alone was enough to keep her happily stepping out with Frank Gellner.

His most recent trip – to Chicago she thought, although she couldn't remember him actually saying – had taken him away for almost three weeks. Now he was back. And, according to the letter which had dropped through the boarding-house door two days ago, surprisingly desperate to see her.

The letter had been sweet, almost romantic in tone, and had implied a closeness between them Anna wasn't sure they had reached. Since the letter had arrived, however, she had begun to wonder if Frank wasn't as much closed as old-fashioned, a believer in slow courtships. She had no objection to that.

My dear Anna,

Forgive me, I seem to be gone far more than present since I met you. It wasn't my intention to be on the road quite as often, but I hope that, once you see what I have been working on, you will understand why I was too often away.

I worry that you must find me secretive or, at best, distracted. I am sorry for that too. The task I have been entrusted with – which has finally come to fruition – has required not inconsiderable discretion. We are launching it here in Yorkville, but it is an initiative that involves our whole country – I am not exaggerating when I say that it is something all good German Americans have been waiting for and can be proud of.

We are unveiling our plans at the Casino on Saturday, and it would make my heart swell if you were there by my side. The main event starts at seven, but you should come at 6.30 and ask for me at the delivery door: there could be crowds at the front.

Until then.

Your (I hope can I call myself that)
Frank

It was all very mysterious. Anna could only assume that, whatever this launch was, it must have something to do with the brewery – a new beer perhaps that Frank had to keep secret from his competitors in case anyone stole the recipe. It was also – with its assumption of crowds and its assertion that all German Americans would be touched by it – rather dramatic. Drama, however, was what was missing from every other aspect of Anna's life, so he had her attention. And now it was five o'clock on Saturday night and she had been ready for hours.

Anna crossed to the window and leaned out. Spring had finally arrived and brought a pretty evening with it. The air was warm and sweet-scented; if she concentrated hard enough, she could smell apple blossom.

Anna decided to take a slow walk to the venue. It was ten minutes at most to the Casino if she went there direct, but it had been a while since she had dawdled through the neighbourhood. Winter in New York had been harsher than any she remembered in Berlin: the snow had fallen in drifts and the wind from the East River had sent ice into her bones. She had got into the habit of scurrying home from the bakery and curling up in the warm parlour in the evening so that she could scour the adverts in the newspapers, trying to determine which of the men advertising there were properly qualified private detectives, and which ones were charlatans.

Fortunately, Frau Möller so approved of her liaison with Frank, she no longer pushed Anna to spend her time running round all the societies the area could offer. It had made for a cosy winter – albeit one with a little too much solitude and time to dwell on her mother and wonder when it might be safe to physically write the letter that she constantly wrote in her head – but now the weather was finally changing, it would be nice to wander, to properly look about.

Anna still felt out of place in America, even in the German-soaked streets of Yorkville. She did not understand her new country's nuances and she needed to change that.

And to organise drama classes. And to sort out the application for my resident's visa, before it becomes a problem that my tourist one has run out. And to work out a way of introducing the Baileys into conversation.

She would make a list the next morning, a heap of new resolutions ready for spring. Tonight she would focus on Frank and decide if growing closer to him might be one of them.

By the time Anna reached the Casino, she was regretting the walk. Yorkville had not stood up well, today at least, to closer inspection. Since the episode six months ago with the backfiring van, Anna had tried very hard not to fill her new neighbourhood with her old fears. Frau Möller had been right: the German sector of Yorkville was a closely interwoven community, and – for those it counted as its own – it was a warm and welcoming place. Everyone who came into the Heidelberg Bakery was a regular. When they learned that she was newly come from the 'Homeland', everyone had treated Anna as part of the family.

The area was a mix of old and new immigrants, but most of the families who filled up the district's fifty square German American blocks had put their roots down in the late nineteenth century. Memories were long, ties to the 'old country' were tight; everyone spoke about their *Heimat* with a sentimentality Anna couldn't share but always smiled at. The political shifts of recent years seemed to be less relevant than old allegiances. If discussion in the café turned to Hitler and the National Socialists, people looked over their shoulders and closed the conversation down. Anna assumed that was because they all shared her disgust at the Party and its ramping-up persecutions. Frau Möller wouldn't permit any mention of that 'awful little man' in her house. Not being permanently tuned to the news and the shifting mood on the streets was an adjustment for Anna, who had spent so much time in Berlin afraid, for herself and for her country. She did not miss living under that shadow.

Life for Germans in America, however, wasn't picture-book perfect. There were rumblings even in Yorkville. Although Anna didn't share her Broadway experiences, she soon discovered that she wasn't the only one whose accent had led to insults. And she soon realised that the experience wasn't new. Some of the older coffee drinkers in the café grumbled about how quickly the 'land of opportunity' had turned on its many German communities during and after the Great War. Many of them had suffered the indignities of being interned, and had then felt forced to Americanise their names in the face of prejudice that did not end in 1918. Many of them felt abandoned by those in power, from district up to Senate level, compared to the Italians and the Irish, even though – as she heard many times a week – 'we make up a quarter of this country'.

A national boycott on German goods had started to bite at the same time as Anna began work at the bakery. It was cheered on in large sections of the – non-German – press as being a protest against Hitler, not an attack on loyal citizens. Few who lived or traded near 86th believed that. The boycott rattled the shopkeepers, and led to a flurry of *Buy German* protest-stickers adorned with Nazi-like blue eagles which had rattled Anna. Those, however, soon disappeared. The papers kept insisting that the boycott was working and teaching Hitler a lesson, but most New Yorkers were happy with their melting-pot reputation and happier than the newspapers to let life roll normally on. Stocks of apple sauce and bratwurst continued arriving with the ocean-crossing liners, sometimes with their labels switched to fool the investigators; more often not. The shopkeepers settled down. Frau Hertig, the bakery's boss, continued to insist that 'no matter where we are from, we are all Americans'. There were rumblings, but the insults and attempts to stifle trade were a drop in the ocean compared to the crushing tactics used against the Jews Anna had seen in Berlin. She had finally convinced herself, therefore, to stop worrying. Then she went out for a peaceful wander, and back the worry flew.

Two signs posted over the shop windows and street lamps had done it – one that she didn't understand, and one that she very unhappily did. The first was a poster designed to grab the eye, its message – *Awake and Act!* – lettered in a jagged red and black script that flashed across the paper like lightning bolts. Smaller type underneath directed the interested to a 'launch at the Yorkville Casino at 7 p.m. tonight'. Anna ripped one of those down and stuffed it in her purse. She told herself it couldn't possibly be anything to do with Frank, but the coincidence nagged at her.

The second sign was smaller, its meaning far more straightforward. When Anna read it, she felt sick. *Don't buy from Jews.* She pulled one of those away from a door frame to see if it had an identifying signature, but there was nothing on the front or the back with any clue to where it had come from. She stuffed that into her purse as well, and wondered how practical it would be to tear them all down. She would have tried it, but the street was busy and no one else seemed concerned.

I should go home.

It was a strong impulse. But so was, *stay calm and stay rational.* No one else being worried most likely meant that the leafletting wasn't a reflection of how the wider community felt but the work of a few out-of-step individuals. No doubt it would be cleared away by the morning. And, obviously, *Awake and Act* had nothing to do with Frank: how could such a dramatic slogan relate to beer? The Casino was huge: any number of organisations could be meeting at seven. Frank, however, might be able to shed some answers on who the troublemakers were, given all the neighbourhood connections he had. Anna had no doubt that – when she showed the offending articles to him – he would find the posters as sickening as she did.

Time had run away with her again: it was twenty past six. Anna snapped her purse shut and hurried down 3rd Avenue. When she turned onto 86th, she stopped as abruptly as she had when she had caught her first glimpse of the street. Frank had been right about the crowds: the sidewalk outside the Casino was overflowing, people standing three deep in the road. Anna could see a police horse circling its edges, and a squad car at the end of the block keeping traffic away. The crowd was quiet enough, and well dressed – almost funereally so. All the men – and it did seem to be mostly men waiting to gain admission – were wearing dark suits and hats. The few women Anna could see wore unadorned black coats. They all looked perfectly respectable. But there were too many of them, all too plainly dressed, to assume they might be attending one of the Casino's dances. And Anna couldn't believe they were all beer fans.

Something is wrong; I need to go home.

'Anna, you made it. Frank will be thrilled. But why are you standing out here? Didn't he tell you to go round to the delivery door?'

'Yes, but I'm not sure that I want—'

Frank's younger brother, Stefan, already had her arm and was steering her towards the building, keeping up a stream of chatter that paid her hesitation no heed. 'We are all that proud of him. You wouldn't believe the running round he's been doing, spreading the word, looping all the smaller groups together. He's been in Detroit and Chicago and Milwaukee in the last few weeks alone. At least Brooklyn and the Bronx are closer targets, so we should have him back for a while.'

Anna had more questions than she could keep track of, but it was pointless asking Stefan to explain what he was talking about; he was too keyed up. She let him whisk her inside the building – where the press of people was as thick as it had been outside – and up a back staircase that smelled of stale air and cigarette smoke. He was half-running by the time they reached the third floor. He pushed open a fire door and started heading down a far quieter corridor at the same tilting speed.

Anna, however, had had enough of being pulled around as if she was on the end of a leash. She dragged her hand out of his and waited until he realised and stopped, which took him a few more paces. She was determined not to go a step further without some sense of what exactly she was walking into. 'Stefan, please. Could you take a moment? Could you tell me what is going on here?'

He stared at her; he could hardly stand still – his feet were virtually twitching. 'We'll miss all the excitement if we hang about. It's the launch, didn't he tell you?'

If I hear the word launch one more time, I will scream.

'Yes, he did. But what launch? Is all this really about beer?'

He frowned. Before he could answer, however, a door opened and Frank stepped out into the corridor. His face lit up when he saw her. He had only been away three weeks; Anna hadn't forgotten how perfectly handsome he was, but the sight of him could still take her breath away. Standing there in his sharp-shouldered black suit and dark grey shirt – a departure from his usual white and a shade that turned his blue eyes navy – he looked like the kind of chiselled-jawed hero UFA would have flung contracts at.

'You're here. That makes the night perfect.'

He held out his hand. Anna wanted nothing more than to grab it, but she hung back. There was something too precise, too uniform-like about his clothes that made her neck itch.

'What's all this about, Frank? All the crowds, all the secrecy. What exactly is this *initiative* you've been spending your time on? Is it do with the brewery?'

He laughed as if she had told the wittiest joke. 'No, not at all. It's better than that – it's the best thing you could imagine. A new brotherhood. A new beginning.' He stepped forward and took her hand anyway.

'What does that mean, a *new brotherhood*?' The phrase was too unexpected for her to make sense of it.

When she didn't move, he tugged her forward. 'Stop trying to spoil the surprise. Now, come on, we have a few minutes before the hall fills up and I want you to meet somebody.'

He didn't wait for her to agree. He drew her hand through his arm and hurried her into a room where a group of men dressed not unlike him were standing. There were two other women there; both of them had make-up-free faces and hair scraped back into braided buns. They ran their eyes over Anna's pink-and-cream coat and flower-trimmed hat; neither of them smiled.

Anna was growing increasingly agitated and very tired of being pulled around and having her questions ignored. She was about to protest, and demand proper answers, not this *surprise* that seemed to cast her in the role of a child, when Frank jumped in first again.

'Do you have a tissue?'

'What?' His voice didn't sound as if he had a cold.

'Your lipstick is a little strong tonight, and your rouge.'

'What on earth are you talking about?'

He turned away from her as the men bunched in front of them stopped talking and separated. 'Never mind. He's not that much of a stickler. He's not particularly worried about women using paint and dressing up as long as they are loyal.'

On any other day, Anna would have taken Frank to task, both for his rudeness about her appearance and his peculiar comments about women. On any other day, she would have stalked out. Today, the angry words wouldn't come. All she could think was: this must be a joke. The man standing in front of her looked like a cartoon version of Hitler. He was wearing an olive-green military-style jacket, brown breeches and leather jackboots. He was overweight, his hair was thinning, his face was lumpen. He was standing so rigidly – stocky legs wide apart and thumbs stuck into his belt – he seemed more cardboard than human. Frank, however, was staring at him as if he was Michelangelo's David.

'*Bundesführer*, this is Anna Brandt. Anna, this is *Bundesführer* Fritz Julius Kuhn: the first man with the vision to unite all the true Germans in this country, and America's next leader.'

He could have repeated the title a hundred times and Anna would still have thought she had misheard him.

Kuhn smiled at her, but he didn't alter his stance. 'Fräulein Brandt, it is a pleasure. You are as lovely as my lieutenant said you were.'

This was worse than *brotherhood*. Surely at some point there had to be a reveal, a flinging back of the curtains and an elaborate punchline?

Anna managed a nod by way of a greeting. Kuhn's smile grew more satisfied.

'And you and he are great "Lindy Hop" dancers he tells me. Not something I imagine our masters in Germany would permit their young people to do, but a perfect illustration of how the National Socialist movement in America must embrace modern customs to win new hearts. I am delighted to meet you, Fräulein. The troops devoted to me deserve the best specimens of our womanhood devoted to them.'

The way he spoke was ridiculous: pompous and self-aggrandising, with one eye on his audience. It was clear, however, that there wasn't a punchline coming. Everyone but her was hanging on Kuhn's words.

Anna stepped back from him, her stomach lurching, wondering if her brain was playing tricks or she had actually heard him say *masters in Germany*.

Frank took hold of her arm again. She was about to shove him away when the doors at the other end of the room opened. Anna could hear music and cheering and feet stamping; a crowd getting restless. And then two rows of men marched in, chins up, eyes front. They were wearing black trousers, caps and neckties, grey shirts and jackets. They stopped opposite Kuhn and their arms snapped up.

'Frank, what the hell is this?'

'Isn't it wonderful, how much devotion he inspires?'

They both spoke together and his voice was louder.

'Quick now. We don't want to miss the crowd's reaction.'

He swept her into the line striding through the open doors behind Kuhn and his entourage, holding her so close she could smell his lime cologne. It no longer smelled sweet.

This has to be some kind of mistake. This is America. How can there be National Socialists in America?

Her mind was tumbling, her thoughts in free fall. She looked frantically for an exit and found herself instead on a stage. The hall they were in was enormous; Anna presumed it was the one that Romy had referred to when she first came to the Casino. It covered the whole of the third floor up to the high arched windows, and it was packed. There were too many people to count, but Anna guessed it was thousands and they were all on their feet cheering.

As Kuhn entered, the voices grew deafening. Kuhn's guard – there was no other word she could think of to call them – moved to the edges of the stage. More men dressed in the same black and grey uniform stepped up to join them. Someone struck a drum. The hall immediately fell silent. The men's voices rose up in song.

Up, up for battle, we are born to battle,
Up for battle, for the German Fatherland.
We are sworn to Adolf Hitler,
And to Adolf Hitler we extend our hand.

They sang it again, then started another verse extolling the Third Reich, their voices soaring, the German words filling the hall. The melody was beautiful; the lyrics were brutal. Anna could feel tears pouring down her cheeks. Frank's eyes were shining.

'I knew it would move you. Especially the music – you have such a feeling for that. That's why I wanted you to experience it this way, with no introduction. This is family, Anna. This is our heritage as true German citizens. Doesn't it make you proud?'

Anna's throat was full, but she couldn't speak.

The singing stopped. The crowd roared. Kuhn raised his hand; the crowd fell silent.

'My friends, all the societies who have come here tonight, who have been waiting too long for this moment: I salute your patience. For years, the German voice has been scattered. For years, right-thinking men and women like us – Americans by birth but Germans by blood – have been promised a new voice that will rise up against those in this country who belittle Germans and Germany, who do not value our great contribution to our adopted land. Now that voice is here and it will never again be silenced. Tonight, my friends, we are united. Tonight sees the birth of the organisation which will remake America: the *German American Bund*.' His voice boomed out the name; he left a tiny pause after each part of it.

The crowd roared again, until he gestured it to stop. He stalked the stage like a puppetmaster, using overblown actions to accentuate his words. Anna knew she was watching a man who had studied his heroes, who saw himself as cut from the same cloth as Hitler and Goebbels. His performance was preposterous; his audience loved it. She was near enough to the front to pick out individual faces: the ones cheering the loudest looked feral and frightening.

Kuhn's speech went on and on, brimming over with all the odious pro-Nazi and hate-filled antisemitic sentiments Anna now expected to hear.

'Our task is to hunt down and remove the Communists and the Jews who will defile our country as they have attempted to do in our homeland.

'As long as there is a swastika, there will be no hammer and sickle.'

She tried her best to block it out. Every time Frank squeezed her hand, she wanted to slap him.

I'll get through this and I'll be done with him. I'll tell him what an animal he is, for being part of this. For thinking that I would want to be part of this.

Kuhn finally stopped. *Sieg Heil* screamed round the hall.

Anna stood statue-still as copies of a pamphlet with the *Awake and Act* slogan were distributed, practising all the insults she was longing to heap onto Frank. She had been afraid when she first realised what she was caught up in, shrinking from the echoes crashing back. Now she was revolted, and furious. That such an organisation could exist here in America; that Frank thought she would be impressed by it, and by him.

'This way.'

The rally had ended while she was lost in her anger. Frank started to move at the same time as the crowd on the floor began making for the doors.

'We'll go out via the main hall – I need to do a bit of meet and greet – and then we're out of here. Fritz has a hell of a party planned.'

And Hell is where you should hold it.

She slipped her hand into her pocket before he could take it again but followed him down the steps off the stage. At least being on the busy floor would give her a chance to wriggle away. She would keep her insults for later, for when he tried to contact her again, which she knew that he would: speaking her mind here could be dangerous.

'Everybody stay where you are. Nobody leaves.'

New uniforms had suddenly appeared, navy blue not black and grey.

Frank turned back to Anna, who was still a few paces clear of him. 'It's the police. The bastards must have sneaked in wearing overcoats. Get your head down; we need to get past them. Don't worry – they won't be after the women.'

But they were.

Anna heard the shout too late, as she was pushing towards a policeman she prayed would get her to safety.

'That one, in the cream coat. She's Gellner's girl. Grab her.'

An arm shot round her waist faster than she could fight her way free.

'We know the names. We've been watching Fritz and his merry little band prepare for this for months. What we need out of you is their plans.'

'Which I've told you, I don't know.'

She was exhausted; she had to concentrate hard to stop her English from slipping. She had lost count of the number of times they had asked the question. Or refused to accept her answer.

'Where have you brought me? This isn't a police station.'

Anna had asked that twice already and got nowhere.

This time, the younger of the two men facing her finally offered some sort of a reply.

'What do you base that on? You don't look the sort who's experienced at being banged up.'

The older man sighed. His irritation, which was clearly with his partner not her, made it easier for Anna to ignore her racing heart and answer as if she wasn't petrified.

'Of course I haven't. I've never done anything criminal. But I have seen pictures.' Anna glanced pointedly round at the yellow walls and red floor, the grey shape painted on the linoleum presumably to look like a rug. If the effect was meant to look less threatening than a cell, it hadn't worked. The attempt to create softness instead made the room deeply uncomfortable. 'And this looks nothing like them. So I'm wondering if you're not the police at all, but something to do with the government.'

It was a poor fishing attempt, far too unsubtle; they didn't fall for it.

'Nice try.' The younger man almost smiled. 'I figured you'd be a bright one. Frank and his Nazi pals might be happy enough to pay for the dumb sort, but they choose a better class to go courting.'

He made it sound like a compliment. Anna swallowed the acid burning her throat. She couldn't think about Frank without her stomach heaving.

The older man glared at his partner again. 'What does it matter what kind of woman she is? All I can see is a Nazi.'

Anna's palms itched to slap him. She slid them under her thighs. 'I am not a Nazi.' She spat out the word as pointedly as he had.

He leaned forward. 'Well, you're certainly not an American. We've checked into you, *Fräulein* Brandt. You came in on a tourist visa, and that's expired. There's no trace of any permanent paperwork. What was the plan? Did the Party send you over to be a good little wife to one of its faithful? To marry Frank, or one of his kind, and raise a troop of soldiers and baby-makers for the Fatherland?'

'No!' Her shout bounced round the room. She dragged herself back under control. 'Nobody sent me. I've never had anything to do with the Party. And I never want to see Frank or any of those monsters from the Casino again.'

'Good. That makes things simple. Wouldn't you agree, Agent Hardy?'

Agent Hardy, the younger one, nodded. 'I do, Agent Nicholls. No goodbyes, no one to come looking. It makes things very simple indeed.'

Anna stared at them, trying to work out the dynamic in their awkward double-act the way she would if she was watching a film. Hardy seemed the less threatening of the two, although she was basing that on the fact that he frowned less. And talked in a marginally less unpleasant tone.

It was Nicholls, however, who continued.

'If you have no ties here, you won't mind being deported. We can have you sailing home by the middle of the week.'

'No! No, you can't do that.' This time, Anna didn't care how wild her voice ran. 'I won't go back; I can't. Whatever it takes to stay, I'll do it.' She stopped. 'That was what you wanted me to say, wasn't it?'

Nicholls picked at a fingernail. 'Wanted is a bit strong. Guessed is probably closer. It doesn't make much difference. I don't see how we can use you… you keep insisting you don't know anything, and you seem inclined to hysterics, which nobody needs. It's nice that you like America so much you're longing to stay, but, all things considered, it would be a lot easier to kick you out.'

Anna knew he was playing with her, that the plan for her had been decided the moment the agents entered the room, possibly long before that. They thought she was powerless, and she was; what they didn't know was that she had been powerless before, and she had survived.

There has to be some humanity here I can appeal to.

'You don't understand. I can't be sent back. I'm half-Jewish. The laws discriminating against Jews have been reported here – you know what's happening. For someone like me to return could be dangerous.'

'Jewish?' Hardy – as Anna had hoped he might when she aimed her plea at him – looked at her with slightly more interest. 'Is that the reason you came here? Have you been persecuted?'

'My father was—'

Nicholls leaped in before Anna could get any further. 'Don't even try, it's far too convenient. Is that your defence, that you're Jewish? Do you really expect us to buy it? You were caught at a Nazi rally. You were carrying Nazi literature in your purse. My partner here might go to temple often enough to be conned, but he'll get over it. And I'm not one for being duped at all.'

Anna took a deep breath. Hardy frowned and looked down, as if he was suddenly aware he'd made a fool of himself.

He saw me as a person for a minute; I know he did. There was a flicker of interest there, not contempt.

Honesty had got her that far, maybe more of it would get her safely out of the door. She sat up straighter and pulled a confidence around her she was a long way from feeling.

'It's true. My father died at the Nazis' hands, and I really am in danger. I was an actress before, in Berlin. I did something that upset Minister Goebbels very badly. If I go back to Germany, I believe he will have me killed too.'

The atmosphere shifted. Both men looked directly at her.

'You were an actress? Were you any good?'

It wasn't the reaction Anna expected, but she nodded. 'Yes, very.'

Hardy looked at Nicholls, who indicated that, this time, he should do the talking.

'That might have upped your value a little. And you're genuinely afraid of going back?'

The conversation was suddenly going where she needed it to.

Anna did her best not to sound desperate. 'Yes. Goebbels wasn't a good enemy to make.'

Hardy pulled out a pack of cigarettes. He was about to offer her one until he glanced at Nicholls' rigidly set face. 'No, I don't imagine he was. But a connection to him couldn't hurt you over here, not if it's used right. Let's try this again. How much do you know about Kuhn and this fascist organisation he's fronting, the German American Bund? What has Gellner told you about it?'

'The answer is still nothing. I met Frank Gellner at a dance four months ago.' Anna stopped; she realised Nicholls was checking his notes. 'But you already knew that: whoever grabbed me called me Gellner's girl – you've been watching me.' The thought of that made her shake, but she made sure they didn't see. 'Well, whatever is in your folder, I had no idea Frank was involved in politics of any kind, except maybe at local neighbourhood level, sorting out community meetings. And I didn't know I was attending a Nazi rally. As stupid as it sounds, I thought I was going to the launch of a new beer.'

Nicholls scribbled something in the file as Hardy continued. 'Say that's true, and you're not one of the faithful, why did Gellner take you with him tonight?'

Anna rubbed at her aching temple. 'I wish I knew. I think he was trying to share it with me, because it was special to him. He presented his work – pulling the *new brotherhood* together, as he called it – as if it was a gift; as though I would be proud of him.'

Hardy believed her – she could see it in the softening round his jaw.

Unfortunately, so could Nicholls. 'Good. And that is exactly how you will behave the next time you see him.'

'What do you mean?' The hair rose on Anna's arms as if a chill wind had blown in. 'I don't want to see Frank again; I don't want anything to do with him at all.'

When Nicholls replied, his self-assurance was terrifying.

'I want Frank, so forgive me if I don't care what you want. Your boyfriend is one of Kuhn's most trusted lieutenants; he's the one who set up this pack of stormtroopers Kuhn stomps round with. He's also your way into the Bund, and being able to get inside knowledge of the Bund is the only reason you matter to us. So, yes, we will ask you to see him on the same terms as before, and you will do it. Or you won't, but you know the penalty for that.'

He raised a hand as Anna tried to speak. 'Stop. This isn't a negotiation. Kuhn and his followers aren't playing dress-up. What do you think Hitler is doing, with his speeches and his purges and his all new Aryan Germany, Fräulein Brandt? Let me spell it out for you: he's rearming. Your country is tearing up all the treaties that were meant to hold it in check after the last war and it's got a new one in its sights. We know there are already German spies here; God knows how much military information they've already got their hands on. Which means every man, and every woman, who joins the Bund and snaps their arm up for the Führer is a threat to America. We don't like those. If I had my way, we would burn down every sauerkraut-stinking street on the East Side and smoke you all out. Unfortunately, that's not allowed yet. What we can do, however, is make Germans like you – with no right to be here and very poorly chosen friends – into our own. Crush the cockroaches from inside the nest.'

Anna's increasingly white face finally registered with Hardy. He shifted uncomfortably and waved a hand at his partner. 'All right, back up. Can't you tell her what we need without all the politics? It's not like she's getting out of here unless she agrees.'

Nicholls grimaced at the interruption and stood up. 'I'll stop caring about politics when you wise up and dump the Kraut friends you pretend you don't have, or, better still, start using them properly.' He turned back to Anna as Hardy swore. 'We're going to drop you back now, to the police station on 77th that's holding the rest of the scum. Tomorrow, when Frank comes looking for you, all puffed up against the *evil police* who snatched you away, you will be tearful and loving. And so incensed by your treatment, you will become the Bund's most fervent supporter. You can do that, can't you? You're a good enough actress?'

Anna nodded; at that moment there was nothing else she could do. She had no intention of obeying him.

Nicholls watched her from the door. 'Don't think you can fool us. You're going to do this, and we have eyes on you to make sure. You report here, to this office, once a fortnight. How you cover your movements is your problem, not ours – if you get caught out by the other side, we'll deny all knowledge of you. Bring us something each time you come; make it something valuable. Or find yourself on a ship. It's your choice.'

'Wait.'

Even as the word came out of her mouth, Anna had no idea what she was going to say. All she knew was that, if she really had to go back to Frank, she had to try and claw something back.

'I need something in return.'

Nicholls stared at her. 'Besides us not throwing you onto the next ship?'

Anna ignored him and focused on Hardy instead. The whole interview had been about what they wanted, and what they demanded. Well, she wanted something too. The FBI – who she had no doubt Hardy and Nicholls belonged to – could make life very hard for her, she was in no doubt about that, but they could also bring her closer to finding Franzi than searching the adverts for a dubious private detective, or hoping one of Frank's unknown contacts would come through.

Anna took a moment to moisten her dry lips, and to let her heart still, and then she slipped on her most confident face.

'There's a couple I need to track down. They sailed from Berlin to America around about July last year, with a baby. I need to find them. You could help me do that.'

'Well, aren't you the brave spark?' Nicholls paused, his hand on the door. 'Okay, just for argument's sake, say we were to play along, do you have any other details about them, for example where in America they might have arrived? And are you going to tell us what your interest in them is?'

If I say I'm looking for my baby, I'm handing them another card.

Anna kept her eyes on Hardy. Hearing Nicholls' sneer was bad enough; she didn't need to see it. 'No, I'm not. And I don't know where they were headed. But I do have a name.'

His laugh was as cruel as his sneer. 'Well, good luck with that. We're done; I've no time for games.' Nicholls stalked out, calling for his partner to follow.

Hardy, however, hesitated.

'What is it?' He took his notebook out. 'The name?'

'Bailey.' Anna could barely breathe as she said it.

Hardy made a note; he didn't ask her anything else. 'I'm making no promises. Don't make the mistake of thinking I'm your friend.'

He left without giving her a chance to reply; Anna couldn't have formed one if he had.

The police officer who drove her back to Yorkville was politer than the one who had bundled her away from the Casino, although the windows of the vehicle he led her to were as darkly tinted. When they reached the station, she was taken in through a back door, and ushered out, very visibly, through the front.

It's your choice.

It wasn't – all three of them knew that.

Anna walked the dozen blocks back to the boarding house trying to envisage a world in which she could smile lovingly at Frank Gellner. In which she could stand without screaming in a room where men chanted *Sieg Heil*. It was impossible to imagine. But being forced onto a boat back to Germany wasn't. Being picked up in Berlin as some kind of traitor to her homeland wasn't. Or standing in front of Goebbels and watching his cruel smile and knowing she was caught. Staying with Frank, becoming a loyal follower of the Bund wasn't what any reasonable person would have considered a choice, but Anna knew she had crossed into a world where *reasonable* didn't hold any weight any more. What mattered was staying in America; what mattered was finding Franzi.

If there was even the remotest chance that doing the FBI's bidding could lead to her baby, staying with Frank was a detail, a bargain she would have to live with. She could do it: she was an actress – what was this if not another role? She could do it, until she had what she wanted, and then she would shake off the watchers and find her way out.

'That place is a swamp. Getting evidence of the filth that's peddled there is your best chance yet to prove you've some real value – don't waste it.'

Nicholls hadn't needed to tack any threat onto that: Anna already understood those all too well.

Anna fiddled with her camera as if she was checking the light. She still hadn't managed to swallow her revulsion long enough to take one shot.

Nicholls would have used up a dozen rolls by now, he'd be so desperate to catch even the slightest shred of evidence.

It wasn't as if she was short of targets. From the veranda of the clubhouse where she was sitting – under a sign which read *Ein Volk, Ein Reich, Ein Führer* in a gothic script – Anna had an excellent view across the central spaces of the 180 acres Frank had boasted made up Camp Siegfried.

She could see the parade ground, where rows of little boys in white shirts and black shorts were valiantly learning to march. She could see the teenagers in brown shorts by the lake, strapping on heavy backpacks, ready to set off on a twenty-mile hike. And the swastikas which fluttered above the chalet-style holiday homes and marched down streets named after Hitler and Göring. And the *Ordnungsdienst* or OD, the Bund's version of Germany's stormtroopers, patrolling the sports field, the jagged silver flashes on their uniforms sparkling in the sun.

Whichever way Anna looked, all she could see was the faithful. And they were all she could hear. The '*Horst-Wessel-Lied*' – the anthem of the National Socialist Party – blared out at regular intervals from the speakers dotted all over the camp. Even the smallest children chanted slogans as they drilled, praising Germany for picking up the struggle and pledging their hearts to the Fatherland. Frank said the noise was joyful; it was warlike and repulsive.

Anna shuddered as another grey-shirted OD troop marched past – their voices raised in an anthem about Jewish blood dripping from German knives – and had to pretend a bee had buzzed too close.

How can this possibly be America?

Camp Siegfried wasn't in a field outside Munich or Berlin, it was in Yaphank, a sleepy suburban town a two-hour train ride from New York. That such a place could exist so close to the city – that such a place could exist in America at all – was preposterous. Or 'a triumph', if she listened to Frank. Which was – according to the FBI agents – what she had to do with a rapt ear and a pretty smile. Following that order had proved the hardest performance of her life, and she had now had to give it many times.

When Anna had done as she was directed and committed herself to the Bund, Frank had been so delighted, he had finally grown talkative. His love for the Bund, for the National Socialist cause, was an obsession. When Anna, carefully suppressing her disgust, asked him why he hadn't told her earlier about his involvement, he had explained about all the attempts to create a viable German American National Socialist movement that had fallen victim to in-fighting before Kuhn took up the reins, and about the oath of secrecy that they had sworn to Kuhn to keep everything under wraps until the Bund was unveiled. He spoke about the new leader as if he were a messiah, and assumed she felt the same. Nothing about Frank was closed anymore, and Anna hated every inch of the man he had revealed. No matter how hard she tried not to do it and scratch at the wound, all Frank's new openness did was point up how poorly he compared to Eddy. There were nights when Anna would have forgiven Eddy anything for another hour with a man who was caring and honest, not one who was driven by dreams that repulsed her.

Now that nothing was secret, Frank stopped taking her to dances or the cinema, although he would countenance trips to the *Deutsches Kino* in the Casino to watch German films. His main mission on their now far too frequent dates was to educate Anna in all aspects of the Bund, an undertaking he delivered in a series of lectures that did not require comments or questions and replaced all other conversation.

Anna dreaded their meetings but was glad all he seemed to want her to be was an audience. The lectures were tedious, their subject matter repugnant, but dancing would have meant an intimacy she would have struggled not to shrink from, despite her acting skills. She survived her indoctrination by treating the sessions as hunting grounds for the information she needed to appease her new bosses, and get one step closer to Franzi. So, when Frank had begun extolling the wonders of the youth camps as soon as they boarded the specially chartered train from Penn Station taking Bund leaders and their wives and girlfriends to Camp Siegfried for the weekend, Anna had given him her most encouraging smile.

'This is where we will raise the future leaders of America. Here at Camp Siegfried and at Camp Hindenburg in Wisconsin, and Camp Nordland in New Jersey. And those three are just the start. Before this decade is done, we will have a camp in every state, and every Aryan child with German blood will spend their summers in one. They will swear allegiance to the Fatherland and we will teach them the skills they need to prepare for *Der Tag* – the day when we must stand and fight the Jews, and the communists, determined to infect America with their poison. That battle is coming, Anna, and it is a battle we will win. All of us fighting together as soldiers in the only cause that matters.'

Der Tag: the Day. It was the first time Anna had heard the expression. Once inside the camp, however, the shorthand for the conflict the Bund was actively preparing for was repeated everywhere. Frank's rhetoric on the train, describing the 'joyous day of reckoning', had run on and on, with a zeal that was worthy of Goebbels. With Nicholls' voice in her ear, Anna had told Frank that, although it was hard not to choke on the Minister's name. Frank had clasped her hand so fervently, she thought he would crush it. Her one consolation was that the train was too public for him to kiss her, although he whispered how much he wanted to. That

Anna was still managing to hold him – mostly – at arm's-length was the main reason she could get through the days.

Keeping him at a distance hadn't been easy. Now that she was a 'loyal Bund member', Frank had become far more physically attentive. Anna had to stand on her honour and remind him more than once of the value the Party put on the purity of its women. When Frank had called at the boarding house the day after the arrests at the Casino – arrests he had rather skilfully avoided – he had been so desperate to hold her, Anna thought she might have to feign her first off-stage fainting fit. The thought of his hands on her body was obscene. Frau Möller, however, wouldn't let him past the front door. And the landlady wouldn't let Anna stay longer than the two days she grudgingly gave her to make new arrangements. Her dismissal had been coldly direct.

'You have disappointed me, or duped me. I am not sure which. But I won't have Nazis under my roof.'

Anna couldn't explain or argue; she couldn't look Frau Möller in the eye. Frank, to her horror, had threatened the landlady and told her it was time for her to learn about loyalty and pick the right side. He had also risen to the role of her protector with an enthusiasm Anna had to pretend was delightful. He had found her a new home the same afternoon: a room in a house on 87th overlooking a pretty park that bordered the river. A house which looked identical to the one Anna had left, except it was festooned with photographs of Hitler and filled with Bund members and felt like a trap.

Unlike her, Hardy and Nicholls had been delighted at the move. It was the only time in the five visits she had made to the headquarters in Foley Square before leaving for the camp when Nicholls' face had come alive.

Anna knew what they wanted from her – they told her every time she passed them the snippets of gossip they already knew. Lists of who in the Bund was travelling backward and forward between

Hamburg and New York. Names of the members who were also agents of *Abwehr* – the German military intelligence service. Which individuals were masquerading as businessmen and intending to steal blueprints for aircraft carriers and bomber planes. On one visit they showed her matchbooks picked up in the nightclubs on 86th. They insisted that the indecipherable red marks, which, to her eyes, could have been wine or lipstick stains, were in fact code names she had to find out how to crack. That was the day Anna had called the men's demands ridiculous. Nicholls had put her into a car and driven her to the docks. She didn't use that word again.

'I want more involvement. I want a real role. Will you help me find it?'

Frank had beamed when she'd asked him, and talked about their strength as the 'perfect Bund partnership'. He promised he would help, although he was quite clear on the limits.

'Women are permitted into the Bund to support the men, and serve as role models for other women's domestic behaviour. They cannot, of course, hold leadership positions or wield authority.'

He had said the last part as if the idea was laughable. Anna hadn't reacted; not reacting had become her most valuable skill.

'But we can be secretaries, can't we? I've done that type of work before. And, back in Berlin, I studied photography. I could take pictures when the *Bundesführer* is speaking, or at other events. Pictures that would help spread our successes.'

Lying about her past was a gamble – she could hardly admit that she had learned basic camera and typing skills to make some of her earlier acting roles look more plausible. Compared to the risks the FBI was demanding she take, however, it barely made the scale. Frank had asked her very general questions about her life before America, and had accepted the sketchy portrait she had offered him of days lived quietly in Berlin. No one else – apart from Frau Berger, who now belonged to a different world – knew anything about Anna at all. And her hastily cobbled-together plan had worked, far better than she had believed it would when she threw the suggestion out.

Frank was valued by the Bund, therefore Anna was too. In May, a week after Nicholls had taken her to the pier and threatened to put her straight on a ship, Anna had become one of the small team of secretaries Kuhn employed to make his office look powerful. The other two women treated Kuhn as if he was a god; Anna studied how they behaved towards him the way she had once studied characters in a script, and flattered him even better than they did. More and more of his work ended up in her tray. So far it had been mainly speeches she was instructed to type, and forbidden to correct. But, over the last week or two, letters to other Bund officials had started to appear, letters that mentioned names and hinted at operations that involved travel to Germany. And he had called her twice into meetings to take minutes, praising her diligence at not missing a word.

Her new job meant that Hardy and Nicholls were marginally less disappointed, and Anna was hopeful. She began to convince herself that, in a little while, if she managed to cement Kuhn's growing trust in her, she might be able to – gently – disentangle herself from Frank without losing her position. She would still be stuck at the heart of an organisation that disgusted her, but she would be one personal step back. It was a small ray of light and it was surely a bargaining chip to keep pressing Hardy with to help her search for the Baileys.

She was hopeful, but she was also exhausted. Worn out from pretending that this twisted world felt right to her. That its prejudices and hatreds didn't sicken her through to her soul. Worn out from the need to balance keeping Frank's interest with her desperation not to be touched by him, by maintaining the 'virtue' they had both agreed mattered. From enduring his kisses when he insisted on 'a proper goodnight' and she couldn't avoid them without arousing his suspicion. She couldn't bathe enough some days to make her skin clean.

'Where are you? You're miles away.'

Anna jumped. Frank had returned from the parade ground while she was lost in her thoughts. He was leaning over her, uncomfortably close, his shadow blocking out the last lingering rays of the sun.

She collected herself and smiled. 'It's the heat. I've been sitting out in it too long; it's made me sleepy. Is your training session done? Is it time to dress for dinner?'

He didn't answer. There was something odd about his expression that she couldn't place, something uncharacteristically furtive. As she squinted at him, he stepped back.

'Could you stand up for me, Anna. Please.'

She did as he asked – it was usually easier to do what was asked and buy time. At least on her feet she could create a space and see past him. There was a crowd gathered on the veranda that hadn't been there before. Anna could see Kuhn among them, and a number of his favoured lieutenants. Some of the wives and girlfriends were dotted among the watching men, and there were OD members as well as the higher ranks, ranged along the steps and the handrails. They were all looking in her direction, but the sun's position meant she couldn't see if anyone was smiling.

What if they know. Oh dear God, what if they know. What if someone has been following me?

She stuck her hands in her skirt pockets and tried to look unconcerned.

I need a cover. What if I was to say that the FBI were trying to help me locate my mother?

It was a ludicrous idea, but her empty brain couldn't land on another.

'Didn't you hear me?'

Frank's voice sounded anxious, which made no sense because Frank never sounded anxious.

'Don't tell me I've got this wrong, not with everyone watching. Let me do it again. Let me do it properly this time, so there's no mistaking.'

Anna stared at him. He was paler than she had ever seen him and seemed to be crouching.

'Frank, what are you doing?'

He wasn't crouching. He was down on one knee, his hand stretched out, his trembling fingers clutching a diamond.

'Now she is looking, so here goes. Anna Brandt, will you marry me? Will you do me the honour of being my wife?'

The assembled crowd began to cheer and gave him his answer.

CHAPTER NINE

Yorkville, April 1938

The envelope was onionskin thin. Anna could see the sharp lines of Frank's handwriting and the black imprint of the *Inspected By* stamp through it. She closed the front door and counted to three. Frau Meyer appeared exactly on cue.

'Another letter, Fräulein Brandt. He writes with such regularity, and yet you said you never reply. The poor man must be growing desperate.'

Anna took off her hat and smoothed her hair, trailing her fingers over her eyes and blinking rapidly as she did so.

Frau Meyer was immediately all fluttering hands and contrition. 'Oh my poor girl, now I've gone and upset you. Shall I deal with it? Shall I spare you the pain?'

Anna nodded and sniffed and followed Frau Meyer into the parlour. She didn't speak until the envelope was safely consigned to the flames.

'You know I would write to him if I could. It tears my heart to think of him locked up in that terrible place without a word of comfort. But the *Bundesführer* was clear: Frank could be in the FBI's pay by now; no one can have contact with him.' She sniffed loudly as the landlady grimaced. 'I know, I know. I find it as impossible to believe as you do. But we can't be sure what pressure they put on him and what they might have promised – or threatened. The *Bundesführer* hates this as much as the rest of us – Frank was his protégé and his right-hand man – but if he can break their bond for the sake of the cause, how can I refuse to?'

'Will you make this sacrifice, Fräulein Brandt? Will you put aside your own happiness for the greater good?'

Kuhn's response last summer when Frank was sentenced to three years' imprisonment in Rikers Island couldn't have gone better if she had scripted it herself. Agreeing she could had been Anna's easiest performance in months.

Frau Meyer wiped her hands on her apron and patted Anna's arm. 'You are an example to us all, my dear. A true believer. Go and rest now before dinner; I'll send Trudi up with some of my coffee cake.'

Anna held her breath until she was safely inside her room. Frau Meyer adored Frank, which was why he had chosen her as Anna's landlady; now she viewed him as a martyr and his conviction as a travesty. Anna couldn't afford a slip in front of her.

What would she say if she knew he was innocent? If she found out it was me who put him in there?

There was a knock on the door; the maid appeared, balancing a plate of cake and a balloon-shaped glass too full of brandy. 'The mistress thought you might need it.'

The girl almost bobbed a curtsey as she backed out. It was how everyone treated Anna these days, with deference, as if her *sacrifice* had made her some kind of heroine. It was almost laughable.

Anna ignored the drink and carried the cake over to the window. The April skies had been leaden all day and the East River was little more than an inky shape, visible in patches where the beam from the lighthouse on Welfare Island raked across it. Rikers Island was somewhere out there in the darkness, where the river curved out past the Bronx.

Anna shivered despite the room's warmth. No one had anything good to say about conditions at the prison complex. One of Kuhn's OD guards – one of the many who had spent time there for offences Anna didn't care to know about – had told her that so much rubbish had been dumped on the island over the years that phosphorescent fires regularly flared up all over the hillsides. He had described the phenomena as strangely beautiful, 'like a forest of fireflies'. She wondered if Frank, after ten months' incarceration, found the sight lovely or hellish.

I hope he's not suffering, no more than he will from being locked up.

She meant it. She didn't cherish the thought of him being trapped in such a desperate place. She rarely, however, allowed herself to feel guilty any more that he was. If the future had played out in the way Frank had drawn it, she would have been the one cornered and broken. She wasn't going to let that happen: she had given away enough of herself to men who had decided her life was their plaything. She would do whatever it took to survive the nightmare she was caught in, but she wouldn't give them her soul.

'Being his girlfriend was bad enough, but I won't do this. I won't marry him; I won't sleep with him. I'll walk away first. Come after me, send me back, I don't care. There are lines I won't cross, whatever the consequences. If you want any more out of me, you have to make this right.'

If Anna had spoken to Hardy and Nicholls that bluntly in the months immediately after they had – in their words – recruited her and Frank had proposed, she would have been on a ship the next day. But by March 1937 – when Frank was pushing for a wedding date and her nerves were shredded from stalling – Anna was, finally, holding a few cards of her own. Her position at the centre of Kuhn's circle was assured. The other secretaries were gone: she was the one sat by Kuhn's side and scribing his secrets. And pouring them straight into the FBI's hands.

What she brought them now was valuable – although she no longer saw the agents in person every two weeks, Anna had delivered enough material directly to them to see how eagerly they consumed it. Her information was no longer snippets of gossip and lists snatched without context; it had a shape.

'These pamphlets were all printed by *Bodung-Verlag*, in Erfurt in Germany. Kuhn was beside himself with delight when the shipment came in: *VB* is Goebbels' favourite publisher and he has a direct hand in the messaging they put out. This lot were smuggled into America on the cruise lines from Hamburg and there's more coming in. What they say will be repeated in every Bund newspaper and pamphlet. Every member will be encouraged to memorise and spread their words.'

The agents' eyes had lit up when she presented them with a bag stuffed with examples of the most virulently antisemitic literature she had ever seen, and the names of the next cohort of carriers. It was a proven link between the Bund and the Party's propaganda machine in Germany, the first one Anna had managed to uncover. The subsequent arrests had stemmed the flow of hatred at least for a while.

Spurred on by that success, Anna had taken a bigger risk than stealing pamphlets or learning lists of names. Hardy and Nicholls loathed the Bund, but they still talked about the organisation as if they were incapable of mobilising on a large scale. The next document she brought them changed that way of thinking.

'It's a copy of the map the Bund intends to use to capture New York on *Der Tag*.'

It was clear from their faces that none of their other informers had made them aware of the term. Anna had to explain it twice before they believed such a plan to take over America could exist.

The map hadn't been easy to obtain. Kuhn was paranoid about its existence leaking out and he counted the copies in and out of the safe in his office whenever they were used. Anna couldn't risk trying to photograph them: she had had to memorise the details in sections instead. It had taken her three weeks to produce the finished article. The *Der Tag* map divided New York into twenty-one districts, and plotted the position of every key location – including police stations, federal buildings and telegraph offices. It was annotated with the number of the armed militia units assigned to subduing each area of the city, and the percentage of trained snipers each counted among their ranks. When Anna had told Hardy and Nicholls that the next stage of the plan was to amass detailed information on every communist and Jew in every sector, and the value of their assets so the Bund knew who to seize first, the two men had turned pale.

It was the third piece of information, however, that had really shaken them both. That made Anna realise she finally had enough power to start bargaining.

'The Bund know about the Senate Committee that's being set up, the one that's going to investigate them for being *un-American*. They're going to target the senators involved – Kuhn wasn't specific how, but you've seen their armed capability. And they are going to change their tactics to make themselves look less like outsiders and more attractive to non-German Americans. They are expecting new recruits to come flocking.'

For the first time in the eleven months she had worked for them – even more so than when they had seen the *Der Tag* map – the agents' mouths had fallen open.

Anna had seized her moment before they could recover their composure, and made it clear what she wouldn't do with Frank.

'What do you mean, *you have to make this right?* What do you expect us to do? We're not the mob; we're not going to drive past his favourite coffee shop and shoot him.'

Nicholls had pulled himself up as square as ever, but then Hardy had told him to shut up and listen, insisting there were things no woman should be asked to do no matter where she came from. Anna could feel him, at least, slipping onto her hook. As for Nicholls: that his first position was murder had shocked her more than she was prepared to show. It had also given her negotiating room.

'That's not what I'm asking. I don't want Frank dead. But surely you could find a crime he could conceivably have done and get him arrested? See to it that he's sent down? That would get him away from me, and make him a liability, which will ensure he can't come back. Kuhn won't want someone close to him who's got himself caught.'

'All right, Lady Macbeth. What if Kuhn clears you both out? Cans you as well as Frank? What use are you then?'

Anna had answered Hardy with a certainty she knew she had no right to feel. 'He won't. He trusts me. I'll separate myself from Frank; I'll make it look like I'm putting the cause first. Kuhn will buy it, I promise.'

Kuhn had. More to her surprise, Hardy had too, and he had persuaded Nicholls. Within a week of their meeting, Frank was arrested and charged with the savage beating of a Jewish shopkeeper in Queens. He was refused bail, and visitors. When he came to trial two months later, witnesses appeared who swore that they had seen the whole horrible incident. And swore that they had been approached by the defendant in a bar the same night where he had tried – drunkenly they had to admit, but very determinedly – to recruit them for an American branch of the German Gestapo that he 'would soon be in charge of, on the orders of Hitler himself'. Frank had sat in the dock white-faced. Anna had spent each day of the trial weeping prettily into her handkerchief. When he was sentenced to three years' imprisonment, she sank to the floor. Then, the next day, she had gone back to her desk, pale but resolute. Kuhn had stood up and applauded. She had kept her position; she was more trusted than ever. And she had kept on feeding the agents information ever since.

Which is why they will have to agree to my next demand.

Anna knew the days of dismissing Kuhn and his followers as buffoons were long gone. Never mind that the FBI now knew the extent of the Bund's ambition, the shifts on the world's stage were too big to ignore a Nazi threat on home soil. Hitler's annexation of Austria in March and his hostile stance towards Czechoslovakia had made the international mood nervous. Nicholls and Hardy were obsessed with the threat to America's national security. And – as German Americans worried about a war America might fight on 'the wrong side' – the Bund's membership was rising, especially across the country's northern cities. Kuhn now claimed tens, potentially hundreds, of thousands of followers; Anna could report no evidence to disprove that.

Its mission to sweep the country free of communists and Jews was also gathering momentum – Anna had seen, and copied, *Der Tag* maps for Chicago and Detroit and had no doubt there were more. Thousands of people were attending weekly rallies in Yorkville, and beyond the neighbourhood's borders as the Bund spread its web through New York. By spring 1938, there were groups established across the city, in locations – and among social classes – as far apart as Park Avenue and Brooklyn. Most weekends saw members marching unmolested, flanked by the OD and waving swastikas. Chanting Kuhn's latest slogan – 'a better America is our goal'. Handing out German American Bund Supporter buttons as if they were candy to every blonde-haired child they passed. The hostile newspaper articles reporting the marches shifted from mockery to discomfort, and then to fear.

The Bund was being taken seriously, and so was Anna. There were no more threats from Nicholls. There was some level of protection. Since Frank's arrest – and the resulting heightened paranoia of everyone in the Bund – she was no longer required to go to Foley Square unless specifically requested. She dropped her information instead at a post office on 80th, via a designated clerk whose shifts she had memorised. In her more positive moments, Anna was able to convince herself that she was doing a valuable job; that she was making the country she had chosen to live in safer for the ordinary people, including her daughter, who deserved to live in it free from the monsters who had ruined her homeland. And then the weight of it – the lying and the fear of discovery and the revulsion she was daily forced to swallow – came back and crushed her. She couldn't go on, month after month, spending her life with the very people whose beliefs she had fled from. She couldn't go on nodding at their hateful views.

I've done what they wanted. I've delivered. Now it's time they did the same. Permanent residency and a promise of an end to this, or I'm gone.

Anna watched the lighthouse beam sweep across the black water. Tomorrow she would go to the FBI offices, and present her handlers with her ultimatum. She had no idea what *gone* could mean. She could only pray they would agree to what she wanted before she had to get that far.

Hardy had shaken his head as if he was disappointed. Nicholls had called her arrogant; he had laughed. Worse he had countered with a task she had never dreamed he would ask. Anna dropped onto a bench at the edge of the square. She didn't check her surroundings; she no longer cared if she was being followed. Being exposed as an informer by the Bund seemed suddenly preferable to the path she had agreed to follow.

'You are very full of yourself today, *Fräulein*. Demanding a meeting; telling *us* what *we* need to do. As if getting Frank out of your hair wasn't concession enough.'

There hadn't been a trace of warmth in Nicholls' voice. Anna had refused to let him intimidate her; she had stood her ground, hoping that, once again, Hardy might be more persuadable.

Which was stupid – he might not be as bad as his partner, but he's been clear enough that he wasn't my friend. I should have walked away. Got on a bus and got out of New York. Called their bluff and run.

A chill wind plucked at her fingers and face – April had so far shown no signs of spring. Anna stayed slumped on the bench; the thought of returning to Yorkville drained her. And Nicholls had stamped on the thought of going anywhere else.

'I told you: we have eyes everywhere. Wherever you run, we'll find you. I'd make it my business to see that we did.'

She believed him.

'What do I need to do? To get my permit? To get a route out of this?'

She had fallen into their hands as completely as she had two years ago. Nicholl's smile had told her that.

'You take a trip.'

He had played with her, stringing the details out. Anna could have the citizenship she craved, she could have an agreed date when her work for them would end. She could, he swore, 'absolutely trust him on that'. All she had to do to secure her release was go back to Germany. From the surprise on Hardy's face, it was clear that this was the first time he had heard the plan. He didn't, however, respond to her horrified gasp. He didn't do or say anything at all.

'You'll be there for ten days, that's all. Add a week or thereabouts on the ship either way and you'll be back in less than a month. And that's the beauty of it: you will be back.'

Anna had looked frantically at Hardy; he had ignored her. So she had got up, and she had got as far as the door. And that was when Nicholls had promised they would find her.

I have to stop letting them be a unit. I have to separate Hardy out.

'Can't you stop this? You're better than him, you're kinder; I know it. You helped me with Frank, you understand about me being Jewish. You took the name from me. Can't you stop this?'

Fear had made her careless. She saw Hardy's face tighten, saw Nicholls' eyes darken with fury, but it was too late to snatch the words back.

'What name? Hardy, what is she talking about? Have you been doing deals on the side?'

'Of course not, what do you take me for? But I thought that, if we put her in real danger – like we're doing now – we might owe her something more than a visa. I took the name of that couple she was on about. I didn't follow up, it's no big deal.'

Hardy kept his voice far lighter than Nicholls, but his tone didn't fool Anna.

He's afraid. He doesn't want to be marked out as a risk, or a traitor. I've ruined any chance of him helping me now.

Hardy's next words to her proved that.

'You're making too much fuss. What we need you to do isn't a difficult job. We're not parachuting you into the middle of the Reichschancellery. You'll be a nursemaid, accompanying one of the youth groups your boys keep sending over to the Fatherland to play with their Nazi compadres.'

'Which is a practice, by the way, you seem to have forgotten to mention in your reports. I'm still trying to decide if that was deliberate.'

Hardy's jaw had tightened at Nicholls' interruption.

'I didn't know about the youth trips. I haven't seen those directives.'

It was the truth, but it didn't matter. Anna knew she had lost Hardy, and, with him, the spark of hope that had sent her with such misplaced confidence into the meeting. It was hard not to crumple as Nicholls continued.

'Or perhaps you're not as thorough as you would have us believe, or not so far inside the inner circle. That, however, is for later. What matters now is getting you out with the next group, which our information says is leaving the week after next. Our other – very thorough – sources suggest Hitler might meet with this one, which is where you come in. I know you think your contribution is valu-able, but, you see, I don't. All we've really had is one connection between the Bund and their German masters – a connection we would have made ourselves sooner or later – a few nasty leaflets and a map that – let's be honest – you could have faked. It's hardly earth-shattering. But these trips are something else – maybe a cover for espionage-planning meetings – so you're going. And you're going to work out who's driving the contacts between Germany and here, and what their aims are, and bring back proof. Do that, and maybe I won't think you're useless after all.'

Anna knew the information she had already passed over was more valuable than Nicholls was pretending, but it was pointless to argue. She had tried instead to persuade them that the plan was impossible, that she would not be able to join the sailing at such short notice. That objection was dismissed as 'your problem, not ours'. Then she had pointed out that Hitler had issued statements denying any direct involvement with, or endorsement of, the German American Bund, so there was likely nothing to the visit but some form of cultural exchange. Nicholls had responded to that as if she was stupid.

'What did you expect him to do other than deny they are linked? The Bund aren't big enough to act as Adolf's army here; the United States government hasn't formally said that they're actively hostile to his landgrabs and his warmongering. Adolf doesn't know if we are going to be friend or foe – although I'd be happy to tell him – so he needs to keep everyone sweet while he gets his battle plans ready. No doubt it's a different story in private, a real love-in between him and Führer Junior.' He paused.

Not knowing what to say, Anna had said nothing.

'Oh, you don't know? Another gap, then, in your knowledge. There seems to be quite a few of them today.'

'Even if all that's true, I can't go back; I've told you why.'

It was a pointless, last-ditch plea for sympathy, and directed at Hardy, who wouldn't meet her eyes.

Nicholls simply laughed. 'Of course, I forgot. Your broken-romance with Goebbels. It stands to reason: he's not had much to do these last three years, so he'll have obviously spent his time brooding about you. Grow up. You were never that important. If you're worried, dye your hair, eat a carton of cinnamon rolls every day for the next week and get fat. He won't know you anymore either way.'

Three years. Nicholls' assessment was crude, but that didn't mean it was wrong. Three years was a long time: why would anyone in Germany still remember her, much less a man preoccupied with persuading the world he possessed its most eloquent voice?

'What we're asking really isn't that bad. We've seen the travel plans. It's two days in Berlin, that's all. The rest of the time you'll be buried out in the countryside. What's two days against the promise of a permanent life here, and an end to work we know is wearing you down?'

Hardy was finally looking at her; his tone was as kind as it could be. Anna knew he didn't dare step in any further, that it would be wrong of her to ask him again for help.

She gave in. She left with her instructions, convincing herself she could do it. And then the enormity of what she had agreed to sank in, and she had stumbled onto the bench without a clue how to get through the days that came next. She needed not to think, or she would drive herself crazy with everything that could go wrong. She needed a distraction, until she could breathe and make a plan that wouldn't sink her.

Go to the cinema. Lose yourself in a film.

It had been her solution to her problems in a previous life – perhaps that was why it had come to her now. She hadn't been to the cinema since the beginning of her courtship with Frank; she hadn't given that world any thought. The Bund didn't approve of American films and she couldn't face the ones they showed at the *Deutsches Kino.* Their programmes tended to be retrospectives, not new releases, and, in the early days of her arrival at least, she had been concerned that she would spot Marika and make a fool of herself.

The wind had begun blowing hard; it was too cold to linger. Anna got up, glad to have made some kind of decision that would at least fill in the next couple of hours. If she caught the subway, she could be in Times Square in twenty minutes – there would be a cinema there she could sit quietly in. It had been years since she had been anywhere close to 42nd Street; it had been too long since she had been anywhere but the confines of German Yorkville and Foley Square. Anna had no idea what the latest releases were, something that would have been unthinkable five years ago. She had no real idea who the latest celluloid gods were either, with the exception of Clark Gable, who even Frau Meyer was prepared to concede was 'rather dashing'.

I wonder if Marika ever made a career for herself here.

The thought brought her to a stop at the top of the steps leading up from the subway. It didn't seem likely. Anna couldn't imagine that Hollywood had been any more receptive to unknown German actresses than Broadway was. She hadn't once considered what might have become of Marika's career after she reached America – or Eddy's. She had been too busy being hurt. But surely it couldn't have come to anything?

Somebody jostled her, somebody else cursed. Anna moved away from the early-evening crush and headed for the corner dominated by the Paramount Theatre's twenty-nine storeys. The more she thought about it, the more impossible it seemed that Marika could have had any more luck reviving her career than Anna had. The Yorkville *Kino* was covered with posters of Germany's top actresses – Henny Porten, Zarah Leander, Lil Dagover – if there was a new German star in America, wouldn't someone have mentioned her?

Anna stopped in front of the Paramount's arched entrance. It was plastered with posters for the upcoming premiere of *Fools for Scandal* and blow-ups of the film's leading lady, Carole Lombard, who had been one of Marika's heroines. The rest of the windows fanning out on the sides showcased a series of smaller movie-star photographs. Anna walked past them, pretending she was picking out the older idols she recognised, but really searching for a picture of Marika. There wasn't one. At least not with the right name. There was, however, a face that Anna knew. A face that made her stop and the world tilt. The hair was darker and more elaborately curled, the contours of the woman's cheeks were slimmer. Everything else was the same.

Anna closed her eyes, opened them slowly; checked the silver-lettered name again. Louise Baker. She stared at the photograph, willing it to be someone else. Its features didn't change.

'Excuse me?' It took a moment for the cashier to look up from her magazine. 'That actress in the picture over there, Louise Baker. Is she famous?'

The woman gazed at Anna as if she was mad. 'Where have you been? Louise Baker is one of Hollywood's hottest tickets – she has been for ages.'

Anna grabbed on to the edge of the booth. The cashier edged back.

'I didn't know. And she's really popular now? Even though she's German?'

The woman put down her magazine. 'German? What are you talking about? Louise Baker is French. Well, she was. She's one of us now, an American. German; as if. Germans talk like they're spitting through a mouthful of gravel. She's got a wonderful voice, all husky. You're the one who sounds foreign. What are you?'

Anna shook her head and stumbled away. She wasn't certain anymore that she knew.

CHAPTER TEN

Germany, April 1938

I must have been out of my mind to think I could do this.

He was three feet away. She could see the weave of his suit – the elegance of those hadn't changed – and smell the musk from his cologne that was as cloying as when he had grabbed hold of her at Bogensee.

Anna clamped her lips shut, convinced Goebbels would recognise the sound of her breathing. She had played every step wrong from the first day to this – one turn now and he would see her; he would be close enough to grab her. One turn and she was finished.

'The Youth Movement trips that we send out to Germany. I want to go on one. The next one. The one that sails for Hamburg in two weeks.'

Nicholls' demands had knocked the wind out of her; Marika's photograph had made her clumsy. Anna had returned to the Bund's headquarters on 85th in a daze and had forgotten to take the care that was normally stamped through everything she did. She hadn't flattered. She hadn't wound her way round a conversation until she could ferret out the nuggets that she needed. She had rushed, and blundered. Kuhn had cleared his office before he answered her.

'You did not knock, Fräulein Brandt.' He waved a hand as she stumbled over an apology. 'No matter. This must be important if it makes you step over our lines. Although I confess, I am surprised.

I have never heard you express any interest in our Youth Movement before, not even when Frank was such a key part of it. And, tell me, how did you know about the sailing? The details of that were not handled here. I do not recall passing you any relevant correspondence.'

He made the enquiry sound casual; Anna wasn't fooled. There was nothing casual about Fritz Kuhn. He slapped backs and pinched cheeks and loved to act the genial host in Yorkville's bars and restaurants. He could be the most charming man in the world when he chose. At his core, however, he was ruthless and he was the undisputed king of his world. That didn't mean, however, that he was content – he was instead paranoid and bitter, and, in the year since Frank's arrest, obsessed with *traitors*. Anyone could be an informer; anyone could be an enemy – as the pressure to wipe the Bund out of existence escalated, he grew convinced more of those he had once trusted were.

In public, Kuhn manipulated the media attacks on him like a master. In private, he obsessed over each hostile word and pulled his circle ever tighter. Anna knew the knife-edge he walked along. She knew no one was exempt from his suspicions. And she knew that the Bund's youth wing was such an easy press target for rousing public distaste that their movements were closely guarded. She had still crashed in with all the finesse of an elephant.

'My landlady, Frau Meyer, mentioned that the son of a friend was travelling with the party, and he had been worried that it might not go because it isn't always possible to find leaders to accompany them. I thought it sounded so wonderful – taking our young people to experience their homeland – that I wanted to help and I got carried away. I am sorry. And I hope that, by telling you this, I haven't got her into trouble.'

Anna didn't care if she had, and there was no time to worry about the lies she might need to tell to wriggle out from this one. All that mattered was wiping that searching look from his face.

To her relief, the luck that had carried her safely past Frank's arrest held. Kuhn dismissed her with a curt, 'I'll look into it.'

When he informed her the next day that one of the female team leaders had a sick mother and would be grateful to be replaced, it was so big a coincidence, Anna assumed Nicholls must have arranged it. She didn't bother to try and check. However it had come about, she had the place on the ship that they wanted, and there wasn't a name on the expedition's list that she knew. That was a small victory, but Anna took some comfort in it: small victories were all she had and they lessened, a little, the enormity of the task that was facing her. No one knowing her meant she could change her appearance without raising eyebrows.

The night before the sailing, she cut off the curls that clustered round the nape of her neck and brushed a bottle of Brownatone dye through her hair until its lights were dulled and its texture roughened. On the day itself, she left the house before anyone else was up. She wore her hair in a straight bob pinned back from her forehead. She left her face make-up-free. She dressed in a shapeless white blouse and a too-long black skirt. She looked severe and dowdy and closer to forty than twenty-eight.

No one knows me; no one will comment. And they won't see me again when this trip is done and I soften back to myself.

She rode the El and the subway to the dock at Hoboken feeling safely invisible. And then she arrived at the pier and there was Kuhn, ready to wave them all off.

'What in God's name have you done to yourself?' His shout turned the whole party round. 'Have you come in disguise?'

Anna wanted to believe the question came from shock and had no deeper meaning, but it still wrong-footed her. She quickly adopted a hurt tone and a hurt look, although her stomach was twisting.

'I wanted to look serious.'

'To impress a bunch of kids? Why? And why do it by making yourself ugly?'

She was saved from answering by the call to board.

As she ran up the gangplank, she heard Kuhn call one of the two male team leaders back. He was still staring up at her when she reached the deck. Whatever Kuhn had said wasn't divulged, but the three other adults kept an immediate distance, and the teenagers – fifteen boys and fifteen girls, all of them blonde and oozing self-confidence – followed suit. It wasn't the start Anna needed, and she did her best to change whatever poor opinion they all had of her as the journey progressed. She led the girls allocated to her in their daily exercise programme with all the verve she could muster. She supervised the discussions of National Socialist policy and suggested suitable topics if they flagged. She mouthed along with the loud rendition of the '*Horst-Wessel-Lied*' which closed the nightly card games and singalongs. None of it worked: the harder she tried, the hollower her efforts seemed. None of the team leaders pulled her up; none of the children were rude, at least not to her face. But no one was warm; no one would let Anna inside the circles she knew she had to be part of.

She spent the crossing living from day to day, trying to salvage her position, refusing to worry about what might be coming in Germany. Even when they left Southampton and began the last part of the journey through the English Channel and across the North Sea, she didn't know how to imagine their arrival without seeing so many dangers they crippled her. And then they arrived in Cuxhaven and the gangplanks were attached, and there were soldiers wearing swastika armbands milling all over the jetty.

'Fräulein Brandt, what are you waiting for? We have a strict timetable to follow.'

The rest of the party had disembarked while she was hovering, her feet refusing to take the first step.

None of this is real. It's all a performance. Eight nights – it's barely a run.

She repositioned her Bund necktie to ensure it was visible over her coat and walked down to join them.

'Forgive me. It has been a while since I was home. Arriving was a little overwhelming.'

Neither Theo – the group's main leader and the man who Kuhn had spoken to – or his deputy, Erich, smiled.

This needs more than vague excuses if I'm going to win anyone round and not give myself away. One more wrong step and all of this crashes.

She waited until the party was assembled in neat lines on the train platform and then she launched her attack.

'I owe you all an apology.'

Theo started to protest as Anna stepped forward. She carried on talking over him.

'I know none of you are impressed with me. That is my fault – I should have been honest with you from the start. I am afraid of the sea. Terribly afraid of it. The crossing was a test of my stamina, and I fear that I failed. I was distracted. I must have seemed lacking in commitment, to our cause, and to you. I hope – now that we are all safe on dry land – you will allow me to redress that.'

She sounded stilted and overly formal, but that was the kind of voice the teenagers were used to, and it had got their attention. One of them – Kristina, the prettiest and most popular of the girls and the one most determined to shine – raised her hand.

'I have a question?'

Anna nodded her to go on, already guessing what was coming.

'Why was the *Bundesführer* shocked when he saw you?'

She shuffled and gave herself a moment before ruefully patting her hair.

'I am a victim of vanity. I had my hair restyled to come on the trip, and it was a disaster. And then I spent too much time trying to fix it, and ran out of time to apply my make-up, or even to bring it. Trust me, Fräulein, I did not plan to look like this. Or to have the *Bundesführer* thinking that I have dropped my high personal standards.' She finished with a shrug and a self-pitying smile.

Theo's stern face didn't soften, but the girls smiled and Frau Dahlman – the other female leader who had been determinedly frosty – made great play of offering Anna a lipstick. Once the girls were won over, the boys followed. By the time the train journey was done, Anna began to believe that her initial mistakes might be salvageable. The teenagers grew chatty, as did Sonja Dahlman. The journey passed without incident.

The little town on the Elbe where they were to be billeted was surrounded by vines, lined by half-timbered houses and pretty enough to have stepped out of an older and softer Germany. Anna's shadows began to recede enough for her to relax her vigilance a little. Admittedly, the mayor who greeted them was wearing a swastika on his arm and lapel, and the teenagers whose families the Americans were twinned with were all in *Hitlerjugend* or *Bund Deutscher Mädel* uniforms. Anna, however, had expected that and didn't falter. She had also expected that the house in which she and Sonja were staying would have a large portrait of Hitler on display in the hallway. She was used to walking past those without flinching.

The time they spent deep in the countryside quickly settled into a rhythm that wasn't, on the surface, as uncomfortable as Anna had feared it might be. She didn't see the children once the daytime activities were done. Sonja was far happier to spend their evenings discussing the endless ins and outs of her love life than Party policy. The days were spent outdoors, hiking and boating. The townspeople were welcoming. Nobody treated her as if she was anything other than she claimed to be. If it hadn't been for the blood-soaked songs the teenagers sang as they marched, or the cards they traded with their new German friends, gloating over the caricatures depicting hook-nosed and monster-shaped Jews, Anna could have convinced herself she was leading a normal scout group. She managed to sleep. She was certain she had managed to fit in.

What continued to evade her, however, was anything that would be of use to Hardy and Nicholls.

No one discussed links between the Bund and the National Socialist Party, at least not in Anna's hearing. When she tried to find out the itinerary for the visit to Berlin which would close out the trip, nobody could provide it.

'I don't think it's finalised.' Sonja gave Anna the same answer whenever she – carefully – brought up the subject. 'Theo and Erich are waiting on something, but they won't say what. I did hear – although don't breathe a word, because you know what they are like about gossip – that there is a chance we could be meeting with Hitler. I don't know if it's true – I overheard Theo say that the *Bundesführer* makes the same request every time a group comes out, and it never happens. It would be something though wouldn't it: us meeting the actual Führer? Can you imagine anything more wonderful?'

It never happens. And I don't want it to this time, but it must. My permit and my freedom and finding my child all depend on it.

Sonja was still waiting for Anna to share her excitement.

Anna grinned. 'I can't, I really can't. But how incredible if that was to actually happen.'

She hugged her startled colleague; it was the only way to hide her face.

The shifts in Berlin were subtle ones. Anna had left a bustling city; she returned to one as vibrant. The pavement cafés were crowded, although April hadn't yet fully warmed the air. Cars and trams filled the roads. People looked purposeful, the city looked prosperous – clean and well-stocked. And yet...

There were uniforms everywhere, not just on the streets housing the ministries, and people in every age group bar the very oldest were wearing some flavour of one. If they weren't, they were sporting swastika lapel pins. Every store window Anna passed had a prominent portrait of Hitler. Every street had a crop of shop names that had been blotchily whitewashed and inked over. And every building and open space she could see bore the sign *Juden Verboten*. In 1935 when she had boarded the train to the docks, the National Socialist presence had been the most visible thing in the city. It still was – two and a half years after she had left, Berlin continued to be swathed in the Party's red banners. But now it was more than signs and symbols. The Party's hatreds had seeped into the fabric of the streets and the people and embedded itself, enabling *Jews Forbidden* to become as mundane an order as *Keep off the grass*. Anna walked along the pavements feeling alienated, her skin crawling at the thought that this place full of prejudice and division had once been her home.

'Anna, keep up. If we don't hurry, we'll miss our space.'

Sonja was pink-cheeked with excitement; she had been bubbling over since Theo had appeared on their last day in the countryside with the long-awaited envelope clutched in his hand. It had at least stopped her asking Anna why she had barely spoken a word since they arrived in Berlin, or noticing how often Anna looked over her shoulder. She grabbed Anna's arm and hustled her over the Schloßbrücke and onto Museum Island.

'Listen to it. Oh please God we haven't missed his arrival.'

She dropped Anna's arm again and began running, shooing the youth group in front of her.

'There they are. Quick, children, get into place.'

Theo and Erich were standing in a small taped-off area at the front of the wide road leading through the centre of the Lustgarten, waving frantically for the rest of the party to join them. Sonja was still shouting about what an honour it was to be allotted such a privileged vantage point. Her words, however, were quickly swept away in the clamour.

Anna wanted to clamp her hands across her ears – the noise was unbearable. There were tens, maybe hundreds, of thousands of cheering people crammed into the space between Berlin's cathedral and the Altes Museum. Far more than Anna could count, far more than she had imagined would be present when an ecstatic Theo had announced that they were going to be guests at Berlin's spring youth rally. For the first time since she had got on the train to the city, Anna took a proper breath. An audience on this scale wasn't what Hardy and Nicholls had counted on; it wouldn't win her any favours when she reported it back. She didn't care.

They promised me a permit for coming, not for what I brought back. And even if Goebbels is here today – which no one has told me he will be – he will never spot me in the madness of this.

'He's coming! He's coming!'

The cry flew up around her at the same time as the arms.

Sonja burst into noisy tears as the open-topped Mercedes came into view. 'It's him. It's actually him.'

The roar was deafening. The officials standing on the steps at the front of the Altes Museum couldn't quieten it. And then Hitler stepped up to the podium and a breath-holding silence fell. Whatever he said slid over Anna. All she could see was the man in the expensive suit standing next to him.

Who can't see me. Who will never be able to see me in a crowd like this. Who can't therefore hurt me.

The sheer relief of having survived a gamble she hadn't thought she could emerge from unscathed spread a smile across Anna's face that was brighter than any she had worn in years.

'I knew you were one of us.' Sonja had turned round while Anna was still staring at Goebbels. 'Theo wasn't sure. The *Bundesführer* asked him to watch you, and he didn't think what you said at the train station about being scared of sailing was at all believable. But I knew you were loyal, and look at you now, smiling at our leader: I've never seen you this happy!'

Her heart dropped. It was an overused stage direction, impossible to translate into a reaction. Except this time Anna felt it. Felt the blood rush through her, too quick and too heavy for her body to balance. Erich was waving to them both, mouthing words she couldn't hear. Sonja stiffened beside her. The Führer's address had finished, but the crowd was still yelling, refusing to let him go.

'He's going to meet with us.' Sonja could barely get the words out.

This time Anna's heart didn't fall, it shrivelled. She said 'Who' simply so her body would be forced to take its next breath.

'The Führer, silly. Didn't you hear Erich? If we go now, to the museum, he will spare us ten minutes. Whoever arranged this will be my hero for ever.'

There had been no way out. By the time Hitler left the podium and headed into the museum – with Goebbels, as Anna now knew he inevitably would be – glued to his side, soldiers had cut a path through the crowd to where the Bund group was standing. They were escorted through the packed parade ground to the back of the museum at a trotting pace. There wasn't a gap Anna could have ducked through; or any excuse she could have offered for leaving if she had tried. Every impulse in her body had screamed 'run', but *the Bundesführer asked him to watch you* formed too tight a shackle.

'You at the back: put your head up and smile.'

Anna jumped at the photographer's shout and followed his order before he could single her out again. This nightmare was too nearly done to risk drawing attention. The meeting was barely a meeting and it hadn't taken ten minutes. The Führer had swept in, shaken hands with Theo and Erich, nodded in the direction of the two women, and thanked – very briefly – the awestruck children for coming. Anna had kept her head down and her shoulders stooped throughout the whole thing, desperate to create the illusion of an old, uninteresting woman. Goebbels had barely looked up from his notebook.

One more minute and he'll leave; you'll be through this.

And then Theo had requested a photograph, and Hitler – to Theo's obvious surprise – had agreed.

'Boys and girls in rows at the front, team leaders to the back. If the Führer could take one side, and the Minister the other.'

The photographer had arranged them efficiently. Anna had shuffled into place, holding her body tightly away from the place Goebbels occupied barely three feet away. She hadn't run the way her body ached to do. She had acted quickly to correct her one mistake and lifted her chin. The camera flashed.

Hitler broke away at once; Goebbels followed him. Anna began to exhale. And then the photographer said something that made both men laugh and they looked round; they looked straight at her.

He knows me.

She took a step back.

Hitler turned away again almost immediately; Goebbels didn't. He frowned.

Why didn't I drop my head?

It was too late to do it now; it would be too obvious. She stopped thinking. She raised her hand to her face, as if she was about to sneeze. Goebbels hesitated. His body angled as if he was about to move forward. Anna braced herself for the moment of recognition that was surely coming, for the shout; for the gun.

'Fräulein Brandt, why must we always wait for you?'

Theo's exasperated call broke the spell. Goebbels shook his head, made a comment to the photographer, who laughed louder than was needed, and was gone. She stared at the space he had left as if his body still filled it.

'Anna, Anna wake up! We have to leave, the head of Berlin's *Hitlerjugend* has invited us all to the reception he's giving. Come on!'

One second earlier and Goebbels would have heard Sonja. He would have heard the name Anna knew he had been hunting for. She had to fight to stop her knees crumpling.

'I can't go.'

Theo was no longer exasperated, he was furious. 'I have had enough of this. You've been out of line with the rest of us – again –

since we arrived in Berlin. Acting as if you hate being here, hiding your face for a photograph you should be proud to be in. This reception is a huge honour. You will come.'

'No. I won't. I'm sick. Give my apologies.'

She was already at the exit. Theo could be as angry as he liked; he could – and no doubt would – report her to Kuhn. Anna couldn't think about that now. Goebbels could still be feet away. He could have heard Sonja. The more Anna thought about that, the more likely it seemed. He had barely left before Sonja shouted and Sonja was loud. What if, right now, he was making the connection? Every rational thought left her. She ran back to the hostel in Alexanderplatz, convinced she could hear footsteps giving chase. She lay dressed under her blanket the whole night, ready to run at the first sound of boots. She was so certain that the train would be stopped on the way to Cuxhaven, or that the ship would be refused permission to sail, she was a nervous wreck by the time the last gangplank was released.

Nobody spoke to her on the return journey. Anna was too overwhelmed – with the relief that she had escaped and the certainty that she was walking into more trouble – to try to win anyone round.

I will apologise for behaving badly. I will say I was sick. Surely when he sees me, Kuhn will believe that was true.

If he saw what the mirror in her cabin saw, he would have to – Anna almost convinced herself of that. She was so drawn and pale after a week spent barely eating or sleeping, she half-expected that her return ticket would be rejected and she would be sent back where she had come from as a health risk. Frau Meyer's horrified reaction when she stumbled into the boarding house seemed like a good omen. Except Anna knew Kuhn was too skilful a manipulator himself to accept something as simple to fake as appearances. Especially when Theo told him what he had seen in the Altes Museum: that Anna had been shaking not with sickness, but with fear.

CHAPTER ELEVEN

The foyer and the corridors leading into what was normally New York's main boxing arena in Madison Square Garden were a hive of activity. Long tables were covered in Bund buttons and pennants and pamphlets; bodies clustered round them, frantically filling paper bags.

'Look sharp, Fräulein Brandt. Every delegate needs a welcome pack, which gives us three hours to finish twenty-five thousand. A mammoth task, but we are nearly there, and we will complete it if all hands are willing.'

Anna was hustled to the middle of a production line and positioned next to a pile of copies of the *Der Stürmer* newspaper – the crude Nazi propaganda tool she remembered avoiding in Berlin.

The supervisor was still waving her swastika-wrapped arm. 'Get started now. One per pack and pass it on. Don't let the line stop moving.'

'This a bit of a comedown for you, isn't it, getting your hands grubby with the workers? Aren't you normally backstage sipping champagne at these things?'

The woman stretching her cramped fingers and giving up her place was one Anna recognised from the pool of secretaries who had once worked for Kuhn, before Anna had replaced them.

She took her seat without answering. Everyone knew her champagne days were long gone. Everyone knew Anna was out of the inner circle and lucky to still be in the Bund at all. Although *lucky* was Nicholls' word to describe her position, not Anna's. Theo – as Anna had guessed such an ambitious man would – had got to Kuhn before she had. A note had arrived at the boarding house telling her not to return to work. That had got Anna out of the bed she had taken an ill-advised refuge in and back to the office. Kuhn's new secretary had refused her an appointment. Anna – with her value plummeting and nothing to lose – had burst through his doors anyway.

'You don't know the whole story.'

His contempt had been scathing.

'No? But I imagine that's what it is: a story. I have no interest in hearing any more of your lies. You begged to travel to Germany on a trip you should have known nothing about and then you apparently behaved as if the whole expedition was loathsome, including – and this I cannot fathom, whichever way I turn it – being in the Führer's presence. What am I supposed to assume, Fräulein Brandt, except that you are not, as you portray yourself, an honest follower of the cause? That you are, in fact, a plant, an informer – although perhaps not as good at the job as your controllers hoped, given your most recent performance. You should be grateful you were simply dismissed. A man would have met a far worse fate; I am not entirely convinced your gender should spare you the same.'

It was the first time Anna had heard Kuhn even vaguely acknowledge the rumours that swirled round the Bund. About men who had talked too freely and disappeared. About the mob connections Kuhn had cultivated to keep his hands clean. Anna refused to let him see she was shaken. She didn't have her reward yet; she had nothing but a promise it was coming. In an ideal world, she would walk into the agents' office and the citizenship papers would be there waiting. Anna had long since stopped believing in an ideal world. She had to stay valuable – to Kuhn and to the agents – until that prize was in her hands. Which meant that she had to tell the truth now, or some version of it.

'It wasn't the Führer I shrank from. I am loyal to the Führer: to be in his presence, to be so close to him was more than an honour, it was a dream. It was Reichsminister Goebbels who unnerved me.'

Kuhn sat back and properly looked at her. Anna ploughed on before he could ask what she meant and trip up thoughts that were barely forming.

'I was a secretary before, in Berlin. I worked in the Propaganda Ministry. The Minister has an eye for women – you may have heard that. One night when I was working late, he made advances, and I refused him.' She hesitated; let Kuhn start filling in the blanks. 'He hurt me, *Bundesführer*. He took my—'

She stopped as Kuhn broke into a perfectly timed fit of coughing, and hung her head. 'What could I do? To bring an accusation against him – and defame the Party by it – was unthinkable. So I ran. And then, there he was, at the rally in Berlin, and all my old fears flooded back.'

She peeped up at Kuhn who was red in the face and sweating. 'I think the fear of him was perhaps why I made myself look plain, and why I couldn't explain the change in me when you asked.' She stopped, dropped her head again and waited. She would have crossed her fingers if she had dared to move.

Kuhn shuffled some papers, cleared his throat. 'You never mentioned working in such an important position before.'

Anna stayed looking down, trying to ignore her pounding heart, and said the one thing she knew he couldn't challenge.

'I told Frank. I presumed he must have told you when you gave me the post as your secretary.' She let the pause stretch and resisted the urge to fill it.

'Even if I am to accept that this… regrettable incident… happened…'

Kuhn's voice had switched to the bluster uncertainty always pushed him into. Anna lifted her head.

'That does not explain why you were overly eager to accompany the youth group. If you were so afraid of seeing the Minister, why on earth would you put yourself in his way?'

She had one shot. She held his gaze and took it.

'Germany is my home, *Bundesführer*. I did not leave it willingly. And my commitment to our young people, our future soldiers, is real. But how can I be a model for them if I cannot conquer my own demons? I put myself to the test. And I failed. I let my fears overwhelm me. And now here I am, admitting and accepting my failure and proving my strength. As I proved it when I sacrificed my hope of Frank and a future. My loyalty is not in doubt, *Bundesführer*; my loyalty is everything.'

Every drama teacher and director she had ever worked with would have laughed her out of the room. Kuhn looked as if he might clap, or cry.

'A most heartfelt speech, Fräulein. Most heartfelt. Perhaps I was too hasty to listen to gossip. I will reinstate you. Not to your old position as my secretary – I cannot be seen to have favourites, no matter how hard it seems to be to replace you – but to the Bund. A lower position, where you can prove your loyalty to everyone, would be the best thing, for a little while at least, and then we will see.'

Anna had thanked him. Kuhn had found her a place in the membership office, on the lowest rung and at half her salary. There had been gossip for a week; when she worked harder than anyone and didn't rise to the whispers, the gossip moved on. She couldn't presume, however, that no one was watching her, so she had waited a fortnight before reporting in to Foley Square. When she arrived for her appointment, only Nicholls was there.

'Where is Agent Hardy?'

Nicholls barely looked up from his files. 'Moved on. Not cut out for this type of work, too sympathetic.'

The one door she had found that could lead to the Baileys had closed. Anna couldn't manage a single word.

Nicholls pushed aside the folder she assumed was hers and scowled. 'And you've fallen from favour.'

It was a game, all of it. He batted an accusation or a demand over, she batted them back. And however hard she played, the outcome was already determined.

Anna said what he expected to hear, and didn't bother to ask herself if she believed it. 'I can work my way back up; Kuhn has made that clear. I assume I won't need to.'

'And why would you assume that?'

'Because I went to Germany like you asked, and you are going to give me my resident's permit.'

He smiled, as she knew he would.

'I thought you might think that. But the trouble is, with all the Krauts desperate to worm their way in here these days, the system's clogged. It could take years to move you up the list.'

Anna had made herself stay calm; she had refused to give him the satisfaction of seeing her break. 'But you could speed it up, couldn't you? If the application has been made, you could use your contacts and hurry it along?'

He hadn't bothered to lie.

'Fräulein Brandt, could you please stop daydreaming? The doors are opening.'

Anna jumped and picked up the leaflets lying untouched in front of her; the supervisor didn't acknowledge her apology.

'Big smiles all of you, hand the packs out and then straight into the hall when you are done. I'm sure none of you want to miss a moment of this.'

It took Anna an hour to empty her station. She could hear the roars long before she was ushered, with the rest of her colleagues, into their reserved seats on the arena floor. A Bund-led rally to celebrate George Washington's birthday: it was Kuhn's most inspired piece of theatre yet, a mass demonstration of just how 'American' the German American Bund had decided to become.

Anna couldn't take her eyes off the stage. The spectacle before her was more shocking than anything the Bund had ever dared to unleash in public before. A thirty-foot-high illuminated image of George Washington dominated the centre, flanked on both sides by giant Stars and Stripes flags. As Anna stared in horror at the way the emblems were being misused, the main arena doors flew open and a five-wide column of OD guards marched in, followed by a band playing a song whose familiar and so out of place notes cut through the cheering. The guards began to sing, their voices raised in a joyful rendition of 'The Star-Spangled Banner'. The thousands packing the stadium threw back their heads and joined in. Anna's stomach lurched at the hateful cleverness of what she was seeing. She would have walked away then, but she was too tightly surrounded.

Every paper will have to report this, even the ones who hate the Bund. And even if they rail at the way the Bund is reinventing itself as being more American than German – which please God they will – some of their readers could read about the flags and the singing and decide that, maybe, American Nazis aren't unpatriotic monsters after all.

The anthem continued to swell its way from the crowded floor to the balconies. It could have been the opening moments of the World Series. If it hadn't been for the OD's stormtrooper uniforms. If the rest of the spotlights hadn't clicked on as the last notes struck and lit up the huge red and yellow Bund banners hanging next to the Stars and Stripes, banners emblazoned with swastikas that rose up like trophies. Or the signs hanging like bunting around the arena: *Wake Up America, Stop Jewish Domination; A Million Bund Members by 1940.*

The American anthem played out, the German one played in. Arms snapped forward, the air bristled with *Sieg Heil.* Anna stared round the ecstatic crowds welcoming their *Bundesführer* to the podium. *A million members.* In this moment, Anna could believe it was coming. Twenty-five thousand tickets had been sold for this event; the demand had been even higher. Every person she had handed a welcome pack to had grumbled about the 'Jew protesters' and the 'heavy-handed' police outside and promised to recruit a dozen more members.

And people will talk about free speech and no one will stop them. And the support will keep coming, and the candidates and the votes. And where will America be then?

She already knew; she had already watched the movement roll over Germany because no one had admitted the danger in time. And now here she was, in a country that should have been safe, standing by, doing nothing, as the horrors unfolded once again. Anna's head was pounding, her stomach doing its usual dance. Whatever came next, whatever the FBI or the Bund threatened her with, she couldn't be part of this insanity for a moment longer.

Anna pushed her way out of the row, muttering about finding a bathroom. The party workers had all been counted in and would all be counted out and the corridors were crammed with security guards – if she left, someone would stop her and start asking questions she was too tightly wound to answer.

She found an empty corridor and sank down. Bomb squads had combed the building before the rally began. Anna wished they hadn't. She wished one of the braver Nazi-haters who had threatened to plant a device had got in, blown the whole place to pieces as Kuhn started speaking and wiped the Bund out of existence. She wished she had planted a bomb herself.

The roars from inside the stadium grew steadily louder. Anna got to her feet and straightened her skirt. Let them try and stop her, let them try and question her, she no longer cared – she was leaving; she was done.

CHAPTER TWELVE

*New York and New Jersey,
March to December 1942*

Maybe tonight I'll meet someone; maybe it's at least time to try.

Anna checked the angle of her new red hat in the hall mirror and smoothed on her silk gloves. The invitation said it was a small party to celebrate the launch of Carlo's new restaurant. His sister Maria, who was Anna's closest thing to a friend at her workplace, had promised there would be no more than two dozen people. She had hinted one or two of the men would be single. A *nice meal and a little bit of mingling*, as Maria had put it; Anna was sure she could manage that.

Perhaps tonight will mark a new future.

A future. She still wasn't used to the thought of it. Three years ago on the night of the George Washington rally, when Anna had walked away from Madison Square Garden, the future was the last thing on her mind. She hadn't imagined having one. She had walked away from the rally and away from the Bund. The next morning, she had packed her suitcase and walked away from Frau Meyer's boarding house. She hadn't made a plan – she hadn't expected to need one. She had assumed that, once she failed to drop her regular report at the post office on 80th and didn't appear in person at Foley Square, the FBI would come searching. She had assumed the eyes Nicholls had threatened her with were still watching. She no longer cared.

There will never be security; there will never be anything other than lies.

Anna had known that after the debacle of the German trip. Sitting alone in the corridor at Madison Square Garden, almost a year on and still without her papers, still surrounded by Bund supporters baying for Jewish blood, she had had to accept it. Facing that truth had been both hard to stomach, and freeing. Their deal – if there had ever been such a thing – was broken. *If I don't do what the FBI wants, they'll deport me* no longer had any power. *If I do what they want, Hardy will help me find the Baileys* had probably never been more than a dream. Once she accepted the truth, pretending she could bear her part of the bargain was impossible. As was pretending that there was any difference between the life she had fled in Germany and the one she had stumbled into in America: the Nazis swilling their poison, and the fools blindly cheering them, were exactly the same. And as for this horror show of a life she had made for herself – filled with lies and the worst kind of people – or the penniless one she was about to walk into, how were either of those worlds fit for a child? What kind of a mother would she be if she dragged Franzi into a misery like that?

She might not have made a plan when she took her blind leap in 1939, but Anna had closed the door on the house on 87th knowing that, whatever came next, she couldn't stay in Yorkville. She wasn't ready to leave New York; that was too big a step, and the only other residential area she had heard of – apart from the unaffordable Upper West Side – was the Bronx, where Mrs Michaels had spent her Sundays off with her husband's extensive Irish family. The Bronx was easily reachable on the Third Avenue El, so that was where Anna went. Drawn by the need for open space, she got off the train at the Bedford Park Terminal and followed the signs towards the Botanical Gardens. Luck seemed to be following her. The diners on Webster Avenue were opening up, filling the air with the tempting aroma of coffee and crisping bacon. The one Anna chose had a board full of room-to-let notices and a waitress who – for the promise of a tip larger than her offhand service should have earned her – grudgingly drew a rough map. There seemed, for the short-term at least – which was all Anna was capable of thinking about – to be possibilities.

The first door she knocked on had slammed in her face. The second did the same; this time, however, the bang was accompanied by a 'we don't need Nazi lovers here'. At the third house, one of a neat row tucked into the end of East 202nd, the first words out of Anna's mouth were, 'I'm Austrian.' That got her across the threshold. A bitten lip and a deliberately vague glossing over her background which included the word 'refugee' got her a room. Anna had been in Mrs Cormac's elegantly neat boarding house ever since, playing a character that was finally close enough to her real self to almost feel comfortable.

As well as she had managed, however, she hadn't got everything right: she had made a mistake that first day she instantly regretted. In the relief of finding a welcoming place to spend the few weeks of freedom she imagined were all that were left to her, Anna had forgotten to create a new alias and had given her name as Anna Brandt. After that slip, she was far more careful. She made sure she responded to any questions about her life before the Bronx with a sadness she hinted was too painful to talk about. Everybody in the house had seen the images of Hitler's troops swarming through Austria. Nobody asked twice. And – despite her fears – nobody came looking.

For the first weeks – as she had done years ago in Kerstin's home – Anna spent her days waiting for the knock on the door or the tap on the shoulder that would uncover her. March passed by without a footstep behind her and turned into April without a summons for anything but meals. She began to stand a little taller. She began to believe that, by some miracle she hadn't dared pray for, the FBI no longer cared about her whereabouts, and perhaps – despite Nicholls' threats – never really had.

As the weather warmed and her stack of money started to dwindle, Anna had emerged from her self-imposed isolation and began looking for a job. By the beginning of May, she had found one in the wages department of a small car dealership. As her world started to widen, Anna even allowed herself to wonder again about finding the Baileys, although, given nearly four years had passed since her daughter's birth, the trail seemed impossibly cold.

The Bronx she moved into, in common with Yorkville, was a noisy and colourful place. Most of the people she encountered were of Irish extraction. There were no Germans – at least not in the neighbourhood where she lived – and there was no discernible Bund presence. Anna stayed alert, but, in the Bronx at least, the Bund was viewed not with admiration but with contempt. Once she recognised that, it was as if a wall had been dismantled. She started to see how different her life could have been if she had stayed in the west of the city and never crossed Central Park, and could have wept. As the threats that had fenced in her life fell away, Anna had moments when she wondered if any of them had been truly as serious as they had felt when she was trapped underneath them. She wouldn't give in to that thought – there was nothing about the Bund or the FBI, or Goebbels, that she could have imagined – but there were days when *maybe I could have walked away sooner* pounded through her head and made her angry, and ashamed.

The newspapers she increasingly pored over told her – although she could not have imagined such a thing happening when she was caught in the midst of Madison Square Garden's cheering crowds – that the Bund was falling apart. That the revulsion it stirred up ran far wider than the Bronx. The opposition voices had strengthened as Hitler's intentions to expand Germany's lands and his power grew undeniably clear.

In the early summer of 1939, the Dies Committee – as the House Un-American Activities Committee was more commonly known – declared that the Bund was no longer to be classed as a subversive organisation but a traitorous one, a direct threat to America's security. Anna was glad of that, even though the ruling meant the search for its members would speed up. She was glad too when Fritz Kuhn was arrested, even if the only charges that would stick to him were embezzlement and tax evasion. The government ruling and the criminal charges were a public acknowledgement that the Bund truly was dangerous, that the threat of the Nazis gaining a powerful foothold in America was real. It meant that the information she had risked her safety – and her sanity – to acquire had been valuable, that it could have contributed to the downfall that was surely coming. Anna took enough comfort in that to prepare her defence ready in case the FBI finally arrived. Nobody came.

Nobody came when war was declared between Germany and the European Allies in September. Nobody came when Kuhn was convicted of grand larceny in December and imprisoned in Sing Sing. By the start of 1940, the Bund had collapsed and no one was cheering the Nazis anymore. The Dies Committee had switched its attention to the communists; the FBI had new spy rings to investigate, and an increasingly anti-German public happy to help.

Anna's new life went unchallenged. She wasn't happy; she had lost too much to be happy: her child, her parents and Eddy, who she knew, deep in her heart and buried away there, was the love of her life. And she had watched the country she had once loved set out to destroy the world's freedoms and impose an order across it that would lead to nothing but more hatred if they won. If she let herself dwell on any of that she would never have got out of bed.

But Anna didn't let herself dwell, and so she had survived and she had reached a point where she could envisage a life that was safe. Or almost. The introduction of the Alien Registration Act – which had to be completed by every immigrant, resident or not – in June 1940 was a shock that almost sent her running again.

'It's a good thing – it will weed out the spies and the trouble-makers.'

Anna had nodded her agreement along with her colleagues, but she had no intention of complying with the request to complete it. She had heard enough about the questions the form asked to know that, if she filled it in honestly, her life in America would be done. It was only when her employer reminded her, for the second time, that she hadn't requested the time off that she needed to 'fulfil her duties' and that, if she didn't comply, he really couldn't keep her, that she finally went to the post office and joined the long line.

I last arrived in the United States at...

I came in by...

I am, or have been within the past five years, or intend to be, engaged in the following activities...

The form's thirty-two questions were as detailed in their probing as the profiling questionnaire Anna had had to complete in Berlin.

And I have to lie on it. As Marika must have lied on it, or wouldn't the world know the truth about her by now?

Marika – Anna still couldn't call her Louise – had become Hollywood royalty: every movie she made turned into gold. Since leaving Yorkville, Anna had sought the films out and done her best not to give in to jealousy as she watched Marika shine in them all. She had also read all the, very few, interviews that had splashed Marika across magazine covers but actually said very little. Marika was a deliberate mystery, Eddy had disappeared – no matter how hard Anna dug beneath the hints Marika threw out about a heartbroken past, she couldn't find any trace of him. Once or twice, in the early months in the Bronx when she was frightened and lonely, she had considered the possibility of *I could get in touch with her and ask for help.* She had got as far as pen and paper before Marika's imagined tearful apology and welcoming hug reformed into a horrified rejection as the actress watched her carefully constructed world collapse.

Marika might be part of Anna's past, but they both shared a talent for reinvention Anna wasn't about to let slip. She collected her form with *if a Hollywood star can do it, I can too* running through her head; she left the post office as a fingerprinted Austrian with an unblemished record. It was another lie, but there had been so many, she couldn't afford to worry about another one. If it wasn't for the fact her employer would see the resulting registration card, she would have reinvented herself completely.

Her luck held. Her papers arrived, her employer relaxed. Life moved on at a pace she could manage. She pushed her old sorrows and regrets and deceptions down into a place she no longer dug at. And then, in March 1942, as she was straightening her hat and finally looking forward to the innocent pleasures of a party, the knock came.

'We are here to see the German citizen Fräulein Anna Brandt.'

Anna knew her world was done. It didn't matter who had ended it: whether it was Nicholls who had caught up with her, or someone in the Bund out for revenge, or simply her outdated papers finally coming to light, there was no hiding from this. There wasn't a moment where she could have begged for help, or run. Two policemen entered the hall before the maid could announce them. Mrs Cormac appeared from the kitchen and froze.

'Anna, what is this? Why would they call you German?'

She didn't answer – what could she possibly say? She focused on the policeman instead.

'Can I take anything with me?'

One of the policemen nodded. 'One case – you have five minutes to pack it.'

Anna went up the stairs; one of the policemen followed. As she reached the landing, she heard the word 'Nazi'. By the time she came back down – her case hastily packed while the silent officer ransacked the room around her – Mrs Cormac was too shocked to look at her or speak.

'I am sorry. I never meant to deceive you. I'm not what you think.'

She was hustled out of the door and into the squad car before she could finish. She managed not to cry until they turned onto the George Washington Bridge.

'Into that line. Don't waste anyone's time with questions.'

Anna was at the docks, as she had expected to be, but there was no sign of an ocean liner. The policemen pushed her towards a smaller pier than the ones those docked at, and into the back of a snaking queue flanked by soldiers in olive drab uniforms. No one spoke, apart from to tell her to move. The men and women surrounding her were a mix of ages and races. Some were clutching children; all were clutching suitcases; all of their faces were drawn and desperate. The silence they huddled in was frightening. Anna took her place.

A few moments later, they were herded onto a small ferry with wooden slats around its decks more suited to a cattle truck. She immediately recognised the style of the boat: she had last seen one from the upper decks of the SS *Hamburg* in 1936, picking up steerage passengers to drop onto Ellis Island.

The sea was choppy, the swell fierce. By the time the short crossing was done, Anna's stomach was queasy and her nerves were frayed.

'Up the stairs, into the registry room. Give your name when you are asked. Keep moving.'

There was no time for questions; there was no one who looked approachable enough to ask what might be coming. The queue was funnelled with conveyer-belt efficiency into a damp-smelling entranceway where their cases were rifled through and up a staircase which was so steep it made her head spin.

The registry room itself was enormous, as dwarfing as the room in which she had first met Goebbels. Its high vaulted ceilings and arched windows were more in keeping with a cathedral than a government building. Despites its size, it was crammed.

Anna's line was pushed into another one shuffling towards long rows of desks.

'Name?'

'Anna Brandt.'

The official consulted his list without looking up. 'Soldier accompanied. Room three.'

'What is going to happen to me?'

He was already waving the next person forward.

The soldier clutching his rifle nodded her down a narrow corridor and into a small square room she tried not to think of as a cell. There was no window. There was a table, with two chairs placed next to each other behind it. Anna hovered, unsure whether to take one. As she hesitated, two dark-suited men walked in, one of them carrying a beige folder. There were no introductions; neither seat was intended for her.

'Why did you claim to be Austrian? Why does this contain no mention of your membership of the German American Bund?'

One of the two men – whose faces and bearing were as similar as their suits – pushed forward her Alien Registration Form. All she could think to do was buy time until the nature of the charges against her, and their possible consequences, became clearer.

'It's complicated.'

'Make it simple.'

Anna knotted her fingers behind her back. 'I haven't had any dealings with the Bund for over three years.'

'That isn't what I asked.' His face was unreadable. 'We have your file; we know you are German. We know that you were an active member of the Bund at least until 1939, and secretary to its leader. What I asked was why you lied.'

Anna was so desperate to find a straw to cling to, she focused too much on the wrong part of his statement; she heard too much hope in it. The two men were far tougher in their manner than even Nicholls had been, but surely they were from the same organisation?

'If you have my file, then you know why. I was an informer. I was working for the FBI, investigating the Bund.' Their expressions didn't falter. Anna's sudden burst of confidence did. 'I reported to two agents, Hardy and Nicholls. They… recruited me in 1936 and I was their informant inside the Bund until, as you said, 1939.'

She paused again, waiting for some sign that they recognised the names. Both men stayed silent. Anna knew she should stop talking, but her nerves wouldn't let her.

'It was a deal. I came into America on a tourist visa, and it expired. They promised me a resident's permit if I co-operated, and threatened me with deportation if I didn't. It wasn't a choice. Being involved with the Bund wasn't what I wanted.'

The second man had produced two more pieces of paper while she was talking. Her interrogator consulted them but kept whatever they said covered. When he spoke, he sounded bored.

'This defence, agents offering residency in return for informa-tion, wore out months ago. The process of becoming an American citizen takes time and numerous checks; it is not in anyone's power to offer – no agent would do it. And the names you gave – Hardy and Nicholls – are not on my list of Bund investigating officers. I suggest this is another lie. They are accumulating.'

It is not in anyone's power. It was the fear that Anna had already grappled with, and had decided to dismiss. Whatever these men said, she knew Hardy and Nicholls and their promises were real. She refused to believe that Hardy at least hadn't meant to try to deliver on them. She suspected that this was simply a tactic to trip her and break her story, and she wasn't about to crumble before it.

'Perhaps they used aliases, I don't know. I do know that I am not a liar. Whether those names are correct or not, I met with FBI agents on multiple occasions at Foley Square. And I used the 80th street drop-off to pass on my reports.'

He wasn't listening. He pushed one of the papers towards her. It was a photograph. Anna's last hope that she could make them listen fell away.

'This is you? In the back, behind Reichsminister Goebbels? Please don't waste our time denying it: you have been identified by too many of your fellow Bund members.'

Anna stared at the picture. Her head was up as if she was proud to be in it. She was looking straight at the camera. The lights had turned her shocked expression into a smile. The image was the lie in the room; it didn't matter.

'I was there, in Berlin, because the FBI instructed me to go.'

It was a waste of breath. He packed the photograph and the papers back into the folder.

'Do you have anyone who could vouch for your character?'

Anna's mind raced, skirting across Mrs Cormac all the way back to Riverside Drive. She couldn't think of a way to explain the mess she was in, not in the limited time she was sure she would be given. When the final name she landed on was the impossibility of *Louise Baker,* her shoulders slumped.

'I thought not. You are indeed a liar, Fräulein Brandt. And we believe you are also a German spy. Countless Bund members have been brought in for questioning since Germany declared war on the United States in December. They all remember you, and your disappearing act. We believe that you jumped ship when it was clear that the Bund was disintegrating, so that you could stay undetected and active. We will be recommending your immediate deportation.'

'You can't do that. No decent person could do that.'

For the first time since they had entered the room, both men looked properly at her.

'I am half-Jewish. Which is Jewish, as far as the Nazis are concerned. So, if you have any humanity, you can't.'

Their faces closed down again, the same as Nicholls' had. Her interrogator sighed; both men got to their feet.

Anna had so little left to lose, she finally started to shout the way she had longed to shout for years.

'You will not walk out as if I have no value. You will hear me. I am not a spy, not in the way you mean. I have lived with monsters, in order to bring monsters down. That has cost me my soul. And now you think you can call me a liar and send me back to a country that I ran from in fear of my life? Where my life will surely be in danger again? No. You do not get to do that. You know what's happening there; every paper has reported it: Jews are being made to wear yellow stars. Have you asked yourselves why? Jews are already banned from every aspect of life, why mark them out unless it is to hunt them? You cannot send me back to that. You won't. Your people have ruined too much of my life; you owe me the rest of it.'

She stopped, her fists clenched, her heart thumping.

The two men let her finish. Then they crossed to the door and walked out.

'What happens to us next?'

'Whatever they decide.'

'When will they tell us?'

'Whenever they choose.'

The questions, and increasingly despairing answers, bounced back and forth in the dormitories, and the dining room, and the wire-fenced exercise yard, measuring out the days on Ellis Island like a metronome. Manhattan was so close it felt touchable, but so did the ocean liners steaming away from its piers. None of the inmates staring out from the compound knew in which direction they would be going.

Because her detention and processing had been carried out with such speed, Anna assumed her fate would be decided as quickly. She crept onto the narrow bunk allocated to her on the first night without unpacking; she climbed out of it the next morning and put on her coat. She did that for a week before she was forced to acknowledge what her roommates had already learned: that time on Ellis Island was elastic. The days were endless and blurred from one into the next. There was order: the gun-wearing guards who never made eye contact ensured that. There was also an attempt at routine, anchored round the unfathomably early lights-on at 5.30 a.m. and the three inadequate meals doled out in the dining hall. Beyond that, there was nothing but hours to fill, with only a wind-whipped yard and an overcrowded and understocked library to spend them in.

At the end of the third grey week, Anna went to the commissary and bought thin paper and envelopes that reminded her too brutally of Frank. She finally wrote to Mrs Cormac. She outlined as best as she could both her deceptions and, most of, the truth. She asked for her forgiveness and help. Mrs Cormac didn't reply.

She thought about writing to Mrs Michaels, but the explanations involved defeated her. She didn't waste time considering Marika.

The days stretched on. Women moved out of her dormitory, women moved in. New faces appeared in the exercise yard just as she had managed to forge tentative connections with the old. March became April became May; the wind blowing in over the sea barely grew any warmer. Anna watched the sky over Manhattan change from winter's grey to summer's blue and wondered if she had been utterly forgotten.

It took them fifteen weeks to get to her name. The man waiting behind the desk this time was in uniform. Anna wasn't asked to sit; the line behind her was a long one.

'You are Anna Brandt, a German citizen, last given address 263 East 202nd Street, New York?'

'Yes.'

'Your case has been heard. The sentence is indefinite internment. Take this paper, put the label round your neck and proceed to muster point C.'

He pushed a typed sheet headed *Internment Order* and a stringed cardboard square bearing her name and a number across the desk and called the next person.

They decide your life as if it isn't yours.

Words she had heard in the exercise yard and refused to listen to.

Anna stared at the documents: he hadn't said *deportation,* for which she was more grateful than she could express, but what he had said left too many questions.

'I don't understand how my case can have been heard without me being present, or what *indefinite internment* means. Please could you take a moment to explain that to me, or at least tell me where I am going?'

His glance flickered over her. 'No questions – move along.'

It was as if she was a piece of cargo. 'I don't think you understand. I am not trying to be difficult, but I've had no information for months and no chance to speak to anyone. Can't you at least tell me what's coming next?'

His stare was so cold, Anna would have stepped back if there was room. He picked up his pen, lingering over his words as if he was enjoying them. 'I can amend internment to deportation if you prefer. The note next to your name suggests that was, for some of the witnesses, the preferred option.'

'No.' Anna whipped the paper away before his pen could touch it. 'No, that's fine. Thank you.'

She stumbled away towards a group of women and small children being tidied into rows beneath a large letter C.

'Has anyone been told where we're going?'

Nobody turned to her; nobody spoke. They all had their eyes firmly trained on the guards and their rifles. While Anna was wondering whether to risk drawing attention by asking again, a soldier stepped forward.

'Move it out.'

It was the first time Anna had ever heard the phrase; it was to become her new soundtrack.

The train had rifle-wielding guards at both ends of the car and black shades pulled down over the windows.

'We're spies. They can't risk us staring out at the scenery and reporting back all the trees we see to Hitler. Don't you know how dangerous we are to America's security?'

The woman had looked pointedly at the baby she was breast-feeding as she spoke. The whole car was full of mothers trying to manage their children; that any one of them could seriously be a threat seemed absurd.

At the first stop, Anna inched the shade up, determined to get some sense of where they were going. A group of children loitering on the platform immediately came running.

'I told you it was one of those trains! Look, they've got labels on them – they're Germans!'

She fell back against her seat as stones flew.

'Leave it down.' One of the guards leaned across her and slammed the blind shut. 'Unless you want to advertise that this is a train full of Nazis.'

When they were finally decanted – at a station called Gloucester City, a name which meant nothing to Anna – it was onto an empty platform. From there, they were bundled into army trucks that jolted them into nausea and their next, Anna wanted to say, prison, but the building they were dropped outside was a large and confusingly pretty Victorian house that wouldn't have looked out of place on Riverside Drive. They were ushered in and efficiently processed, their cases and money locked away 'for safekeeping', their clothes replaced with plain cotton dresses. It wasn't until the lights were out and the children were finally sleeping that the women in Anna's dormitory – all of whom were German in some degree or other – finally recovered their voices. The stories they shared were all the same: homes raided, husbands seized, an immigration system that was deaf to their accents.

'He was snatched at four in the morning; it took me two months to find out where he'd been sent.'

'They ransacked my house, broke all of my photographs, dragged Dieter away while the children were screaming.'

'His was the only wage and I've three mouths to feed – how am I supposed to manage?'

'When we kicked up a fuss for too long, they brought us in too. They call this *voluntary*, but does it look voluntary to you?'

Everyone was waiting to be reassigned to the family detention camp thousands of miles away in Texas, where they had finally been told their men were. Everyone was desperate to be American, and afraid to be marked out as German: love of *homeland* had been replaced by fear of deportation. 'How can we go *back* to a country we barely remember, where our children have never been?' was the room's most common refrain. And everyone assumed Anna's story was the same. She fell back on nods and sparse details and silences and didn't contradict them. None of the women were the hard-faced *Abwehr* informants the security services had cast them as, but, beyond that, Anna knew nothing about their beliefs or their contacts in the German American community. They didn't know her, but they had included her; that was far more important than trying to explain the truth of her life.

Once the women adjusted to the new regime, the Gloucester City house – on the surface at least – was a far kinder place to be than Ellis Island. The outdoor areas had grass to sit on and trees to sit under. There were handicraft classes and the opportunity to sell what was made if the inmate was skilled enough. None of the wardens carried guns; some even made an effort to learn and remember names. It was still, however, and despite first impressions, a prison. There was a fence surrounding the property through which passers-by could – and did – stare and jeer. Anything coming in was censored and there was constant surveillance: no letters were private; no room had a lock. No one was allowed to wear their own clothes, or manage their own money. The term of their detention never shifted from *indefinite*.

Boredom and the weight of confinement left too much time to think, and to question. As the months passed, Anna had to stay increasingly vigilant about policing her past. At first, her lack of the censored letters and supervised visits the others lived for won her pitying looks. By the time six months had dragged by, the looks had switched to nudges and raised eyebrows and an increasingly unsubtle prying she struggled to duck. Anna began to feel vulnerable, she began to withdraw. And then, on a snow-dulled December morning, the shout to 'move it out' rang through the house and she was back to being one of the herd.

CHAPTER THIRTEEN

*Crystal City Detention Camp,
December 1942 to February 1947*

The train journey to the detention camp took a week. No one was foolish enough to raise the shades this time. Anna had no conception of Texas beyond the sweeping skies and steer-roping cowboys she had seen in the movies. She couldn't hear the name *Crystal City* without imagining Dorothy and the Tin Man.

The cowboys turned out to be real – the guards patrolling the perimeter fence were kitted out in Stetsons and riding on horseback – but there was nothing glittering or beautiful about the Crystal City compound. The first thing Anna saw as the buses drove through the gates – as she was sure was intended – was the fence. It stretched out and stretched up and was topped with vicious barbed-wire curls. Guard towers presided over by machine-gun-wielding soldiers sat at the corners and spotlights bigger than any she had seen at UFA ran down its whole length. The dirt road they turned onto brought her in sight of buildings that were little more than rough wooden huts. There was no greenery. There was mud everywhere, thick and sticky and – as the children quickly discovered – so deep in places it could swallow unsuspecting legs up to the knees. The air, too mild for December, was thick with the damp earthy smell of it.

The new inmates were given no time to stop and stare or adjust to the disconcertingly spring-like climate. Their travel-cramped legs were urged off the bus at a trotting pace and into a low-roofed reception hall. Women asking about their husbands were told to shut up. Suitcases were removed and swapped for bundles of faded clothing that hadn't been selected for size. Anyone asking when their belongings might be returned was ignored.

Anna shuffled along, determined to listen and not speak. When she handed her papers over, however, the guard frowned.

'You shouldn't be here; you've no husband waiting. You should be in the single women's facility at Seabrooke.'

Anna forced herself not to notice the whispers rustling down the line.

'There must have been a mistake. Perhaps he was here and now he's been deported.'

It was a ridiculous lie; it couldn't possibly hold, but her audience needed something.

The guard looked over at the women and crying children still waiting to be processed and sighed. 'What there's been is lazy paperwork which I don't have time to deal with right now. There's a single-room hut free – take it. Keep your head down and maybe no one will care.'

Anna didn't need telling twice. She couldn't face another move. She needed to stand still and gather herself up and work out what routes back to normality, if any, were open to her. The women she had travelled with, who were still whispering, might think she was odd, they might think she had something to hide, but they weren't unkind. They hadn't excluded her in the house despite their reservations, and Anna doubted they would do it now without serious provocation. She was, however loosely, part of a community and that was all that mattered. In the nine months since she had been snatched out of her life, that was the most valuable lesson Anna had learned: any kind of detention was bad, but detention endured alone was unbearable.

The months passed. The German detainees kept to their side of the compound, the Japanese inmates – who had been detained at

Crystal City first – kept to theirs. Anna and the women she had arrived with began to explore their new home, which, although rough and clearly not ready for as many people as were now crammed into it, was set up to be more like a small town than a camp. It had shops and services as well as the crude buildings being used as housing. It also had guards and watchtowers and a curfew and no way of getting out. And the worst climate Anna had ever encountered. When the mud dried up, it was replaced by dust which coated the throat, and made the eyes sting, and sat in a fine film across every surface. The warm air turned hot and the heat kept rising until the tin-roofed, tar-papered huts turned into ovens. Rattlesnakes and scorpions slithered through open doors and gaps in the walls. Nights became sweaty sleepless things spent trying not to think about nocturnal visitors.

Anna kept her head down, made herself useful and didn't complain. She was never late to line up for the three daily roll calls, even the 5.30 a.m. one whose shrill whistle blasted the detainees too brutally into their day. She did extra shifts in the laundry and the grocery market when mothers with sick children were called away. If she cooked more than her tiny icebox could hold, she gave it away to families with more mouths than their rations could comfortably stretch to. She managed, she was treated respectfully, but she was desperately lonely.

As the camp expanded, the detainees worked together to build the facilities the compound lacked that would give them at least the semblance of a normal life. A snake-thick reservoir was cleared and turned into a swimming pool. Some enterprising chefs opened a German restaurant and a beer garden, and everyone pretended there wasn't a prison wall less than ten feet away.

Anna heard the laughter and the splashing every evening. She never went. They were family places, filled with children whose presence – especially the six- and seven-year-olds who were as lively and curious as Anna hoped Franzi would now be – made her loneliness deeper. She painted her hut instead. She watched the Japanese detainees transform the plots round their homes with flowers and shrubs and became a gardener. Once a week, she played cards with women whose children were teenagers and happy not to be watched over. She worked very hard to ignore the guards who patrolled the compound every hour. She pulled her curtains tight at night before the spotlights snapped on and turned them all into specimens. She made sure to keep busy enough to keep the *Gitterkrankheit* away – the *fence sickness* the doctors in the overstretched medical unit called laziness or malingering but its sufferers knew as a creeping depression brought on by confinement and isolation and a loss of control.

As the authorities rounded up more and more of the country's alien populations, the camp continued to grow. Its inmates' censored lives, however, shrank further and further. By the summer of 1943, Anna had stopped asking what *indefinite* meant. She had trained herself to live day by day; she had trained herself to forget and to be forgotten. And then she walked into the dining hall on a sweltering June day and all her carefully constructed defences shattered.

Fritz Kuhn was standing by the serving counter, staring straight at her.

Everything changed with his coming. Anna had told herself that no one in the camp wanted to be anything but a good American, that everyone hated the Nazis and their view of what Germany meant as much as she did. With Kuhn's arrival, however, old hostilities and hatreds resurfaced. A new breed of men came into the camp, men who were hardened from prison and quick with their fists. Who saw *pro-American* as *anti-German* and *traitor*. Who tore the Stars and Stripes down from the flagpole and replaced it with a swastika, and did it again and again despite the solitary confinement and reduced rations it led to.

Their poison seeped out. Some of the original detainees – the ones who had been carefully hiding their fury at being imprisoned by a country they thought they belonged to – embraced older allegiances. A new kind of order swept through the camp, one that required a black market and protection money and was backed up by bullies who swaggered round brandishing clubs and saluting the Führer.

The new inmates not only brought their anger with them; they brought reports of the war. After years of being denied radios and newsreels, the inhabitants of Crystal City lapped these reports up, never realising they were as heavily censored as the few newspapers and magazines that made it through the fence. Kuhn and his men crowed about Germany's total occupation of France and the continuing *purge* of the Jews. They dismissed any discussion of Hitler's crushing defeat by the Russians at Stalingrad, or Mussolini's collapse, which Anna and some of the other inmates had overheard the guards whispering about, as being carefully stage-managed American lies to break German morale. Then they taught anyone who dared repeat those *traitorous rumours* some very uncomfortable lessons, so the rumours died. Shoulders went up; for too many, *Heimat* once again became a word dripping in pride.

Faced with this new swaggering, those whose hearts had never been Hitler's retreated and began shunning the public spaces. Anna was one of them, although she knew hiding was pointless. Kuhn had seen her. Their confrontation was merely a matter of time.

He waited a fortnight before he kicked her door in. Nobody came running at the noise, although it was long past curfew – the nightly patrols had apparently melted away. He brought two men with him, both square and brutish. They separated out as they entered, flanking her one on each side, leaving the centre of the floor to Kuhn.

Anna stood up and folded her hands behind her back. She had never been more frightened, or more determined not to show it. 'What do you want?'

Kuhn stepped closer. His breath was spicy and stale. 'A confession.'

She kept her eyes on his, blocked his henchmen out. 'To what?'

'To the truth. That you were an informant. That you passed on our secrets. That you had one of our best men arrested and imprisoned on a trumped-up charge.'

Anna flinched at that; she couldn't help herself.

Kuhn nodded to his men.

'Frank was released early, although you wouldn't have known that, because you had already run. He had time in prison to think, and he made contacts who were happy to do a little digging, a little surveillance. He brought me quite a dossier, about your trips to Foley Square and the spies' post office. He knew you were behind his arrest. I wouldn't be surprised if you were behind mine too.'

'I hope I was.'

Anna could have stopped the words before they came out of her mouth: she had had enough practice at covering her feelings and lying. Except that she didn't want to stop them and, despite what came next, she was glad that she'd said them. That she had stood up for herself and against the Reich and let Kuhn finally know just how well, and for how long, she had fooled him. He had expected her to beg – that was written in his arrogant smirk. Instead Anna balled up her fists and she thought about Franzi and how much she loved her, and how much she hated men like Goebbels and Kuhn and all their twisted little acolytes, and she spat in Kuhn's face.

'I hate you. I have always hated you and the Nazi scum you attract. You are not America's saviours – you are evil, the same as Hitler is evil, and I pray every day that the Allies will win this war and destroy every last trace of you.'

The first blow knocked her to the ground. The second knocked her unconscious. In the fleeting gap between the two, Anna felt lighter than air.

'Your shoulder was dislocated and has been reset. You have three broken ribs, extensive bruising and possibly some internal bleeding – we are waiting on tests. It was a savage beating. Do you want to file a report?'

Anna, very carefully, shook her aching head. She had no intention of enduring another assault.

The doctor sighed. 'Whoever did this is dangerous. When the alarm was raised and the patrol officer found you, he thought you were dead.'

Anna tried to sit up; the pain was excruciating. 'Perhaps if he had come when the trouble started, I wouldn't have got into this mess.'

The doctor's face hardened. 'Don't put the blame on us. Personal issues between detainees aren't the patrol officers' concern. They are here to protect the outside community from you, not you from each other.'

Anna didn't bother to answer. No one had ever attempted to escape from the camp: the fence was too high and they were reminded at every roll call that the penalty for trying was death. And, apart from the houses the camp's employees lived in, there was no outside community to protect. From what she had heard, the town of Crystal City was nothing more than a handful of boardwalks, and San Antonio – the nearest settlement of any reasonable size – was over a hundred miles away. The lack of any decent shops or cinemas or bars near the camp was one of the reasons most of its employees hated working there, and was another reason too many of them hated its inmates. But the fiction that everyone in the camp was dangerous had to be maintained, or what reason was there to keep them locked in?

The doctor waited – Anna could imagine the note he would make on her file if she chose to argue. When she stayed silent, he moved on.

For the four weeks it took her to heal, Anna played the good patient and was left largely alone. It was hard to push away the echoes of the Charité Hospital. It was hard not to be dragged under the weight of the past and whatever Kuhn decided would be her future. Within a day of her discharge, what that would be became abundantly clear.

Kuhn, it appeared, had more in common with Goebbels than his ability to manipulate an audience: he understood the power of isolating his target. When Anna arrived back at her hut, it had been emptied. There wasn't a can in the cupboard or a sheet on the bed. She dragged herself to the German grocery store, clutching the plastic tokens she still had in her pocket which passed in the camp for money. Kuhn's men and their threats had got there first. No one would serve her. No one would speak to her. She tried the camp's general store instead. The servers were all Germans; the response was the same. Hungry and refusing to be beaten, she went to the dining hall. Someone knocked into her tray and toppled it.

For three days, Anna could get nothing to eat or drink apart from the milk that was delivered daily to every door. On the fourth day, she fainted and was sent back to the hospital. The pattern went on for weeks. In the end, Anna sought out the circle of women she had lived with in Gloucester City, broke down and wept.

'I wasn't a Nazi, but I was an informer. I got sucked into a deal with the FBI because I was on a blacklist in Berlin and was terrified of being deported. And because I'd lost my baby, and was foolish enough to think they might help me find her again. I shouldn't have done it, and I am sorry for all the deceptions working for them dragged me into, but this punishment is too much. Can't any of you help me?'

There was some sympathy, especially for the loss of a child, but there were also a lot of shrugs.

'Is it true that you had the FBI make up charges against your fiancé – that he didn't do what he was sent down for?'

When she answered yes, most of the group got up and left. The few who didn't could barely look at her.

'You've told such a lot of lies, Anna, we don't know what to believe. There's some here who hold with Hitler; there's plenty who don't. But there's none of us who would betray an innocent man.'

Anna knew then that what Frank had been, or what her reasons were, didn't matter. If she argued that they were judging her against the wrong standards, they would all walk away. All she could say was 'I'm sorry', so that was all that she said. It won her more kindness than she expected.

'Three of us will take it in turns to leave you food. If our husbands find out, we will stop.'

They kept their word; Anna kept going. No one hurt her again, although her nights were broken for months worrying that someone would. Kuhn made sure that she was ostracised, watched her fade and turned his attention elsewhere. By the time he was shipped away in the spring of 1944 – to a more secure facility where he could do less harm – Anna was able to buy basic food again. The damage, however, was done. Her weight dropped below a hundred pounds; her nights were wrecked by insomnia. Fence sickness set in. She was plagued by bouts of fatigue and a wave of chest infections that, in the December of 1944, turned into pneumonia. She was admitted to the hospital, not expecting to come out again; the illness, however, saved her life.

'I don't care that she's on the list. She will never pass a medical and to put someone this sick on the transport risks jeopardising the whole thing. Do you want to be the one responsible for keeping our boys in German POW camps?'

Anna was such a quiet and biddable patient, none of the doctors or nurses lowered their voices when they were near her cubicle. She had spent most of the previous fortnight too sick to care about their gossip. Now, however, the penicillin was finally working and her attention was caught.

'And we'll get a replacement easy enough, more than one I bet. We've fed them with so much propaganda about how great the war's going for Germany, they're queueing up to go back. What

I wouldn't give to see their faces when they get off the boat and realise the Reich is finished and Hitler's done.'

'Do you think it's wrong, what we're doing?' The second voice sounded younger and more hesitant. 'Making them think they're returning to a flourishing country when they're just pawns to get our prisoners back? And with Germany in the state it's in? The photographs of Dresden and Berlin are terrifying – there's nothing left there but ruins. Should we really be sending women and children into that?'

The answer was lost in a flurry of shouts and calls for the cardiac cart.

Anna lay rigid, trying to make sense of *there's nothing left* and *pawns*. Repatriation was what they called it now, not deportation; a large group had already left. Anna knew another was scheduled to leave in the New Year; she hadn't known she was part of it. Or that Germany was *destroyed*. She closed her eyes, visions of black-clad SS men cornered like rats flooding her head, and prayed that her mother had made it safely to Hamburg and that city wasn't another broken Dresden or Berlin.

They won't go down without a fight; they'll take everything and everyone they can with them.

Anna pulled the covers around her and poked at her fingers and arms. She wasn't quite as thin as she had been. Rest and regular food had started putting weight back on her bones.

They're not taking me. If sick is all it takes to stay off the lists, that's what I'll be.

She ate as little as she could to function. She failed medical after medical. And then, the war ended. Anna heard the news of Hitler's suicide, and then Goebbels', and she sobbed with relief. And when she finally saw the photographs of Berlin with its beauty all pounded to dust, she sobbed again.

The camp stayed open, the *repatriations* continued, although there were voices now all across America saying that they shouldn't, and the guards treated their inmates with a compassion few of them had shown before. Anna, however, had nowhere to go and no one outside to call on, so she stayed in the camp and she stayed thin. She failed another medical. And then, in February 1947, there were no more medicals to fail.

'You have to sign this. All ex-inmates are bound by it.'

It was an official oath demanding that she never speak about what had happened in the camp. The guard had the grace to look shame-faced as he passed Anna the pen.

'Move it out.'

The Crystal City Camp closed. Anna's life rolled back five years and put her once more onto a ferry bound for Ellis Island, where failing a medical meant a ship sailing away from Manhattan.

All that effort to stay alive and to stay sane just to get back to where I started.

The thought ran through her as sharp as the pains that stabbed at her chest as she tried to climb the steep staircase up to the registration hall.

Goebbels is dead. The Nazis are gone. Germany is clean again. Franzi is lost, there's nothing here for me, but perhaps there will be something there.

She tried to hold on to that instead, but it was too hard. There was no propaganda about the state of Germany anymore – everyone knew the truth. The country was in ruins; it was starving; it was struggling under the weight of camps that made Crystal City look like paradise, under the guilt of the millions sent to them. Anna knew she no longer had the strength to confront whatever *Germany* and *German* meant now.

The second set of stairs defeated her. She sank down, waiting for the shout to move. Instead, she was met with strong arms and a smile.

'Come on now with you, sweetheart. We can't have you sitting down here. Let's get you to the top, see what can be done.'

Anna found herself in a chair, wrapped in a blanket, a mug of the best coffee she had tasted in years warming her hands as conversations whirled over her head.

'We can't stick her on one of those ships bound for Germany. She wouldn't make the journey; if she did, she wouldn't last a minute over there with the mess things are in. I wouldn't do that to a dog, never mind an old woman on her own.'

An old woman? I'm thirty-seven.

Anna didn't know whether to laugh or cry. And yet they were right. The last time she had looked in a mirror, the bony and worn-out face peering back had looked thirty years older than she should.

The man who had half-carried her up the stairs bent down. 'Do you really have no one we could call, who could speak for you? Who could get you back on your feet a little and help you sort all this out?'

His voice was lilting and soft and rolled round the words.

A brogue he spreads as thick as butter.

The words popped up from nowhere.

Anna put down her cup. Pride and the impossibility of explanations had stopped her before, there was no point in clinging to them now.

'There might be, but I lost contact with her long ago…'

It was too slight a hope to put any real faith in. When the immigration officer rang Riverside Drive, the house was closed up except for a new housekeeper who had never heard of the old one. Anna told him about the policeman husband and off he went again.

She won't remember me, or she won't want to remember me. He will have retired and gone.

Anna curled up in her blanket and let the fates be; she no longer had the strength to try and outwit them. An hour passed, and then another. She stopped counting, started to think instead about her mother and the possibility of finding her again if they did send her back. That was a ray of hope that might make the days bearable. And then Anna heard her name, and there was Mrs Michaels standing in the hall with her arms flung wide.

'Dear God, you poor girl, what have they done to you? Come here, pet. Let me take you home.'

She had never heard anything sweeter.

PART THREE

CHAPTER FOURTEEN

Los Angeles, October 1957

Los Angeles Times
9 A.M. FINAL

Friday Morning, October 10, 1957 Daily 10c

WAS LOUISE BAKER GOEBBELS' MISTRESS?

HOW A HOLLYWOOD LEGEND REWROTE HER NAZI PAST
By Peggy Bailey

'What do you know about Louise Baker?'

Film fans have been asking that question since the star first burst onto American movie screens in 1936. Given that the actress has spent the last 20 years carefully cultivating an air of mystery, the usual answer is 'not much'.

> **Soviet spy Jack Sobel sentenced to 7 years.**
> Full details page 3.

Now new revelations about Miss Baker's life – as one of the shining lights of the **Nazi** cinema in **Germany** under the leadership of **Third Reich Propaganda Minister Joseph Goebbels** – may explain why she has gone to such lengths to keep her past secret.

The feature looked far more stark set out on the page than Peggy had envisioned. It was also far more damning than the version she had, in the end, decided to write. There was no sign of *daughter* or *search* or *missing mother* in the opening paragraphs. Instead **Goebbels**, **Mistress** and **Nazi** flew black and angry out of the printing presses and onto the whirling conveyer belt.

'They're pinning a lot of hopes on this edition; the boss thinks it might break the million-copy mark. That's quite a feat for your first time out. How in hell did you hang on to the byline?'

Peggy didn't bother to reply: the supervisor's leer told her he had already come up with an answer far more entertaining than the truth, which was 'sheer bloody-mindedness'. She took a step back from the churning machinery, finding its relentless speed unnerving. The print room was a far less comfortable place to be than the office. Peggy had been in it once before, as part of a whistle-stop tour of the building on her first day in the job. She had been permitted in there tonight because it was her first published article: watching the newspapers fly out of the press – at over 40,000 copies an hour – on the 11 p.m. production line was a reporter's rite of passage. The noise, however, was overwhelming: a constant whirring and grinding she could feel more than hear. And the smell – of iron-tinged hot metal and faintly musky, woody ink – was almost feral. Standing in the middle of the presses was like standing in a beast's lair.

A beast I'm about to unleash without any hope of keeping control.

Tomorrow morning the papers would hit the city's newsstands and her words would be out in the world, to be chewed over and repeated and – as Peggy was starting to realise – reshaped.

But, however they are interpreted, they will be read, which is what I wanted.

And it was. Except, looking at the headline the editor had run with, it was hard to shake off the *wasn't it?*

Peggy had taken half-a-dozen journalism modules in college, and she had still forgotten the most fundamental rule: *the story that runs is the story that sells.* Charlie had tried to remind her of that before she ran off to the paper all revved up, but Peggy had been too carried away with her plans to take any real notice.

'Even if they let you write it – and that is a very big *if* given you've no experience and how many noses would be stuck out of joint in giving you a byline – that doesn't mean you'll recognise what ends up on the page. I had articles that could have run as a two-page spread cut down to two lines, and others where the first sentence was the last one I'd written, which made things far more black and white than they were in reality. I've also made more than one pitch where the premise fell apart as soon as I got past the first paragraph. The frustration of having my work constantly messed with was one of the reasons I got out.'

Peggy had snorted, but he hadn't shut up.

'I get it, I've been there. You think you're too good a writer to have your work messed about with, and that your hunches always play out. All right, Dorothy Parker, here's hoping I'm wrong and at least one of those misconceptions is true.'

Now Charlie had every reason to say *I told you so*, although Peggy hoped he had more sense than to try. Her article was completely reshaped, and as for her hunch that Louise was unreservedly wicked and needed exposing… Peggy remembered *whatever is coming to her, she deserves it*, and would have cringed if the supervisor hadn't still been watching. She had meant every word when she'd said it to Charlie at the restaurant. She had still meant it when she'd pitched the article ripping Louise's reputation to shreds. What she hadn't realised, however, was that somewhere between turning up all bright-eyed at the newspaper and actually doing the writing, she would find a narrative that didn't come neatly packaged in black and white, but was shot through instead with grey.

'I am here to see the editor, Mr Williams. I have a proposal for him that, trust me, he will want to hear.'

Peggy had been as ignored on her first approach to the desk as she had expected to be.

On her second, she added, 'And I am prepared to wait all day,' and was ignored again.

In the end, it had taken five hours sitting in *The Los Angeles Times'* draughty lobby, and five politely phrased requests, before the receptionist finally gave in and placed a call to the impenetrable upper floors. It was less time than Peggy had steeled herself for. Charlie had warned her that the first time he had gone there with his résumé, it had taken him two days to be seen, and less than twenty minutes to be ushered out again. *The Los Angeles Times* was California's biggest-selling newspaper and the largest paper anywhere outside New York, which was why Peggy had chosen it. She had no intention of her exposé disappearing into the muddle of scandal and gossip which filled the pages of most of Hollywood's press.

As befitted such a powerhouse, everything about the paper's headquarters on West 1st Street was designed to keep mere mortals away. The huge entrance was ringed by pillars that could have graced a classical temple. The legend *The Times* was carved in giant letters across the stone frontage, as if the newspaper was the one shaping every minute of them. Despite the constant flow of people, the entrance hall was as hushed as a mausoleum.

Peggy, however, had pictured herself taking her first step into the magical world of newsprint for far too long to be cowed. The only female journalist she knew of at *The Times* was the legendary show-business columnist Hedda Hopper, who was famed as much for her elaborate hats as her scoops and her film-star contacts. Peggy had considered wearing a showstopping headpiece herself but rejected that when Charlie creased up with laughter. She had dressed instead as she imagined a successful reporter would dress, in a green tweed sheath dress and matching waisted jacket, and a black Juliet cap with a satin green trim. The outfit was stylish and businesslike and had turned appreciative heads as she entered the building, which was precisely the effect Peggy had intended. She was carrying a slim attaché case into which she had tucked the photograph and her notes on Louise, plus a spiral-bound journal the girl in the stationery shop promised all the reporters used and a selection of pencils and pens. Peggy had never felt so prepared, or so professional. Or so unprepared for the greeting she received when the receptionist's call was finally answered.

'Dear Lord, who have you come as? Have you seen this one, boys? Rosalind Russell's turned up to hold the front page.'

The jacketless man bowling up through the lobby wasn't the editor: Peggy had memorised every detail of the elegantly posed photograph she had found of him in the library. The man approaching her was pouchy-eyed and pouchy-framed and clearly had no respect for quiet, or for elegance.

The security guards laughed; Peggy, to her annoyance, blushed.

Ignoring the grins, she stood up and stuck out her hand. The barrel-shaped man ignored it.

'My name is—'

'Peggy Bailey. Yeah, I got it. And that you've been here for hours pestering the girls. Okay, you got me down here, well done for that. Now give me your story, or your résumé, or whatever it is that's so earth-shatteringly important, and I'll give you a call when I've read it.'

'No you won't.'

The man's double take was exactly what Peggy needed to pull her confidence back.

'You'll throw it in the trash. Or you'll go through my notes and lift what you want and never give me credit. I told the desk I have information that will interest Editor Williams, and it's him I'm here to see. If you can't make that happen, I'm happy to keep waiting for someone who can.'

There was a pause Peggy managed not to fill.

The man looked her up and down, burst out laughing and finally held out his hand. 'All right, short-stuff. It's a slow day; he might be glad of the entertainment. Come on.'

He led her via a busy lift to a crowded floor bristling with desks and alive with the sharp ping and percussion clack of typewriters going at a speed Peggy realised she was a long way from matching. The editor's office was in the far corner, its windows shaded from prying eyes. Peggy followed her guide's fast trot, dodging overflowing in-trays and waving telephones, trying to pretend that being finally inside a newsroom wasn't making her giddy.

The man, who she had worked out from all the shouting voices was called Bernie, turned round as they got to the threshold of the inner office.

'All right, Miss Peggy Bailey, you're up. He's a good one. Go in and impress him – which you're not half bad at – and he might even listen.'

He knocked, pushed the door open and was gone again, tearing round the desks, calling out for the copy-boy, grabbing up typed sheets in a whirl of energy Peggy longed to bounce after.

'Well, you got past Bernie, which was your hardest challenge. What is it you want from me?'

The man behind the desk was as sharp-suited as his picture, beautifully spoken and exactly what Peggy wanted a newspaper editor to be. She grinned.

'A job.'

'Williams was grabbed, I could see that at once. But he was hesitant. He wanted to give it to a senior reporter, like you said he would, but I refused. I told him: "It's my story to tell and it's my story to write."' She gave a little bow as Charlie laughed. 'And then he offered me a crazy amount of money for the information we've already gathered. And I still said no. So he gave in. I have four weeks to back up my pitch with enough evidence to get it past the lawyers, and to write an article that's good enough to print.' She finished in a breathless rush.

'And?'

Peggy's smile almost split her face.

'And I got my job. It's local news, the bottom of the heap – spelling bees and bake sales – but I'll be a reporter. A proper reporter. My mother – Joan, I mean – would have been so proud of me: it's what she always said I would be.' Peggy stopped, suddenly desperate to call Joan and tell her the good news, and horribly aware that she couldn't.

'She would be, and I am.' Charlie had caught hold of her then and swung her round, and then, somehow, he was kissing her and it was exactly as delicious as she had hoped it would be.

'I can't be distracted – there's too much at stake.'

'I know. You don't have to explain the importance of nailing your copy to me. I get it.'

He did. It was one of the, very many, reasons Peggy had grown to like him as much as she did. So she had stopped talking about the article and let him distract her, for a little while at least.

Once Williams bit, Peggy's first stop had been to go back to Clara Sokoll with another full purse. It took longer this time to extract the details that she wanted – everything had to be written down and signed, which Clara was reluctant to do until Peggy counted out more bills. She came away with pages of gossip about Goebbels' dreaded ministry teas, his affairs with the actresses Luise Ullrich and Lida Baarová, and the casting-couch weekends at the Bogensee villa, which the old lady described as a brothel. She did not, however, collect anything of any use about Louise.

'Everything she said was still rumour and innuendo. I kept pushing her, and then she got angry and we didn't part on good terms. And the thing is, after listening to all the horrible stuff she had to say about the way the film industry was run, I'm not as sure as I was that what happened with Louise is exactly how I imagined it – with her as the villain, I mean. She was young and Goebbels was… predatory is the best word I can think of. Clara said he was known as the *Babelsberg Goat*. She also told me a stomach-curdling anecdote about a girl called Renate Müller, who she says Goebbels had murdered – pushed out of a window – because she wouldn't sleep with him or star in his propaganda films. Do you think that could be true?'

Charlie stared at her.

'Do I think that one of Hitler's most trusted advisors, a man who murdered his own children, and was a major cheerleader for gassing Jews could have had an actress killed on a whim? I don't know – it's a hard one.'

Peggy managed to resist throwing a pillow at him. 'Don't be sarcastic; it doesn't suit you. I know how dumb that sounded, but I've been going in circles. If Goebbels controlled every aspect of the film world – which, obviously, he did – maybe Louise didn't do whatever we think she did with him out of choice.'

Charlie was immediately back in step with her thinking. 'Which changes the tone of the article. *Actress hides past because she was terrified of Nazis* isn't quite the piece you were looking for.'

'Exactly. And it's not what I pitched, or what will keep me in a job. The added problem is that there's no way of tracking down anyone else we could talk to – Clara is our only lead here – and there's no time to start hunting out actresses in Germany who might have known her, or got involved with Goebbels themselves.'

'Eddy didn't come up with anything then, when you wrote and told him your suspicions about Louise?'

Peggy shook her head. 'His reply was like his first letter: more going on under the surface than in the actual words. He didn't appear to have heard of Louise Baker, and the news that she was Marika was clearly a shock. He made a cryptic comment about having had as many reasons not to search for Marika back then as he had for trying to find Anna. And he asked me to stay in touch, same as last time. He didn't add anything. I haven't written to him since, although I should maybe warn him about the article before it comes out, in case it gets picked up by one of the papers or TV channels over there.'

'And you still haven't told him that he might be your father?'

'No.' Peggy shrugged. 'I can't. Not with all the uncertainty still around Anna.' Her attempt to sound casual didn't fool Charlie. He pulled her into a hug she was very glad to curl into.

'What are you going to do, Pegs, about the article? You were so angry when you came up with the idea. Are you still as determined to write it the way you said?'

It was a good question, one that Peggy had been wrestling with. She still wasn't sure of the answer.

'I'm less certain Louise is as wicked as I painted her to the *Times*, when it comes to being a Nazi, I mean. But I still think she's hiding more than we've found out, and that the gaps in her story are where I'm going to find Anna. What was that thing she said: *You're certainly as easy to fool?* I'm still angry with her; that hasn't changed. And I'm still as determined to find my mother. Given Louise won't co-operate, and I'm done offering her chances, there's no other way to do it than this. I'll soften the article, I'll be more speculative. I won't set out to destroy Louise, if I can help it. But I'm not backing away.'

Peggy had done her best. She had made more of Louise's youth; she had made more of Goebbels' viciously predatory nature. She had angled the piece to make it more about the friendship between Louise and the missing Anna, about a daughter's search for her mother, than a legend's destruction. She had written what she thought was a balanced, investigative article.

But she hadn't been in control, she had been naïve, and all of her efforts to be fair had been stripped away in favour of **Goebbels' Mistress** and **Nazi.** Not that anyone but her was concerned.

'Isn't anyone worried about her lawyers anymore?'

By the time Peggy managed to ask the question, it was clear no one was.

Bernie carried on topping up her glass with the champagne they had cracked open to celebrate the paper's record-breaking circulation.

'Why would we be? We dropped in enough question marks to avoid a libel suit. And, besides, why would she stoke the fire by responding? Word is, she legged it out of her mansion before the second edition appeared. The great Louise Baker has gone to ground, and, if even half of what you wrote about her and that bastard Goebbels is true, then good riddance. I hope she'll be licking her wounds for months.'

Peggy sipped her champagne. She didn't argue; there was no point: Bernie had already danced off in search of another bottle. She didn't, however, agree with him. Louise Baker slapped and snarled; she fought back. If Louise really had disappeared, then it was surely to work out her next play. There were many things Peggy could imagine a woman who could reinvent herself as perfectly as Louise doing – including carrying on a dangerous flirtation with Goebbels. Licking her wounds in silence, however, wasn't one of them.

CHAPTER FIFTEEN

'Peggy, are you awake?'

Peggy rolled over and grinned up at Charlie, who was attempting to carry a tray piled with coffee and pastries at the same time as reading a newspaper. It was a precarious juggling act destined to end in failure. She sat up and grabbed the tray before its contents crashed.

'I am now. Why? Is there something you'd like to distract me with?'

He grinned back at her, whatever had caught his eye in the paper momentarily forgotten. In the two months since their first kiss, getting distracted with Charlie had become one of Peggy's favourite activities. She put the breakfast supplies onto the bedside table, pulled the quilt aside and patted the bed. He sat down and reached for her. Then he hesitated.

Peggy pulled her very best pout and flicked her hair across one eye. 'What's the matter, lover boy? Are you bored of my charms already?'

His hungry look told her he wasn't, but he didn't move closer.

'As if. And don't think I'm not tempted, but you need to see this first.'

The paper he handed her was *The Daily Variety*, Hollywood's bible for insider movie news. The woman in the cover shot was Louise, but not a Louise the public – or the industry – had ever seen before. The tumbling hair and heavily lipsticked half-smile was gone. Louise had been photographed in profile, with pale lips and hair that was swept sleekly back and curled under one ear. Her dress too was different from the vampish numbers she normally favoured: it was a plain black shift, with a simple, not too low, V-neck, which she had accentuated with a single strand of pearls.

'She looks the spit of Jackie Kennedy.'

Charlie sat back down on the bed. 'Doesn't she just. It's clever. Anyone looking at it will make the connection with America's apple-pie sweetheart far faster than they'll think Nazi.'

'*Louise Speaks,*' Peggy read the headline out and groaned. 'That's perfect too. *Louise* to imply that we all know her, and what a choice of verb for someone best known for her silences.'

'Plus the noble pose looking off into the distance, as though she's about to divulge some great truth to the grateful masses. Maybe she did learn a trick or two off Goebbels after all. Here, read this.' Charlie flipped through the paper to a page he'd marked with a folded corner.

> **After four lonely weeks away from the spotlight, trying to come to terms with an unprecedented attack on her good name, Hollywood legend Louise Baker is finally ready to face her public. Hear *her story* – in *her words* – exclusively on *Tonight Starring Jack Paar*, Friday November 8 on NBC.**

Peggy put the paper down and reached for one of the cooling cups of coffee. The piece was short, but it spoke volumes.

'She's coming out all guns blazing, and going straight for the sympathy vote. Look at the language: *lonely, attack, her words.* And I think, given the way she wraps men round her fingers, she'll at least have Paar on her side. It's obvious why she's doing it – she needs to win her public back – it's certainly going to be interesting to see how she puts up a fight.'

*

It was more than interesting – the interview was a masterclass in how to win over an audience. Peggy had sat down in front of the television set, pencil poised, ready to make copious notes. She had got no further by the time the half-time commercials started than *the lighting is subtler than usual, clearly meant to be flattering.*

'Hold your nerve. There's another twenty minutes to go after the break. They wouldn't have booked her on as the only guest if the second half was going to be a puff piece.'

Peggy waved away the glass of wine Charlie was trying to buoy up her spirits with, although keeping a clear head seemed increasingly pointless.

'Based on the first half, it could well be. Which means I'll have nothing to offer Bernie and I'll be stuck on the back pages covering dog shows for ever.'

Peggy had rushed off to sell her follow-up article to Bernie and Williams fired up with the prospect of making more headlines. *And so full of my own abilities, I forgot how long Louise has been in this game, and how well she plays it.* The memory of how she had breezed into the editor's office, as if she had twenty years' experience, not a twenty-two-year-old's overconfidence, was not a comforting one. The recollection of how she had insisted she was the only one who could write the human-interest angle which would be different from the competition and therefore sell more papers wasn't much better.

Neither Bernie nor Williams had bitten her hand off – as she had rather implied to Charlie that they had. They were convinced that Louise would simply deny the allegations, and there would be nothing left to report beyond that. They were also, however, businessmen and shifting copies was what mattered, so they had given Peggy the possibility of another front page, providing there was some new revelation, and she could pull off 'a piece that wasn't hollow or soapy'. Peggy had left the office clutching her second big break – two more than her age and experience should have allowed her. And now the screen had cut to the Colgate commercial and the confidence she had hurled around in the office had totally fallen away.

When the interview had begun, Peggy hadn't been certain that Louise would be able to take control the way she had imagined the actress would have from the programme's billing. Louise had walked on set to applause that was muted rather than welcoming; she had, however, remained perfectly composed. She was dressed demurely – still 'more Jackie than Jackie', as Charlie had put it – in a simple dark dress with a boat neckline and a bell-shaped skirt that swayed as she crossed from the wings to her chair at Jack Paar's side. If the less-than-enthusiastic audience reception had unnerved her, she didn't show it. She looked serious and steady, and the programme's normally light mood had shifted to accommodate her. There had been no chatty preamble, no comedy or musical moments the way Paar normally welcomed his guests. There was a simple exchange of *hello* and *thank you*, and then he had launched straight into his first question.

'Miss Baker, it's been quite a month for you. Tell me, if you can, how it feels to have gone from icon to – and, trust me, I take no pleasure in saying this—'

'Monster?' Louise had plucked the word out of his mouth so delicately, she knocked the sting right out of it.

'That was too neatly done. They must have practised.'

Peggy was in complete agreement, but there was no time to discuss it. She shushed Charlie as Louise carried on talking.

'How it has felt is simple, Jack: overwhelming. And frightening. A reminder of why I fled the nightmare my home country had fallen into in the 1930s to come here. To America and to safety.'

The camera had panned to the audience as Paar asked his next question. Some of them were so obviously eager to hear the answer, they were mouthing it along with him.

'You *are* German then? Not French as you have always claimed? That part of the paper's revelations were true?'

Louise nodded. Paar looked at his notes as the audience muttered.

Peggy stabbed her pencil into her pad. '*That part.* He's set the next answer up.'

As if to prove Peggy right, Paar softened his voice. 'And could you explain that decision to us, and then address the rest of the allegations that have been made against you?'

Louise took a deep breath and turned to face the faces intently watching hers. The camera zoomed in so close, it was practically caressing her.

'Look at her eyes – they're luminous.'

Charlie snorted. 'Blue eyedrops. All the actresses use them: they make the whites glow. I bet she's made the camera man rub Vaseline onto the lens as well.'

Louise was speaking again, her gaze roaming the tiered rows of seating, resting her glance here and there. Everyone she lingered on, even though it was for barely a second, leaned forward.

'I changed my identity when I first came here because I was too ashamed to be who I was. Being German was such a burden then. Every time I opened my mouth, people heard Hitler in my accent. That was a dreadful thing to live with. Lots of people like me, who couldn't face the prejudice that was widespread then, pretended they came from somewhere else. Often it was Austria, or Hungary, something close to our native voices, but I became French – I had French relatives and I spoke that language fluently, with an accent that wouldn't have worked in Paris, I'll admit, but that sounded convincing in Hollywood. None of us were Nazis; we weren't hiding anything. We just wanted acceptance and a quiet life.'

A ripple had run round the audience at the word *Nazis.* Paar waited for it to settle.

'Before you go on. You mentioned relatives in France: wouldn't they have found your new identity confusing? Are you still in contact with them?'

Louise shook her head. 'Europe was a mess in the war. Much of it is still trying to pick itself up, as many viewers with ties there will know. I can't find any trace of my family. My father was Jewish; my parents went to Paris in 1935 to escape the Nazis. I don't think it's difficult to imagine what happened to them once France was occupied.'

She paused. For a moment she looked lost. Peggy sat forward, sensing the frown that puckered Louise's face wasn't intentional. And then it was gone again and the actress recovered. 'So yes, you asked me if that much was true and it is. I am German. As for the rest of what was said… it is also true that I was an actress in Berlin and that, yes, I did I know Joseph Goebbels.'

The audience gasped. Peggy clutched her pencil.

'Here we go. Keep your fingers crossed this is more than some blanket denial he doesn't dig into.'

Paar let the audience quieten again. 'That is quite an admission. Can you help us understand what you mean by *know*?'

Louise clasped her hands on the top of the desk as if she was steadying herself. 'I will try. Surely I don't need to tell you that, if there is a *monster* anywhere in this, it is him. The terrible things he – I'm sorry, but it is hard for me to say his name – advocated against the Jews; the murder of his own children before he took the coward's way out and killed himself. We all know the horror stories, and I am sure there are more terrible revelations to come. What you don't know, however, is the man himself; not in the way I did. He was brutal, a beast. I was terrified of him. Every actress in Berlin was terrified of him. He…' She hesitated briefly and then gave herself a visible shake. 'Goebbels ran every media outlet in Germany, and the cinema was his favourite. We were his property, and if we refused his demands, well… At best, careers were destroyed, at worst…'

She stopped again. The audience was completely silent. 'There was an actress I knew in Berlin, Renny, who Goebbels wanted as his mistress. She was a sweet girl who was in love with a Jewish boy. Goebbels made her life miserable and she became hooked on alcohol, and morphine. Her acting suffered and he had her committed. And then – if the rumours about her death are true, which I believe they are – he had her murdered, thrown from a window. Her neck was broken for saying no.'

There was a noise from the audience that sounded to Peggy like a sob.

Louise bowed her head and continued. 'Renny was on a list of his favourites, and so was I. I was never his mistress, but I was next in line. Which is why I ran, and came here. Being German was bad enough – if people had known I had been in Goebbels' inner circle, even though I never wanted to be there, they would have said… well, they would have said all the cruel things they are saying now. So I made up a new life for myself. That wasn't a crime. But staying in Germany, refusing to be what that man wanted me to be… that would have been my death warrant.' She stopped.

The silence continued, and then Paar had started to clap, and the audience had joined in and Peggy was left with an uncomfortable feeling of guilt and nothing to write.

'It was a very convincing performance.' Charlie came back out of the kitchen, clutching a huge bowl of chips Peggy had no appetite for.

'Because it was the truth.' She shifted over as Charlie sat back down. 'Whatever else happened, and however my mother – Anna – fits in, I believe Louise about Goebbels. She's a good actress and the show is in her pocket, but that was heartfelt and it echoes what Clara Sokoll said. If Williams lets me touch this story again – which

I doubt he will – all he's going to permit is an apology. Which, given the way my article portrayed her, I think she deserves.'

The show's theme tune started up again – Peggy realised the song they were playing was 'Everything's Coming Up Roses' and started to laugh. If anything fitted Louise's talent for self-preservation, that song was surely it.

The camera switched from the opening shot of the audience back to the interview desk. Louise was sipping at a glass of water while Paar patted her hand. Peggy couldn't tell if the actress was distressed or perfectly in control.

'Miss Baker, I am sure I can speak for the whole audience – here and at home – when I say how brave we all think you have been.' There was a huge volley of applause he had to wave back to quiet. 'But I have another question I think we would all like an answer to: why do you think this journalist – Peggy Bailey – came after you in such a malicious way? Is it jealousy? Is she a failed actress perhaps?'

The audience laughed; Louise allowed herself a small smile. It was such a shock to hear her own name, and in such an unpleasant context, Peggy dropped her pad onto the floor. She was still scrabbling for it as Louise answered.

'It did feel malicious, didn't it? And, no, as far as I know she isn't an actress, failed or not. The truth is she is too young to really be anything. As her article said, I have met her – although her recollection of the brief time we spent together is a little fanciful at best. Miss Bailey is barely out of school; she is completely inexperienced. I am genuinely surprised that any editor, much less the editor of *The LA Times*, would allow a novice like her to run with such a damaging story. But I suppose sales matter more than the truth nowadays.'

Peggy groaned as she heard her prospects at the paper go up in smoke.

'However, although I said her behaviour *felt* malicious, I don't actually believe that. Miss Bailey is clearly naïve and misguided…'

'Oh my God, she's going to ruin my career before it's started.'

'But I don't think destroying me was her aim, even if that was, almost, the result. I think, if you asked Miss Bailey, you would discover that this *exposé* was never really about me. It was always about the missing mother the poor girl is desperate to find. She did allude to that in her article, but it hardly has the same headline-grabbing impact as *Hollywood star was a Nazi's mistress*. No. The poor thing attacked me, I believe, because it was the only way she could get any attention.'

'We can turn it off if you want. If it's making you uncomfortable.'

Peggy wanted to. She felt so exposed, she could hardly bear to watch. She gestured to Charlie to sit back down and leave the set on.

Back on the screen, Paar was nodding, his face a picture of concern. 'Her missing mother, yes, let's turn to that. I know Miss Bailey believes this was a friend of yours, and that was how she linked her article to you. But what I am astonished at – given how the young lady has behaved – is what you told me in the break. That you want to help her with her search. Is that really true?'

Peggy went rigid; Charlie stopped eating.

'I do, Jack, yes. What Miss Bailey has done to me was terribly unkind, but I am not without blame here.'

For the first time since the interview began, Louise looked directly into the camera. 'Peggy, if you are watching this, which I am sure you are, I am offering you my help. The woman you believe was your mother, Anna Tiegel, was indeed a great friend of mine. I don't know what happened to her after I left Berlin, but I think it is possible that she came to America. And I have a confession to make. When I ran away, I hurt her very badly. There was a man she loved, who loved her, who I think may be your father. I used him to get here, and I caused him to abandon her. There is no excuse, except that I was young, and afraid, and desperate. But I caused her pain and perhaps, by that, I caused you pain too. I want to help

you find her, Peggy. I want to bring your family back together. I
do hope you will let me.'

Peggy sat in stunned silence as the audience clapped its approval.

The last moments of the interview were given over to a set of
carefully managed questions about Louise's future hopes for her
career, and effusive thanks for her 'brave candour'. And then the
credits began to roll and Peggy still couldn't hold a clear thought.

'Do you think she meant it?' Charlie was coiled on the edge of
the sofa, the chips reduced to a shower of crumbs round his feet.

'I don't know.' Peggy grabbed her untouched glass of wine and
took a big gulp. 'Maybe. Or maybe it's an elaborate publicity stunt.'

The telephone rang as she was trying to work out which.

'It's going on eleven – who on earth rings at that time? Unless
its Bernie telling me that being labelled as *naïve* and *misguided* on
a major TV show means that I'm fired.' She got slowly up from
the sofa and unhooked the receiver. She got no further than *hello*.

'You saw it?'

'Louise?' Peggy leaned against the wall, shushing at Charlie,
who had jumped to his feet. 'Yes, I saw it. But I don't understand.
You turned me away when I came to you. You denied knowing
anything. Why would you get involved now?'

Louise took a sharp breath, which made her sound irritated, as
though Peggy shouldn't have needed to ask. 'Because mud sticks,
especially the muck you threw. That was quite a hatchet job you did.
I lost two film offers and a lipstick endorsement I was counting on.
I can't afford to lose that kind of money, never mind the damage
to my reputation. And I can't have the name Goebbels popping up
any time anyone mentions mine for the next God knows how many
years.' She sighed. 'But, despite my performance out there, there'll
be as many who believe what you wrote as the ones this won over.'

Peggy swallowed. The words didn't come easy, but they had to
be said. 'About the mistress thing. I'm sorry—'

Louise cut straight across her. 'I don't want, or need, your apology. What I need is to win back the public. And what better way to achieve that than to find Anna, do a bit of penance and give everyone their happy ending? My next call will be to your editor, to get him to fire up the search in return for all the exclusives, which you, my dear, will write. He'll lap it up. If he doesn't, then I'll remind him that's it a lot better than the libel suit I could hit him with. I will be back in LA on Monday, and you and I will do a photo shoot. Present a pretty, and forgiving, united front to the world to get the ball rolling. Agreed?'

None of this is about Anna or me; it's all about her ego.

It didn't matter; Louise could boost her ego as big as she wanted if it meant finding a pathway to Anna.

Peggy nodded. 'Agreed.' She hesitated. She could sense that Louise was done with the call, but she wasn't. 'Do you think that, even if she is here, Anna will come forward? What if she has a family she's never told about me? What if she doesn't want to be found?'

Louise's response was so sharp, Peggy almost dropped the receiver.

'What has that got to do with anything? *I* need this. *She* doesn't get any choice.'

CHAPTER SIXTEEN

'You look like she's holding a gun to your back.'

Peggy hadn't argued with Charlie's assessment. The photograph which Louise had very carefully choreographed in the *Times'* newsroom was hardly flattering, to her at least. Louise, who was dressed in a black-trimmed powder-blue Chanel suit, had one arm looped round Peggy's waist and looked effortlessly elegant. Peggy's smile looked painted on.

'It was the dress – how could I look anything but miserable in that?'

Louise had brought that little number with her. It was a wide-skirted, windowpane-check, taffeta-lined monstrosity that she insisted made Peggy look *charming.* Both of them knew that was code for *too young* and *naïve* and was there to set the power balance. Bernie had spilled his coffee when he had seen Peggy wearing it.

'I presume the headline was her doing as well?'

It was. *Bring Anna Back Home for Christmas!* The tone was so melodramatic, so unlike the *Times*, Peggy had assumed Bernie would take his red pen to it. Louise, however, had charmed him – and Williams and the rest of the office – into printing whatever she wanted. Her appearance at the paper's headquarters had been as much of a masterclass in managing people as the television interview had been. For the first hour of the visit, Peggy had stood quietly on the sidelines and watched the actress perform. Louise was on her sparkling best. She was bright and funny and engaging.

She turned everyone she switched her attention to into the most important person in the room. It was a side of Louise Peggy had never seen before – off-screen anyway – and it was impossible not to warm to her. As the morning progressed, however, glimpses of the side Peggy was more familiar with kept spilling out. Louise had her temper in check, but she was still mercurial, only comfortable if she was the one in control and as quick to snap shut as she was to appear friendly and open.

'She had her usual entourage of lawyers and lackeys with her, but she doesn't need them: no one gets close. It's like there's a force field hovering around her, one she slams down the second she thinks she's let herself be the slightest bit vulnerable.'

Peggy had left the office on the Monday after Louise's visit completely exhausted. She had been called in early, as she knew she would be, by a phone call that was so curt she had expected the worst. She had barely hung her coat up before Bernie appeared and began tearing a strip off her for letting 'some ageing, about-to-be-forgotten actress make me and the paper look like idiots for hiring you'.

Peggy had been so rattled by the day's events, she had barely been able to fork up the chicken tetrazzini Charlie had produced when she stumbled through the door, even though it was from her favourite Italian restaurant.

'And then the said *about-to-be-forgotten actress* arrived, flashed one smile and there Bernie was, trotting behind her like a lapdog. Talk about looking like an idiot, I swear I don't know how I held my tongue.'

'I'm kind of glad that you did, or your career would really be toast.' Charlie had already started on the plate Peggy had pushed away. 'Do you still think it's a publicity stunt to save her career?'

'I don't know.' Peggy had taken her wine and gone to stretch out on the couch, leaving Charlie to polish off the pasta. The amount such a beanpole of a man could eat still mystified her.

'Partly, yes, of course I do. She said as much; she certainly behaved as if that was her agenda. She's been very clear that the paper – and by that she means me – needs to take a sympathetic line, and print whatever she chooses to tell. And if she doesn't choose to tell, then there's to be no digging into anything she's fenced off as private. That – surprise, surprise – includes her marriage and how she survived between arriving here and making her first mark in Hollywood. The good stuff, in other words. I don't know anything more about the husband than the sketchy details anyone can find – he was in finance, he was a lot older than her, not in good health and he left her well provided for. As for the missing first year here… she says it was spent working on her accent, taking acting classes "to be more American" and doing waitressing jobs. It's the same line as a hundred other girls who came to LA desperate to be a star would sell you. I'm sure it's a version of the truth; I'm equally sure she's buried any skeletons very deep and paid them well to stay there. But there's more to it than a stunt; there's more to her.'

It hadn't been easy to explain what she meant. How there had been times during the day Louise had spent charming the office when her polished veneer had slipped. How she hadn't been able to say *Anna* or *Eddy* without a slight pause or a fleeting shift in her face. Peggy doubted that anyone but her had noticed the tightening round Louise's lips, or the wash of doubt in her eyes; no one else was watching the actress with such a clear gaze.

'She feels guilty, I can sense it. She's put the timeline of my birth and her leaving Berlin together and worked out that Anna must have been pregnant. It was clearly her who persuaded Eddy to run to America, not the other way round. She's hazy about that bit, but it's very apparent she doesn't like thinking about the consequences. I don't think she's ever let herself do it before, or at least not until I appeared at the studio.'

That feeling had persisted from the launch of the elaborate, and nationwide, campaign to find Anna and on through the two weeks of exclusives that followed. Apart from on one occasion when her assistant was held up, Louise never spoke to Peggy completely alone. All the interviews took place in an office at the newspaper's headquarters and they never strayed beyond the topics Peggy had been told she could discuss. Louise set the agenda, kept Peggy at a deliberate arm's-length and told her nothing beyond what she wanted Peggy to hear.

Some things, however, could not be glossed over or spun better. It was obvious, despite Louise's guarded responses, that she had somehow tricked Anna – and Eddy – to make sure it was her who had accompanied Eddy to America to begin the preparatory work on Max Reinhardt's *Dream* and not his long-standing girlfriend. Louise had tried, at first, to cast it as a sudden love affair that blindsided them both. Then – on the morning when it was briefly just the two of them in the room – Peggy asked what had become of the romance in America and Louise's myth-making ran out of steam. She opened up so suddenly and unexpectedly, Peggy could barely scribble fast enough.

'I was desperate to get to America, for my career, yes, but also because I was genuinely afraid of Goebbels. I never wanted Anna here – although I pretended to Eddy that I did – I didn't want the competition. And then, when it became clear that I would have to reinvent myself, I was glad she hadn't come; she would have got in the way.'

'It wasn't about you and Eddy at all then?'

Peggy had hesitated before asking, but Louise didn't skip a beat.

'No. I didn't love him, although I acted like I did. I spun his head so brilliantly, I even managed to convince him it was for the best when Anna didn't show up, for a little while at least. But he was always hers; I could never have kept him. Not, in the end, that I tried.'

'You left him then almost as soon as you got here?'

Peggy had rattled out the question with one eye on the door. Louise had nodded.

'Pretty much. And I didn't know he had gone back to Berlin. That was a shock when Max told me. And then he said Eddy couldn't find Anna, that there were rumours she had come out here too. I didn't know what to believe.'

'But you never looked for either of them?'

Louise shook her head again, slower this time, as if even that slight movement was tiring. 'There was no one in Germany I wanted, or dared, to contact. And as for Anna... I did try to find out what had happened to my mother and father in France, that was true. The records were in such chaos, it was hopeless. And it was a stupid thing to try. The private detective I hired started getting suspicious, even though we did our best to hide my name. I couldn't go searching for Anna; I couldn't risk everything I'd built. Maybe if I'd been better at trusting people... But then the last person I trusted, or who trusted me, was your mother and look what I did with that.'

It was the first time Louise had used the word *mother*, or been so nakedly honest.

Peggy was on the edge of her seat, poised to ask *why did you do it to her* when she suddenly realised what Louise had said. 'Wait a moment, what did you mean by *when Anna didn't show up*?'

Before Louise could answer, the door flew open and her assistant reappeared, covered in apologies.

Louise had immediately pulled back, her eyes snapping open as if she had been in a trance. She reverted at once to the distance she normally kept, and ordered Peggy to tear out everything she had written. Peggy did as she was asked, but they both knew that Louise couldn't make her unhear what she had said.

'Do you like her? You've spent a lot of time with her; you must have an opinion by now?'

Charlie had asked her that, as had Bernie. It was an impossible question to answer – the response could change in a moment. Peggy had been as truthful as she could: 'Sometimes; I want to, but she's such a mess of contradictions and secrets, I don't know how.'

The answer didn't satisfy her, never mind them.

Luckily, Peggy was far too busy to have any time to waste analysing her conflicted feelings about Louise – or to try to uncover the woman her mother must have seen inside Louise's hard shell and been friends with. Anna was finally centre stage in the story, and the possibility of finding her blocked everything else out. Even Charlie's well-meant but infuriating, 'it might not happen, or not how you want it' couldn't discourage Peggy's hopes.

The campaign – and the $500 reward Louise had pledged to 'make Christmas special for the sweetheart who finds my best friend' – meant that the phone on Peggy's desk never stopped ringing. Everyone in America – including the shocked residents of her old Rhode Island neighbourhood Fruit Hill who were the most eager to talk, despite knowing nothing – seemed to have picked up on the search. If the calls were to be believed, there were more Germans called some variation of Anna living in America than there were in Germany.

For the first week Peggy had pounced on the phone every time it rang, *This could be my mother* singing through her head. She wouldn't let a single caller go, even when she had exhausted their tales of the cashier in the supermarket with the 'guttural accent', or the Anna who made the most incredible Black Forest cakes for the church bazaar. She wrote every detail down and checked and checked, and even rang some of the more plausible callers back. None of them led anywhere; they all fell apart on the first probe. Most of the women identified weren't even German.

Peggy kept her spirits up for a second week. By the start of the third, she was having to be reminded to answer the phone. So, when what felt like the four hundredth call came in, late on a Wednesday night when the office was virtually empty, Peggy was tempted to let it go. She still had Louise's latest revelation to type up ready for the 11 p.m. print deadline and she was barely halfway through. It was a piece about Goebbels' casting-couch villa, which Peggy knew – if she could word it carefully enough for a family newspaper – the readers would love. The phone, however, kept on ringing.

'Answer the goddamn thing can't you, before I pull it out of the wall.'

Peggy snatched the receiver up as another reporter on a too-tight deadline yelled across the room.

'What is it?' She was sharper than she should have been, in no mood for any more stories about an amateur-dramatics-loving neighbour, who spoke with a lilt and was 'so good she must have been a professional'.

'Am I speaking to Peggy Bailey?'

There was an unusual hesitation to the voice that made Peggy sit up straighter and forget her unfinished copy.

'Yes, you are. Who is this, and how can I help you?'

There was a pause on the other end of the line.

Peggy was about to repeat herself when the woman spoke again. Her lightly accented voice was still soft, but the hesitation was gone.

'My name is Annabelle Brand. And you can help me by stopping this search.'

'I know this sounds stupid when I say it, given how hard I've been looking for her, but I don't think I realised until now that she was actually real, not just a figure I'd conjured up out of my dreams. That she had a whole life that wasn't at all connected to mine. A life that was hers to keep private, or share; not mine, or Louise's, to meddle in.'

Peggy closed her eyes as the plane began its descent into New York's Idlewild Airport. The truth seemed no less foolish now than it had when she had admitted it to Charlie after Anna's – Annabelle's – first call.

My name is Annabelle Brand. And you can help me by stopping this search.

Of all the first words she had imagined coming out of her mother's mouth, none had ever sounded as hollow as those.

Because the words you imagined hearing were all about you. Peggy shifted in her seat as another uncomfortable truth hit her.

Oh, my darling, how I've longed for this; how I have prayed every day for this. The declarations she had dreamed of were pulled from bad B movies; they weren't drawn from real life at all. Annabelle's phone call had made that brutally clear. The tear-soaked embraces and exclamations Peggy had been running in her head for months had fallen apart in the reality of Annabelle's terse demand and her tentative 'Are you her? Are you Anna?'

The silence that had followed that question had stretched out so long, Peggy had grown convinced that the next sound she would hear would be the receiver's click.

'If I answer that, will you forget about this? Will you stop looking?'

It had been Peggy's turn to hesitate then. She couldn't say *no*; she couldn't agree to forgetting. She had fallen back instead on a shaken 'If that's what you want.'

'Yes, it is. And yes, I am Anna Tiegel. Or I was.' Annabelle had stopped.

Peggy knew it was the truth, as certainly as she had known all the other calls weren't. She had waited, too choked up to speak, hoping desperately for some more personal declaration. But then Annabelle spoke again and it had felt like a slap.

'And my life is not anyone's to pick over, especially not her. I never asked to be found. I never wanted to be.'

Not even Peggy could twist that into a joyful reunion: never mind the finality of the words, she could hear nothing in Annabelle's voice but pain. Peggy had stared at her notepad as she tried to find a way back into a conversation she knew was about to close. The lines scribbled across it were full of Louise.

I need her to be. She doesn't have a choice. When Louise had spat out that declaration, Peggy hadn't considered that it might not be true. She hadn't considered anything except letting Louise drive the story on, never thinking that it might do the exact opposite of what Peggy had intended and push any hope of her mother even further away.

Louise's voice has been too loud from the start. This can't be about her anymore; this has to be about us.

'Not found by anyone? Not even your daughter?'

Peggy had blurted that out, refusing to let herself think where the question might lead; not knowing how she would get up from the desk if the answer was *no*.

She opened her eyes again and gazed out of the airplane window where Manhattan's skyscrapers were slowly appearing through the rain-streaked clouds.

Charlie had been holding tight to her hands when he had asked her how Anna had answered, as if he was afraid she would run. He had been a bundle of nerves from the moment she had appeared at his door, her eyes red, her mascara smudged; unable to say anything at first beyond 'I spoke to Anna, the real Anna.' She had been glad that, when she finally told him, he hadn't tried to make anything better; he had simply pulled her into his arms.

'She said the strangest thing.'

Peggy watched the sunlight dancing across the bay below, remembering what she had repeated to Charlie, wishing she could push the memory away. The sadness, the emptiness, in Anna's response still reduced her to tears.

'She repeated the word *daughter,* and then she said, "I'm sorry. Whatever it is that you hoped to get from me, I don't know what to do with that word."'

The phone call had ended almost immediately after that, although Peggy had managed to keep Annabelle – she was still struggling to hold that name in her head – on the line long enough to give her Peggy's home phone number and to beg her to call. Annabelle hadn't agreed, and she hadn't volunteered her own details. Peggy had known instinctively not to ask: she had sensed there would be no more communication until some measure of trust had been established. That, whatever came next, Annabelle needed to be the one in control of it. Charlie had felt the same way.

'Carry on doing what you're doing: going into work as if everything is normal, telling no one what's happened, including Eddy. She's made the first move. If she doesn't hear from anyone else and if nothing appears in the paper, she'll get back in touch. Whatever she said, Peggy, she will have been thinking of you. I promise, in another few days you'll be as mad with me as you normally are for always being the one in the right.'

It had taken more than a few days for Annabelle to resume contact; it had taken a week. The waiting had been agony. Going into the office every day and pretending to be interested in phone calls she knew were nonsense. Listening to Louise talk on and on about herself as if anything she said mattered. Sitting by the phone night after night as if the force of her longing would make it ring. Not knowing what to do with herself when it did.

'Thank you.'

Annabelle's first words when Peggy picked up the phone had opened a future back up.

'I had to wait. I had to see if you would do as I asked or if you would write that you'd found me. I assume from the lack of headlines that you didn't tell your editor. Did you tell anyone?'

Peggy had wondered if Annabelle meant Louise, who she had kept as much in the dark as everyone else. She was about to say 'no one', but there was something in Annabelle's clipped tone that suggested she would know that was a lie, and that she would disappear for good if Peggy tried to fool her.

'One person. My boyfriend, Charlie. He's been part of this from the start, and he won't say a word.'

There was a pause Peggy had desperately wanted to fill with promises, but she held her nerve, and her tongue. When Annabelle spoke again, she knew her decision to be honest had been the right one.

'I am glad you told me that. And I am glad you have someone in your life you are able to trust. I lost that ability a long time ago. I don't expect to easily recover it, even with you.'

It was the *even with you* that had given Peggy hope. That had given her the courage to ask for what she really wanted.

'Do you think we could meet? Somewhere quiet, where you would feel comfortable? When you are ready, I mean.' There had been a pause when Peggy asked, but not an immediate *no*, so Peggy had ploughed on, trying not to let her longing make her clumsy. 'This isn't about the paper, or Louise. This is about us. And I won't tell a soul, I promise.'

'Not even Charlie?'

For the first time since they had first spoken, Peggy had heard the trace of a smile in Annabelle's voice.

'I don't have to. But I'd rather: I don't like secrets; I've had enough of them.'

And that was how she had ended up on a flight to New York, ten days before Christmas, brooding over the few conversations she had had with Annabelle, her stomach in knots, repeating over and over to herself: 'Don't charge in, don't have expectations, take this steady.'

Although Annabelle had agreed to the visit, Peggy knew she could back out as easily. When Peggy had called her back to finalise the arrangements, Annabelle's voice had sounded so tense, Peggy had feared the hope of them meeting would end with the call.

When she didn't cancel it, Peggy resolved not to phone again and risk a rebuttal – even though she woke every morning yearning to hear Annabelle's voice.

She bought her tickets. She managed to persuade Bernie to let her take her Christmas break early in order to pack up her family home in Rhode Island and get it ready to put on the market. It was a task that was long overdue so, although she wanted to rush straight from the airport to Annabelle's home in Greenport, Long Island, she slowed herself down by going to Fruit Hill instead.

She slipped in and out and managed, to her relief, to avoid all her old neighbours. She sat in the house for a little while, and she cried for a little while, and remembered the happy days that had filled it. She let herself grieve, and she let herself say a proper goodbye to the parents who had raised her with so much love. Then she piled the hire car with the personal items that were all that she wanted and left herself with nothing to do but set out.

It was a far shorter journey than the one Peggy had embarked on five months earlier. It was less than seventy miles to Greenport – a journey that would take hours, not days. If she left before lunch, she would be there long before the December light faded. It was a far simpler thing to do altogether than cross from one side of the country to the other. Except this time, Peggy knew who was waiting and the stakes were much higher, and it was proving just as impossible as it had done back then to start up the car.

CHAPTER SEVENTEEN

Greenport, Long Island, December 1957

The house was all windows. The view of the sky and its mirroring water was endless.

'I like to be able to look at the world uninterrupted.'

The woman who had opened the door of the cottage nestled at the furthest end of Greenport carried no traces of the girl who had been captured in a photograph twenty-five years ago. She was slight to the point of elfin, her features finely drawn on her lightly tanned face. Her hair was a mix of faded browns and pale greys, and she was simply dressed in a navy fisherman's sweater and blue jeans. There was an elegance to her – she carried her body like a dancer's when she moved – and beauty in her bone structure. Peggy could see that with the right clothes and more make-up than the slick of pink lipstick she was currently wearing, she would look as lovely in her own way as Louise. Nothing about Annabelle's manner or home suggested that would matter to her. The cottage was simply and practically furnished, its walls painted white, the sofas and chairs all covered in the same shade of eggshell blue. Although it was close enough to Christmas to warrant any number of gaudy decorations, the hallway and the main room that looked out onto the Peconic River lacked any adornment, apart from a series of vibrantly coloured canvases which took Peggy's breath away.

'I discovered a talent for art late in life. One of the local galleries sells enough of them to locals and the odd passing tourist to keep the wolf away.'

Annabelle had invited Peggy to sit on the sofa facing the picture windows, but she was too transfixed by the paintings to move.

'There's no name on these. You don't sign them?'

Annabelle began unloading a tray carrying a coffee pot and a plate of cookies that she had disappeared to prepare within a minute of inviting Peggy inside.

'No. Names don't carry that much meaning for me anymore.'

'But you are Annabelle now, not Anna? And Brand, not Tiegel?'

Peggy finally sat down. She didn't know what to do with her hands. She didn't know what she should ask – beyond the safety of a question she already knew the answer to – or what she should offer about herself. From the way Annabelle was now perched on the edge of the opposite chair as if she was about to fly from it, Peggy didn't know how much time she had to ask anything. Her inability to leave the Rhode Island house meant she had arrived late and she hadn't booked a hotel, or looked to see if the small community even had one. She had driven off the New London to Orient ferry blindly hoping that, if she made no other arrangements, Annabelle might invite her to stay. Watching the nervous woman in front of her, a drive through a snowy night back to the city now seemed more likely than the offer of a bed.

'Yes. I became her when I finally got my citizenship papers. She sounded more properly American than—' Annabelle stopped, stared at the coffee pot as though she had forgotten she was still holding it and put it carefully down. 'I don't know how to do this. I have spent twenty-two years longing for you and training myself not to think about you, and… now that you are here… I don't know what to do next.'

That pain in her voice again. Peggy wondered if she had stirred it up, or if it was never that far from the surface. She said the only thing she could think of to say. 'I had a good life. The couple you gave me to raised me with love.'

The relief that swept across Annabelle's face wiped years from it. 'Thank you, for telling me that. When I had you... when she came for you in the hospital... I didn't want—' She stopped abruptly again. 'I am glad. I am very glad. That was all I ever wanted you to have.'

There was much more. Peggy had felt the layers in the pauses, in the heartfelt *she* and *I didn't want*. She ached to dive into them, to loosen Annabelle's tightly held feelings. She didn't know how or where to start. There was so much already unsaid, the weight threatened to silence them both.

Stop thinking about her as your mother. Think of her as a stranger you have been sent to interview, who is fragile and needs coaxing. Peggy didn't know if she could separate herself out from her emotions and follow her training, but Annabelle was such a closed book, she had no choice but to try.

'Have you always lived here in Greenport?'

It was personal, but clearly not as personal as Annabelle was dreading. Another look of relief crossed her face.

'No, although sometimes it feels like it. I came here close on nine years ago. I had been... ill. The friend who I was with at the time brought me here as a break from the city and I fell in love with its space, and its quiet. Greenport keeps itself to itself and I like that.'

Peggy nodded as she tried to pull out the clues. 'By the city, can I assume you mean New York? Was that where you lived when you first came to America?'

It was like watching shutters come down. Annabelle stared away from Peggy and out of the window. The threatened snow hadn't started falling yet, but the sky and the wind-swollen waters had grown increasingly dark.

'Mostly. I was... further south for a while.'

'Whereabouts were you in New York?'

Annabelle's shoulders hunched. Peggy could feel her resistance, but she needed to find some kind of a connection and the possibility of shared locations seemed to offer the best one.

'On the West Side at first, near the Hudson, walking distance from Central Park and then…' She hesitated, but Peggy had already cut across her, unable to contain herself.

'That's where I was – on the West side, near the park, I mean! Off Columbus Avenue, by the Planetarium.'

The colour leached from Annabelle's face. 'But you work for the *LA Times*. I thought that meant you lived in Los Angeles.'

'I do now, but I've only been there for the last few months. I lived in New York until I was twelve. I loved it. I must have played in Central Park every day. If you were there in the mid-1930s – which I assume is when you came over here, given when I was born and Louise's timeline – we might have actually lived close to each other.' Peggy was so delighted with the turn the conversation had taken, she didn't stop to think about the impact her words might be having, or to notice how badly Annabelle was shaking. 'You said the West Side at first, where did you go after that?'

'The other side of the park. It doesn't matter.'

'But which street? Not that I would probably know it. We hardly ever went to the East Side, especially once the war started. Pop said it was full of Hitler fanatics. We got caught up in a Nazi march once, when I was little, and he went crazy. Not that I remember much except a lot of banners and shouting—'

'Stop it!'

Annabelle was on her feet, gasping, her hands wrapped round her body. Peggy suddenly realised what had come out of her mouth and was horrified.

'Oh my God, I'm sorry. It's because of your new name: I forgot you were German…' She stumbled to a halt. Annabelle was holding her stomach as if she'd been winded.

'You have no idea. You have absolutely no idea. You started this stupid campaign to flush me out without a thought about what that could do to me. You blunder in here, all excited because we *maybe lived close*, without thinking how much it might hurt me to hear that. And talking about *Hitler fanatics* when you've no clue what that means. I should never have called you. I should have stayed hidden, reinvented myself again. I should never have let you in.'

Peggy had never felt so utterly out of her depth. Annabelle was right: she hadn't thought through anything and she had forgotten all her promises to herself not to charge about, to tread carefully. 'Really, I'm sorry. It wasn't meant to be like this…'

And then Annabelle's temper really flared and she was as blind to Peggy's distress as Peggy had been to hers. 'What was it meant to be like? Some great Hollywood-style reunion? Everyone stepping away from their nobly tortured pasts into a softly lit happy ending? Didn't Marika's – or Louise's, or whatever you call her – story not teach you anything about the mess we were in when we ran from our home? We were friends, we were both actresses: did it never occur to you that I could have been in the same danger as her, or that I never found my way out of it? No. You saw her with her dreams all in place and you assumed I was as lucky. Well, I wasn't; I'm not. I lost you. That tore my heart out. And then I came to America and I lost my soul. And now you want me to relive all that to sell a few papers? It's impossible, it's disgusting. I need you to go. I need you to leave me alone.'

Her fury was frightening. But the words Peggy heard louder than the anger and the dismissal – *I lost you. That tore my heart out* – weren't; they were balm. Peggy knew that this was it, that this moment was her last chance, and she wasn't going to let go of it until Annabelle pushed her out of the door and ripped it away.

'I can't. I won't, not unless you physically make me. I know I've made a shambles of this whole thing. It was about me, and then it was about Louise and about headlines and my career, and you – the one thing that really mattered – got lost somewhere in the middle. But – when I first started looking for you, before I ever met Louise – then it was about *us*. And, yes, probably at first I was foolishly hoping for some movie-script ending. But don't hate me for that, or for trying to find you, or for bringing all this upset to your door. Get as angry as you like and I'll make it up to you in any way that you'll let me, but don't hate me, please.'

And now Peggy was the one winded and crying, and Annabelle stopped shouting and finally looked properly at her. She didn't run to her side, or take Peggy in her arms, but she did, finally, say the words Peggy had been desperately waiting to hear.

'Oh Peggy, how could I possibly hate you? I'm your mother.'

Peggy didn't go back to the city that night, or the next. Annabelle's past didn't unfold easily, or entirely. Her account of Goebbels' predatory behaviour towards Louise matched the one Peggy had already been given. Her halting description of her father's death and the threats she had been left to face, and had buckled under, made Peggy never want to speak to Louise again.

Annabelle wouldn't speak about the circumstances of Peggy's adoption, beyond, 'I named you after my father; I would have kept you if I could.' When Peggy pushed – sensing there was more to what she was being offered than a carefully managed handover – Annabelle had snapped at her to be 'kinder to Joan's memory' and cut the topic dead. Peggy quickly learned that Annabelle was a master at that. If she didn't want to talk, she didn't talk, and no amount of subtle, or unsubtle, persuasion could move her. Once Peggy started to understand her mannerisms however, she gradually came to realise that the refusals stemmed more often from fear than from stubbornness. Peggy didn't point that out, and she didn't dare ask if Annabelle's fear came from a dread of being judged or a dread of not being believed, but she stopped pushing.

The little Annabelle revealed about her time in Yorkville and how she had got caught up in the German American Bund was so shocking, Peggy finally grasped why Annabelle had needed, and still needed, to live an undiscovered life. It was barely twelve years since the war had ended. For many families, the grief of loss was still raw. For many, the circumstances of their loss was still unknown: the truth about the extent of the killing campaign the Nazis had unleashed across Europe was still revealing itself in numbers that no one could digest. It was hard for Peggy to argue with Annabelle's hollow, 'I know the war is done and that most Americans are good people who know the difference between Germans and Nazis, but what if there are still places where prejudice lingers? I couldn't bear to be hounded or shunned by even one person; I couldn't live through it again.'

Over the course of the three days and nights they spent starting to learn their way around each other, Annabelle took Peggy as far as Brooklyn and then she wouldn't be drawn any further.

'I signed papers. I promised not to tell. I can trust ordinary people, Peggy, but not the ones in power. If they come for you, there's no defence, no protection. I was out of my life for long enough for me to think I would never get back into it, and that's all I can tell you. Don't ask me again.'

She was insistent on that. She was also insistent that there would be no reunion with Louise.

'I don't trust her. How can I? She won't be able to help herself: she'll throw my life to the public to keep hers in the spotlight. She'll be sorry when she's done it, but that won't stop her. And what would I do if I saw her anyway? Scream at her for stealing Eddy? Blame her for the misery my life became? She made choices; I made choices. They are in the past, and so is she.'

Peggy knew Annabelle was right. If Louise got wind of her whereabouts, she would promise all the discretion in the world and then turn up with a camera crew. She also knew that Louise wouldn't give up the search as long as there was a breath of publicity left in it.

'She's unstoppable, you know that. And whip-smart. If she gets one hint that I'm no longer as devoted to the campaign as she is, she'll know something's up and she'll pounce. I don't know how to manage that.'

Peggy had left it to the last morning, as they were packing up the car for her return, to admit that. Annabelle's walls had come down so far, Peggy was certain now that this new relationship they were building would flourish. She was also certain that all her loyalty going forward belonged to this woman, who was slowly shaping not into her mother in the way Joan had been, but into a different kind of mother entirely. One she shared a bond of blood with, but also the promise of an adult relationship between two women who liked and admired each other, the deepening in the relationship between mother and daughter that had been snatched away from her with Joan's death. Louise, and Bernie, and Williams, however, still believed it belonged to the paper. The puzzle of how to take the next steps had left her sleepless. To her surprise, Annabelle – who was still awkward when it came to touching her daughter, although each tentative embrace had grown a little stronger – put down the bag she was about to stow in the trunk and took both Peggy's hands.

'Yes you do. You're Peggy Bailey, the twenty-two-year-old junior reporter who was clever enough to grab herself a front page. What you do now is what you are best at: you take charge of the narrative. You tell the world I am dead.'

CHAPTER EIGHTEEN

*Los Angeles and Berlin,
December 1957 – March 1958*

I need to take the story back where it started. I need to take it back to Berlin.

When the idea had first popped into her head on the plane somewhere between New York and Los Angeles, Peggy dismissed it as ridiculous. She decided that Annabelle's demand to be killed off – and the cascade of lies that would inevitably stem from that – had scrambled her brain.

Instead, therefore, of blurting it out the minute she saw Charlie, Peggy filed the thought away and concentrated on what she needed to say and do to keep Annabelle safe while she came up with a more workable plan. She went back to the office and answered the phone calls still claiming new sightings with a better attempt at enthusiasm. She continued her interviews with Louise, who – conscious that the Christmas deadline was almost upon them – insisted on ramping up the publicity. The campaign, however, despite all Louise's efforts, was ticking down. It was such a relief, Peggy began to think she might be able to ignore Annabelle's request.

'The search is going to die a natural death, I can feel it. If there's no meaningful lead by the New Year – which, obviously, there won't be – Bernie will let the whole thing quietly drop.'

Charlie hadn't been so easily convinced. 'But Louise won't. I'm sorry, Peggy: I know it's not what you want to hear, but she still needs her win. What if the paper gives up but she goes and hires a private detective? She could start tracing your movements, and Annabelle's been writing to you – that wouldn't be hard to track.'

It wasn't at all what Peggy wanted to hear. Neither was the call from Annabelle echoing Charlie's worries and asking for an ending Peggy still couldn't see any safe way of delivering.

'How am I supposed to do it? If I tell Bernie that Anna's dead, he'll want my source; when I can't give him that, he'll get suspicious and won't buy it. And Louise won't stop drilling until she's down to my contact's eye colour and shoe size.'

She stopped. Suddenly going to Berlin didn't seem ridiculous after all.

'Unless I say that the tip came from Germany. That the call was placed from Berlin and was definite, but anonymous. Louise would hardly dare follow something like that up, especially if I hinted to her I suspected it could be Eddy. She definitely doesn't want to see him again, and she might have got away with her past here, but I doubt she wants to test it out in Germany. And if Bernie goes for it, then I can tell him what I really want to do, which is to go to Berlin myself. To go back to the start of this and give my mother's story – and mine – a proper ending by understanding how it all began. And then I tell Annabelle I want her to come with me. Does that sound crazy?'

Charlie shook his head. 'No. Not to me. But I know the truth. I've seen how close you're growing to Annabelle and how happy that makes you – and how frustrated you get when she still pushes you away. If going to Berlin gets you more answers and a stronger bond with your mother – and maybe your father – then do it. But I'm not the hard sell here: it's Bernie you've got to convince, and it's Annabelle.'

Peggy tackled Bernie first: at least she knew the right way to approach him.

'I believed what the caller told me. There were things he knew about Anna that Louise told me too but that we never printed. It really felt like he knew her. And I've been doing some research: thousands of Germans were shipped home from America between 1941 and 1945 and even after the war ended. It makes sense – especially since we've run into nothing but dead ends here – that Anna could have been one of them. I think it's true, but I'd like to go over there myself and be sure.'

Bernie had accepted the existence of the call, but he had been far more resistant to the rest of it.

'Hold on. If you believe your mystery German, why don't we print what he said and be done? Why do you need to go chasing off to Berlin?'

Peggy knew that the honest answer – the one Charlie had understood and that she prayed Annabelle would too – would slide straight off her boss.

Because Berlin is part of my mother and part, therefore, of me. It's where I began. And the urge to go there, to breathe its air and feel its stones, keeps getting stronger.

She couldn't imagine saying it: she could imagine all too clearly how he would snort if she tried. Rather than make a fool of herself and have the whole plan dismissed, she told him the other part of the truth.

'The whole world is watching Berlin, Bernie, you know that. What is it, nine years since Germany was split into two countries? The East German government is even closer to Moscow than it was in 1949, and, if Russia really is going to push us into another world war like we and every other paper is claiming it will, Berlin will be right on the front line. You've seen the reports the same as I have. Giving half the city to East Germany and half to the West has never worked. It's getting increasingly complicated for people to move between the two sectors, and now there's rumours the East will turn its checkpoints into a permanent barrier and block off their part. If they do that, no one knows if West Berlin can even hang on, given how marooned inside East Germany it is. What kind of a message would that be if it fell? If I tell this right, it's got everything: a proper finale for a search we've been leading with for weeks, rather than just letting it peter out; an eye-witness account of the Communist threat to democracy everyone in America is scared witless of, and all with a—'

'Don't tell me, I get it: a *personal angle.*'

He sounded as sarcastic as ever, but Peggy could see he was wavering.

'All right, Eleanor Roosevelt: stop campaigning me. Even if there is something in this – and I'm not saying that there is – why wouldn't I ship the whole kit and caboodle over to one of our stringers on the ground? That'd be a damn sight cheaper, and probably safer, than letting you off your leash.'

'Because it's my story, Bernie. It's always been my story, and no reporter worth the name would give up on that.'

He muttered, but her passion spoke to his and she had him. And – with Bernie's support and a 'source' no one could get to – she also had Louise.

All Peggy had to clear now was the hardest hurdle: persuading Annabelle to go home.

*

She is my daughter.

Every time the thought struck her – which it did too many times a day to count – it glowed. Peggy was… Annabelle could barely gather up all the things Peggy was. She suited her name; Annabelle was certain of that: Franzi was too soft for such a bright-eyed girl. And she was beautiful, and clever, and brave – and fearless when it came to making her dreams real. All the things the Anna Tiegel who commanded Berlin's stages had been.

And she is destined to be disappointed in me if I can't summon up some of that courage again.

Annabelle – which was how she had determinedly thought of herself since Gretchen Michaels had helped her fill in her citizenship application – put Peggy's letter down. It was the second one pleading with her to at least consider the proposed, impossible trip to Berlin. Annabelle hadn't replied to the first one: she couldn't corral the panic she had felt onto paper. She had said such an emphatic *no* when Peggy attempted a follow-up call, the conversation had come to an abrupt and uncomfortable halt. She wasn't surprised that Peggy had tried again – there was a tenacious streak in her daughter Annabelle would have been very proud of, if she wasn't the one trying to wriggle away from it. She knew that, if their relationship was to continue to grow in the way she wanted it to, she couldn't push Peggy away with another hard *no*. What she also couldn't do was explain to such a fearless creature how terrified she was.

Maybe you should try: what damage could it do? Your first contact with her – never mind your first meeting – could have been a disaster, but you both got through that.

The memory of her call to the newspaper office still woke Annabelle in the middle of the night, or, more precisely, the memory of the way she had so abruptly snapped those awful words, *not found by anyone, even your daughter* still woke her. She hadn't meant to sound cold, or dismissive. When she had stumbled across Louise's interview and realised who Peggy might be, her first instinct had been to jump on a flight to Los Angeles and run to her child. And then the fear of being sprung from her hidden life had kicked in. That fear had won then; it was still winning now.

The year and a half Annabelle had spent living with Gretchen and her family had saved her life. Gretchen hadn't pushed her to fill in the blanks of her life since Annabelle had walked away from Riverside Drive. When Annabelle had finally found her voice, Gretchen had listened without the judgement Annabelle feared.

She had also understood why, in a post-war world still soured by suspicion, Annabelle was desperate to hang on to her secrets.

Gretchen had nursed her through the physical toll the camp had taken, and then through the deep depression she sank into, whose causes went far further back. Once she re-emerged into the world, however, Annabelle quickly realised that the Bronx's bustle was too much. Greenport – whose population of two thousand was a fraction of the million crowded into the New York neighbour-hood – had provided the wide open spaces and safe haven she needed. She had moved to the little fishing village as soon as her citizenship papers, and her last new identity, arrived.

Gretchen had been reluctant to let her go at first, fearing the quiet she was moving into would set back Annabelle's recovery. Then she had watched Annabelle standing in the tiny clapperboard cottage, unable to drag herself away from the wide window and sweeping sky, and had handed over the first six months' rent before Annabelle had needed to ask for the loan.

Annabelle had constructed her days to be easily lived in. She took long walks; she swam when the water in Pipes Cove was warm enough; she worked on the painting skills a sympathetic doctor had suggested she develop to keep her demons at bay. She had made friends – carefully and gradually – with locals she was happy to share meals with, but not her past. Her canvases had become good enough to show, and then to sell. The nightmares had faded. And then Louise Baker had leaped into the limelight to save her skin and her career and spun Annabelle's life back off course.

Annabelle hadn't seen Peggy's original exposé: if she read a news-paper, it tended to be a local one. She was, however, something of a fan of chat shows and particularly liked Jack Paar's gently amused approach to his guests. After a day spent wrestling with a sunset she couldn't translate onto the canvas in the way she had seen it, she had poured herself a whisky and slumped in front of the set. Only to be confronted by Louise, imploring America to go 'looking for Anna'.

She had panicked. For the first time in all the years she had lived in the cottage, Annabelle had pulled all the curtains tight shut. She couldn't go out for days. Eventually her cupboards ran so low, she was forced to venture to the village store. The shock waiting for her there pushed Louise's performance out of her head: the photograph she hadn't seen since she had stuffed it inside her baby's blanket was everywhere. She would have run, but her legs wouldn't listen to her head, and the press of people was, for once, too solid to find a pathway back through. The *scandal*, as Annabelle heard two of the chattering women describe it, had brought everyone together, eager to pick over the gossip. The store bubbled with it, particularly Louise's 'generosity' to the 'silly little journalist stuck on finding her mother, she didn't give a thought to the damage she caused'.

Annabelle had heard herself ask, 'What journalist?' She had managed not to collapse when the store's owner pulled out another front page and pointed to a girl in a too-young-looking dress. Annabelle had forgotten the groceries she needed. She had taken the paper home and worn the photograph thin, staring at a face whose eyes and curved cheeks looked exactly like her own mother's. And she had worn herself thin, battling with a longing to call the number at the bottom of the article that was so fierce it consumed her, and the visceral fear of having her life split wide open.

The nightmares came back. Annabelle went to bed and dreamed of swastikas and songs thick with blood. Or she lay awake imagining backs turning as she tried to explain the unexplainable confusion a chance encounter in a dance hall had plunged her life into. She watched from behind the curtains as the mailman walked his morning rounds, waiting for him to deliver the letter that would take her citizenship back. She relived all the guilt and unhappiness she thought she had buried deep enough to never have to face it again. She stopped being able to swallow, she was so full with it; she knew she was starting to drown.

So Annabelle picked up the phone and called Peggy. Not to tell her all the things she ached to say. That giving up her baby had almost killed her. That she had spent over twenty years carrying the pain of a loss that was baked into her bones and had never stopped hoping that one day she would find a path to the Baileys. Not to say the magic word *mother*. But to tell Peggy to stop, to forget her; to let her go. That wasn't blunt, it was cruel. That they had moved from that place to one where love was possible – where it was already surely, unspokenly there – was a miracle.

And one I risk wasting if I can never let her properly in.

Annabelle picked the letter up again. It was written in such a scrawl – Peggy's letters always were, as if her hand couldn't keep pace with her heart.

This isn't all about getting the story right for the paper, I swear – although I'd be lying if I said that wasn't part of it. You know we have to make your 'death' watertight if we're going to keep Louise off the scent. Bernie – who honestly doesn't know a thing – can spin the search out a bit longer before everyone gets bored, but he needs me to write the piece that I promised would give it the right ending. So I have to go to Berlin soon. And I really, really want you to come.

I don't know what being born German means to me; I don't know if it means anything, but I'd like to have a go at finding out. And Berlin is your city – even if you don't think that anymore. I want you to be my guide. I know you're afraid to go back. I get that, I do, even from the little you've told me. But what if it helped? What if it laid some of your ghosts to rest? What if that helped us?

Some of my ghosts.

Annabelle closed her eyes and let the faces come. Not the nightmare ones, but her mother, and Kerstin. And Eddy. The last time she had been in Berlin, she hadn't thought about them – she hadn't had space in her head for anything except the faces she feared. But what if she could go back and walk with her head up along the streets they had once shared? What if, despite the destruction the bombs had wreaked and the divisions that now split the city, she could find some trace of them? Or of the girl who had once been showered with applause and adored, whose dreams had been sprinkled with stardust not haunted by swastikas?

Annabelle got up and crossed to the phone. She didn't know if she could do it; when it came to the possibility of finding Eddy, she didn't know if she wanted to do it. She didn't even know if she could get on the plane. She picked up the receiver and dialled Peggy's number. Whatever her fears, this was what the daughter she had spent half her life longing for wanted. A trip back to the past but taken together, supporting each other whatever their searching uncovered. Wasn't that enough reason to try?

'I can't get a bearing anywhere.'

On the first day, Annabelle had blamed her inability to map the city on exhaustion from the long flight, which had taken them first from New York to Frankfurt, and then via Air France into Berlin's Tegel Airport. The combination of her first time flying and the destination was enough to keep her awake on the plane. Then, somewhere over the Atlantic, Peggy had revealed that she had been in contact with Eddy and lost Annabelle any hope of sleep when they reached their Charlottenburg hotel.

'I couldn't tell you sooner; I didn't want you to have an excuse not to come. And I didn't know if Eddy would be an excuse.' Peggy had suddenly grown tongue-tied, a state Annabelle had never seen her in, and had passed her two thin letters. 'He doesn't say a lot, but he feels really guilty, and he tried so hard to find you when he got back to Berlin.'

Annabelle read the letters through slowly, trying to find reasons in them to dredge up her anger, but her anger was all gone.

'Do you know what he has been doing all these years?'

Peggy nodded. 'He's not in films anymore; he's a photographer. It seems like he kept on working as a film director, in the late thirties and into the war, but…' She hesitated and then handed over a page of notes. 'Here. His name is credited on some of the Third Reich's banned movies, including *Jud Süß* and *Ich Klage An*, but there's nothing after 1945. I have his address, but I haven't told him we were coming.'

Annabelle had taken the notes from Peggy without commenting, and stowed them away to read later, without Peggy watching. Charlie's brief summaries did not make pleasant reading. *Suss the Jew* was a virulently antisemitic piece disguised as German history. *I Accuse* was a pro-euthanasia propaganda film whose aim had been to create public sympathy for the Nazis' T4 killing programme, which Charlie had described as the planned – and carried out – killing of the incurably ill and the physically and mentally disabled. Both films had been commissioned by Goebbels, both had been watched by millions of German cinema-goers, and both had been banned in 1945.

Two days into the trip and Annabelle still didn't know what to do with the information; all she could hope was that Eddy's participation in the films had been as involuntary as hers had been with the FBI and the Bund. To think anything else entailed a rewriting of the man she had loved that was impossible. Annabelle was confused by Eddy, and she was deeply confused by the city.

'Berlin used to be beautiful.'

She had kept saying it. Peggy had believed her when they walked down the elegant Kurfürstendamm. Then they would turn a corner and be confronted by wastelands or houses that were still little better than rubble, where political divisions had slashed through the city's rebuilding. Peggy had grown silent at those; Annabelle had lost heart.

It wasn't just the broken buildings that they both found unsettling. Annabelle was unprepared for the city to be full of soldiers and flinched every time she walked near one. And both of them were unnerved by the process of crossing from the Western sector into the East. Their American passports secured them a day pass through the crossing point at Friedrichstraße easily enough. However, the warnings not to miss their midnight curfew, and the instructions not to mix too freely in the East, put both women on edge. As did the far closer scrutiny Peggy's accent subjected them to when they presented their papers at the heavier-manned East German checkpoint a few yards further down the same street.

'I am German; I am from here. My parents lived in Mitte; I once lived in Prenzlauer Berg. We have come to revisit my old homes.'

It had been so long since Annabelle had made any claim to be German, the words didn't sound real to her. The guards, however, finally stopped treating Peggy as if she was a potential spy and waved them through.

They were barely round the next block before Peggy came to a stop.

'It's too drab. We've hardly walked a quarter-mile from the West and yet it could be a different city. There's no colour, and it's even more broken down.'

Peggy had been right, and it was from that point on that Annabelle lost her bearings in the parts of the city she could once have walked in her sleep. Every landmark she had known had been ruined or razed. The goddess of victory and her four horses and chariot had vanished from the top of the Brandenburg Gate. The palatial Hertie department store where she had once bought the latest Paris fashions had disappeared from Alexanderplatz, its windowed elegance replaced instead by a concrete box of a building covered in signs offering discounted dresses, which, from what Annabelle could see of the dusty displays, all looked the same. Museum Island was a locked-up mess of debris and shuttered or smashed windows. The Winter Garden Theatre was gone.

After three hours of increasingly aimless wandering, which had reduced Annabelle to tears when she realised that, not only was there no trace of her family home or the cinema, there was no trace of the streets they had once stood on, Annabelle had let Peggy drag her into a café and admitted defeat.

'I don't want to do this anymore, Peggy. I was afraid to come back, in case the memories overwhelmed me, but there's no memories to find. I may as well be wandering the surface of the moon for all the connection I feel to this place. The Berlin I knew is gone and everything I lived through here – the good and the bad – is gone with it. Maybe that's a blessing, I don't know, but I can't keep poking through the past like this.'

Peggy pushed away the coffee which didn't taste of coffee and the cake which tasted chemically sweet. 'But what about the Charité? It's still there, and the map says it's close. You said it was one of the places we would definitely go. Can't we do that at least?'

Annabelle didn't know whether to laugh or to cry. Peggy sounded so young, and so petulant. It was as if she had suddenly had a glimpse of the child she had never known, and it choked up her throat. She nodded and let Peggy pay and lead the way out of the café without answering, afraid that, if she tried to speak, she might give in to tears she wouldn't be able to stop.

The Charité was still there, but it wasn't the Charité. The maze of old turreted buildings had gone, the same as everything else Annabelle knew, replaced by another faceless concrete slab.

'It's as if nothing of my life before ever existed.'

It was one shock on top of too many. Annabelle sank onto a bench and turned pale enough to make a passing nurse insist that both she and Peggy come inside.

'Even if you won't see a doctor, you are going to come and rest in the warmth. This is a showpiece hospital – it would be quite the scandal if I let you faint in its grounds.'

She was too kind, and too determined, to ignore. Annabelle allowed herself to be led to a waiting area and be fussed over.

'They still prize kindness in the nurses here then. That, at least, hasn't changed.' Annabelle sipped her sugary tea and smiled as the nurse frowned. 'I was a patient here a long time ago. There was a nurse who looked after me, Kerstin Pohl, who was one of the best women I have ever met. It's been over twenty years, but I have never forgotten her.'

'Frau Pohl?' The nurse looked at Peggy. 'Did she deliver your daughter?'

Annabelle nodded.

The nurse clapped her hands. 'But that's splendid – she is still here! She is our head of maternity. Do you think if I called her to come down, she might remember you?'

That Kerstin was alive and unharmed – by the war or by the retribution Annabelle had always feared helping her escape Goebbels could have led to – was such a miracle, it broke down the last of Annabelle's defences. She cried so hard when the lift doors opened, Kerstin had threatened to admit her. Then Kerstin had realised who Peggy was, and had out-cried Annabelle. Once the tears were done, the reunion had been more joyous than Annabelle could have imagined, particularly when Kerstin showed her the photograph of the man she had met and married the year after Annabelle had left, and the baby girl who had arrived another year later. Knowing Kerstin had found happiness took one of the burdens she had carried for too long from Annabelle's shoulders. It also made her realise how much she needed to put her other ghost, somehow, to rest. The hardest thing was explaining her feelings to Peggy.

'I know you're eager to find him and I understand that: he's the biggest gap still left for you. But as for me… I don't know if he's the one I've blamed the most, or the one I've missed the most. He's my past; in some ways he is the best and the worst of that. I have no idea if he has any place in my present.'

'And you want to go and find him on your own.'

'I'm sorry, Peggy. I don't think there's another way I can do it.'

To Annabelle's relief, Peggy smiled. 'It's fine. It's the right thing. I want to see him – of course I do, he's my father – but that's just a word at this stage. You need to see what, if anything, he still is to you before I come blundering in. And if one meeting with him is enough for you, then I can make my own way through whatever he is to me.'

That's just a word. She had said almost the same thing to Peggy about *daughter* barely four months ago, and now that word was everything.

'I will tell him about you, and about who you are to him. Whatever you have already said about yourself, he deserves to also know you through my eyes, and to meet you.' Annabelle stopped, unsure what to do with the feelings flooding through her. *She's your daughter, tell her.* 'And he deserves to be as proud, to be as lucky, to know you as I am.'

The snow had stopped by the time Annabelle emerged from the subway station on Gneisenaustraβe, but the wind was bitter. She huddled inside her coat and hurried towards Chamiβoplatz and Eddy's shop. The area – Bergmannkiez at the western end of Kreuzberg – wasn't a district she had been to before, but it was the closest Annabelle had come yet to old Berlin. The streets she turned into were cobbled; the balconied and stuccoed buildings that were still painted in unmarked creams and yellows were softly lit by the wrought-iron lamp posts that had once lit the whole city.

It was the first place Annabelle had been since they had arrived where she couldn't feel the war or its aftermath.

It took less than ten minutes to find Eddy's address. The narrow studio was tucked between a chocolatier already full of papier-mâché Easter eggs, and a cosy-looking Italian restaurant. The photographs on display in the window were all formal shots, posed pictures of nervous brides and awkward grooms and babies lost inside ornate christening robes. Annabelle couldn't see anything in them of Eddy.

Why would I? What would he see in me of the actress he knew twenty-two years ago?

The thought kept her hand from the brass door handle. That and the realisation that she still had no idea what she would say if she even made it across the threshold. She had sat on the subway waiting for the words that would explain what her life had been since he had sailed away from her. That would make him explain that decision. Her head was still empty.

Because this is a mistake. This isn't Kerstin. This is a ghost I shouldn't disturb. Let Peggy meet him. Let Peggy make whatever relationship she wants with him; I don't need to be any part of that.

Except that – sending him the daughter and refusing him the mother – was as impossible as her walking into the shop.

'I'm sorry, were you wanting to come in? I was about to run an errand, but it can wait.'

A heavy overcoat hung from a frame that was thicker than the one she remembered. His hair was far more salt than pepper. But his eyes were still that treacle shade of brown, and his voice was still Eddy's.

'Wait. Do I know you?'

Annabelle muttered a *no* she could barely hear and began to walk away. This was too big, too much. And then he gasped and she heard his keys clatter.

'Anna? Oh my God, is it really you?'

She turned slowly. Looked straight at him. Kept her hands tight in her pockets so she wouldn't reach out the way her memory was aching to do. The big body she didn't know had crumpled; the new ruddiness in his complexion had drained away. He looked like the boy she had loved, and he looked like a stranger. Annabelle watched his eyes fill with tears and wished she had a better answer to give him.

'I don't know.'

The restaurant next door to the shop was empty. It was too late for lunch and too early for dinner, but the owner knew Eddy well enough to give them a table and bring coffee and wine. They sat opposite each other, hands fiddling with cups and glasses, neither of them drinking; neither of them knowing where to start. In the end, it was Eddy who plunged in. Annabelle was so relieved the silence was broken, she let him run on, not caring he had started somewhere in the middle.

'I stayed in Hollywood for six months. I didn't do well there… I was too German, Hollywood was too much. Marika…' He stumbled slightly on the name but continued when Annabelle refused to react. 'She disappeared within a month of us arriving. I don't know if she had planned that; she certainly saw how much Hollywood was stacked against us long before I did. She started telling people she was French, and then she was gone. Although I gather she's reappeared, or was always there. And that she started a search for you. I can't make a lot of sense of it.'

He stopped again. Annabelle said nothing. She had promised herself she was not going to discuss Marika with him and nothing he had said was going to change her mind. Eddy watched her face set and hurried on.

'Anyway, *A Midsummer Night's Dream* was a flop. We ran too fast and made decisions we shouldn't have. Everything was a mistake – the sets we spent too much money commissioning were all wrong;

letting the studio persuade us to promise Jimmy Cagney the part of Bottom the Weaver when all he'd ever played was tough-guy killers. Max came out, saw the chaos we'd got ourselves, and the production, into and he knew a disaster was coming. He sacked me. I came home. I tried to find you.' He paused.

Annabelle knew the questions he was waiting to hear: *why did you do it, why didn't you tell me, why didn't you write at the very least?* Asking any of them suddenly seemed pointless. What did the *whys* matter when the thing had been done so long ago? What could he say? *Because I was a fool; because my head was turned; because I thought I was being a hero.* They were answers she already had. She asked him a different question.

'Was it worth it? Was the life you got worth the one you threw away?'

His head dropped. The apologies she could sense he had been desperate to offer dried on his lips. When he looked back up, she knew it wasn't the first time he had heard that question; she knew it had been haunting him for twenty-two years.

'No, Anna. It wasn't. I lost you. And I lost myself. I went to Hollywood with the wrong person. I came back – stupidly and arrogantly and far too late – to find the right one, and I didn't realise how much emptiness and hatred was waiting for me.'

And then he stopped and looked properly at her. 'Why did you say that I threw it away? I waited for you. I wasn't going to get on the ship. And then Marika broke down and admitted you weren't coming…'

'What?' Annabelle knew there were walls around her, that she was sat on a chair and leaning on a table, but suddenly nothing felt solid. 'Why on earth would Marika say that?'

'Because that's what you told her.' A thin sheen of sweat spread across Eddy's face as Annabelle slowly shook her head. 'We had to change the crossing at the last minute, because Max had arranged a new set of meetings. She went to your flat with your ticket for the revised sailing, but you told her that you didn't love me anymore and you weren't coming.'

'I never said that. She never came.'

'No. No, don't tell me that, Anna. Please don't tell me that.' He was crying. The tears rolled fat and slow down his colourless cheeks. Annabelle could feel every one of them.

Did Max tell you about the changes, or did she?

The question was pointless; every question she had was pointless.

When Eddy began speaking again, the pain in his voice burned for them both.

'I searched everywhere. I couldn't find you, not a trace. And then I was arrested. Goebbels had me thrown into Plötzensee Prison and beaten every day for weeks, until I couldn't stand. He said I had to work for him again, that I owed him. That there were "important films" still to be made and, luckily for me as he put it, "plenty of actresses who weren't traitors ready to make them". I refused. He had my father brought in. He had him… beaten to death in front of me. He promised me my mother would be next. So I did as I was told and directed films that shamed me. Now I am blacklisted and forgotten, which has to be a good thing. If anyone did remember my name, it would be linked to *Nazi*.'

He stopped, reached for the wine the waiter had poured for them both and couldn't pick up his glass. 'All that loss, all that waste, and it's all my fault. I did throw you away, you're right. I chose to believe the wrong girl. Please God tell me that at least your life went better, that it was only mine I destroyed.'

Annabelle couldn't lie to him; she couldn't lie to herself. Part of her wanted to tell him the truth. To tell him how closely the horrors he had experienced mirrored the ones she had faced. Offering herself up like that, however, was too soon and too intimate and she did not need the burden of his guilt.

'What about now?' He frowned at the question. 'That was then, what about your life now?'

Eddy ran an unsteady hand over his chin. 'I have my shop and enough commissions to keep me. I have friends I can pass pleasant evenings with. I have no wife, no children. That was the life I discarded when I got on the boat to America; the one I couldn't remake without you.'

His voice was the same as when he had recounted the revenge Goebbels had taken: weary and broken, but not pleading for pity, not pleading for anything. Something inside Annabelle loosened. There was no price to be extracted here: he had already paid it. There were old wounds, and new ones she hadn't yet allowed herself to feel, but none of them would kill her.

I thought the past would sweep back and drown me, but I'm too strong for that now.

And she knew why, and why she wasn't lost anymore.

Annabelle put her glass down. She reached out and took Eddy's hand. He jumped but he didn't pull away, or hold on too tight. She swallowed hard and looked into his eyes.

'There is something I need to tell you…'

*

The plane was quiet, most of the passengers – including Annabelle – were dozing. Peggy put down the pile of notes she was still trying to sort into an article. Her head was too full to concentrate. Seven months ago, she had buried a mother she loved deeply and she had felt too small for the world. Now she had a new family, and the world barely felt big enough to contain all that meant.

Annabelle had come back from Bergmannkiez and gone straight to her room. The next morning, however, she had appeared at breakfast and sent Peggy to Eddy.

'I don't know what my relationship with him is, or what it will be, but that cannot cloud what you could have. He's waiting to meet you – go to him. He's a good man, Peggy; it will be worth it.'

They had been shy with each other at first, her lack of German and Eddy's long-unused English a barrier. But they had stumbled through the parts of their lives they were ready to share and formed a connection Peggy knew they would build on. When she returned to the hotel, she had told Annabelle that and was glad when she smiled. She hadn't asked what her parents had decided their next steps would be, or if there would be any next steps at all. Whatever her own thoughts on the matter, Annabelle would reveal her decision in her own time, which was something Peggy well knew could not be rushed.

She turned to look at her mother. There were shadows under Annabelle's eyes and her eyelids were twitching as though her sleep wasn't a restful one. It was hardly surprising: there had been so much for her to absorb, and so little time to do it in. Not only the changed state of Berlin and reconnecting with Eddy, but now too the possibility of retracing her own mother, which Eddy had promised he would try to do.

Peggy picked up her notes again, suddenly seeing a shape in them.

All these new starts for us, but what's coming for Berlin except endings?

Annabelle had been lost in Berlin, unable to find anything familiar to hold on to; Peggy had felt the same sense of dislocation spread across the whole city. There had been a wariness in the streets, a sense that the political division currently loosely held up by checkpoints and passes was about to harden into something far more chilling. No one would talk to her in the East, which told its own story. The ones who would talk in the West were nervous for friends and family living in neighbourhoods they could feel shifting away. And they were far more fearful of the war they believed was coming than the one they had too recently lived through. Peggy thought about Eddy – whose home in Kreuzberg was so close to the East, it would be on the front line if the city's worst fears were realised – and shivered. She had gone to Berlin partly to see if the circumstances of her birth would make her feel German. She didn't; she wouldn't pretend to. But whatever the city's fate was destined to be, Eddy's presence there connected her to it.

The tannoy cut through her thoughts, announcing that the plane was about to commence its landing into New York. Annabelle stirred and opened her eyes.

Peggy nodded to the window and the skyscrapers coming into view. 'We're back.'

And then Annabelle smiled and took her hand and Peggy's heart soared.

'No, not just back. We are here together. Which means we are home.'

EPILOGUE

Hollywood, March 1959

The Pantages Theatre on Hollywood Boulevard was packed, the atmosphere inside so tense the air crackled.

'I told you it was crazy, didn't I? This is the Oscars of the newspaper industry, all the great and the good, and the not-so-good, champing at the bit for recognition. And you're up for an award straight out of the gate. It's amazing – you're amazing.'

Charlie had been leaping with excitement since the letter announcing Peggy's nomination had arrived. Now it was time to announce her category, he could barely sit still.

'I'm not going to win. The competition's too fierce.'

Peggy said it because she felt she had to. The same way that she had practised her not-winning-but-fine-with-it face in the bathroom mirror and prayed she wouldn't have to use it. She was so desperate to win, her stomach hurt.

The ceremony's host – the English actor David Niven, whose impeccably cut-glass accent gave Peggy butterflies – raised his hand to silence the room. 'And now to our next award: the best feature article by an industry newcomer. And here to present it is a lady who has been no stranger to the news herself, particularly in the last year. Ladies and gentlemen, please give the warmest welcome to Hollywood legend, and legendary beauty, Louise Baker!'

Charlie burst out laughing as the applause thundered. 'Oh that's priceless. Now you have to win.'

Louise walked slowly across the stage to the podium, acknowledging her reception with her trademark smile. The demure dresses she had favoured during the Nazi headlines had disappeared: the midnight blue gown she was wearing clung like a second skin. She let the whistles die down and slowly slid the silver envelope open.

'The winner of the Best Newcomer Award goes to… Peggy Bailey, for her feature article in the *LA Times*: *A Beginning and an End in Berlin.*'

Charlie exploded from his seat. Peggy did her best not to run to the stage.

Louise handed her the crystal sphere, kissed her cheek and made eyes at the audience while Peggy gulped back the tears she hadn't expected to shed and ran through her short list of thank-yous.

'And finally, I would like to dedicate this award to my mothers. To Joan, who refused to let me give up on my dreams, and to Anna who gave me Berlin. Thank you.'

Louise joined in the applause and then looped Peggy's arm and led her off the stage. 'She's alive, isn't she?'

Peggy stopped dead in the wings, her heart thudding. She ignored the stage manager's frantic wave for them to move and switched on her best smile. 'Who is? What are you talking about?'

Louise laughed. 'Stick to being a journalist, sweetie – you'd never cut it as an actress. Anna, who else? I've had my eye on you the whole time since her *death* was announced. You were never sad enough, and then you bounced back from Berlin with too much of a spring in your step. She went home, didn't she, like you said, but she didn't die. I don't care if that's what happened: I don't need her anymore. But I'd like to know.'

For a fleeting moment, Peggy wondered what would happen if she told Louise she was right. If she got Annabelle's latest letter out of her evening bag and let Louise read all her mother's hopes and excited good wishes for the ceremony. Let her read about Annabelle's most recent trip to Hamburg, where Eddy had discovered her mother – Peggy's grandmother, who she planned to fly out and meet in the summer – in her seventies and not in the best of health, but as delighted to be reunited with her long-lost daughter as Annabelle was with hers. And about the visit Annabelle had also made to Berlin, and the hopeful steps she and Eddy were making back to each other.

My mother is alive, yes, and she is healing and happy.

It was tempting, but Louise was Louise – that, at least, would never change.

Peggy unhooked her arm. 'You're wrong. If I've never seemed sad it was because I'd learned the truth, and I'm done with the past. It's a great feeling. You should—' Peggy stopped. There were a dozen things she could say, but, with everything she had in her life now, winning points against Louise was too hollow to matter.

Charlie was hovering at the edge of the wings, grinning his ridiculous, lovable grin. Peggy had no idea where she and Charlie were going, if they were going anywhere at all, but she knew the journey would be a lively one and worth taking. She waved at him, then she looked at Louise with her tight, attention-seeking dress and her tight, empty smile, and she grinned.

'You should be happy, Louise. You should move on with your life and be happy.'

And with that Peggy turned her back and walked away from a past that no longer claimed her, towards a future she couldn't wait to begin.

A LETTER FROM CATHERINE

Hello,

Firstly, and most importantly, a huge thank you for reading *The Lost Mother*. I hope you enjoyed reading it as much as I enjoyed writing it.

If you want to keep up to date with my latest releases, just sign up at the following link. I can promise that your email address will never be shared and you can unsubscribe at any time.

www.bookouture.com/catherine-hokin

I have been fascinated by film since I was a child and my father introduced me to the great technicolour Hollywood extravaganzas he had fallen in love with in the 1950s. As I got older, I also became fascinated by the impact the movies could have on an audience, not just by making us fall in love with the costumes and the characters and the stars, but also as a propaganda tool. Many different regimes have made use of this, but Goebbels really was – in the darkest of ways – a master. If you are lucky enough to be in Berlin and want to know more about this period, I really recommend a visit to *Die Deutsche Kinemathek – Museum für Film und Fernsehen.*

As anyone who has read my previous novels will know, I spend a lot of time in Berlin and love to walk where my characters walk. With this novel, I was also able to write about some of the special moments I have experienced in America – the wonderful architecture in Rhode Island, that moment when you first come face to face with the Pacific and the insane distances when you embark on a road trip, which, like Peggy, I was lucky enough to do. With this novel in particular, it wasn't just the characters who were real to me, but the places – I hope you have also felt a sense of that.

If you have a moment, and if you enjoyed the book, a review would be much appreciated. I'd dearly love to hear what you thought, and reviews always help us writers to get our stories out to more people.

I hope too that you will let me share my next novel with you when it's ready – I have a new set of characters waiting to meet you…

It's always fabulous to hear from my readers – please feel free to get in touch directly on my Facebook page, or through Twitter, Goodreads or my website.

Thank you again for your time,
Catherine Hokin

@cathokin

Cathokin

14552554.Catherine_Hokin

www.catherinehokin.com

Acknowledgements

As every historical fiction writer does, I immerse myself in the time frame I am writing about. As always, I have read a huge number of books while writing my novels, and watched, this time in particular, a lot of films.

The story of German internment and the activities of the Bund in World War Two is one that has only really started to emerge onto a wider public stage in the last ten years or so, and the sources for that have been particularly fascinating. I have used too many resources to single them all out, but those I would like to particularly mention are: *The Ministry of Illusion* by Eric Rentschler, *Popular Cinema of the Third Reich* by Sabine Hake and *Filming Women in the Third Reich* by Jo Fox; *Before the Deluge* by Otto Friedrich and *In the Garden of Beasts* by Erik Larson for 1930s Berlin; *Goebbels* by Peter Longerich, which is an incredible read; *Swastika Nation* by Arnie Bernstein, *Under Cover* by John Roy Carlson, *Nazi Spies in America* by Leon Turrow and *The Nazi Movement in the US* by Sander A. Diamond; *The Train to Crystal City* by Jan Jarboe Russell. One small historical note – Goebbels was officially given the Bogensee Villa in 1936; for the purposes of the narrative I have moved his occupation of it to 1934.

I owe thanks to many people. I always say it, but I always mean it, those thanks in particular go to Tina Betts and Emily Gowers, my wonderful agent and editor, for their insight, patience and hard work – this book has, once again, been a great collaborative experience. To the whole team at Bookouture who got behind it,

CATHERINE HOKIN

especially Kim and Sarah in the marketing team. To my son and daughter Claire and Daniel, my trusted beta readers, for their never-failing love and support and to the wider writing community I'm lucky to be part of who cheer on every success. And, lastly but never least, to my husband Robert who I couldn't do a step of this without. Much love to you all.

Printed in Great Britain
by Amazon